TANT OF OLD

BOOK ONE OF THE TANTRIC TRILOGY

KRISHNARJUN BHATTACHARYA

FiNGERPRINT!

Reprint 2020

FiNGERPRINT!

An imprint of Prakash Books India Pvt. Ltd.

113/A, Darya Ganj, New Delhi-110 002,
Tel: (011) 2324 7062 – 65, Fax: (011) 2324 6975
Email: info@prakashbooks.com/sales@prakashbooks.com

facebook www.facebook.com/fingerprintpublishing
twitter www.twitter.com/FingerprintP, www.fingerprintpublishing.com
For manuscript submissions, e-mail: fingerprintsubmissions@gmail.com

Copyright © 2014 Prakash Books India Pvt. Ltd.
Copyright Text © Krishnarjun Bhattacharya

This is a work of fiction. Names, characters, places and incidents are either product
of the author's imagination or are used fictitiously, and any resemblance to any
actual person, living or dead, events or locales is purely coincidental.

All rights reserved. No part of this publication may be reproduced, stored in a
retrieval system or transmitted in any form or by any means, electronic, mechanical,
photocopying, recording or otherwise (except for mentions in reviews or edited
excerpts in the media) without the written permission of the publisher.

ISBN: 978 81 7234 522 8

Processed & printed in India

For Kolkata

Where I was born

Land of pujos, crowds, madness

Land of tales and fantasy

Land of loud stagnancy and quiet movements

Land of irresistible charm

The forgotten city never forgets
And neither will I, her lost son come back
I will seek out her mysteries, her death pangs, her kiss
In her filth, her cracks and her inky blacks
Her debri'ed embrace, her sludge-stagnant feel
My poem drinks up, piecemeal, piecemeal

PRONUNCIATIONS

Adri Sen— O-dreeSh-eyn

Aurcoe— Aww-r-ko

Ghosh—Gh-oh-sh

Sural— Shu-raal

Aman— Umm-unn

Fayne— Fay-i-n

Mazumder— Mo-joom-daar

Ba'al— Bay-l

Arshamm— Aar-shum

Kali— Kaa-li

PROLOGUE

The skies were red. The boy watched from behind the curtains, hiding. No one passing the castle could have seen his face. He could not fully understand the beauty of a sunset back then, but it mesmerised him nevertheless. Explosion. Colours. So many windows in thick stone. So many.

The boy in the castle watched the sunset and thought of escape. He thought of the other children he wasn't allowed to play with. The children who did not belong to the castle, the ones who ran about outside. He could only watch them and suffer alone as he did. Walls. Padlocked doors. Torches burning. And the dank, musty smell that had become a part of him, the smell he had grown up with—amidst the torchlight, amidst the darkness.

He wanted answers. But most of his questions stayed just that—questions. The few people who knew him and talked to him, the people of the castle, they treated him well, though. He wondered about many things, and though having expectations was not something he was able to grasp fully then, he was aware that all the people who knew him, somehow, *expected* something. From *him*.

The books were proof enough. After he had mastered reading in the three languages—the Old Tongue being the most important, of course—giant books were deposited in his room, routinely. At first, the thickness of the books scared him—the pages old and frayed, abandoned rather than preserved, the binding hard, dark, worn. Intimidation.

But the boy, with ennui threatening to grip him harder than ever before, had eventually started reading. He had started with History and Geography, but had soon moved on to extremely specific studies of the Old Tongue. He was bright. He could understand almost everything that was there in the books, picking up things and remembering them with surprising ease. If there was anything he could not understand, he would ask his father, who came in once every week, and his father would answer all his questions—except for the more daring ones, the ones whose answers evaded him the most. He had begun studying runes and call-signs dedicatedly. Symbols and figures; runes and scratchy diagrams the books called call-signs, drawing and redrawing them until he almost knew each curve and each stroke. Practice, the books urged. Learn by heart, repeat in dreams. Madness, he thought. Madness inculcated by madmen, inculcated into books with trembling hands. Shaky writing. Occasional dark stains. He forced himself to trust the books, the madness, for there was nothing else. But nothing was constant, not even the written word. When he got comfortable with his books, a new bunch of books would always find themselves in his room.

The sun had set, the evening arrived, and with it the darkness the boy did not like. While he was free to roam anywhere in the castle that he pleased, he never went where no torches burned. Thoughts occupied his mind as he wandered around the castle tonight. Thoughts that almost stopped him from seeing the tiny light at the end of the west wing. Almost. He stood at the entrance of the dark hall, looking at what had caught his attention: the light at the end of the long, stony corridor, flickering uninvitingly, like the dying breath of something in pain. A dying torch. An open doorway. A narrow flight of steps leading down, somewhere out of sight. Enough to spark his curiosity.

Descending cautiously, the boy heard sounds. Human voices, talking amongst themselves, creating a sense of urgency—things being moved somewhere, furniture being shifted, a noisy affair, yet hushed. The sounds got louder. And louder. He could discern snatches of conversation now.

'. . . the incense, is it in order yet?'

'The hour . . . it is almost here . . .'

The boy softly stepped off the last stair, creeping towards the door which stood ajar in front of him.

A tinkle of breaking glass. Then a high pitched cry. A voice that had long done its time.

'Curse you, Souvik! Is this the amount of care you have for Aujour?'

With the old man bellowing and another man hurriedly muttering apologies and scooping up the pieces of whatever he had dropped, no one noticed the boy as he entered the room and crept off to stand behind a pillar. Something about the whole surreptitious nature of this—whatever this was—told him it was wisest to stay hidden. There were five people in the room, he saw, all in the familiar black robe of the castle uniform, white runes on the black. The one giving all the orders was old and wrinkled with a mane of dirty, white matted hair on his head. The others were younger, and they scurried around obediently, following his terse instructions.

The room itself, circular in shape, was quite large. A colonnaded ring surrounded the main area that stood a step lower than the pillars. Torches burned all around, making the room appear quite bright, but the secrecy of the affair lent it a very ominous touch. Something moved near the wall at the far end of the room and the boy squinted to see what it was. There, in the shadow of a pillar, was a chair and someone seemed to be sitting on it.

'And which incompetent son of a vulture left the door open?' the old man roared again. 'Have you no understanding of simple rules?'

One of the minions hurried towards the door to shut it. He latched it and turned a giant key in the keyhole. The boy stared at the door. He knew he should not be in the room, but he had never been stopped from going anywhere in the castle. If anyone caught him here, he would just tell them who he was before trouble fell, and he'd be escorted out of the room with nothing more than a few harsh words. For now, therefore, he was safe. And curious.

'We are done, Malik,' someone addressed the old man. 'The room, I believe, is set.'

The old man's face, illuminated by the quivering light of the torches, was grim and impassive. Carved out of rock. 'Countermeasures?' he demanded.

'They are ready,' the man named Souvik replied, looking at the other three for a confirmation. They then withdrew strange-looking metallic devices from within their robes and pried them open with faint clicking noises.

'Fire and light. Check, everyone,' Souvik spoke.

'Check,' the others muttered in unison.

The old man's hand now subconsciously went to his neck. The boy caught the movement and saw a tiny locket he wore around his neck. He recognised it. It was a rune sign, the one called Audakha. He did not, however, know its purpose.

'Quite so, then. Let us begin. Suddho, draw the circle,' the old man commanded and walked to the centre of the room, the others following him. They stood close to each other, and the one called Suddho bent down and scratched a circle all around them on the floor with chalk. When he finished, the old man inspected the circle and nodded.

'Bring her,' he said.

Souvik went across the room to the chair the boy had spied earlier, and yanked someone up. He pushed the person into the light and the boy saw that it was a woman. He did not understand beauty, or he would have seen that the woman was beautiful. No, what he did notice was that she was unusually pale and silent, and she staggered, losing her balance as Souvik dragged her across the room—he had to catch her twice to stop her from falling. The old man caught her as soon as Souvik thrust her at him. He caught her hair roughly and forced her to fall to the floor, keeping her well outside the circle. Souvik stepped inside the circle once more, and the old man now spoke, 'We begin. If anyone has questions, I would like to hear them now.'

'None, Malik.'

'Then make sure all of you keep your mouths shut and your trigger fingers ready.'

The boy inched closer now. All the men stood inside the circle, but a little beyond the circle, he now spied something else drawn on the floor as well. And as he leaned forward to see what it was, he realised breathlessly that he had seen it before. He knew it well. He had drawn and redrawn it countless times himself. It was a call-sign, perfectly etched, right down to the sharp, confident strokes.

The old man began to speak. Old Tongue, the boy registered. He could understand snatches of what was spoken, but it did not make much sense to him. Words, invocations, greetings, everything spoken in a strange sequence. The old man's voice echoed throughout the room—rumbling with confidence, precision, and experience, at times reaching a feverish pitch, and at others, dropping to a low steady mumble. And all the while he chanted, the old man held on to the woman's hair in a vice-like grip. He declared and he drawled. And the boy watched, fascinated. Finally, after what seemed like an endlessly long hour, the chant slowed in pace and intensity and the old man finished off the incantation with two syllables that he screamed out loud, and with the last one, a blade flashed in his hand.

The boy did not scream as the woman's throat was slit. Or as the old man kicked the corpse towards the call-sign and stepped further back into the circle. The boy simply froze in his place. He did not fully understand what had just happened—the taking of a life had never been explained to him—but he perceived, a little vaguely, the ungodliness of the act. The air around him seemed to throb with certain vibes he sensed weren't good for him, and a growing numbness spread itself through his body and mind. He wanted to melt into the pillar in whose shadow he stood. Yet he stood. Watching. Everything had fallen quiet. The torches continued to burn, casting an eeriness on the picture—the five men standing inside a chalk-drawn circle, motionless but tense, and the corpse of a young woman, sprawled on the floor, just outside the circle, her blood slowly travelling across the floor, mixing with the call-sign, a star within a circle.

'Ma-Malik?' someone stuttered.

'Quiet!' the old man hissed.

The lights started to dim. It happened very slowly, hardly discernable to the eye, but the intensity of the flames slipped down steadily, and finally, one of the torches went out with a faint hiss. Another torch in the room followed suit. Then another.

The men in the room followed the torches with their gaze as they went out. No one spoke. A slight, gentle wind blew out of nowhere, and then stopped. All the torches, except for one, were in darkness now. That one still burned, feebly. The boy, still hiding behind the pillar, felt very, very uneasy in the quiet. The dreaded feeling that darkness often inspired, now crept up his spine. To his advantage though, he was still so disturbed by what he had seen that this fear could not take hold of him completely. He deliberately made himself look away from the corpse on the floor and watched the call-sign.

Long moments later, something stirred in the depths of the shadow that the call-sign lay in. It was black, pure black. It rose from within the call-sign and arranged itself in a shape, that of a tall man without any features. Even in the dim light of that lone torch, one could see that its entire body seemed to be made of something akin to black glass. It stood to its full height, towering above the tallest man in the room, and surveyed its surroundings silently. The men watched, preparing themselves. The boy watched.

'Demon,' the old man spoke. The Demon, as addressed, stopped surveying the room, and slowly turned its neck to face the old man.

'Accept your sacrifice, creature of Shadow,' the old man spoke further, addressing the form. 'Satisfy your hunger, and then we will discuss things further.'

The Demon said nothing. It looked down at the body at its feet. A shadow from within its self reached out, like a stream of water, and enveloped the body, and when the shadow retreated back into the Demon, the woman was no longer there.

The old man nodded, acknowledging the acceptance and began again, 'Your task is an assassination. The target is none other than the famous—'

'Wrong,' the Demon spoke for the first time, interrupting the old man. Its voice was barely a hiss, an inhuman hiss that crawled up the boy's body and made him shudder.

'What do you mean?' the old man asked, mildly surprised.

'She did not satisfy my hunger.' Its words, though in a sentence, were disjointed, as if it was trying to learn to speak.

'Oh very well,' the old man spoke, and grabbing Souvik by his collar, threw him out of the circle. Souvik screamed as he hit the floor near the Demon.

'Take him,' the old man said, gesturing to Souvik, who was fumbling desperately with the metallic device in his hands.

The Demon bent down in front of Souvik, hiding him from the boy's view. The next instant, a sound was heard, something like a sharp rip. A scream. Silence. Then the Demon stood up again, facing the old man. 'I've seen this since a long time. Your kind trying to be Summoners, thinking they can command our kind. Necromancer,' the Demon spoke, 'you forget your place.'

'Do not try to judge my abilities, Demon,' the old man said. 'Tell me of your hunger.'

A pause. One of the men behind the old man fidgeted.

'My hunger yearns for the taste of your old flesh, Necromancer,' the Demon replied in a low drawl.

A sharp intake of breath. The old man moved his fingers in the air in a pattern. 'Away with you!' he spoke in the Old Tongue. The Demon did not react. The Necromancer looked at the creature with unbelieving eyes, repeating the gesture, chanting the words, a little frantic now.

The Demon laughed, and the boy felt his blood run cold at the sound. He covered his eyes and pushed himself deeper into the shadow of the pillar.

Loud slashing noises. Men screaming. Tissue tearing, bones snapping softly. And then, silence.

The boy slowly removed his hands from his eyes and peeked out from behind the pillar. Everyone was dead and the Demon, the Demon was hunched in front of the old man's body, right inside the circle.

'I can see you, you know?' it spoke slowly.

The realisation that it was addressing him was terrible and merciless. It hit the boy like a hammer, and heart pounding, he watched as the Demon turned around to face him.

And Adri Sen woke up with a start.

16

1

Adri was sweating. It was the first thing he noticed, the cold sweat all over his body. The second was that it was morning and the sun had been up for quite a while now. The third was Death, sitting at the edge of his bed.

Adri's apartment, tucked away in one of the busiest and most crowded neighbourhoods of New Kolkata, was easy to miss if one didn't know where to look. It lay somewhere in the midst of a labyrinth of stalls and small shops, an area of the city where one wouldn't come looking for anything. It was also the only part of the city that couldn't be called perfectly *clean*; New Kolkata, as claimed by its makers, was an example of a completely controlled, clean city. It was also white. From the wide streets of white concrete, the white walls of the houses to the giant white walls that ran all around New Kolkata, everything was white. Within these giant white walls, everything ran with immaculate order and precision, something MYTH had done properly, as far as the role of rulers was concerned; the people, well-protected from the rumoured terrors outside the walls, functioned with full efficiency; they had almost everything they desired— the economy was in great shape, they were happy in their existence, and were free to do what they wanted. Good pay for good work.

Except for the forbidden arts. But then again, when most people were content being bankers and engineers, making themselves useful to society, why would anyone want to dabble in the supernatural? Curiosity in the forbidden arts, after all, could hardly be generated, leave alone sustained, when the alternative was a safe, well-paying job. No, let MYTH handle the Necromancers, the Tantrics. Isn't that what the government was all about anyway? Protecting the people from magic. With magic. No one was complaining.

Adri wasn't one to complain aloud either. All these years he had kept a low profile, living among the everyday people—people scared of magic and of the supernatural. One look at his apartment, and anyone would've known that he, Adri Sen, was a Tantric. It was a one-room flat with an attached bathroom, crammed with all kinds of oddities. Books fought for space everywhere—not just the old leather-bound volumes holding myriad secrets, but also bestsellers, cookbooks, and medical journals. In the middle of the room lay a shelf, crudely dividing the space into two parts, stacked with vials and vessels and bottles. Some had old, tired-looking plants growing within them, some were filled to the brim with strange powders and liquids, and odd vapours swirled inside some. A lamp made out of human skulls conjoined together hung surprisingly low, casting light out of the eye sockets and open mouths. On the free space available on the stone floor, etched with a sharp object, was a pentacle, and a few hundred candles, now put out, littered the area around it. Snakeskin dried along the windowsill of the single window in the room, and next to it was a small bed. Two figures currently occupied this bed—one half prostrate, and the other sitting on the edge, watching the first, intently.

The one half-prostrate on the bed was Adri Sen, having just woken up from one nightmare to another. He would've sighed if he was older—having known the life of a Necromancer better by then—but he was just twenty-three and he could find no casual remark to throw at the creature in front of him. No, Adri was shaken, and visibly so.

Death was facing him. Smell. Decay. Little girls singing sadly. Old men gazing beyond the horizon in long, lingering, final looks. Shackles binding dreams. Death knells. Feasting crows. Piles of corpses. Stories and warnings. The mask of rust. The cloak of chains.

Adri was overwhelmed. An aura was penetrating him. Killing his thoughts, leaving none save dread. Trance.

Adri looked at the mask. Rusted metal held together with punched bolts. Grates for the mouth and dark holes for the eyes. Ugly. Heavy. Consuming. Eternal. A deformed skull. A tomb. Adri looked for the eyes within, but could not see them. Something moved in the hollow. Liquid. He could not take his eyes off the mask. It drew his gaze, forced him to look at what it was. Decay. The mask stood for everything that had given way to the marches of time, everything that was no more, everything that had been. Broken apart, torn down to the bones, until life itself was swallowed, devoured by the rusted skull that sat before him. Adri tore his eyes away from the mask. A shawl covered the upper body, tattered, dry. Black. More metal over dark robes. Leggings, rusted. Gauntlets, rusted. Bloodstains, dry. Chains trailing down the body, twisting, turning, running along like hair, spreading on the floor, trailing across it. Thin darkness, slithering around its body. Like fluid. A snake. A shadow. Dark and viscous. Death.

Adri's mind began to slowly recover from the aura. This wasn't a spirit, he realised. It was a Horseman, one of the four. Death, to be more exact—an old being, spoken about in stories and lore, an entity beyond anything he had ever witnessed.

'Forgive me, this is the only place I could find to sit,' Death spoke slowly. His voice carried a grated, cold, dry edge. Like a razor. It was the eeriest voice he had ever heard, and he had heard many—Demons used many voices to frighten and impress.

'You're a Horseman, aren't you?' Adri asked slowly, sitting up.

The creature nodded slowly. 'I am Death,' it said.

Adri wondered—not with the lazy air of a stargazer, he wondered, and wondered fast—why Death was here. The only answer that presented itself was not a reassuring one. Of course people died all the time in New Kolkata—they got hurt, they fell sick, they met with accidents, and old age caught up with them. Death itself, however, did not come for them. Never. It was unheard of. Ridiculous even, that a being of such rumoured power would run around collecting people whose time was up. The universe did not work that way. No, there had to be something else, something more. He tried to break through the rising panic in his mind and look at things logically. Adri's time wasn't up. He decided to ask.

'Your time is up,' Death replied.

'What? What do you mean?' Panic engulfed him in entirety.

Death took its own sweet time to reply, observing Adri closely. Adri felt it pulling at his existence, pulling him and everything he was towards itself with its very gaze. 'You must die, Adri Sen. I have come for you. I will personally take you across the River.'

For the first time now, Adri noticed ash flying all over the room, covering it like a blanket. This death of his to be, was it because of his smoking?

'Why?' he asked Death. 'Why must I die?'

'Because it is your time.'

Adri blinked hard. Had he imagined the mask grinning?

'I have been searching for you all this while . . . and now, I have finally found you.'

Searching for him? Was Death warming up to him in a dark way? 'Horseman,' he spoke, 'to be honest, I haven't dealt with your kind before. Hell, I haven't even *seen* a Horseman before. The salt keeps the Demons out, and the Coven, thankfully the Coven doesn't have access to these areas.' Reaching into a bedside drawer, Adri withdrew a pack of cigarettes and a lighter. He lit a cigarette and took a long, deep drag. Death watched. 'So what

I want to ask,' he continued, 'is how does one keep a Horseman out of one's house?'

'You cannot keep Death out of your house,' Death replied.

Adri was thinking fast. He wasn't ready to die. No, not yet. A plan began to formulate in his mind; not brilliant in particular, but it would have to do. It was decent, given the circumstances and the kind of pressure he was under. It would involve pain, something he did not like. But anything was preferable to death. Literally or otherwise.

Adri reached beneath his pillow, as slowly and stealthily as possible, and withdrew his shooter—someone had taken a revolver and modified it to hold a gemstone inside, one with a powerful magical essence, turning it into a magical projectile firearm. Adri's shooter was silver with a brown handle, a light blue glow seeping out from its insides—in the next instant, quick as lightning, he pointed the shooter at Death's face, the barrel mere inches from its forehead, and without word or breath, pulled the trigger.

CLICK.

Nothing. No smoking barrel. No screams. No Death clutching a bleeding head. Nothing. An unforgivable mistake. Adri stared at the shooter in disgust, feeling incredibly foolish. He kept the shooter under his pillow for obvious reasons, but he hadn't loaded the damn thing. Across the room, in a wooden box, lay the ammunition that the accursed weapon was missing. Before he could think any further, Death's gauntleted hand reached over and snatched the weapon from his grasp.

'Curious,' Death spoke, turning the shooter around in his hands, examining it from all angles. 'I have seen these before.'

Adri stared incredulously at Death as it handed him the shooter back.

'It is of no use, human. Weapons do not affect me.'

'There's been a mistake somewhere,' Adri spoke.

'Your words do not affect me either,' Death replied. 'Your soul is mine.' It stood up then, nine feet tall, the chains across its body rattling and clanking as they were pulled up from their resting places. An extremely tall, terrifying creature, old, powerful, dominating, it loomed over him. The shawl fluttered in the afternoon breeze. The darkness beyond the mask pierced into him. Adri felt fear. Real, raw fear. This was it.

'But not today,' Death concluded. 'As per the rules, and my personal touch of sympathy, I give you twenty-four hours to make your peace with the Gods, to say goodbye to your loved ones, and to undo your wrongs. I will be where you are tomorrow to take what is mine.'

Adri stared as Death turned to leave, hunching to avoid the skull lamp. At the doorway, it paused and turned around. 'Oh, and I guess your *plan* was to shoot me with your concoctions, which would not have had any effect on me whatsoever, then jump out of the window, crashing rather painfully, I might add, in the alley below, pick yourself up along with your broken bones, and *hobble* away from *me*? Laughable.' It started on its way, but Adri interrupted.

'Horseman,' he said, 'I need more time.'

'That's what they all say,' Death replied.

It bent down and moved out of his doorway. Adri heard it descending the staircase, the chains rattling. Beyond earshot then. Beyond sight. Whatever. How did Horsemen travel anyway?

He heard a loud neigh and wanted to kick himself. Horsemen. Right. Adri did not move. He needed to think. Lighting another cigarette, he lay back in his bed.

The young Tantric was not typically handsome, but he did have a rugged sharpness to him that warranted a sly, second look. He was slim and muscular, apart from the slight belly trying to burst out, that is; luckily, he was good at holding his breath, managing to pull his stomach in at the most crowded of places, not that he looked the social type. His hair was long, dark, and unkempt, and he was mostly always unshaven. He was tall and lean, old writing tattooed all over his arms, curling serpentine towards his back. He caught the attention of women at times, but he never allowed things to go beyond that. Ever. Tantrics couldn't afford to form intimate bonds with too many women—the very mention of a Tantric was enough to make anyone nervous. But Adri's quiet, reserved demeanour helped him blend in with people who weren't Necromancers. The tattoos were a dead giveaway, of course, but Adri mostly wore full sleeves.

He slept naked though, and he looked down at himself now with sudden horror—he had been naked all this while in front of a mysterious, ancient entity. Had he glimpsed rotten teeth beneath the grates? He hurriedly gathered his bedclothes about him, trying very hard to shrug off this feeling of embarrassment. There were more important things that needed to be taken care of. He needed to save his own life, for one.

Until this morning, he had not known that Horsemen truly existed. He knew nothing really of their weaknesses, nothing of their powers. There were, of course, the old books, the ones that spoke about them in the occasional reference, as ghosts, as monuments forgotten—but they offered no real knowledge. And as it was with every being he had ever fought against, knowledge was the first step. He needed to know more. And he needed to know *why*. Death had dropped certain keywords, certain phrases that indicated that its presence in his room was more than the usual *I-have-come-to-take-your-life-away-mortal* grind. While the words did not make sense to him, they might just do so to another. Someone he knew. An old being, not of this earth, but the only one who could possibly help him now.

Stubbing the cigarette out, Adri got up. Tick-tock, tick-tock. He was living on borrowed time. He had no intentions of saying any goodbyes to anyone just as yet. No. He had no choice, he would have to turn to this being, and seek him out.

Adri hurriedly got dressed—jeans, the usual kurta, the lockets around his neck clinking against each other—and picked up his shooter. Walking to the wooden box at the other end of the room, he took out a fistful of bright red bullets, tucked three of them into the hollow grooves of the shooter, and stuffed the rest into his pockets. He put the shooter inside a leather sling bag, flinging it over his shoulder before slipping into a pair of red slippers. A huge key, shaped like a leaping frog, hung on a nail next to the door. He picked it up, stepped out of his room, locked his door, and headed down the staircase, out into the street.

The new Coffee House was nothing like the old one, not that MYTH had tried recreating the environment either. This was more like a New Age fast-food joint—clean, organised, and well-maintained. The charm of untidiness was not something MYTH would understand. Disarray was not to be found here, not even a speck of it. The waiters were strapping young men bouncing about with trays of food, models of efficiency with uniforms to match. The feel was that of the new and the squeaky clean. The damn place was air-conditioned, Adri observed with discomfort as he made his way up the marble staircase. Still, it had throngs of people, which made it a safe place for a meeting. Crowding Coffee House were people of all kinds, people from everywhere—from the young students of Presidency University and wanderers of College Street, to old timers who came from all over Kolkata just to sit and talk about old times. Forgettable middle-classers would be found discussing politics, MYTH's administration, and the future, while brash film-makers crunched the latest new wave and plans to use actual magic in their films. As Adri wove his way in, overhearing snatches of every conversation conceivable, he wasn't noticed by anyone except his contact.

Aurcoe raised a hand. Adri saw him and made his way towards the young man sitting calmly at a table in one corner of Coffee House. This place was just as noisy as the old one, Adri noted as he reached Aurcoe. It helped the secret conversations. Drawing a chair, he sat down. Aurcoe smiled at him.

Aurcoe looked like any other man in New Kolkata. There was nothing unusual or striking about him. Chubby face, intelligent eyes sparkling from behind a pair of rimless spectacles, thinning dark hair, and a well-fed countenance with belly to match. Very normal, very ordinary. But Adri was a Tantric, and therefore, a bearer of the natural gift of Second Sight, and he could see the creature in his true form—the pearl-white skin and the dry branch-like stumps behind his shoulders.

'Infusion,' Adri barked, and a nearby waiter nodded and rushed off.

'I take it this is not a pleasure meet?' Aurcoe enquired in a completely normal, human voice. He was still smiling.

'No,' Adri replied. 'With your kind it's always business, isn't it?'

'Sen, Sen . . . what could I have possibly ever done to you to earn your disfavour? I am but a humble creature here to answer *your* summons.' Aurcoe added a little tilt of the head, a mock bow.

'Sure. And I am Harry Houdini, come here to pull rabbits out of my—'

Aurcoe laughed, interrupting Adri. 'I did not mean to be sarcastic,' he said, voice dripping with sarcasm. 'But if we do not talk about business, my mind does tend to flicker. I might, for instance, begin to ask you how your father is doing, the great adventurer that he is. *He* though, was miraculously quick where his deals with *me* were concerned . . .' Aurcoe's voice trailed off.

'Save it,' Adri muttered. The creature had a habit of bringing up things one would rather shy away from, rattling skeletons in one's closet. Knowing everyone's secrets made it an effective blackmailer and an expert manipulator, deceptively innocent at first glance, but sly and deceitful to the core. Yet, Adri thought regretfully, the only one capable of helping him. Hesitation. 'I need your help,' he said at length.

'Obviously,' Aurcoe replied. 'I'm not an idiot, Sen. Tell me.'

Adri looked at Aurcoe seriously. A moment of silence. Adri took a deep breath. 'Have you heard of the Horsemen of Old Kolkata?'

Aurcoe did not reply immediately. He looked at Adri, his eyes fast, calculating. His smile was gone. CLANK. The waiter had appeared with Adri's coffee. Adri took a sip and burnt his tongue.

'Four,' Aurcoe said, grim. 'Four Horsemen. War, Death, Famine, and Pestilence.'

'What else?'

'Not much. The usual rumours of their connection to the Apocalypse. Their functions are unknown, most information being old wives' tales. But contrary to a lot of ghost stories, they are for real.'

'Tell me about it,' Adri sighed. 'Death paid me a visit this morning.'

'The Horseman came to your apartment?'

Adri nodded.

'What did it want?'

'My fucking soul. It has given me twenty-four hours to make my arrangements.' Adri hated being straightforward with Aurcoe, and more than anything, being honest. His kind would never reciprocate. They had no honour. Information was like a weapon for his breed, and Adri was handing Aurcoe an arsenal. There was no way of knowing if this creature was lying about the limits of his knowledge about the Horsemen, but one thing was certain—his mention of the Horsemen had caught Aurcoe's attention. This was not a routine affair. Irritatingly, however, Adri could not help but notice that Aurcoe's annoying smile was back.

'You *have* a soul, then?' Aurcoe smirked.

'The clock is ticking, damn it,' Adri replied, irritated.

'I knew this would be about you. Self-preservation, yet again. Tantrics, you know one, you known them all.'

'Are you going to help me or not?'

'Twenty-four hours? By now it's what, twenty-one left? You honestly *think* I can help you?'

'So I'm wasting my time?'

'If the Horseman wants your soul, the Horseman will have it. Who am I to hold him back? And to tell you the truth, Sen,' Aurcoe shuffled closer, 'I think you fully well deserve it. The things that you have done—'

'Have no place in this conversation,' Adri finished, unmoved. 'And look who's talking.'

'Ouch! That hurt, Sen!' Aurcoe pretended to wince.

'I haven't even started yet, Aurcoe.' Adri put his leather sling bag on the table with a soft thud. He knew Aurcoe would sense the magical energy emanating from within and easily identify the shooter in the bag.

Aurcoe glanced down at the bag, and then up again at Adri. 'Like father, like son. Surprising how quickly even Victor would resort to cheap threats.'

Aurcoe had hit something, and Adri recoiled. 'Look,' he said, barely controlling himself, 'I don't have either the time or the patience for your little games. I hate your kind and I hate how you twist words and facts and everything else. In fact, Aurcoe, I hate you. I hate your guts. And nothing would give me more pleasure than to see the things you want the most, denied to you. But that has nothing to do with this. My life is in question and you're the only one I trust to have enough knowledge to pull me out of this mess.'

'You been practicing that?' Aurcoe chuckled. 'In front of a mirror? Doesn't change anything, you know. I told you—'

'What you told me has no place here either. You think I don't know you, Fallen? It's not a question of what *I* want.' Adri looked at Aurcoe, gravely. 'The question here is what do *you* want?'

Aurcoe burst into laughter, clapping his hands ecstatically like a child. 'Oh very good, very good indeed, Sen! I love your hate. I *feed* off it, in fact.' His eyes twinkled. 'Well, now you need to tell me more. Why shouldn't Death have come for you?'

'Because Death does not come for everyone. People die every day.'

'So it's come for you. Maybe it decides to be random.'

'Nothing is random. You know that.'

'What are your leads?'

'Something the Horseman said. Somethings, actually.'

'Elucidate.'

Adri took a moment to recollect. 'Death said it had been *searching* for me. And that's not all. It used the words "as per the rules" while telling me that I had twenty-four hours to settle my affairs.'

'So there are rules,' Aurcoe pondered.

'Exactly,' Adri remarked. 'There are rules, and he was hunting for me. This is planned, and this has been done before.'

'Someone is setting you up.'

'I think so, yes.'

'So who did you piss off last?'

'I can't say I remember. I have many enemies.' Adri regretted saying the words the moment they left his mouth.

Aurcoe did not let it pass. 'I have many enemies,' he mimicked in mock seriousness. 'Look at me, I'm so dramatic and serious and mysterious and dark and cool.'

'I generally piss off people and all other kinds of entities, all right?' Adri sighed, raising his hands in the air.

'Not much to go on though,' Aurcoe remarked, mostly to himself.

Adri looked at him. If he knew the creature well, Aurcoe would soon make his demand, and if he did, Adri could rest assured that the pest was capable of finding out what he needed to know. The Fallen were very confident, but fickle. However, Adri could still not be sure if Aurcoe was really interested, or if everything said so far had been worth Aurcoe's time.

'Very well, Sen,' Aurcoe declared after a pause. 'I can get you the information you want and I can point you out in the right direction as well. But—'

'What do you want?' Adri was desperate to hear this bit. He did not want Aurcoe to recite the favourite fantasy of the Fallen. There was, however, no escape.

'What else, Sen? What else can a Fallen possibly want?' Aurcoe smiled broadly.

'C'mon Aurcoe. Not that. Why *that*?' Adri voiced a feeble protest.

The Fallen were a cursed race. Having fallen from the grace of all things holy and pure, and finding no refuge among the ranks of the unholy breeds either, they were a condemned species that lurked midway between the two, fuelling conflict and solving problems for a price, trying to either win their way back into the higher order, or commit deeds low enough for them to be accepted into the nether orders. They had once been Angels, proud and powerful, but their wings had been ripped off, their skin not retaining the sheen, their blood losing its magical value and rendering them powerless as warriors. The Fallen were damned, but their salvation was always at hand—an essence that they could not procure themselves, yet was the simple path to the restoration of their power and honour. A simple solution for instant redemption.

'The blood of an Angel,' Aurcoe whispered, and Adri thought he saw the want in his eyes, the desperation, the thirst.

'Why now? You haven't asked for it before,' Adri said.

'You haven't asked for *this* before,' Aurcoe snapped. 'What I'm getting into isn't normal, Sen. Even with your limited human senses you should be able to see that. This is big, possibly bigger than you. And if little old me is endangering his existence with this whole poking around business, I might as well get the ultimate reward.'

'Why not ask someone else? This is not the only deal you're making, I'm sure.'

'I'm cancelling my other appointments the moment I get into this, Sen. Make no mistake, this will eat up all my time. And I'm asking *you* to get it because I know you'll manage it. Not praise, mind you. You're pathetic, but you'll manage nicely, I think.'

'The fact that you're *still* a Fallen proves that people don't succeed often, Aurcoe.'

'What, you want praise now? Look, Sen. People have failed, yes. It's not an easy thing to get. But I know what kind of birds you Necromancers are, the whole lot of you. And I've seen you go to any lengths to protect your measly little lives.'

Adri drew back grimly. The blood of Angels. It was twisted—a dirty job, not to mention tough as hell. A lot of lying was involved. Lies and life risks. But that's what came out of associating with the Fallen. Adri took another sip of his coffee, now cold. 'I take it that you have an Angel in mind?' he asked.

'Yes. But you know how tricky they are,' Aurcoe said.

'After dealing with your kind? Hardly.'

'I will pretend I didn't hear that. But you do know the magical formula that guards their presence, don't you?'

Adri knew. It was complicated magic, meant to prevent anyone from discovering the Angel's true form, even with Second Sight. There were two exceptions to this though—one, if the Angel

32

chose to reveal himself, then he would be seen as he was. The second, they could be traced through their siblings from the human families they led their disguised, earthly lives with. Adri would, in other words, need a sibling of the Angel in question.

'You will need a sibling,' Aurcoe said. 'I will give you a heads up. The gracious donor is a powerful warrior Angel called Kaavsh. He will be found near the outer borders of the Lake of Fire. Old Kolkata.'

Adri groaned. 'Can't you find someone lesser? Someone easier to get to? The Lake of Fire is where the war is right now, isn't it?'

Aurcoe stared. 'The point,' he said, 'is to get blood with good, strong magical power. And the territory wars are happening in a lot of places, one of them being the Lake of Fire. *You* should be able to survive in Old Kolkata.'

Adri looked at the Fallen, restraining himself from strangling the creature.

'On the other hand,' Aurcoe continued, 'Kaavsh's sibling is quite close. A girl in Jadavpur University.'

The creature was crossing a line now, Adri realised in horror. It was taking a personal delight in arranging certain things for him. 'I am *not* dragging a girl across Old Kolkata,' Adri said stubbornly. 'Not happening. And there is no way this girl will even agree.'

'Hypnotise her for all I care,' Aurcoe retorted, equally stubborn. 'She's your only ticket, Sen. I don't care how you do it. Her name is Maya Ghosh.'

'Maya . . .' Adri repeated. He didn't know hypnosis. 'Is that all? How do I even contact you?'

'When you do have the blood,' the Fallen said, 'I will find you.'

'I cannot reach the Lake of Fire in a day, Aurcoe. Even if I start now, it's impossible.'

'Concentrate your energies on the girl for now. I will take care of your deadline. Meet me in Old Kolkata tonight. The station. Try and make it before dawn.'

'You really need to take care of the deadline. If something happens to me, you stay Fallen,' Adri said, a final reminder.

This seemed like the only way out. Aurcoe was not to be trusted, but he'd take care of it. Unless Adri's enemies had already hired him earlier . . . Adri shook his head, trying to push back all the horrible thoughts. They were not helping. The task at hand was a curious one—he was not good at convincing people, especially girls.

Aurcoe teleported out of the joint, a convenient exit. Adri had to face the crowd again, jostling and apologising.

2

The plan was simple: Get into the university, get Maya Ghosh, and get out. A problem though—Adri did not know what she looked like. Then there were the Guardians, watching over the gates. Adri had been lurking around Jadavpur University for a while now, mixing with the crowds to avoid the Guardians' eyes, even though he knew they wouldn't make a move unless he crossed the university gate. Of course, there was also the fact that the university was very well protected. MYTH, Adri mused, appeared to value the youth and their education, and Jadavpur University was supposed to be quite good. It offered a huge variety of courses, everything non-magic, of course. MYTH did not encourage the common people to be anywhere near magic, or to have anything to do with it. Adri had never been able to decide whether this was a pity or a good thing, for magic had done a lot of harm as well. And magic was the reason he could not enter through those gates right now.

Guardians were magic hunters, instinctively attracted to magical residue or vibes of any kind, be it emanating from a weapon, an artefact or simply a person who had magic in his blood; they would catch on to it, and in most cases, catch the person as well. Magic had been outlawed, and the Guardians were to make sure it stayed that way. They had a natural shield against magic, making it near impossible to use raw magic to take them down—and as far as physical attacks were concerned, Guardians were trained for years in physical combat and swordplay before they were allowed to serve MYTH. Skilled with their main weapons—the broadsword and shield—they wore a traditional flawless white armour that covered every inch of their bodies, leaving only their faces visible.

Adri knew he gave off a lot of magic, and so did the shooter in his bag. If he crossed those gates, they would be on him like starving wolves. He stayed out of their direct line of sight therefore, watching them carefully. They stood above the university gates, atop the pillars on which the gates were hinged, unmoving, silent like statues, their broadswords pointing downwards, hilts on the underside of their palms. Their eyes, of course, were closed. Bloody magic hunters, sensing everything in the vicinity.

Adri's mind raced. He had never needed to infiltrate an educational institution before; he would usually be seen in places darker and dirtier, greeted by beings far nastier than the noble Guardians of New Kolkata. Adri had taken on Guardians in the past though—the law did not allow him to live in New Kolkata, and occasional encounters with these law-keepers were inevitable. Almost every time he had ended up in jail—every time that he couldn't run away, that is. Adri went to a roll shop and bought a chicken roll, mentally figuring out his options.

The university had several gates, but there were sure to be Guardians on all of them. Adri munched on the chicken, looking darkly at the gates. The old JU, the original university in Old Kolkata, had a secret entrance underground, one that he knew about. Adri looked around with great distaste, at the students with their blind trust in MYTH, their illusion of independence. But that was another business altogether. A girl, having ordered a roll and waiting for it, had been occasionally glancing at him. Best not let this pass. 'Excuse me, er, Miss,' Adri fumbled. 'Would you happen to know a certain Maya Ghosh? I'm supposed to get n touch with her, it's quite urgent, but I happen to have lost her contact information.'

The girl looked taken aback for a few seconds before she recovered and asked warily, 'Which department is she in?'

Bloody Fallen hadn't mentioned that. 'I have absolutely no clue,' Adri spoke, attempting a smile. He wasn't very good at this.

'It's actually a very big university,' the girl said. 'I don't know her, but if you go in and ask around near the central field, you might find someone who knows her.' She got her roll just then and hurriedly walked away, betraying her eagerness to get away from the strange man with long hair.

Not much of a plan, Adri thought, glum. *Think, man. You deal with Demons, this is just about finding a girl.* Time was ticking, he had better come up with something fast. When the idea finally hit him a couple of moments later, Adri cursed himself for not thinking of it earlier. He looked around for a restaurant. There, above him, on the first floor of a building. Striding in, he made a beeline for the bathroom. He locked himself in an empty cubicle and sat down on the commode. The bathroom was spanking clean, Adri noted, yet another example of MYTH's penchant for perfection. A hurried search of pockets. Chalk. Circle swiftly scratched on the floor. Furiously quick. Star, runes here and there. Pentacle.

'Arrive,' he spoke in the Old Tongue. A deafening siren sounded throughout the building almost immediately. A Familiar had materialised, hovering in front of Adri inside the cubicle, waiting for orders. The smoke from its body had set the damn fire alarms off. Adri heard rapid footsteps. 'Meet me on the roof,' he barked, and the Familiar nodded, making its way towards a ventilator. Stamping out everything he had drawn, Adri stepped out of the bathroom right into a sea of distressed people. It took ages to cross that sea, answering queries, denying accusations of smoking in the bathroom, and shirking responsibility for setting off the alarm.

The Familiar was waiting for him on the roof. A humanoid form of smoke and gas, it hovered on the roof silently, looking like the discharge from some ancient diesel machine. Adri approached the Familiar. 'Distraction purposes mostly. You are to enter the gates of the university, and lead the Guardians on a chase so that I may gain entry. Understood?'

The Familiar nodded. Drifting closer to the edge of the terrace, it peered at the university gates across the street, and then, turning back to Adri, it spoke in a murky rumble, 'There are two Guardians as I see, my Master. Only one of them will come after me.'

'Split yourself.'

'I understand, my Master. But when they catch up with me, I will be submitted to questioning. And as you must be aware of—'

'You do not lie to any man, yes. You have permission to dissipate before they get too close. A few minutes are all I need.'

'Very good, my Master.'

The Familiar melted to the floor, a thin carpet of smoke at foot level. It crept alongside Adri as he made his way down the stairs through the crowds, towards the university gate. Adri stopped at a safe distance from the gate as the Familiar continued. It split into two just before it reached the gates, and passed through, picking up speed.

The twin Guardians opened their eyes together. 'INTRUDER' one thundered, as they leapt off their pillars, landing on the campus grounds, their swords and shields ready. Dust erupted as they recovered from their jumps, straightening up and looking ahead. The Familiars swooped away like shadows of a cloud. The Guardians gave hard chase, running surprisingly fast for their size. Someone screamed as the Guardians pushed past them, but most of the students simply fell back in silence, giving way—none of them had spotted the Familiars; they were far too stunned to see the forever-still Guardians move.

Adri was already inside. He walked past parked cars and bikes, heading deeper inside towards the academic buildings. Students stood in groups all over the central field, talking and gossiping. Approaching them, Adri began asking questions, for some inexplicable reason, introducing himself as a journalist. When he finally found Maya, she was busy in conversation, and Adri was curiously inspected by three of her brawny friends as he went and introduced himself.

'Journalist?' Maya asked suspiciously. Olive-complexioned, long black hair tied back in a neat ponytail, and sharp features, Maya had a certain calmness about her. It made one think of quiet places immediately. Coupled with the intelligence in her eyes, one would probably add knowledge to the equation, knowledge of some sort. A library in the lonely, pretty forests, Adri thought. That's what she reminded him of.

And so he was meeting a girl, rather pretty, right before setting off on a long, dangerous journey into a treacherous land. Adri shook his head and ignored the cliché. He just wished her male friends would stop glaring at him. He hated fistfights. For a second he wondered darkly if the Fallen had intended one to happen.

'Okay, no. Tantric,' he replied.

The girl's eyes widened. Her burly friends drew back. Whispers erupted as distrust turned to awe, and on to deeper distrust. *Good. At least they know what a Tantric is capable of.*

'Am I in trouble?' Maya asked. She had lost her calm. Far behind her, he saw a Guardian still on the chase.

'No,' he spoke. 'I . . . um . . . I need your help. Something important.'

She did not look entirely convinced. '*My* help? Why me?' A part of her wondered if this was a joke. Adri did not look familiar. 'Are you with MYTH?'

'I'm sorry, but I can't say anything in front of all your friends.'

'Then where?'

'Anywhere. Your friends can stay around if they don't eavesdrop, that's all.'

'How 'bout Banerjee's classroom?' someone prompted, evidently excited about the idea. Much more than Maya. 'It's empty.'

Maya looked unsure. 'Fine, but my friends will come along and stand right outside the class,' she spoke.

'Please,' Adri said. 'Lead the way.'

The group moved together and Adri shuffled a short distance behind. He could hear them whisper. Adri was secretly quite satisfied with the developments so far—it seemed he was not altogether incapable of having conversations with young women after all. Still, too many of the common people nursed all kinds of grudges against Necromancers. They were going to a lonely spot—it was best to be careful, he thought. He kept looking around nervously for signs of Guardians, but thankfully there were none to be seen.

A confusing jaunt across college buildings, a flight of stairs, and a few corridors later, they reached a spacious classroom. The group turned to look silently at Adri, who entered without a word. Their eyes went to Maya. She looked nervous.

'Just stick around, okay?' she said.

'We'll be right here, if he tries anything,' one of the guys growled.

'I don't think so,' Maya replied. She entered the classroom.

Adri was sitting in the back row of the class. She sat down on another bench, keeping distance. He looked complicated, she thought. Adri was looking down at a desk—evidently thinking of how to begin. This had better be good. She doubted his claims of being a Necromancer. Anyone could pretend to be a Tantric. 'Are you with MYTH?' she asked again. A lot depended on his answer.

Adri, however, continued to look at the desk in front of him. A smile dawned on his face. 'They don't let you guys write on the

40

desks anymore,' he spoke suddenly. 'Like everything else, even these are clean and white. Untouchable.'

Maya was taken aback, but she caught on. 'You've seen the old desks? The desks in New Kolkata have always been like this.'

Adri looked at her. 'I've seen them,' he said simply.

Maya looked at him, her eyes a mix of curiosity and suspicion.

'And no,' Adri continued, 'MYTH has not sent me. I have been banned as a practicing Tantric for many years now.'

'Don't mind me,' Maya began, 'but I don't take things at face value. If you want me to believe you, prove it.'

Adri was beginning to like how she was. Logical rather than emotional. Curt, yet she'd been polite so far. Maybe this had a chance of working out. He rolled a sleeve of his kurta back.

'Tattoos of the Necromancer,' she spoke softly, looking at the black, swirling writings. 'Fine. I believe you. Go on.'

'My name is Adri Sen, and I have been involved with the magical arts for a long time. But right now, I need help, help from a certain person who's quite close to you.'

'Who?'

'Your elder brother.'

'Abriti?'

'Yes. Abriti. He has something I need, something that will get a certain *debtor* off my back.' Adri had never been any good at simplifying things, and this was all that he could come up with at the moment. It wasn't the worst explanation in the world, and it left a lot of questions unanswered, but for now, it would have to do.

'What does Dada have that belongs to you?' Maya asked. Dada was a term of respect and endearment for an elder brother, and betrayed Maya's closeness to him.

'I'm sorry, but he wouldn't want you to know,' Adri replied. It worked. Maya looked a little less suspicious than before.

'Dada's not here,' she said after a pause. 'He works for MYTH. He's in Old Kolkata, working in one of their protected research camps.'

Research camps? Adri thought. His human guise must be that of a scientist or something. The part about him working for MYTH, however, was true. For now, the Angels, the Necromancers, and the Sorcerers were all fighting against the Free Demons under MYTH's banner, in a battle that had been raging in Old Kolkata for about ten years now, with neither side showing any signs of a definite victory. It made sense, Adri realised, for the Angel to tell his adoptive family that he was working for MYTH—lesser cover-ups and alibis to come up with.

'I know he's in Old Kolkata,' Adri said. 'But I can't get to him.'

'Obviously,' Maya replied. 'They don't allow us outside the gates.'

'The problem isn't Old Kolkata. The problem is MYTH. I have been banished by MYTH. If I am found anywhere near a MYTH facility, they'd do me in.'

'They will do that to any civilian,' Maya spoke. 'The Old City is anyway out of bounds for civilians of New Kolkata.'

'They'll go easier on civilians. And besides, not if we disguise you as a random civilian of Old Kolkata, then they won't.'

'Disguise *me*?' Maya exclaimed, surprised.

'Ah,' Adri said. "Ah" hardly cut it though. He hadn't mentioned that she would be tagging along to Old Kolkata with him—she had simply, and quite naturally, assumed that he was just seeking information. The revelation of the extent of her involvement had been fast and brutal. He should've broken the news more slowly, more gently, perhaps. But Maya's eyes were brightening.

'*You're* asking *me* to go to *Old Kolkata*?' she asked, her voice thinner.

'Was about to ask, yes,' Adri ventured.

'But that's incredible! You know how to get there?' she asked, clearly betraying excitement.

Adri stared at her. How did he get so lucky? Maya was practically *dying* to get to Old Kolkata. With a complete stranger, even. Maybe she wasn't as mature as she had seemed. But Adri wasn't complaining.

'I can get us to your brother,' Adri spoke.

'Old Kolkata is dangerous,' Maya said, her enthusiasm unabated. 'Will we see Demons?'

'Hopefully not,' Adri replied. 'Like I said, I can get us to where your brother is. All *you* have to do is bring him out to me. I need to talk to him.'

Maya turned thoughtful all of a sudden. 'Look . . . er . . . . Adri . . .' she began awkwardly.

'It's fine, call me Adri,' Adri stated impatiently.

'Yes. Adri. Thing is, I don't know you. You could be anyone, any rogue Tantric who takes me out there and . . . er . . . does black magic on me or something.'

'Why are you so keen on going then?' Adri asked her. 'You're obviously interested in Old Kolkata. Weigh that with the risk.' He had given Maya an ultimatum. He expected it to work.

'I need time to think about this,' Maya said.

Adri nodded understandingly. 'I can give you half an hour.'

'Half an hour?' she repeated, incredulous.

'I have to reach Old Kolkata before dawn. It's a *very* strict deadline.'

Maya got up and walked towards the blackboard, her fists clenched. One of her friends, a girl, came halfway into the classroom. Maya gestured that everything was all right and her friend went back. After a while, Maya followed her outside. Questions. Whispers. Giggles. Adri suddenly realised everything had been dead quiet so far. Bloody eavesdroppers.

It was an hour later that Adri hurried down the stairs, with Maya in tow. One hour. An entire hour, half an hour more than he had bargained for. This wasn't good, Adri thought. He couldn't afford to be *this* lax with his time, not with what was waiting beyond the deadline.

'My friends hate me,' she panted.

'They don't trust me,' Adri murmured.

'*I* don't trust you,' said Maya, shaking her head. Maya's friends were watching darkly from the second floor. She waved to them cheerfully, while Adri walked on. She was carrying a backpack. Must be books, Adri thought. Reaching the college grounds, Adri began scanning the area for Guardians. None could be seen. Only students.

'Where are we going? I need to pack my stuff,' Maya said.

'Fine. Where do you live?' Adri asked.

'Near Ruby.'

'I need to pack my stuff too, and I live closer. Let's go to my place first.'

'Okay, where do you—'

'Gariahat.'

'That's pretty close.'

They continued walking fast, occasionally conversing, until all of a sudden, Adri stopped dead. Then he turned around, and walked back briskly. Puzzled, Maya looked ahead only to see the twin gates of the university in the distance.

'What is it?' she asked, following him.

'Is there a bathroom around here?' Adri asked. Luckily, he had remained just outside their range, or they'd have been on to him by now. He should have known that they'd be back on their pillars. It had been more than an entire hour, for heaven's sake. He needed to distract the Guardians again.

'A bathroom?' Maya repeated.

Adri was not even listening to her as he looked around frantically. Maybe in one of the buildings—

'Is it the Guardians?' Maya asked.

Adri stopped. 'Yes,' he replied. 'They will sense me easily.'

'Okay,' Maya spoke. 'We'll jump the wall.'

'We'll do *what*?'

The low wall was a long walk away. Adri could see the neat pile of white bricks the students had placed beneath the structure to make the jump easy. There were no Guardians here, he observed, jumping the wall and landing on the other side, close to a busy intersection he knew well. They could get a bus from here easily.

'See? Wasn't so tough, was it now?' Maya said, out of breath. 'Why were you looking for a bathroom?'

There was no way Adri was going to tell her about his Familiar trick now. A low wall? Seriously?

On the bus they sat on separate seats. Maya fished out a book from her bag and started reading. Observing her, Adri realised this was going to be a strange journey. Maya had, for the moment, agreed to come—he was glad about things working out this easily. She did not seem like the average girl though. No, it would definitely take time to understand her, and he needed to understand her to manipulate her. She was doing him a favour; he couldn't let things turn sour. He couldn't be rude, for one. Adri did not prefer being this calculative about people, but it had become second nature. An unforgivable profession, Necromancy. The matter at hand was a delicate one. He *needed* Maya.

Just like its predecessor, New Kolkata too had a lot of traffic; the bus took its time to travel the short distance to Gariahat. Adri did not like it. He could feel each second, every moment, the entire day almost, scrape past slowly but yes. The traffic lights irritated him, as did the other vehicles that slowed the bus down. He needed to move faster, dammit. They got off, only to get swallowed by the crowd—a whirl of people and colours, hawkers screaming their prices, flashy goods brushing against shoulders, multitudes gushing through narrow streets. Claustrophobia. A pickpocket's paradise. Something like the Esplanade of the Old City, thought Adri. He was used to it, and fighting his way through the crowd, he cleared out a passage for Maya. She followed gingerly. Once or twice they almost lost each other in the crowd.

Maya didn't see the sudden gap between the two buildings, a narrow crevice, almost undetectable, until Adri slipped into it. She inched in behind him, carefully avoiding the adjoining sewer, until Adri took a sudden right and disappeared. A small opening. A flight of stairs. Adri wasn't visible, but she could hear his footsteps, climbing up. Looking around for a second, Maya followed him. An open door greeted her on the first floor landing and she peeped in, delicately. Adri was pottering around his small one-room flat.

'You didn't lie about being a Tantric,' she spoke, awestruck, as she stepped in, leaving the door ajar. Adri's room was strange. Maya looked around, her gaze travelling from one object to the next, eyes wide in wonder. She touched things, lightly, gingerly, briefly.

'Be careful,' Adri spoke, looking at her. 'Don't go around touching everything you find mysterious, or harmless, for that matter.'

'Sir, yes, sir,' Maya whispered, staring fascinatedly at the skull lamp. She inspected the pentacle on the floor with great interest, moving on to the numerous scrolls scattered all over the single table in the room, most of them rolled up and sealed with black wax. The air smelt of some peculiar incense, she realised. Or this guy smokes a weird brand, she thought, spotting an ashtray.

Adri moved off to a corner near the bathroom door and pulled something out from beneath a tomb of books. A backpack. Dusty. Carrying it to the window, he slapped it against the sill, dusting it noisily and vigorously. Long trapped dust exploded, fleeing its confines, making Adri sneeze.

Maya's gaze had turned to Adri—to this twenty something Tantric, no older than a college student, sneezing away. Old Kolkata was a dangerous place, she had no doubt; but her doubts about Adri rose, about his ability to protect her as promised. Maya knew a lot, but knowledge was not enough to survive in the Old City, she needed someone with experience. And Tantrics were supposed to have a lot of experience. Were *supposed* to. Adri sneezed again.

She was losing confidence in Adri. But going to Old Kolkata was imperative for her—she wasn't an idiot to run off on adventures with complete strangers. The young Tantric seemed like the perfect vessel to get to the Old City. Once there, she would find a way to take care of her business, it was a city after all, roughly modelled the same way as New Kolkata. Even if she had to ditch Adri, with luck she would find her way around. Right now, however, Maya needed Adri. She had tried to leave the city before and had failed. Besides, she was curious to know if he would live up to his boast.

She hated the fact that he was a real Necromancer though. She was hoping he would turn out to be a fraud, his tattoos temporary; she wanted him to be someone who would just take her into the city and disappear. She didn't want him to be a problem later on. Tantrics were a tricky lot, and people who managed to offend them did not live to tell the tale. She was wary of him, but her doubts about his abilities kept her reassured. It was best to keep Adri thinking she was an innocent curious kind of girl. This room held no signs of a girlfriend; Adri didn't seem experienced at all in dealing with the fair sex.

An oblivious Adri had finished dusting the bag. He started packing. Some spell-books, pocket-sized, bound in brown leather. A couple of glass vials, different sizes, all packed carefully within the folds of a soft cloth. Some clothes. A few wooden cylindrical containers, painted black, dropped carelessly. There was nothing methodical about his packing.

It was while throwing in a couple of dried human bones that he heard it. A creak, against the door. Very slight, but enough. Adri whirled around and rushed past a startled Maya, disappearing outside the doorway. Sounds of a scuffle. And a moment later Adri was pulling in a struggling figure. The fight ended, the newcomer landing hard on the floor and Adri crashing against a stack of books.

The figure on the floor was that of a youngster. The most startling thing about him was his pearly white hair, a confused fuzz stacked atop his head, each individual strand a viciously tight curl. Dressed in a formal shirt and jeans, he was handsome, with a striking face and fair built, though there was not a trace of muscle anywhere on his body. He was gasping for breath on the floor, his eyes shooting daggers; but not at Adri.

'Gray!' Maya exclaimed, eyes wide.

'Who's he? Do you know him?' Adri wheezed from the floor.

The newcomer turned to look at him. 'You can say that,' he muttered, his voice resounding with anger.

'Boyfriend?' Adri asked wearily.

'Younger brother,' said Maya. 'Someone who has a lot of explaining to do right now.'

'I knew it, man. I *so* knew you were going out with some . . . some . . .' Gray looked spitefully at Adri.

Adri glared back. This wasn't the Angel. This was the younger brother. So there *was* a younger brother in the family, someone capable of finding Kaavsh. And yet the Fallen had skipped this little detail, pairing him up with the girl instead, making the job so much more painful. Fallen's little joke. Adri thought of retaliation, but Gray's accusations reached his ears, withdrawing him from the recesses of his mind.

'He's *not* my boyfriend, Gray,' Maya spat. 'And even if he was, it does *not* give you any right to follow me around like this! What were you thinking?'

'Excuse me, but I think I have the right to know who my sister is dating,' Gray muttered defensively, sitting up.

'I will *slap* you,' Maya told him.

'You can't. Not after you've been caught with this bloody Necromancer!' Gray stated.

'Hardly *caught*. You don't know *caught*,' Adri said, rolling his eyes. He was still spread-eagled against the pile of books.

'I'm not dating him, Gray.' Maya felt her anger slowly ebb away. She was the one who would have to do the explaining; curiosity and protectiveness were no sin. She detested what Gray had been up to, but she loved her brother.

Gray stood up. 'Oh God, there's hardly any space here,' he complained, making his way to the bed and sitting in a corner, arms crossed against chest. 'Explain.'

Maya was quite fair about it, telling him about Abriti and how Adri needed his help, ending with the part where she'd have to go along to get their brother out to a safe distance, beyond the reach of MYTH, to a place where Adri could talk to him. Gray did not remain quiet during the explanation, coming up with a thousand questions. But much to Adri's relief, he swallowed the story in the end.

'So you're off to Old Kolkata?' Gray asked in a tone of great disapproval when Maya finished.

'Yes. And *your* permission is the last thing I'm bothered about,' Maya replied.

'Not necessarily,' Adri intervened.

The siblings turned to Adri.

'I need only one of you. So, either of you can come with me. I'm assuming Abriti will recognise Gray,' Adri said matter-of-factly.

Maya looked at Adri with growing horror, and Gray's eyes widened with unexpected surprise. As they began to argue, Adri looked on. Gray had taken the shameless bait he had thrown.

College kids, surely bored, probably thinking the Old City is some tourist spot. Adri wasn't eager to paint the real picture. No. He would obviously prefer Gray on this journey, and his conscience did not speak otherwise. Maya would be a liability, and would not be used to the hardships they would certainly face on their journey. Adri naturally assumed that on grounds of impending dangers and possible wear and tear, the male would win the battle between the siblings. He was wrong.

Maya was adamant. No one could try and stop her from her sojourn to the Old City, *especially* not Gray; she wasn't a little girl anymore, and could take care of herself—something Gray needed to understand. Gray, on the other hand, refused to let his sister go off to Old Kolkata with someone he did not trust, a Tantric to boot. A responsible brother, he claimed rather righteously, would never allow this. He would have to go instead; to keep a watchful eye over the man as he led him to Abriti, who would most certainly know how to deal with him.

Adri left the siblings to squabble and resumed his packing. He was almost done, stuffing in some mercury branches at the last moment, when Maya called him. 'A conclusion?' Adri asked, turning around to face the siblings.

'Take both of us,' Maya said. Her eyes were not meeting his.

'Do I happen to look like a tour guide?' Adri raised an annoyed eyebrow.

'C'mon man. You can take an extra person,' Gray said meekly.

'No. I take you, or I take her. That city is risky, I'm not pulling two people through that.'

'Look, I'm not letting her go alone. And she's not letting me go alone. Give me a solution that's as practical.'

'Toss a coin,' Adri suggested.

Gray considered this, but Maya had started protesting. 'Adri, it's either the both of us . . .' her voice trailed off.

Adri looked at them. Brother and sister, standing side by side, looking back at him. He needed them to find the Angel. What choice did he have anyway? 'I will give both of you fifteen minutes to pack your things. We leave this place in five, beeline to your house.'

Adri picked up the last and the most important thing in his kit—a long, fairly large wooden casket, the size of two shoeboxes piled on one another. There was a custom-made place for it on one side of his backpack; tying it in place firmly, he grabbed a shirt, and headed off to the bathroom.

Neither sibling was too pleased about the other tagging along, but they were temporarily satisfied with the Necromancer's reply. Fidgety, Gray stood up and moved about the room, eyeing everything suspiciously. Maya watched her brother for a moment before turning her attention to the pile of books Adri had crashed into earlier. Neat, black, leather bound books, all identical. She bent and picked one up. The paper was old—like parchment, but not quite—and the book was surprisingly heavy. She opened it. Untidy scrawls crowded the pages. Maya read a few lines and realised what the books were. Diaries. Adri's diaries. At least a hundred of them. She picked another one up. A diary again. How much did this man write? Her curiosity got the better of her and without so much as a second thought, she quickly put a few of them into her bag. There were things to be learnt.

Gray had not noticed. He was busy examining a wooden hand that he had found. He moved the fingers, examining the metal joints.

Adri came out ready, and picked up his backpack. 'Let's go then,' he said. 'We have to travel a lot in the—Oi! Put that down!'

'What is it?' Gray asked, unabashed. 'Is it dangerous?'

'Valuable,' Adri said. 'It's from Ahmedabad, City of the fabled Warlocks.'

'Far West,' Maya murmured. 'Those who make the sun set.'

Adri nodded. 'A long, long journey, thankfully nothing we need bother ourselves with. The Old City is mere hours away. No, what is tough is the walk once we enter.'

'What about food? Do we pack food?' Maya asked.

'Canned stuff,' Adri replied.

'Can I have a weapon?' Gray asked.

'Excuse me?'

'You know, like a magical weapon or something. It's going to be dangerous out there, right?' Gray asked.

'You are not getting a weapon,' Adri spoke, shaking his head. 'Let's go.'

Gray hadn't expected a weapon. He just shrugged and stepped out silently with Maya, and they watched as Adri put out the lights and locked the door behind him.

'Why is the key shaped like a frog?' Gray asked.

'It's a cursed object, it protects my place,' Adri replied, irritated.

'What does it do if someone breaks in?' Gray asked, evidently interested.

'Stop asking so many questions, idiot,' Maya interrupted.

Adri felt a tinge of gratefulness, but it did not last as Gray snapped back, and soon enough the siblings were quarrelling again. Adri descended the stairs rapidly, keeping as much distance as he could from the two. They followed, still bickering.

3

No one knew much about the old storyteller. He would appear, as was his custom, on the dirt road leading to the Settlement once every month, welcomed by the old people and the children. He would find a place to sit, and the little ones, having spotted him from their windows, would come trickling out of their homes, running to him, surrounding him, fighting for a place close to him. He wouldn't stay for very long; after sharing a stock of stories he would leave once more. The hardworking folk did not pay him any attention—for them he was simply an old man with too much to talk about; though everyone did admit that his stories had a certain power of drawing in an audience immediately, not all of whom were children

No one could really remember when he had first appeared in their Settlement, but in the beginning everyone had been wary of his wizened old face, his long white beard, and the sharp eyes beneath those overgrown eyebrows. Every time he visited them, he would be wearing that same white dhoti and kurta, and carrying that same wooden stick as old as he. But over time they had warmed up to him; sure the rumours about him persisted—that he was seen in many places at the same time, that he had been a powerful sadhu once. There were always the more ridiculous whispers that he had the power of prophecy, for which he had traded away his soul, and that he was one of the seven deadliest warriors in the world.

People knew which rumours to be inclined to believe though. He was definitely harmless, a cheerful old man who loved children and greeted everyone with a smile; and he had never spoken of the future, only of the past. His knowledge in folklore and legends was unparalleled, and a gifted storyteller he was. He was said to roam throughout the burned lands, moving from place to place, Settlement to Settlement. He had been seen as far as Ahzad in the far north, and even at Kanyakumari—the holy communion of the three seas in the south, always in the same white dhoti-kurta, always unharmed.

Right now he was in the realm of Old Kolkata, in the Settlement of Barasat, a Settlement that fell in the shadow of the Shongar Ruins. He had hobbled into the Settlement as he usually did—the peacekeepers lowering their customised weapons to let him pass without a second thought—and he had found himself a place beneath one of the old surviving banyan trees of the area. The kids gathered around him immediately.

'Story, Dadu!' they shrieked. 'Story!'

The old man laughed with delight, keeping his stick on his lap as he sat cross-legged among the children. 'You want a story, huh, Mira? And you too, eh, Jyotish? A story you shall hear, then!'

He always remembered all the children's names. Never did his old age slip up his memory, not unless it was a deliberate act in his storytelling when he did not want to give something away. The old storyteller scratched his beard and looked up, his eyes unfocused as he recollected.

'Story, Dadu, story!' the children chattered excitedly.

The old man began: 'Back in the days when the sky was blue, there lived a Dragon. Not a shape-changer, but a true Dragon of the Earth, hatched from an egg blessed under the seven constellations of the powerful. His name was as old as the Earth itself, a name carved in granite and gold—a name we still whisper in our dreams to protect us from nightmares. Dhananjay,

54

the greatest hunter to have ever lived, was closest to the Dragon and a very good friend. They used to hunt together, and cook, and talk about things old and forgotten.

'The Serpent of the Ondhokaar was born soon, fuelled from all the hate and the deceit in the world at that time—growing up stealing cows and goats from herds, it soon grew powerful and strong. The Serpent of the Ondhokaar hated the Dragon, and challenged him to many fights, all of which it had to escape from for fear of its dreaded life. The Dragon never pursued it back to the Ondhokaar—he let it live, partly out of pity for the corruption that fuelled its existence, and what his other reasons were we will never know, as he was a great and powerful creature, and is said to have only shared his thoughts with the Hunter.

'The Serpent hated the Dragon, and knew it would never equal the Dragon. So, it conspired. With several creatures of shadow, it hatched a plot to claim the great being's life.

'On that day of great sorrow, while the Dragon slept, they covered his earth-brown hide with black shadow. Meanwhile, Dhananjay, having heard so many complaints about the Serpent from the people he protected, was tracking it—and the Serpent led him to the cave where the Dragon blissfully slept. The black skin clouded the hunter's judgment and mistaking the Dragon for the snake, he let loose a well-aimed arrow of such power that it claimed the Dragon's life in three breaths it took. The Dragon had time to open his eyes, however, and see the face of his killer. Eyes wide open in shock, he gazed upon Dhananjay and then his eyes closed forever, his giant body an unmoving heap.'

The children listened, caught in the story, their young faces betraying both wonder and fear. A dead silence descended on the little group.

The old storyteller began again: 'Dhananjay realised the treachery involved. Devastated, he wept and he wept beside the body of his oldest friend until he could take it no more. Taking out a dagger, he was about to plunge it in his own heart when he was stopped by a voice. A sage, a sadhu had been meditating in the same cave and he had sensed everything that had happened. "Take not your life for this sin, Hunter," he said. "The guilty are still free, and they will be capable of many such acts if your arrows do not stop them." Dhananjay faced the sadhu and asked for his means of redemption. "You have slain an innocent," the sadhu replied, "and for that you must pay the price with your own death. But death comes in many ways, and in that you have a choice. For now, avenge the great creature before you and put an end to the sly Serpent, for it is as responsible for his death as you are."

'Dhananjay broke off a single scale from the Dragon's body, and sawed off a single fang from its mouth, and then, working for months, he fashioned a sword out of the fang, and a piece of armour from the scale. He wore the armour and took the sword in hand and went into the Ondhokaar to find the lair of the beast. He killed it after a long battle, finding his redemption through the Dragon tooth that pierced its black heart, and the Dragon scale that protected him from the Serpent's venom.

'But the Ondhokaar was a maze, and by the time Dhananjay could find his way out, years had passed. He made his way back to the cave and buried the Dragon, burying the sword and the armour along with him. The sadhu was still there, and Dhananjay first sought his blessings and then asked for his permission to seal the mouth of the cave from prying eyes so that his great friend could rest forever. The sadhu granted him the permission to do so, and Dhananjay did, sealing the sadhu in as per the sadhu's wishes. But he left a back door to this tomb, one to which he alone had the key, this entrance prepared for a specific reason.

'For hundreds of years Dhananjay hunted, but his mind was not at peace. He missed his old friend, but that was not what plagued him—no, what bothered him was the thought of what the Dragon had seen in his dying moment. He had seen the hunter, holding his bow tight, the freshly released arrow now deep within his own heart. The Dragon had not said anything. Dhananjay was proud of their friendship, and could not bear the thought of what had gone through the Dragon's mind as he died. Was it the horror of betrayal? Dhananjay screamed to the skies in agony of this thought, and the very gods were scared—they sent storms and rain to calm him down, they sent great and vicious monsters for him to hunt. But nothing seemed to quench this thirst of the Hunter. He travelled the earth, hunting and looking for something he didn't realise. Until he heard of them.

'Dhananjay had been hunting frost giants in the North when he heard about a curious trio of men. They were called Necromancers, Talkers to the Dead. A village shaman told the hunter what he needed to know—they were powerful and secretive, and would not divulge their art to anyone; all three had ascending levels of power in their art.

'Dhananjay went to where the three lived, in the depths of a forest surrounded by graveyards, called *Pai-jinoshk*. Dhananjay had been warned by the same shaman that the graveyards were infested with revenant, but they were nothing he hadn't dealt with before, and he cut hundreds down as he made his way deeper into the forest. Finally he did meet the three, and he had to answer three questions for them before they would talk to him. He answered the questions correctly, and the Necromancers asked him what he wanted. "I want to talk to a dear old friend," he replied. "Someone who is already dead."

'It was not an easy task to recall a Dragon's spirit into the world of the living, but that was the power of the Necromancer, as it is to this day—they were the ones who could see spirits and talk to them, and the most powerful among them could even command them. So first, the *Doresh el ha Metim,* the man who questioned corpses, tried to call the spirit, but it did not reply. Next was the *Yidde'Oni*, the second Necromancer, the gainer of information from ghosts. He too was unsuccessful. Then it was the *Ba'al Ob*'s turn. The master of spirits held a powerful summoning that lasted for months, and finally the spirit found the doorway it needed and appeared, its spirit form face to face with its old friend. Tears came to the hunter's eyes, and he explained what had happened that fateful day, and how the Serpent was now dead.

'The Dragon heard everything and then in his eyes, Dhananjay saw him smile. The Dragon shared its thoughts with Dhananjay again, like times gone, telling Dhananjay that he had forgiven him the instant he had died—and the proof of course was the fact that the hunter still breathed, for a Dragon's death curse is always fatal. Dhananjay, moved, reached out to hold his old friend's head, but his hand passed right through the silvery creature. The Dragon smiled then and told him to come to the other side when he would. There were many creatures there for them to hunt together. And then the Dragon was gone. Dhananjay stood rooted to the spot of the summoning for the next three days—tears fell from his eyes, freely, and he breathed in old memories of their time together. Then, he turned to the three Necromancers.

'He was very happy with them and he demanded of them that they take apprentices so that the art may be passed on to others. As the Necromancers considered this in the dead of night, a Cyclopidian chimera attacked their camp. It was intent on devouring all three of the dead-talkers; but luckily, after it had killed and eaten the *Doresh el ha Metim* and the *Yidde'Oni*, Dhananjay woke up and fought the beast. It was one of the hunter's toughest fights, the chimera being one of the strongest that roamed the ancient lands. The remaining Necromancer, the *Ba'al Ob*, summoned a thousand and one spirits and sent them to help the hunter, and together they finally slew the chimera. "I fought not for myself, not for you, but for your art," Dhananjay told the Tantric after the battle was over, and with these words the dead-talker realised that he must pass on his art. And so he did. With the help of the hunter, the Necromancer spread his art through the ancient lands. Necromancy, the Art of the Tantric, became better known, better respected. It was much later that Dhananjay died, peacefully, as an old man, and rejoined his friend in the spirit world. They hunted together once more, and their great friendship is seen in the stars even today.'

The old man pointed at the skies and all the children followed his gaze. 'Next Wednesday, children,' he spoke. 'Look to the skies at night and you will see the constellation we call the Twin Hunters. Man and Dragon.'

'Are there Dragons around, Dadu?' a child asked.

'Yes, can we see a Dragon?'

The old storyteller shook his head. 'No. He was the only Dragon there was, there have been none others.'

'Tell us his name, Dadu!'

'His name is not known. He was the only one of his kind, you see,' the old man explained. 'So his name is not needed to remember him.'

'We want to talk to his spirit!'

The old man laughed heartily. 'Ah Jyotish! I am not a Necromancer,' he said. 'But he was a good Dragon,' the storyteller continued. 'I'm sure he would have loved to meet all of you lovely children.'

'Where are the Necromancers then?'

'They run the government of New Kolkata, most of them. Do you understand what government means?'

'Yes, it is what rules us. Isn't it?'

'Yes. It is called MYTH. Have you heard of it?'

'Yes we have!' they replied in unison.

'If any of you ever go to New Kolkata, it is very important to listen to them and obey them. Them and your parents. Do you understand?' Some of the children nodded. 'Good. It is very important that all of you grow up safely and be strong men and women.'

It was afternoon, the streets mostly empty. The sun was up, and the heat bore down on everyone. The old man and the children, in the shade of the giant banyan tree, were comfortable. He continued telling them stories, one after the other, but somewhere in the middle of the fourth one he stopped and looked at the empty street before him. The children were confused. Dadu never stopped in the middle of a story! They urged him to continue, but he did not respond to them, steadfastly peering instead at the street in front of him. Winds blew, scattering leaves and swirling up dust in the afternoon heat and in its midst, the old man saw someone walking down the road towards them.

The figure came closer. A little girl, dressed in a skirt and a top that was a faded white and purple. She was very young, about six, with bright, gleaming skin, and dark black hair. Her face however, was not visible, for she wore a mask. It was a dark brown wooden mask of a grotesque being, a *rakshas* of some sort, with bulging eyes and little eyeholes, and horns and huge teeth carved skilfully. The little girl walked towards them, stopping when she saw the storyteller. She surveyed him silently, and he looked back at her. Then, after a very, very long pause, she turned and walked off into a side alley.

The old man looked at the children. 'When did Kaveri get that mask?' he asked them.

'Some days ago. She wears it all the time now. We're all scared of her,' the boy named Riku spoke.

'How many days has it been?'

'Two or seven,' the boy replied confidently.

'Does she ever take it off?' the storyteller asked. The children looked at each other, shifty, uncomfortable. No one replied.

'No,' Minti answered at length. 'I used to play with her. Now she doesn't take off that scary face so I don't play with her.'

The old man looked down the street wordlessly. It was empty once again. He got up, grabbed his stick, and bid a hasty goodbye to the children. Then he hobbled off towards the headman's house. The biggest house in the Settlement, it lay in the centre—the old man climbed the stairs to its front porch, his steps slow and painful, and knocked sharply on the door. There was no reply for the longest time, but the old man kept knocking relentlessly until the headman, finally awakened from his afternoon siesta, answered the door.

'What is it, old man?' he asked, irritated.

'Something more important than your afternoon sleep,' the old man replied.

'Don't teach me—' the headman began, but was cut short by the old man's next words.

'Your Settlement is in grave danger.' The old man's eyes burned seriously.

'Danger? From what?'

'You wouldn't know if I told you, and you wouldn't believe me if you knew. But I am sure.'

'Look, storyteller. I allow you to come here, I allow you to stay, to sleep. I grant you shelter, but that doesn't mean you feed me your foul legends. I think you've been out in the sun too long.' The headman looked at the old man in disgust bordering on anger.

'No,' the old man shook his head sadly. 'You must send out a messenger in search of a travelling Tantric. If you do not get a Tantric here in time, you are all undone.'

'Leave this Settlement, old man,' the headman replied. 'I have no use for your stories of doom, neither do any of the people here. Leave now. I do not kick you out because I respect your age.'

'I am bringing the first Tantric I might be lucky enough to find,' the old man spoke, turning around and hobbling out. 'And if you are fortunate,' he said, his back towards the headman, 'then it might not be too late.'

The headman said nothing. Leaning against his doorway, he watched the old storyteller walk the lonely deserted road for a couple of minutes. Then he shouted out loud, 'What should I watch out for, storyteller? What threatens us?'

The storyteller slowed down and turned halfway. 'Do not approach the little girl in the mask,' he said with finality, and continued walking.

The headman watched him go in silence. No one needed to know any of this—and he would be damned the day he let a dead-talker cross the gates of this Settlement. Little girls were not what he was afraid of. It was magic, something he did not understand.

4

'Magic is everywhere,' Adri spoke. 'In the air you breathe, inside the ground your boots are stepping on. Inside that statue, to the brim' —he pointed— 'pretty much everything you see around you has magic. And the thing about magic' —Adri paused as he, Maya, and Gray crossed a busy road and continued walking— 'is that it is *chaotic*. This is what most Necromancers and Sorcerers do not grasp. Magic is not out to help you; it's there to make things go wrong. It's a powerful, destructive force. There is *nothing* good to be found in magic in its purest form.

'We try to wrestle with something that isn't rightfully ours, and in all our hypocrisy, we trivialise it. Sorcerers and Necromancers have tried to control and channel magic the most. Their work has led to the channelling of magical artefacts as energy sources, of all things, in day-to-day life, in things you see everywhere and use every day.' He stopped. In front of him was an arch, white marble like everything else, with steps leading down. The passage was illuminated in bright neon. METRO—broad letters declared at the head of the passage. 'The Metro, for example, runs on magical energy,' Adri said, descending the stairs. Maya followed, and so did Gray, hanging on to every word.

The Metro was almost empty; the last train was due in a few minutes and there were no more trains to be caught after that. A few people lingered here and there, the occasional beggar sleeping on the landing. They walked past the ticket counters and Adri vaulted over the ticket machines. Maya looked around for Guardians and Law-keepers, only to realise that Adri would have sensed them before her. Gray had already vaulted over the machines, copying Adri, and without so much as a glance at her. She followed.

They headed down to an empty platform. Clean, white marble, with the occasional wall-mounted television broadcasting films; news channels had been down for years. There was no one else on the platform. Adri took a seat. Maya followed suit, while Gray preferred to remain standing, taking off his backpack.

'So it's a Metro train?' Maya asked.

'Yes,' Adri replied. 'They will never open the gates of New Kolkata for anyone. This is how people travel in and out.'

'When does this train come?' Gray asked.

'One hour after the last one,' Adri replied.

'One hour to kill, then,' Gray said.

The siblings had packed fast without complaint, while Adri sat in their apartment and played with Maya's kittens. He had not seen either of their parents in the house and he did not ask. His only objection, though, was to Gray's violin case. 'Wait, wait. You're taking a *violin* along?' he had asked, his head swimming.

'I thought we could do with some good music at times,' Gray had replied.

'I'm sure the Demons will love it.'

'Look, I need practice. It's been a really short while since I started.'

'Which means you probably play horribly,' Adri had sighed.

Gray had slung the damn thing alongside his bag, while Adri had been left to rethink his decision of taking these two along. Maya, meanwhile, had been trying to decide what books she should carry. Finally they wore their boots, ready for the journey.

The nearest subway station was only a little far off, and they had to change two buses and then walk a bit, avoiding Guardians all the while. Adri had explained to Gray how Guardians functioned. Maya had spent her time wondering how much of the information was true, whereas Gray drank everything in.

Adri looked around the deserted platform once again to make sure there was no danger, even though he didn't really expect any until they reached the Old City. Seeing no one, he leaned back with a tired sigh and put a cigarette to his mouth. Maya and Gray looked at him, their faces blank.

'I know it's not allowed here,' Adri said. 'A lot of things aren't allowed in New Kolkata. Both of you, for instance, are not allowed to go to the Old City, but here you are, waiting for the train to Old Kolkata, and here I am, smoking in the new.'

'You said you have been banned,' Maya said.

'Yes.'

'So you're not supposed to be here in this city?'

'Correct.'

'So why are you here?'

'I wonder about that myself,' Adri murmured.

'Pardon?'

Adri did not answer, and continued smoking. Maya looked at him, and then looked the other way, her hair covering her eyes with the sudden movement. Adri let the silence brew for a few moments more before he spoke.

'Maya.'

She turned to look at him.

'What's your branch of study?' Adri asked. 'In college,' he added, clarifying. Maya remained silent. Adri did not prod again, and Gray, looking up and down the Metro tunnel, got steadily uncomfortable about the silence. No one spoke for the next half-hour or so, and Gray's footsteps echoed through the empty platform as he walked its length. They heard the sound of the metal shutters clattering shut at the entrances. It was time, and the maintenance people never checked the platforms. One never knew who, or *what,* was bound for the Old City.

'Will the lights go?' Gray asked Adri. 'Cause, you know, I kind of hate the dark.'

'The lights should stay on,' Adri replied.

And they did. The silence maintained itself as well, and Gray wondered if he should get some violin practice done. He hated complete silence almost as much as he hated darkness. He tried making conversation with his sister, but she was taciturn. Giving up, he finally sat down next to Adri.

'This will not be easy, Gray,' Adri said.

'I know. She's really mature, but extremely moody at times.'

Adri looked slightly annoyed. 'I wasn't talking about your sister.'

'Oh.'

'Old Kolkata is not what you are expecting it to be. I have no expectations from the both of you, but you will see things magical, unbelievable. Remember your sanity, and hold on to it like a precious thing. You might see things that will catch your beliefs by the collar and throw them right out of the window.'

Gray looked a little uneasy. 'Things like what?' he asked.

'I can't prepare you for it, believe me,' Adri replied. 'Old Kolkata is a city that does not forgive. Neither does it forget. It is dark.'

Gray felt a tiny buzz start in his tummy and make its way up to his brain. Anticipation. His life in New Kolkata had been more eventful than his sister's, but it had never been enough for him. He had always wished to see the much spoken about Old City. He wanted to breathe in its secrets, to understand how his ancestors had lived there. His city of dreams, unapproachable in its distance, its silence, its invisibility in the city new. Until now. And yet he was apprehensive. His sister's safety was important, and perhaps it was the nudge he needed to embark on this journey—he asked himself if he would have gone otherwise. He did not find an answer. 'Can one photograph magical beings?' he asked Adri after a moment.

'Yes, most of them.'

'Good. I've taken my camera along. I'm a student of photography, actually,' Gray ranted on. 'And being able to photograph the Old City . . . well, it's something I've thought about often.'

MYTH had banned all visual representation of Old Kolkata; and the citizens of New Kolkata had never gotten to see the city. Of course, there were the occasional rebel photographs that leaked out; but no one could confirm whether they were really of the Old City. Speculations, therefore, ran amok.

Adri raised an eyebrow. 'Photographer? I took you for a musician. With your white hair and everything.'

'I was born with the white hair. It is random genetics, nobody's been able to explain it. The violin is a hobby.'

Adri nodded. Most curious. But then he didn't have any friends or acquaintances of his own age. People he knew were much older, some a few centuries old; he couldn't remember the last time he had tried talking to a college-goer. He didn't understand this generation, neither did he want to, for that matter. But it was interesting nonetheless. He hoped he could keep both of them alive while they negotiated the Old City. Adri lit another cigarette. This was going to be stressful, this whole affair. Had to happen to *him,* of all people. If the Fallen ultimately confirmed that all of this wasn't a conspiracy of some kind and that he had been chosen randomly by Death, he wouldn't be surprised. Not at all. He'd only be angry at his typical dumb luck.

The worst part was that he couldn't instil the fear of the grisliest things that could happen in Old Kolkata into the siblings; he *needed* them to come along. He couldn't scare them off. And yet his conscience would not let him push them into the city unprepared. Small warnings, he decided finally. Small tidbits of information to keep them on their toes.

And then, soundlessly, the lights started to dim. Slow, steady.

'The lights!' Gray yelped.

Adri stood up, grabbing his bag. 'Our ride's here,' he said.

Maya had heard it coming before the two of them. She had been walking up and down the length of the platform once her brother had sat down and she was near the mouth of the tunnel when she heard the noise. Before she had time to walk back to Adri and Gray, the train zoomed in, screaming right past her. It wasn't what she had anticipated, though she wasn't expecting the typical New Kolkata train.

'It's not air-conditioned?' Gray asked, looking at it with bulging eyes, as Adri, still smoking, fitted three rounds in his shooter.

The train was a wreck. It looked like a tangle of disfigured metal with rough holes punched in, held together with nothing but prayers. The compartments were old and beginning to rust; most of the windows had no safety bars, and old tube lights struggled to stay alight inside. The compartments were endless, they continued down the tunnel till they ran out of sight. The train stopped with an almighty sigh, the clanking and cluttering finally coming to a stop as age-old brakes screeched. The platform lights remained dim, making the train look creepier still, with its devastated exteriors and lights within.

'Does this thing actually run?' Maya asked incredulously as she picked up her bag.

'There's no AC,' Gray groaned.

Maya spotted what Adri was holding. 'Hey, is that a—'

Adri entered a compartment without answering, sliding open a rusty door. Shooter raised, he walked in, surveying the seats and the overhead baggage compartments with sharp eyes. Apart from a man sleeping in a far corner, the compartment was empty. The siblings crept in after him, and stared as Adri approached the sleeping man, weapon raised.

The man appeared to be a homeless—old clothes, cap pulled over face. Adri stood in front of him and slowly eased his weapon barrel towards the man's forehead. The siblings watched, frozen. Adri gently lifted the cap with the barrel until he got a glimpse of the man's face. Then he turned around and lowered the shooter.

'It's okay,' he said.

A chair car. The seats weren't in as bad a condition as the train itself, and Maya and Gray sat on the other side of the aisle from Adri. Every available inch of the compartment was covered with old, frayed leaflets and posters, scratched messages, and amateurish graffiti. The windows were open; the shutters had long broken away. The platform lights were so dim by now that they could see nothing but darkness outside.

'How long is the journey?' Maya asked, peering out of a window.

'About six hours,' Adri replied.

'Not that long, huh?' Gray commented.

'Gets boring,' Adri said, leaning back into his seat, his bag on the empty seat beside him.

Gray turned around to look at the man in the back row, still sleeping. 'What did you suspect him of being?' Gray asked. 'A Demon?'

'He could have been a lot of things, Gray,' Adri replied, shifting in more comfortably.

'You mean the train isn't safe?'

'Even New Kolkata isn't safe. Nowhere is safe.'

Maya spoke up. 'You're always so vague.' She wondered if the Tantric was concealing information, or hiding his ignorance. Either way, it was about time she got to know a bit more about him than he intended to reveal. His origins or background wouldn't be a bad start. Any information was crucial, just in case he turned on them later on. She had already bound Adri's diaries in brown paper—now she readied one inside her bag, keeping a watchful eye on the young Tantric. He looked ready to sleep off. She would wait until he was, in case he felt any magical vibes from the book or something—she could never be too sure. The train started, sluggishly at first, picking up speed soon. They rushed into an endless tunnel, the darkness outside deepening. Gray peered out of a window, while his sister seemed to hunt for something in her backpack. All he could see was black—the New Kolkata tunnel lights had clearly not been installed on the way to Old Kolkata. He wondered if this train was a secret from MYTH, or if they allowed it to run. The next instant, he froze. A figure was moving towards them through the aisle. A huge man in a blue uniform, the cap pulled over his head, casting his face into shadow. He was built well, his muscles pushing against the uniform's fabric as he walked. He blocked the lights with his size as he approached.

'A-A-Adri!' Gray stammered, looking to his left. Maya was staring at the figure, while across the aisle Adri was sitting straighter and searching his bag for something.

The figure stopped in front of them. Then, in a voice that was more like a grunt, something Gray heard over the noise of the train, he spoke. 'Tickets.'

The siblings looked at the man with their jaws hanging, eyes wide in surprise. In the darkness of the man's face, something moved.

'Here you are,' Adri said.

A red cloth bag, tied at the mouth. The man took it, felt its weight, and grunted.

'All three of you?' he asked.

'All three,' Adri replied, praying he hadn't miscalculated.

The figure moved past them towards the sleeping man in the back.

'Who was that? You paid for us?' Gray asked, while Maya looked on.

Adri took a moment before he replied. 'He's called the Driver,' he said. 'We do not talk about the Driver while we're on the train.'

'What was in that bag?' Gray persisted.

'Later. Believe me, now is not the time. His hearing is *quite* sharp,' Adri replied, leaning back again. Shuteye. This was probably the last opportunity to grab a few hours of good sleep. If only sleep would come, if only that infernal ticking would leave. Tick, tock, tick. Every second. Leading to the dawn. His death. Death. A Fallen's promise; what was it even worth? He could not sleep, how could he, when his life was literally in the hands of someone he could not trust? Adri frowned, despite himself. He counted the seconds with mad helplessness.

Gray turned around and looked behind him, at the door that the Driver had gone through. It was solid metal. For an instant, just for an instant, he had a mad urge to run to the door and throw it open. He looked outside again. Darkness. It was going to be a long trip.

5

Adri wasn't happy. He didn't trust Demons and he didn't like summoning them. Besides, under more normal circumstances, no boy his age would be expected to summon Demons. But then he had seen things not normal. Things he would remember for life.

'I don't want to trust a Demon,' Adri spoke with finality. His voice was young. Untarnished. Innocent.

'It's like a formula, Adri. A mathematical formula. You put things on the board, you do it right and perfect, and there is no reason why the Demon won't carry out your task,' Victor explained for the hundredth time.

'My Familiars can handle my tasks, Father,' Adri spoke with the air of someone clutching at straws.

'Familiars? Ha!' Victor scoffed, turning away towards a giant window, as big as an entire wall. 'They can't even keep your secrets, can they? Not to mention their amazing fighting skills.'

'I don't want to call Demons,' Adri insisted.

'Are you afraid of them?' his father asked.

'No.'

'Really, Adri?'

'I'm not afraid.'

'This is the age you have to start at, my boy. By the time you are my age you shall be perfect, you shall be flawless. Undefeatable.'

Adri remained silent.

'Adventure is the ultimate aim, Adri. Experience. See it all. Do it all,' Victor spoke with enthusiasm, turning back to his son.

'I'm interested,' Adri admitted. 'I'm interested in what I learn, Father.'

'Then why not Demons?'

Adri was silent once more. 'I've heard bad things,' he spoke at length.

'You've heard that they kill Summoners even though all the conditions have been fulfilled. You've heard that our protective measures don't work against them at times,' Victor said.

'Yes,' Adri muttered.

'You heard wrong. Nothing steps inside the circle. Nothing! You are always safe within it if the other measures were correct, if your incantations were correct, if the pentacle and the sacrifice were correct. Anything goes wrong, feels wrong, banish the Demon immediately.'

Adri was silent.

'Seven hundred and sixty-two summonings, Adri,' Victor continued, his voice now barely audible. 'And as you can see, I'm still alive.'

'Father,' Adri asked, 'have you ever summoned an elder Demon?'

'Several,' Victor replied.

'Have you ever summoned one from the realm of shadow?'

The question hung in the air. 'Have we been reading forbidden books, then?' Victor asked softly.

'No books are forbidden to me, Father,' Adri replied gently.

'This is exactly the kind of attitude I want from you,' Victor said. 'You must know more, much, much more than is expected from one your age. I am happy.'

Adri nodded politely.

'You question is an important one, but you do not corroborate it with research. Demons of shadow do not heed our call. They are not bound to human summoning.'

'And if one is called?'

'If someone is silly enough to call a being they cannot control or banish . . .' Victor shook his head. 'I'm not telling you to do as you wish. Read the books, ask me questions. Learn the rules. But what I've been trying to tell you is that Demons can't just be read about in books. You have to summon them, talk to them, see them for real, breathe in their stench, look into their eyes. *Then* you will begin to understand the power of the Tantric.'

'I have been doing some summonings,' Adri spoke.

'Spirits. Yes. And you are impressive in calling them. You might even be *Ba'al Ob* one day if you keep carrying on like this. But you sharpen the arrow and do not attend to the bow. You are a Necromancer, and you must understand that you *have to* know by code everything there is to know about summoning, banishing and exorcising both Demons and spirits. Incompetence in either one will make you fail. And in our line of work, failure can be rather *grisly*.'

'I will not disappoint you, Father,' Adri said softly.

'Start with the younger Demons, the weaker ones. The inexperienced ones are easier to catch, faster to summon.'

'I really need to work with Demons, is it?' Adri muttered, mostly to himself.

'Stop running away, boy. Remember the basic summoning rules.'

'Yes, Father.'

'Well, what are they?'

'Higher power, The Telephone Call, and Precautions.'

'Excellent. Demons are the best keepers of secrets, always remember that. If a Demon does something for you, not a soul gets to know. That is the only reason Tantrics use Demons. That, and their massive reservoir of unholy power. Powerful creatures they are.'

'What is the most powerful Demon you've met, Father?'

Victor was thoughtful for a long time. 'The one which had destroyed the city of the Kushanas alone,' he replied. 'Ba'al. A Demon of incredible power, and I think it was young then, as far as Demons are concerned.'

'Did you summon it?'

'Yes. It took a couple of days to make all the arrangements and preparations, but yes, finally it was me who summoned it. The city had to fall, and we knew it could get the job done. It did.' Victor's eyes were cast to all the years back, to all the blood and the killing. Sigh. He missed those days. Adri didn't miss the sigh.

'This was before you were born,' Victor added, all of a sudden. Adri said nothing. He had Demons to summon.

Maya looked up from the diary. Adri was sleeping, and looked more vulnerable than ever. Maya gazed at his face, one that had evidently been forced into prematurity. She had no clue as to how Necromancers were trained, or what they had to go through, and the diary was vastly interesting to her. About the young Tantric she now knew a bit more than before. It felt curiously good. She looked to her right and saw Gray snoring, head against a lone window grill. She turned around. The sleeping man hadn't moved. What was it with everyone sleeping? Was the train so safe after all? The Driver, he had given her the chills; who was he anyway? *What* was he? Did he leave the wheel to collect tickets while the train sped? And why had Adri kept his magical weapon raised and ready as he had entered the train? Evidently they could be in danger. And now Adri was fast asleep, as was Gray. So-called protectors. Not that she needed protection, but danger could be anywhere.

The compartment door up front slid open again. Maya caught a brief glimpse of the empty vestibule beyond as an old woman entered and slid the door shut behind her. She was old, undoubtedly in her seventies. She walked with a curled walking stick and wore black—a twisted, curving sari. Wrinkles cut deep and strong on her face, almost like scars; there must be a million of them on the face alone, thought Maya. Her hair was a dirty white, neatly tied in a bun, and her eyes, steel grey, looked at the three of them with interest. She did not approach them, choosing a seat right next to the door.

Maya decided to start reading the diary again. She opened it, and the lights flickered. She looked up. Strange. The lights seemed fine. Suddenly, another flicker. Then again. And again. And again.

Maya was wondering if she should call Adri. She looked behind her. The sleeping man hadn't noticed. Nor had the old woman, though Maya could just see the back of her head. The tube lights crackled as the electricity in them shorted. Bursts of dark overpowering the feeble flickers of luminance.

Darkness. Light. Darkness. Light. Darkness. Darkness. Darkness.

'Adri!' Maya called softly. No response. Gray's snores continued, uninterrupted.

Light. A moment of clarity. The old woman was not in her seat anymore. Disturbing. Uneasiness built steadily within Maya. Darkness. Yet again. The train continued moving at its unnervingly high speed.

Another sudden spark of electricity. The lights flared back, this time staying for a fraction of a second. Maya's eyes, reeling from the flash, glimpsed the old woman. She was on the *ceiling*, nestled among the fans, on all fours, her hair hanging, her clothes billowing.

Maya screamed.

Her scream was cut off as a strong hand clamped itself firmly over her mouth. As she desperately tried to fight the hand away, a voice whispered in her ear. 'Sssshhh!'

Adri's voice helped Maya overcome her hysteria. 'Adri!' She shrieked in relief, but his hand tightened down on her mouth. Maya, even in panic, realised that the Tantric wanted her to shut up. She was relieved to have him, have someone to help her overcome what she had seen. She wanted to hug him and bury her face in his shoulder and not face the darkness, but Adri whispered again, and she struggled to listen.

'Maya! Maya, I need you to be brave,' his voice spoke in the dark. 'You have to trust me, trust what I say. Everything . . . *your life* depends on it.'

Tears were running down Maya's cheeks, and she nodded.

'First of all, silence. Whisper, don't talk,' Adri continued, still covering her mouth. She nodded again, and Adri slowly relaxed his grip, letting go.

'Hold my hand, Adri. I'm scared. I'm so scared,' Maya whispered, her voice thin. Adri did.

'Listen to me. This is important.' He paused. No sounds, nothing except the occasional loud snore from the still-sleeping Gray and the jangles of the speeding train. 'What you saw, the old woman, she is a Dyne. She cannot harm you here, but neither can I harm her while we're on the train.'

'Wh-what does she want?' Maya stammered.

'She wants your *scent*. And we have no choice but to give it to her.'

'My scent?'

'Yes, your smell. She is a smell collector, and she wants to collect from all three of us, if I'm not wrong.'

'So-so what will she do, Adri? What—'

'She will creep over and smell all of us, one by one. It's *very* important, Maya, that you pretend to be asleep when she does. Do not react under any circumstance, no matter what she does. She cannot harm you while you're on the train, but I do not want her to give you the Mark. And that is something vile, I assure you.'

'I-I can't do this!'

'You can. Maya. Listen to me, you're strong. You can do this. And we aren't even in the Old City yet. Now, buckle up!'

Silence, for a while. Then Maya spoke slowly, 'She can't harm me?'

'Not here, no.'

'What is the Mark?'

'I will explain later, I promise. Right now let's concentrate on *not* getting it, shall we?'

Maya nodded after a moment, though Adri didn't see it in the darkness.

'All right, Adri,' she spoke, her voice almost inaudible.

'I have to go back to my seat,' Adri spoke, an apology creeping into his voice.

'Oh.' She gently let go of his hand.

'I'm here. Don't worry. Just sleep off right now if you can.'

Maya knew she wouldn't be able to sleep. That hair-raising flash of light had made her a wreck. She shut her eyes tight, wishing for the image to go away. She prayed to her God with burning urgency, feeling guilty about not being a more regular devotee. But she called his name and she did it again and again and again, trying to dispel the darkness. He would see her through this, she hoped and prayed. Her mind was a whirl of emotions, contrary to her body which was playing dead.

And then she heard a sniff. Right next to her. Then another. She turned extremely rigid, slowly, not even daring to breathe; and in the silence, she waited. Something cold touched her cheek. She almost screamed. It retracted, then touched her forehead, something icy and soft. It stayed for a while, then retreated once more. Biting her lip, Maya readied herself for the next touch; it did not come again. She heard the sniff a moment later, but to her left, where Adri was. It took Maya more than a moment to realise that the worst had passed, that the thing, the Dyne had moved on. But still she lay as one dead, not daring to move. For how long she sat like this, she did not know, nor did she know when the tears started to slowly make their way down her cheeks. By the time the lights came back on, however, she had regained her composure completely, her eyes and cheeks dry as rock. The Dyne was gone. Gray was still sleeping and looked untouched—much to her relief. Adri was looking at her.

'You okay?' he asked.

'Yes,' Maya replied, embarrassed, not meeting his eye.

'Don't feel ashamed. Their kind has what we call an *influence* over our senses; they can affect us in various ways, the most common being the sapping of courage, of will. How you reacted wasn't your fault entirely.'

'How were you so calm?' Maya asked, as she realised why she had panicked.

'Training. And all the experience with their kind.'

'What are they?'

'Witches. Dynes. One of the most terrible races out there in the Old City. I don't know why this one was on the train. But they can't transform here, not on the train, and thus we were comparatively safe.'

'Transform? Transform into what?'

'Their true form. They're not human.'

'*What* are they, then?'

'Savage beings ruled by a hunger for flesh. One of the damned races, also one of the most feared.'

Maya was quiet. 'We aren't even *there* yet. And look what's happening already,' she spoke.

Adri nodded. 'It's certainly not a good start.'

'Why did she smell us?' Maya asked. 'You said she's a smell collector. What does she do with the smells?'

Adri looked into his bag, searching for something. He groped around till he finally withdrew a clutch of bullets coated in what looked like silver. 'You're not going to like the answer,' he replied drily.

'I suppose I must know,' Maya said. 'If I am going with you all the way to where my brother is, then it's best I start preparing.'

Adri nodded in understanding. 'Witches,' he said, 'are predators. And this one has taken our smell because she intends to hunt us down in Old Kolkata.'

'My God. Silver bullets, they kill witches, then?' Maya asked hopefully.

Adri laughed a short laugh. He had laughed after a long while, and it felt good. 'They aren't werewolves, and this isn't silver. It's mercury inside crystal with a couple of more ingredients thrown in.'

'Is it meant for the witches?'

'Yes,' Adri said, removing the current rounds from the shooter and putting in the mercury bullets.

'Okay. I'm glad to know you have *some* sort of defence against them.'

'Not enough. I will need to buy ingredients in the Old City. I need to make more bullets.' Adri pocketed the last two shots for ease of access.

'Will we be okay?'

'Yes, hopefully. I'm not planning to take us through witch territory yet, so if we're lucky they won't bother us again. They're quite territorial, Dynes.'

Maya felt a bit better. Her opinion of him, she had to admit, was beginning to change. Where she had been sceptical about his claims of being a Tantric, she now knew that he had evidently been trained in Necromancy, and trained well—so far he had proved knowledgeable and dependable. And calm in the face of danger. No, he was definitely no pushover Tantric. Sigh. It would be tough to take care of her little business in the Old City. It was something even Gray did not know. No, she knew she would have to move alone. No Gray. No Adri. She needed a map of the Old City, she realised. She considered Adri, taking them along for his own ends and thus, she did not intend to feel guilty about ditching him. If all went well, maybe his problem would get sorted out as well. But her problems had the upper hand for now. The Tantric was never generous with information anyway; he kept to his own devices. And she realised she preferred a taciturn Adri to a talkative one. He had not told them why he stayed in New Kolkata. She realised that he must have had his reasons.

'Adri,' she spoke, 'I didn't tell you back then, I'm a student of Demonology.'

Adri was surprised, incredibly. The study of Demons was not something MYTH would allow easily. It was almost like studying magic—but not quite so—by limiting it to a certain race with magic in their veins. Demons. 'How is your government allowing that?' he asked.

'MYTH has scruples about the idea. But we have a very stubborn HoD, and that is why negotiations with MYTH are still on. The department might shut down any moment, which doesn't make it a very popular subject.'

Adri figured that only the rich and the curious would take a chance with Demonology. Most parents would want their children to study something safer, something with better career options.

'Demonology is safe,' Maya continued, as if she had been reading Adri's mind. 'It's just theory, about everything on Demons.'

'So where do you see your future?'

'The only place the department promises to send us to is MYTH, as advisors to the Sorcerers. Seeing that the Tantrics are Demonologists themselves.' True. For Necromancers it was one of the compulsory degrees they needed to have.

'Yes,' Adri nodded. 'We needed to get the degree early.'

'Were you coached at MYTH Castle?'

'Yes,' Adri paused. 'Which year are you in?'

'My fourth.'

'Hmmm. So you're supposed to know about most Demons by now.'

'I've read a lot of fifth level books as well,' Maya admitted. Like you did in your childhood, she thought.

'Your time in the Old City will not be as dull as we had thought then, Miss Ghosh,' Adri replied, a smile slowly forming on his lips. 'You will be able to recognise a lot.'

'Never seen them,' Maya said. 'Read everything there is to read about them, but I've never actually seen a Demon. Yes, the physical descriptions are there, but MYTH has banned all visual representation. So no photographs, no sketches.'

'They're not pretty,' Adri said. Maya laughed, despite herself.

They talked more. Not that they had much to discuss, the only thing in common being Demons; but it didn't take long for Maya to understand that Adri did not mingle with people much. It was a good conversation though.

Adri was shamelessly making sure she wouldn't back out. The witch incident had unnerved him even more than Maya; if the siblings got scared enough to take the train back to New Kolkata, there would be nothing he could do to stop them. He thought he had the capabilities to protect them and he did not want them thinking otherwise. He had to placate them. Being nice to Maya was a start, and Adri didn't even have to feign interest in what she was saying. He knew little about MYTH's current education plans and agendas and it was good to catch up.

Gray was the one who interrupted them, muttering in his sleep. Maya stopped mid-sentence and turned to him to find that he had woken up and was very, very confused.

'I screamed and you did not wake up,' Maya told him immediately.

'Whaa?' Gray mumbled, disoriented.

'It's probably the influence that made him sleep this strong,' Adri suggested. He had never seen a witch's influence do that to anyone before, but if his guess averted another loud fight between the siblings then he was all for it. Luckily, Maya believed him.

'I guess it's not your fault, then,' she told Gray, who rubbed his eyes.

'*What's* not my fault?' Gray asked, scratching his head. 'God, I'm stiff all over.'

Maya recounted the details, and Gray's eyes bulged.

'No way! You guys are ripping on me for sleeping—' he began.

'She has your scent now, cretin,' Maya cut in. 'That bloody witch will be after us in Old Kolkata.'

Gray looked at her unbelievingly. 'What exactly is a witch?'

'Something MYTH tries extremely hard to keep out of New Kolkata. The great walls were built exclusively to keep out their kind,' Adri explained, careful to keep the panic meter in check.

'Are they photographable?' Gray asked.

He sounded excited.

'Put an address on that damn camera though, so they can mail it back after they find it. I give up,' Maya spoke, and taking out a bottle from her bag, took a drink of water.

Adri looked outside the window and saw a wall-mounted light zoom by. Then another. The train was slowing down. The Old City was coming, and with it a whole lot of accompanying emotions that crowded his mind.

It wasn't just the journey ahead that was bothering Adri. His apprehension was about dawn, and Death's promise to hunt him down in a few hours after sunrise. *Wherever* he was. He could not outrun the Horseman, certainly not in Old Kolkata. No, his life now lay in the undependable hands of a Fallen. A dark smirk edged up Adri's lips. His situation could be laughed at, and if it weren't happening to him, he would have certainly laughed his innards out. Life, it seemed, had a very twisted sense of humour. A joke perhaps, one he was struggling to live through. One thing he was still sure about, though—his companions could not know about his personal agendas. He needed them just long enough to get the Angel's blood. Nothing more. That done, he could make arrangements for their safe return. Perhaps the Angel himself would do that. They were his earth siblings, after all. Who knew?

Right now it was too early to think about the future. Right now, he needed to survive the dawn. And he needed the Fallen to be there, at the station, with some miracle. Adri looked down and realised his hands were shaking.

The train lost speed as it neared its destination. If anyone bothered to stick their heads out of the window and check, the station would initially appear in the distance as a dull speck of light, growing larger. The three of them gathered their things, waiting. Adri seemed tense to the other two, and they kept the silence brewing in return. When the train finally slowed to a halt, they made their way out into the platform's flickering light.

The platform was desolate. Lonesome figures made their way out of the train, shuffling towards the exits. The engine shut down, rendering the whole atmosphere silent. Maya looked around. Dirt, filth, newspapers, garbage, plastic bags, leftovers of things old, all strewn around. Abandonment. The walls old, the plants creeping through brick. There were no electrical lights; a series of ancient torches instead, flickering fire along the crumbling walls, casting light and strange shadows over the dead train and the dark tunnel beyond. The place seemed unbidden, forgotten, and for someone who had grown up in the neatness of New Kolkata, a very cold welcome indeed.

Gray did not waste too much time looking about. Fumbling around in his backpack, he withdrew his camera and busied himself. Maya looked at Adri, he was stationary, looking at something carefully, but not at the surroundings—no, Adri had definitely been here before. He was peering at a group of homeless people huddled together in a far off corner of the platform, paying absolutely no attention to the three of them. Maya had seen such people before. She wondered what Adri was looking for.

She found out soon enough, but not before Gray caught the attention of the entire group of homeless with a blinding flash from his camera. Instant apologies about how it had gone off by mistake did not please Adri. Just as the young Tantric was beginning to worry, a figure detached itself from the shadows of one of the exits and began walking silently towards them. It wore a dark blue hooded jacket, face hidden beneath the hood. Adri was more than relieved to see the Fallen approach them.

'You guys are really good at maintaining a low profile. Camera flashes attract witches faster than blood,' Aurcoe spoke smoothly.

Adri turned to the other two. 'I have to talk to him for a minute,' he said and holding the Fallen's shoulder, led him away.

'Real funny, Aurcoe. The information about Gray Ghosh *slipping* your mind,' he snarled.

Aurcoe's eyes glowed a light blue in the darkness of his hood, and there was a ghost of a smile on his face. 'C'mon, Sen, I don't see you complaining. You now have *two* chances at that Angel instead.'

'I bet you're really happy about it.'

'Only if you can get the blood. If you fail, our deal is off and your story has a short ending.'

'I know what I'm up against,' Adri said.

'No you don't, Sen,' Aurcoe smiled slyly. 'You have *no* clue what you're up against, but I'm going to find that out for you. *If*.'

Adri felt anger quickly take over his sense of relief. His mistrust of the creature was rearing its head again, but he couldn't let that make the decisions for him.

'I'm on your side. Relax, Sen,' Aurcoe spoke, lowering his voice. 'I've got something for you, something that will save your behind.' The Fallen reached into his pocket, withdrew something, and handed it over.

Adri looked at it and drew in a sharp breath. It was an amulet, a pendant—a small pentacle carved out of what appeared to be silver—hanging from a thin silver chain. A piece of beautiful craftsmanship, extremely fine, exquisite work, miniscule writing inscribed all over it. Adri turned it over in his hands, studying it, not able to believe his eyes. 'Is this—'

'Ai'nDuisht? Yes, it is.'

'The Pentacle of the Crescent Moon,' Adri whispered. He tried reading the inscriptions, squinting in the dim light.

'It's real, you don't need to check,' the Fallen snapped.

Adri looked up at him. 'How does it work?'

'It's an artefact of the moon, so it'll shield you, but it can only shield you from the *gaze*; wear it, and the Horseman won't be able to find you. If he's close enough he can sense you though, so don't go dancing naked in front of Death. It does not grant you invisibility, it merely shields your aura.'

'How did you get this?'

'No, no, no, Sen, you got it wrong. This is where you're supposed to say thanks.'

'How is the *Ai'nDuisht* with *you*?'

'Look, I don't ask you where *you* get your stuff from—'

'You know everything there is to know about me! It's your job to know!' Adri cut in. 'And now you have an artefact of such power with you; Fallen, you do not make it easier for me to trust you.'

Aurcoe smirked at Adri's outburst. 'It is going to save you from the morning. I *could* tell you where I got it. I promise you that you'll still take it, perhaps with a heavier conscience.'

Adri glared at Aurcoe, realising the truth in the Fallen's words. The amulet was exactly what he needed. He didn't need to know how many throats had been slit for this. It was saving his life, and for now that was what he needed. He wore the amulet quickly, and immediately felt its power radiate in a magical throb as it recognised its new owner. Then it lay perfectly still, hanging from his neck like any other trinket. Adri slipped it inside his shirt.

'It's not a gift,' the Fallen spoke. 'I shall want it back after this ordeal is over.'

'Fallen can't wear amulets, right? Your damnation saps the magic away immediately,' Adri said, a touch of savage pleasure in his voice. 'This is just a pretty object for you.'

'If you do your job, Sen, I do not intend on staying among the Fallen for much longer,' Aurcoe said.

'How do I let you know when I have the blood?'

'I'll find you.'

'You better have all the information ready by then.'

'Calm down, my child. Composure, composure. After all, the owner of the pretty little necklace should be kept happy, isn't it?'

'You have me over a barrel, freak.'

'Yes I do. What's your move now?'

'A Dyne got our scents. I think I'll avoid witch territory completely and go around the longer way. Right now, we're going to my place here in Patuli.'

'Witches. Great, just great. Say hello to Victor for me when you get home.'

Adri grunted in reply.

'You guys should settle your differences, seriously. Ah, all the pain,' Aurcoe said.

'You keep out of this one,' Adri shot back.

'I'm leaving then. Sen?'

'Yes?'

'Blink.'

Adri blinked his eyes. Aurcoe had disappeared.

The miracle he had wanted was hanging around his neck. Aurcoe had, despite all his fears and the evident lack of trust, given him the means to run. An extension to his death sentence, a very generous one. Relief washed over Adri in warm waves. The world momentarily felt normal again. He could think clearly now and plan his next move. He breathed deep, and it felt good. *God*, it felt good.

He turned back to find Gray hopping around a burning torch, photographing it from every possible angle. Maya was sitting under the torch and reading a book bound in brown paper. Adri lightly wondered if it was a sleazy novel. 'Let's go.' He motioned to the two of them. 'We need to get a move on.'

'He left? Who was he?' Maya asked, hurriedly stuffing the book into her backpack, further raising Adri's suspicions.

'An informant. Some general stuff, nothing important,' Adri replied.

'I've never seen a burning torch before. This looks incredible!' Gray chimed. 'Just look at this picture! I'm going to have a lot of photographing to do!'

Maya looked at the picture. Adri turned to Gray. 'Conserve your camera batteries; you will probably see better things than old burning torches.'

Gray missed the sarcasm. 'That's cool, I'll charge whenever—'

'Old Kolkata does not have a central transformer. There is no electricity to be found here.' Adri jerked a thumb at the torches as he moved towards the exit. 'That's magic burning.'

Gray's eyes widened and he looked at the torches again, stunned. Even Maya cast an interested glance before they carried on. A dark set of stairs, lit by a distant torch, led them to a long, sinister hallway at the end of which there was yet another staircase, this one illuminated by first light. Stepping forth from the mouth of the subway, the siblings got their first glimpse of Old Kolkata as the young sun rose to greet them in the eastern skies.

6

A city that is old, a city that has been
To write for you is the toughest thing
You have resisted, kept away
You have hidden your secrets
from me, from those you have not trusted
How does one earn your trust?

So I am born of you
And I, here, with you
I bathe in your sunshine
I breathe in your rain
I pick up your earth once again, once again

Where is it that I can look for you?
I talk to you, I tell you things
I stand tall above your crumbled buildings
I stand deep beneath your darkest recesses
I am here where you are

In your stagnancy I smell life
In your arms I will feel death
In your embrace I will breathe my last
I will return to you, from whence I came.

7

Only a few people were visible as the trio walked through the streets of Old Kolkata. These few mostly walked in groups, or were loners, and everyone kept their distance; there was an aura of discomfort in the air. Maya could feel eyes watching them from behind barred windows. She did not like it. Adri constantly kept glancing over his shoulder in a guarded manner. It didn't help things. They walked in silence as a morning breeze blew, its gentle swoosh the only sound breaking the quiet—things were unnaturally quiet, and they were sure that it would be easy to overhear them even at longer distances.

Gray, wanting to talk, whispered, 'It's unnaturally quiet.'

'Yeah,' Maya agreed. Both of them looked expectantly at Adri as they walked, searching for an explanation. He didn't disappoint.

'The Old City is mostly like this.'

'Ghost town,' Gray said.

The entrances to almost all the buildings they crossed were secured by massive chains and padlocks and metal shutters. It effectively looked like a city in lockdown, afraid of the daylight and all that came with it. Everything was dead silent, except for the occasional dim sound of music playing, or films running, hidden away inside structures, and other hushed voices making hushed conversation in places unseen.

'Old Kolkata is like this all the time?' Gray asked.

'Gariya is like this. The landscape of the Old City is quite drastically diverse; you'll find every kind of place here. Before its expansion it was just a city, but it's like a small country now. It's still called the Old City though, which makes it the largest city in the world at present.'

'The only city in the world without a government,' Maya said.

'That might change soon,' Gray spoke. 'MYTH is trying hard to take control, right?'

Adri shook his head. 'The territory wars are a more complex matter than that.'

'Complex as in? It's MYTH versus the Free Demons,' Gray argued.

'You forget the Coven.'

'The who?'

'The witches. They hold quite a lot of territory here, and as far as I know, neither MYTH nor the Demons have tried to negotiate with them. And anyway, even if MYTH wins they will not gain control over all of Old Kolkata. MYTH has allied with the Angels in the territory wars, and the Angels will obviously want something back from MYTH. And MYTH has also been attempting a Great Purification rather unsuccessfully for quite some time now; the Old City, as I told you before, is as big as a small country and there are far too many dangers tucked away.'

'Wasn't the first Great Purification the political term for what they did to New Kolkata in the beginning?' Maya asked. Demonology had always kept her away from current affairs.

'Yes,' Gray answered her. 'It's the term they use for the complete eradication of anything that can harm the common people.'

'A slow and thorough process,' Adri added. 'They send patrols of Commandos and Guardians, headed by a Sorcerer or a Tantric, into every single building, every single street and alley, covering every single square inch of the land, and kill anything magically dangerous, even remotely so. They move with a calculated plan, with great precision, and clean up the city like a wave; it takes a *lot* of manpower and good planning, not to mention time.

'MYTH was about to launch one in Old Kolkata when the Free Demons opposed them and the territory wars began. I guess you would know about the Free Demons.'

'Of course,' Maya said. She did. Every word.

'New Kolkata was far easier to purify because all it had were spirits,' Adri continued. 'But this city? This city hides too much under its breath. No one, not one soul, knows all of this city's secrets; and I personally think a purification is impossible.'

'Ah, they'll do it,' Gray spoke with confidence. 'The Demons have to either die or get out of their way.'

Adri smiled to himself. Gray did not know Demons. After all, there was a reason why the war had been raging for ten straight years now; it was a different matter that the war itself wasn't covered by the New Kolkata newspapers, except for the occasional vague article. The territory wars had been strictly declared as government business, and no citizen had a right to its information. Not that the citizens wanted to know anyway. Old Kolkata was too dangerous and unattractive a city for most people, and its fate did not bother them. All they wanted was for their government to stay strong so that it could continue protecting them as it had, and if it won the war, it would only get stronger. And MYTH was an incredibly strong government already. Adri had been a part of it in the past and he knew the extent of MYTH's power. He had seen the sheer number of forces MYTH had at its disposal; yet it was forever training new Commandos and making Guardians— Necromancers and Sorcerers were fewer in number, but that was so only in comparison with its standing forces. The fact that MYTH had continuously been waging a battle for a decade proved this point if nothing else.

'I must admit that after studying Demons I have more respect for our government,' Maya spoke thoughtfully.

"Exactly! MYTH *is* powerful. And you *have* to be strong to fight Demons!' Gray finished triumphantly.

'You ever fought one, Adri?' Maya asked.

Adri simply smiled and continued walking. He felt more comfortable here in the streets of the Old City than he did anywhere else, especially New Kolkata. Sure, there was danger looming over his head. Sure, Death itself was after him. But he was on familiar ground now, a city which he mostly knew, and knew better than most. Danger lurked everywhere here, but it did not give off a false sense of security like New Kolkata; there was a charm to the lawlessness here, a certain beauty in the sense of chaos. It was something that could be admired only by those who had lived here and could defend themselves—the rest had moved or were dead. Adri's mind naturally began connecting old memories to the familiar landscape that he saw, and the young Necromancer entered a pensive, lonely mood. He looked at tree stumps that had once been trees, at old hideouts and places where unexpected and amazing things had happened. He walked a little ahead of the other two, wanting to breathe in his city once more. *I have come back to you.*

'He was born here, but was moved to New Kolkata as a child,' Maya told Gray softly.

'He stayed in that one-room flat?' Gray asked incredulously.

'No. He was coached in his arts at MYTH Castle. Then he went back to Old Kolkata for a while supposedly.'

'When did he get banished?'

'I have no clue. I more interested in knowing *why*, though.'

'He seems okay to me,' Gray shrugged. 'I don't see this guy murdering the both of us.'

Maya nodded. 'He's more learned in his art than I thought. You know the popular saying about young Tantrics?'

'What, the girls' thing?'

'No, the rumour that they make too many mistakes. And *what* "girls' thing"?'

'Nothing, nothing,' Gray muttered in reply.

'There's something about him, Gray. Something I can't get a hold on.'

'Something like what?'

'I can't really describe it. It's like a feeling in my gut. Adri is *more* than he seems to be.'

'You've just met your first Necromancer, I bet you're just tripping on the whole magic thing.'

Maya threw him a dirty look. 'I *know* what I'm talking about.'

'No, maybe it's in your subconscious or something, but you've just met a guy who can practically *summon* the very creatures you have spent four years studying about. I would say you're just thrilled.'

Maya thought over what Gray said instead of retaliating. He was correct. She *was* quite fascinated by Adri because of his craft, and now, even more so because of her growing realisations of Adri's knowledge; but that had nothing to do with this feeling. It had clung to her after her first conversation with the Tantric. Something about Adri—the way he walked, the way he began a conversation or chose to reply. It had nothing to do with attraction—she could not quite put a finger on it and argued with her brother about it. Gray agreed to try and notice this thing if he could in the future, but he had to admit that Adri looked perfectly normal to him. As normal as a Tantric could be anyway. He trusted his theory, but did not bring it up again.

They continued walking for a couple of hours and the landscape remained the same—empty roads, boarded up buildings, and a few people scattered here and there, most of them being homeless. They walked on until some water bodies came into view. There were roads that led by them. The water in the ponds was dark and murky and lay perfectly still, the land at the water's edge choked with weeds. There was no sign of life beneath these waters and they looked dreadfully ominous, even in the morning sunlight. They walked some more. More ponds. And more roads along their edges.

Adri seemed confident about the roads and gave no warning about touching the water, so the siblings were not particularly worried. Not that they wanted to go near the water; Gray stopped to urinate along one such pond at one time, while Maya politely turned away. Adri waited impatiently. He now seemed most eager to reach the house he had talked about. 'It's not far now,' he said. 'We're in Patuli already, my house is in the next sector. Just one thing' —here Adri's enthusiasm seemed to dampen a bit— 'my *father* will be home. Don't get, err, offended.'

'Offended? Why?' Maya asked, confused.

'He's quite *delicate.*'

'That's not a problem at all,' Gray said. 'You should meet *our* dad sometime. I promise you you'll live the rest of your days a lot happier, eh sis?'

'Absolutely,' Maya smiled. 'I'm looking forward to meeting your father, actually. It'll be nice to see your house as well, I guess.'

Adri nodded as they walked on.

'What does he do?' Gray asked.

'You'll have heard of him,' Adri replied, rather drily. 'His name is Victor Sen.'

Gray and Maya stopped in their tracks, their eyes wide in shock.

'*The* Victor Sen?' Maya asked.

'Yes. Him.'

'MYTH's hero?' Gray asked, not daring to breathe.

'MYTH's poster boy,' Adri said. 'I told you, yes. Can we walk?'

Maya wondered what was wrong between father and son. It was not just about awkward introductions and the following embarrassments as she had initially thought. There was more to this; there was a reason behind Adri's reactions. Probably his father's fame overshadowing his growing up years—Adri might have always been told that he was not as good as his father and of course, there was the bit about his banishment from MYTH. Now that it turned out he was the son of Victor Sen, everything changed. Everyone who had ever heard of MYTH had heard of Victor Sen, the hero, the Tantric said to be the most powerful of them all.

That seemed like the most likely answer, though Maya knew all the answers were perhaps written away in the diary she carried. It gave her curiosity a temporary gratification, knowing that she would soon be able to carry on reading it, and what she had read before made greater sense now that she knew who the father was.

Gray had heard about Adri's father in equal measures, if not more. He had heard that MYTH's hero still lived in Old Kolkata, and his mind's eye had always created visions of an impenetrable fortress of sorts. He was slightly disappointed when Adri, on being literally hounded by him to do so, described his home as a simple duplex with a small garden. Doubtless, Gray consoled himself, the great Necromancer had other unseen forces guarding his house. Gray intended to talk a lot with Victor Sen and was extremely happy he had brought his camera. 'Adri,' he began hesitatingly, 'will your father allow me to photograph him?'

'Look, you can ask him yourself,' Adri snapped, a bit tired after all the questions Gray had been asking. 'You see that building there? My house is right around that bend.'

Maya was feeling extremely tired herself, and was glad they had arrived. She hadn't slept on the train, and after walking for this long, she now felt her body protest. She would find a bed and sleep off, first thing for sure. She forced herself to walk the last long stretch she would walk in a while. They took the last turn, and it was then that Adri stopped short. The other two followed his gaze, and did not know how to react.

In front of them, at the end of a long road, was a house. It was not in the condition they had expected it to be, however. The entire facade of the house had fallen away, like a cut-out from a cake; debris stood testament. The two floors they could see openly were black, charred beyond recognition. From where they stood, it looked like a house devastated from a bombing run; except in this case, it had evidently been a fire.

They stood looking at the ravaged thing for the longest time. No one spoke. Then Adri started walking towards the house, silently looking at it as it came closer. The garden was gutted, devoid of any plants still alive. Glass crunched beneath Adri's boots as he neared the house and he noticed the broken windows, their frames hanging loose, remnants of burnt curtains trembling in the afternoon winds. Wordlessly, Adri stepped in through the doorway—there was no door there anymore.

'The building can collapse, right?' Gray asked Maya. 'Maybe he shouldn't go in there.'

'He won't listen,' Maya replied, still recovering from the shock. Both of them walked towards the house slowly.

Ground floor. Burnt objects. Objects recognisable, objects belonging to Adri's family, to his father. The library was in ashes, an irrevocable loss. His father, no doubt, would have done anything to prevent this from happening—and Victor Sen was no pushover. Adri carefully crept up the wooden stairs to the first floor; half of the stairway had crumbled away and one had to stick to the wall.

The first floor told a very similar story, but the more important thing was that Adri could not find, try as he might, a burnt corpse. There was still a chance then, he thought. *Father might still be alive.*

He relaxed, his tense muscles calming for a bit as he slowly began looking for things that weren't ashes. His father's wardrobe was completely gone, as were almost all pieces of furniture. Some magical artefacts had survived, but his father had a habit of casting very strong security measures on these. Adri did not try touching them. Possessions did not matter here, most of his own belongings were back in New Kolkata, but Victor Sen had been a connoisseur of a lot of things, and he would never allow them to burn away. Not like this. Adri's mind drew a possible explanation—captured, but alive.

He looked around and examined the ash. It wasn't too fresh, but not too old either. Still, he needed to know what exactly had happened here.

He drew a quick pentagram on the floor with a chalk and added runes. 'Arrive, Familiar of this house,' he spoke in the Old Tongue. Nothing. Adri had anticipated this. He made his way down to the ground floor once more. Maya and Gray were waiting quietly by the kitchen.

'He's not dead,' Adri said as they looked at him anxiously. 'It takes more than this to kill my old man.'

'What happened here?' Gray asked.

'Not an accident, that's for sure. The house spirit is missing, he must have been removed.'

'What about your mother?' Maya asked.

'She passed away a long time ago. My father lived alone.'

'I'm so sorry!'

'You didn't know.'

There was a pause.

'Um, so what now?' Gray asked in a low, polite voice.

'Right now, I need to know what happened here. We'll have to wait till nightfall.'

'How will you know?' Maya asked. 'Everything is in ashes, right?'

'I'm a Pyromancer as well,' Adri said. Maya's eyebrows jumped, but Gray was still looking for an explanation. 'Fire Reader,' Adri explained further. 'It's very much possible you haven't heard of it.'

'I have,' Maya said. 'The art is said to be lost.'

'I knew someone who knew it; grew up practicing. I need to wait till dark, however.' He looked at Maya. 'Why don't you get some sleep? I don't think you slept at all last night, did you?'

'Yeah, I sort of need to sleep,' Maya replied.

'Do that then. Gray, watch her. I'm going to do some asking around. We had neighbours in those buildings' —he pointed across the pond— 'and I think they should've seen *something*. And please don't touch anything that might seem remotely interesting. A lot of my father's possessions are cursed.'

He left. Maya pulled a bed-sheet out of her backpack. She wandered rooms until she saw the spacious library, and lay down, away from the ash of books burnt. She was asleep in seconds.

Gray checked on Maya once before he began to wander the rooms himself, camera in hand. The house was now dead, but had once been home to one of the best Tantrics in the land, and his son, who seemed to have too many surprises up his sleeve. Gray was not cautious about Adri any longer, now that he knew Victor Sen was his father; he had a house to see as well, albeit a devastated one. No, Adri was definitely who he claimed to be, and impressively so. Gray found Adri's calmness at this turn of events quite inspiring.

His gaze fell on a series of burnt, black frames on a wall. They had once held photographs, or paintings perhaps. Gray started clearing away the bits of brick and rubble near the base of the wall, poking around in the ash until he found what he was looking for—an edge of a photograph, freed as the rest of it burnt. A mere corner it was, the edges of a side burnt. Gray looked at it for a long time before stowing it away in his shirt pocket. He stood up then, dusting his hands, and raising his camera, took a picture of the wall.

Seeing a closed door opposite the wall, Gray opened it. He froze. He could see stairs leading down to what must be a basement. He didn't think Adri had checked the basement in his hurry; he couldn't have checked both upstairs and downstairs in that short a while. He looked down at the darkness. Gray hated darkness.

He would wait for Adri's return, he decided, upon which he would present Adri with knowledge of the basement's existence. Yes, wait for Adri while Victor Sen might just be bleeding to death down there. He cursed softly. Maya was too tired to be woken up right then; he was sure she wouldn't even hear him call. Or scream for help from the basement. He cursed again. His imagination wasn't helping him; but something had to be done. Gray walked to the front of the house and surveyed the long road. Adri was nowhere to be seen, doubtlessly still questioning people. He sighed and walked to the kitchen where his backpack was.

A beam of light pierced the darkness of the basement. Gray played the light around a bit, but all he could see were the wooden steps. The fire clearly hadn't reached the basement. He tried to dismiss all the scary basement stories from his mind—it was afternoon, for heaven's sake. He took the first step. The wooden floorboard creaked loudly with a slow drawl to it, and Gray froze again, waiting a full minute before he took the next step. He nervously flicked the light everywhere as he descended—the basement seemed to be fairly large, and his beam of light fell on shelves of what seemed to be books. Gray checked out the walls and the corners of the basement, but shelves blocked his view. He took time to descend, listening for any sound at all, but the basement was dead silent. It didn't help matters.

'Mr Sen?' he called out nervously. 'Victor Sen? Are you in here?' He kept descending, finally reaching the bottom. He didn't move, and chose to stay next to the stairs, calling out into the darkness, slowly moving his light around the room.

'Your son is here, Mr Sen,' Gray called further. 'Hello?'

Something moved rapidly near him. Instinctively, Gray moved the light and caught a glimpse of what seemed to be human skin—before a shelf collapsed with a deafening noise.

'Aaaah!' Gray screamed and sped up the stairs, dropping the torch.

'You will die!' a voice screamed after him.

Gray almost tripped once, but made it to the door, which he slammed shut behind him and slid the lock in place. Then he lay against the door, panting, but not for long. His uneasiness forced him to move away from that room, and into the library where Maya still slept. He was sure he hadn't imagined the voice; it had been a male voice, rather strained. Perhaps it was Victor Sen himself, somehow holding him responsible for the destruction of the house. Who knew? All he knew for sure was that he wasn't going back there. He would wait for Adri.

It was hours before Adri returned. His enquiries had been unsuccessful, difficult. No one had seen anything; they could tell him that it had happened about two days ago, and that was it. No one knew where his father was, no one had seen him during or after the fire. He was thinking about his next move as he made his way through the kitchen—plonking the packets of packed food he had brought on the kitchen counter—into the main hall, at the end of which was the ruined library. It was here that he found the other two, Maya still fast asleep, and Gray looking visibly shaken. Something had happened.

'Adri, there's someone in the basement,' Gray told him as soon as he entered.

'Basement? What do you mean, *basement*?'

'There's someone in there. Might be your dad, I don't know.'

Adri reached for his shooter. Opening it, he shook out the mercury rounds onto his palm, then groped in his bag until he found bright blue rounds, with which he loaded the weapon.

'What bullets are those?' Gray asked.

'Take me to the basement,' Adri replied.

Gray led Adri to the room with the frames and pointed to the door in the wall.

Adri stared at it. He walked over, touched the edges of the wall and felt the burnt plaster there. 'This door was covered by a layer,' he spoke, almost to himself. Then he turned to Gray. 'I never knew it was here.' Without waiting for a reply, he opened the door almost angrily and walked down the steps, shooter in hand. Gray stared after him, but didn't follow.

Adri reached the bottom and looked around in the total darkness. He shut his eyes and sensed magic. Basic magic, near what seemed to be the far wall. A torch. The artefact powering it still had juice. Good.

'Ignite,' he spoke in the Old Tongue, and the torch burst into flames. It took Adri a moment to adjust to the light, and he stared at what he saw. A man stood metres away from him, holding a torch in both hands, looking at him nervously. He was old and short, and hunched prominently as he looked at Adri. He was bald, but had a huge, unkempt grey beard. He wore rags. An old, moody buzzard with a beard. He was not Adri's father.

'You will die as well!' he spoke in a voice cracked with age. He spoke suddenly; it was more like an outburst, catching Adri off guard. Adri lowered his weapon. 'Who are you?'

The old man's eyes shifted rapidly as he nervously contemplated his answer. When he spoke, it was again all of a sudden. 'It does not matter.'

Adri's eyes burned with Second Sight. This just seemed to be a harmless old man, he had no other form and Adri could sense no magic from him. The only thing radiating magic in the room was the burning torch on the wall. Adri could see now that it was on a wall mount and had been used before, and there were other torches mounted as well, the magic in them dried up.

'What are you doing in Victor Sen's house?' Adri asked, a bit more forcefully.

'You do not understand. You do not. What is your name?'

Adri paused before he replied. 'Adri.'

The old man's eyes flickered around the room, straying occasionally to the steps where Gray was making his way down.

'Who in the seven hells is this?' Gray asked, and was immediately cut off by the old man.

'Nine, son. Nine hells. Don't get it wrong. You should know. You're going there.' He spoke with a crazy fervour, occasionally pausing and catching up in his speaking, always maintaining the bursts of exclamation. 'Look, Adri. Look. You cannot possibly know. So yes. So no.'

'He's not, er, he's not mentally . . . stable,' Gray whispered to Adri.

'Evidently mad,' Adri simplified. 'But he might know something.'

'Yes, yes,' Gray agreed. 'I was thinking the same thing.'

'What don't I know?' Adri asked the old man loudly.

The two parties were still keeping their distance. The old man hadn't moved from his place. He still didn't move as he spoke.

'The end. No one knows about the end. But I do. And I know where you will be.'

'Where?'

'One of the hells. And hell will be right here in the Old City.' The old man's eyes were wide, frantic, as he spoke.

'Okay, I got his number,' Gray whispered. 'Another Doomsday prophet.'

'Inevitable, like the great truth. You must believe me,' the old man ranted.

'Oh we do,' Adri replied softly. 'But come on up, old one. Eat and drink.'

'But the end?'

'Surely the end will let you have a good last meal? Come on.'

The old man looked unsure for a while, his eyes flitting between Adri and Gray with dizzying speed. Then his posture slumped, his shoulders sagged. 'I'm hungry, I am,' he spoke.

103

Adri and Gray led him up the stairs. The old man did not react at all on seeing the half-destroyed house. Not a word, not a look. He simply followed Adri into the kitchen and when Adri, after rummaging through the food packet, handed him a paper plate with *luchi–torkari*, he took it wordlessly and sat down in a corner. Adri sat in the opposite corner and took out his packet of cigarettes, leaning against the wall.

That the old man was hungry was evident from the way he wolfed down the meal. Adri lit a cigarette and watched him eat. 'What's your name?' Adri asked after a while, as simple a question as any.

'Vishwak,' came the reply through a mouth full of food.

'Vishwak. So you like the food, Vishwak?'

The old man continued eating, and then he nodded.

'Good,' Adri said. 'Eat well, there's more if you want.'

But Vishwak did not want any more, and after he finished, he continued sitting in the corner, refusing any more food.

Adri leaned forward. 'Vishwak, tell me what happened to this house?'

'It is only a warning, like the Goshtias got before their life soul was scattered. The end comes, and it comes fast. We all have our time, but now there is not much left! Listen to me, son. You are young. If you have things to do then do them, we do not have much time.'

Adri leaned back again and did not waste his breath. There was no point. Vishwak was crazy, and there was clearly nothing to be had from him, except for his visions of doom. No, he would have to wait for darkness. He looked outside through a partially collapsed wall; the sun was slowly setting. Not long now before he could find out more, hopefully.

Gray walked in. 'Anything?' he asked Adri.

Adri shook his head.

'Thought so,' Gray said.

'Maya still asleep?'

'Yes.'

'Okay. I got us some food, feel free to eat, you'll need your strength.'

Gray nodded. 'What's our plan then?'

'If nothing changes then we stay here overnight, and tomorrow we move further into the city.'

Gray looked inside the packet and starting arranging food on his paper plate. 'Does the Old City have no transport except walking?'

'There are trams, but that's near the heart of the city.'

Gray paused. 'Oh wait, Adri, I found something. Wanted to give it to you.' He reached into his shirt pocket, walked over to Adri, and handed him the photo fragment. Adri took it and looked at it with interest. A photograph of him—he was a young child, not more than ten to twelve years of age. There he stood in the faded photograph, looking expressionlessly at the camera, dressed in neat white, obviously for some occasion he couldn't remember. There was a hand on his shoulder; firm and confident—the sleeve led up to nothing but a burnt edge. Irony. Complete and utter irony. He got up and left the kitchen, intending to finish the meal in the library.

Gray looked up, and then followed him, carefully balancing the food on his plate. Vishwak had not moved. He leaned against the wall as before, his eyes now shut.

Adri paced through the dead house like a spirit, waiting for the sun to leave. Thoughts rushed to him as he looked at the house, and the realisation that it had been wilfully destroyed sank in, only deeper than before.

You were once a complete house, protected by strong magic. What happened here? You had my father, you protected him; and in the end you failed. Where is he? I am here now, I, his son. If he is dead then I am the owner of this ruination. And I command you to tell me what went on here inside your walls. Tell me why doors were hidden from me, tell me what secrets you kept for my father. And tell me the story of your end.

Adri wanted to know, and this thirst was making him impatient. The sun was still visible over the horizon, cruel and unmoving—the house remained silent. Adri went down to the basement again in his agitation. The torch was still burning. He looked at the rows of books on the shelves; and he opened one in the dim, dancing light.

8

Maya woke up to the sound of violin. It was rather cruel and imperfect, the music, but she could tell where Gray was getting better. He did practice rather earnestly when he did, and that alone stopped her from telling him to quit. One thing Gray had was dedication.

She opened her eyes and saw a mounted torch burning on the wall. She yawned and stretched and her stomach sent her panic signals of hunger. Gray sat a few feet away from her, his entire attention focused on the violin.

'Gray!' she called. Gray stopped.

'Food's in the kitchen,' he said before he started playing again.

Maya took a bottle of water out of her bag and got up. Her knees felt shaky, she hadn't eaten in a long time now. She walked out into the dark corridor, the music following her. Striding outside the house, she washed up, blinking away the drops of water as she made her way back in. It was evening already and her eyes took time to get used to the darkness and the dead silence—apart from the screechy violin in motion. She took whatever food was left for her—there was enough of it—and she carried it outside, where she looked at the surroundings as she ate.

A certain cold was in the air, and lights were burning away in other windows. The lights flickered and she guessed the source was fire. The violin's notes crept out and gave her a constant feeling of unease; luckily the mistakes Gray kept making frequently snapped her out of these phases. She stood at the foot of the dark water of a pond, looking at the long road leading away from the house. Behind the house there was nothing but untended land for what seemed to be kilometres together; looked like a swamp, the weeds growing taller than her. Beyond the patch of land she could see other buildings, but they were quite far away, shimmering in the evening air like illusions. No, there was certainly only one viable entry and exit to this place. Sigh. She didn't like the way their little adventure was going so far; Adri was beginning to gain her sympathy, and that, of course, did not help her future plans. Where was Adri anyway? Probably still away. Gray would know.

She went back into the house and moving slowly and carefully in the darkness, made her way back to the library where she finished off the last bite. Gray paused and looked up at her. 'You okay, sis?' he asked.

'Yes. I think I feel better after the food. Where's Adri?'

'He's in the basement, and he's apparently not to be disturbed.'

'The basement? What's he doing there?'

'He just said don't disturb me, no matter what. You know, in that usual to-the-point way.'

Maya sat down next to her bag. Fine, she would wait for Adri to finish whatever the hell it was that he was upto. A well-fed stomach would make it easier, and from what she knew of him, he'd explain when pushed. She pulled one of Adri's diary out of her bag, and the action caused her more guilt this time around. She waved her inhibitions aside temporarily, and started where she had left off. *Lets learn some more things about you, Adri Sen.*

'I wanted to do a lot of things, you know,' Aman said. There was an obvious and understandable sorrow to his voice, something Adri could relate to.

'Yeah, well, the others miss you,' Adri said.

There was silence, except for the soft burning of candles.

'What about Natasha?' Aman asked. 'Does she miss me?'

'We don't really talk much,' Adri replied truthfully. 'Sorcerers and Necromancers have their reservations.'

'I need you to deliver a message to her. Can you do that?' Aman asked. Adri shook his head. 'Why not?' Aman persisted.

'This is the unpleasant part, Aman. You should know this. The advanced rules cover this,' Adri spoke. How come Aman hadn't read up? He was supposed to know. He had been studying as a Necromancer too, after all.

'No, I was more interested in Sorcery. I used to read more of their books.'

'You were?'

'Yes. I wanted to switch.'

'You know MYTH wouldn't have let you. Your Tantric studies had started too early. It's not just a *subject* you were learning, you knew that.'

'I would've tried, Adri! I was ready to convince even the Seven if needed.'

'Fool. You never wanted Sorcery. You wanted Natasha.'

'Yes I did, and I do!' Aman sounded angry. The furniture in the room rattled, as did the windowpanes.

'Easy, Aman.'

'But I do. I love her. I need you to tell her that. For me.'

Adri shook his head once more. 'You are bound here by the thoughts of her,' he said. 'And more importantly, by the thoughts of her reciprocation.'

'What has that got to do with—'

'If she tells me she never had feelings for you, if she insults your memory, Aman, then your spirit will automatically be condemned to walk the earth for eternity until freed.'

Aman was silent. So was Adri.

'That is not what I want for you. You were my friend,' Adri continued, after letting his words sink in. 'It will be tougher to leave the Plane with your question unanswered, but you have the option of leaving.'

'I don't want to go without knowing,' Aman said slowly.

'Maybe it's better this way.'

'No, Adri. It's not. I would *want* to walk the earth forever. For *her*. Don't you see that?'

'It'll get tiresome after a couple of hundred years, Aman,' Adri warned.

'I want that message delivered,' Aman replied stubbornly.

'What is the message then?'

'What? You'll deliver it?'

'The message!'

Aman cleared his throat. 'Natasha, it's me, Aman. I wanted to tell you that the time we spent together meant everything to me, and that is what solely keeps me from fading away right now. I love you and I suspect I always will.' He stopped. 'Did you take that down?'

'I was considering binding you from these words,' Adri spoke slyly.

'If you bind these words I swear I will kill you. You know I'm capable,' Aman replied.

'You wouldn't kill *me* over a girl.'

'Adri, you *obviously* don't understand. It's all some summoning game to you, isn't it? Or is it practice? You doing this for MYTH marks, man?'

'I don't understand love,' Adri confessed. 'I've never really been loved.'

'Your mother,' Aman said. 'She loved you, I'm sure.'

'She died during childbirth, Aman. She never knew me.'

'You don't get it Adri! Love is not logical, that would be stupid. Your mother loved you for the months you were growing in her womb. I know she loved you. I can feel that aura around you.'

'Then WHY does she not come when I call?' Adri shouted in a sudden outburst. 'You think you're the only one I summon? I have called out to my mother's spirit hundreds of times, Aman, since I learnt the art of summoning! I have called out to her again and again, yet she defies all the rules. She shows me no sign of her existence, she does not reply, she does not arrive! Why?'

Aman was silent.

'And it's the same story with you spirits, isn't it? All of you know why she does not reply, but none of you will tell me.'

'You are not *Ba'al Ob*, Adri,' Aman murmured under his breath.

'No, but I will be. And I *will* know,' Adri said. 'But I do not understand love until then, Aman. There is no proof, no matter what things are being hidden from my eyes.' He waited for a few seconds, silent. 'I am now going to bind you from that message you wished to pass on to Natasha.'

The knife on the table began to vibrate softly. 'Do not interfere, human,' Aman spoke noiselessly.

'There is no such thing as love,' Adri spoke through gritted teeth. 'You cannot harm me for something non-existent.'

'This is my last warning to you, friend,' Aman's voice was steadily growing colder and higher.

Adri slowly raised his right arm—and the door behind him opened. His father stood there, hand on the knob.

'What's happening, Adri?' Victor asked.

Adri lowered his arm. 'A routine summoning, Father.'

'Hmmm. Talking to dead friends again, I see. Who is it this time?'

'Aman.'

'Hello, Mr Sen,' Aman spoke, his voice now normal once more.

'Hello, Aman. How are you these days? Restless?'

'I'm afraid so.'

'Well, you made some glasses break downstairs, and I loved those glasses. I will not tolerate something like that happening in my house. Do you understand?'

'Won't happen again, sir,' Aman replied, a sense of embarrassment in his voice.

'It better not. And Adri, I would expect you to keep a tighter leash on your spirits. If he is bypassing you and causing damage downstairs, your hold on him is weak. I don't care if he's your friend or whatever, the hold *must* be strong.'

'I had lost *focus*, Father.'

'You could get people *killed*, you idiot. You are evidently not ready for Demons yet. What use is all the training if you succumb to basic emotions like puppy love?'

The knife, as if in response, vibrated again.

'You even *think* about it, spirit,' Victor spoke calmly, glancing at the knife, 'I will make you burn in eternal fire. Do you understand me?'

'Yes, sir,' Aman replied in a whisper, his tone indistinguishable.

'You better know that you are in *my* house. I have demolished more spirits than you have *seen* in that Plane of yours. You will not think of even touching my son with your incompetence.'

Victor left, shutting the door gently. Adri raised his hand and performed the binding of the words. Aman never spoke words of love about Natasha ever again in his afterlife.

Maya stopped reading. Her head swam for a second, and she felt disoriented—she did not know what to think. She looked up and saw Adri standing in the doorway of the library, looking at her.

'What are you reading?' he asked.

'Nothing, just some old notes,' she replied slowly, hoping her voice did not give her away. Apparently, it didn't.

'You wanted to watch the Pyromancy, right?'

'Yes, I did.'

'Even I want to watch,' Gray spoke up, putting his violin back in its case hurriedly.

'I shall do it here then. But keep quiet,' Adri said. Turning away from the siblings, he fished around inside his backpack and withdrew a small hip flask; then, looking around, he found a piece of un-burnt wood among the ashes. Clearing a circular space on the floorboards with the palm of his hand, he put the piece of wood down in the centre. It had once been part of a chair. Maya and Gray shuffled closer, in silence, watching Adri as he poured a clear, odourless liquid from the hip flask onto the piece of wood. Then, striking a match, he set the wood on fire.

It burned like anything else would, but Adri peered into the flames with a different kind of understanding. His eyes shone like liquid in the face of the flames and his lips moved softly as he read in the Old Tongue. He saw random words initially— the burning of an object confused its memories, and irrelevant information, the outermost layer, was always the first to burn off—Adri ignored it and started reading within, in the deeper layers of the flames. He read deeper and deeper in the dancing fire, until he reached the heart of the blaze; there, nestled within the outer inferno, was the inner fire, the true flame. There it crackled, calmly, slowly, gently eating up the wood which fuelled it. His eyes watered, but he did not blink, for then he would lose it—he stared at the pure fire and read the most recent memories of the burning piece of wood. He read it disbelievingly, he it read again, and then the strain on his eyes was too much—and he blinked.

Instantly the fire was just a fire again, the words, the language it had spoken to him drowned amidst the flames. Adri slowly sat back, thinking and wiping his eyes which were watering.

'Are you okay?' Maya asked. 'You were so close to the flames I was afraid you'd—'

'I've done this before,' Adri said. 'Don't worry,' he added.

'So you *read* the fire?' Gray asked.

'Yes. And I saw what has caused this, something I can't believe myself,' his voice trailed off into deep thought.

'A Dragon!' Gray exclaimed.

Adri looked at him coldly. 'The only Dragon that ever was belongs to legend. This creature is far more real. It's a Demon.'

'Which kind of—'Maya began, but she had already guessed the answer.

'An Infernal,' Adri said, grim.

'A Demon born of fire,' Maya spoke slowly. 'They haven't been around for quite a while now.'

'Nearly impossible to appease. But *this*, this is its handiwork.'

'What else did you read?'

'Nothing about my father. Just the Infernal.'

'What do you plan to do now?'

Adri knew something was afoot, and if it involved a fire Demon it was even bigger than he realised. However, he was in no position to investigate any further, at least not now. He felt the weight of the *Ai'nDuisht* around his neck. It was doing its job well; he was still alive, but for how long he did not know. Death must be hunting for him; it was unwise to delay. *I will come for you, Father, wherever you are. But what good am I to you dead?*

'I have to sort out my own problems first,' Adri said. 'I need to meet your elder brother urgently. I will see you safely back to New Kolkata—maybe your brother can help me there—before I figure this deal out.'

Gray nodded.

'What do you want from Dada?' Maya asked.

'We've been through this, Maya. He has something that belongs to me.'

'You're not going to harm him in any way, right?'

'No, I'm not,' Adri spoke wearily. *I just need some of his blood, that's all.*

'When do we leave?' Gray asked.

'It's risky, starting at night. We'll wait till dawn. There's enough food in the packet for dinner.'

A long wait. Everyone retreated to their corners in the giant room. Vishwak stumbled in just as they were settling down—Adri explained to a shocked Maya who he was—and squatted in the only empty corner of the room, wordless all the while. Adri took out a notebook and began to write in it. One glance at it told Maya that it was one of his diaries. She pretended not to notice what Adri was doing, far too nervous to bring out the diary in her possession and resume her reading; instead, she took out one of her Demonology books and began to look up Infernals in greater detail. Gray took out his violin once more, but he didn't feel like playing and kept it back in, cleaning the instrument for a minute so that he wouldn't look like an idiot. Not that anyone was watching. The only person idle was Vishwak, the old man was murmuring and humming something in a low voice. Gray took out his camera and began looking at the photos he had taken.

'Adri?' Maya spoke up suddenly.

Adri stopped writing and looked at her.

'Where had you gone?' she asked. 'I mean, before this?'

The flickering light played on Adri's face, half cast in shadow. 'I found some of my father's old books down in the basement,' he replied. 'I was reading, and remembering him.'

'I don't mean to be inquisitive, but are you, are you sure you're okay?'

'My father has disappeared, Maya. I'm not okay.'

Adri's blunt reply stung her, but she realised she was prying. Heck, she had started prying with the diary itself. She felt guilty. But then she did not know what to think of Adri. She saw someone before her, and she read about someone in the past; and she could not blame Adri for his actions. The diary spoke volumes about Adri and the way he was brought up, about Victor Sen and the house, and about Adri's loneliness. She thought about his mother; about his anguish through his words, through his recollection of that particular summoning with Aman, even though Adri was never too expressive in his diary entries. Still confused about the state of things, she went back to her book.

Night gradually stole into the house, and a sense of ease and relaxation crept over everyone as they seemed to realise how tough time was to kill. It was silent, apart from the crickets, and the moon was visible through a patch in the partly broken roof. Adri could not write any more. He put his pen down and looked at the others. Maya was still studying her Demonology book; Gray had dozed off, and Vishwak was still humming his tune, louder now and with more confidence. Adri lit the usual cigarette and leaned towards the old man, trying to hear his song better.

Go to sleep my son
There's nowhere left to run
The sun does set, blood red
The final day is done

Don't tremble so, just sleep
Make no noise, don't weep
They are here as promised, hear
And promises, they keep

The earth shall crack open, they said
Fire shall rise in each riverbed

The music shall bell, the tunes of hell
Walk among us they will, the undead

The creature will rise from the Lake of Fire
Blood on its head, flesh its desire
Men will turn, the city shall burn
Burn after death, a funeral pyre

The air shall be thick with venoms of old
Wrath shall rain through hearts ice cold
Those so far lived will be hunted down swift
No legend or lore shall live to be told

Blood bone darkness steel shall mould
Powerless shall be the Tantrics of Old
With each one that dies, the four will rise
The Horsemen will ride again as foretold.

'WHAT?' Adri cried out as the old man began humming his song all over again. 'What did you say?' He leapt across the room and hunched in front of old Vishwak.

Vishwak looked confused. 'Adri. Adri, look. I'm not a prophet, like your friend accused. He accused me, Adri, but wrongly.'

Adri shook his head violently. 'The *Horsemen* will ride again as foretold? Isn't that what you just said?'

'This is a warning to the wise, Adri. A warning.'

'What do you know about the Horsemen? Tell me. TELL ME!' Adri grabbed the old man's collar and shook him roughly, losing control for a second.

'You can only kill me!' Vishwak gasped. Adri stopped, and stared into Vishwak's blank eyes. He let go and the old man slumped against the wall, fighting for breath. 'Adri, you don't understand.'

'What?' Adri snapped. 'What do I not understand?'

'The warning! This was a warning, and I carry it. You are fortunate enough to have heard it.'

'You are a crazy old man,' Adri spoke, taking deep breaths. His anger was slowly ebbing away. 'You are a crazy old man and I'm a blooming fool.'

Vishwak burst into laughter, showing dirty yellow teeth.

'You know about them, but I can't get it out of you,' Adri told him, his look turning into grim amusement as Vishwak went on cackling with laughter. When the old man did calm down, Adri had him sing his warning once more. He did, and Adri slowly memorised it—years of memorising incantations and an entire dead language gave one an excellent memory, if nothing else.

Ignoring the siblings' stares, Adri moved back to his corner, repeating the song over and over again in his head. He thought about it. Interesting. Especially the fact that it involved both Necromancers and the Horsemen in a swirl of all kinds of horrible predictions. He needed to dig for information about the Horsemen, and the one person he had hoped would clear his doubts was missing. As if he didn't have enough troubles already.

The first scream, rapidly morphing into a screech, unholy and inhuman in its very essence, yanked him right out of his thoughts. A screech that stayed in his ears long after it had receded. He had heard these before. Gray and Maya were sitting upright, alarmed; Vishwak hadn't reacted. Adri quickly formulated their next move. It was wisest to visit *him* now. Adri had planned this visit for the next morning, but now it seemed their departure would be more rushed than usual.

'We leave *now!*' he spoke, his voice urgent, but hushed.

'What was that?' Gray asked, his eyes wide with fright. Another screech ripped the night air, this time considerably louder. Closer.

'Keep your voices down!' Adri hissed. 'Maya, let's go!' Maya, who had frozen, hurriedly stuffed her book in her backpack.

Adri checked the bullets in his shooter, then looked at Vishwak. Vishwak hadn't moved, showing no reaction to the noise or their panic. 'You planning to die here, old man?' Adri asked. 'We don't have much time, let's go.'

Vishwak's eyes twinkled in the semi-darkness as he turned to look at Adri. 'Thank you for the meal, son. But I must stay. The warning, my life, everything comes together at last. Everything makes sense.'

'The witches will rip you apart, old man!' Adri barked in an undertone. 'I'm asking you for the last time, because I can't carry you!'

Vishwak grabbed Adri's shoulder, old fingers digging into flesh. 'Sometimes,' he whispered, 'you must do what is crazy. Others might think you crazy for it. But when you see what's coming over the horizon, that is exactly what you must do.' He gave Adri a push, causing him to stumble back. 'Now go! Go before they catch you.'

Adri tried pulling at Vishwak's arm, but he only got pushed back again. There was no time. Adri couldn't think. The old man's words ran in his ears and he swept them aside as he gestured for the siblings to leave. Blindly grabbing his backpack, Adri led them through the house to the back door, out into the night. Grass, seven to nine feet tall, lay before them, illuminated by the moon. Adri dived in. Maya and Gray followed. They started moving through the tall growth, Adri leading the way, parting the grass as fast as he could. Their progress was rather slow, but it was progress nonetheless as they put the house behind them, as fast as they could, not daring to speak.

The grass swallowed them most eagerly; it was everywhere, like an ocean, and gave them refuge for the moments that the witches chose to scour the house instead of giving chase.

'I trust they're not slow old women right now?' Maya panted, stepping on Adri's heels more than once in her hurry.

'Stop stepping on my heels,' Adri panted back. 'And no, right now I would call them a lot faster. Keep up.'

They ran onward, blind, into unending grass, and Maya was reminded of the wilds of Africa—the grass in which the lions hunt the gazelle. She imagined herself to be one of the gazelle's kind, galloping away in an unplanned direction, heedless of all but escape. The image did take her mind off the current situation for a while, her body running mechanically while her mind drifted—though not for long. More shrieks split the night air, bringing Maya's attentions swivelling back to ground zero.

'Shit, they're already done,' Adri cursed as he ran. Maya and Gray were having trouble running; their legs were beginning to burn. They weren't used to so much running, they were normal college-goers with junk food diets. Adri though, was used to running, the Guardians giving him constant practice in New Kolkata. No, his problem here was the dry grass that was ceaselessly brushing against his face as he ran.

'What do you mean, *done?*' Gray shouted.

'What do you think I mean?' Adri snapped back in an equally loud shout, throwing caution to the winds in his irritation.

'The old man—' Maya started.

Adri felt them then. In the grass. Behind them. Gaining fast. Running like a pack of wolves. The grass slowing them down only momentarily. He shouldn't have shouted back at Gray. *Think. There is no time. They are coming.*

'Do they have a weakness for fire? You could set the grass alight—' Gray shouted again.

'Quiet, you little rat,' Adri hissed. 'This way.'

He broke pace suddenly and took a sharp left. It would buy them a few seconds at most, not enough. The Dynes were after them because of their scent, Adri thought. They could not outrun them; nor could they lose their scent right now. Fighting them was out of the question; there were far too many. No time to do any real summoning; well except maybe—

Adri burst out of the field. A construction site lay before him. He dived to the ground, a chalk already in his hand, and began to draw as fast as he could. Gray and Maya skidded to halts next to his crouched figure, panting. They didn't question him, but kept looking behind them, into the field. They could hear rapid rustling in the silence of the night; their pursuers weren't very far away. Maya looked at Adri, and bit her lip as he furiously finished the pentacle, checked the runes once, then spoke in the Old Tongue, 'Arrive!'

The Familiar appeared in seconds and stood silently waiting for orders. Maya and Gray stared at the smoky figure with unbelieving eyes, and somewhere inside, Adri was disappointed that the first summoning the siblings saw in their lives had to be that of a measly Familiar. But now was not the time.

'Dynes! Distract them, lead them away. Use a smell,' Adri whispered. The Familiar nodded and almost instantly began to radiate thick smoke. Its smell began to change as it glided back into the fields, its aura firmly parting the grass around its body. Adri turned to the two. 'We don't have much time. Let's go!' They started running again, towards the construction site. It looked abandoned, like most things in the city, but they could see their way clearly as the moon was full. 'My Familiar, that's a slave spirit, will not be able to distract them for long, even with a full odour of blood. I have a friend who lives not far from here.'

'How did the witches find us? Is your house in their territory?' Maya asked.

'No. I don't know how they turned up there! And it's not important right now!'

They entered the labyrinth of pipes and concrete, roughly maintaining a general direction as they navigated through the construction site. Shadows everywhere. Adri kept a sharp eye out for any kind of movement, even in speed. This was a better place for evading the bloody Dynes; there were many twists and turns, multiple alleys. Since their smell was being used to track them, the Dynes would probably come down the same path, perhaps slower. Nothing broke the silence for a long while except for harsh, ragged breathing as they ran.

'I, I need to rest,' Maya panted, and Gray nodded in agreement.

'There is no time,' Adri shot back.

'We'll die, man!' Gray exclaimed; he was wheezing now, and was so loud that Adri reconsidered.

'A few seconds,' he spoke and stopped. The siblings held on to blocks of concrete as they regained their breath. Both of them were totally out of shape, Adri realised, catching his breath himself though he could have run for longer. Not their fault.

'I think, I think, we lost them,' Gray panted, looking behind him.

Adri shook his head in firm denial. 'We'll have to run again, right now.'

'I can't, not right now,' Maya replied, still gasping for air.

Adri looked up and down the path with a calm but nervous bearing. They couldn't move as fast as was needed to get away. There was nothing around, no sound, no footsteps, nothing. It all seemed wrong to him. It was impossible that the witches had lost their scent, not at this range and speed. They were easily audible too, with all the panting and the coughing, and they were under open sky. No, something else was happening here. Adri realised it a moment later. They were being herded.

Extremely slow, he looked up, so as to not draw any attention to his action. His eyes furiously searched the unfinished scaffoldings, the pipes, and the pillars. He saw her soon enough. There she was, sitting atop an unfinished pillar. A black shape, crouched on all fours, tattered clothes flying in the night air like ragged wings, and clumps of long, tangled hair part of the silhouette. Her eyes burned bright red in the darkness, watching them as the moon lent some colour to the grey hair and the dark rags. She sat like the perfect predator, muscles ready to spring, frozen, mayhap in wait for the perfect moment, next to invisible, merging with the darkness. Adri's eyes roved around but he could not see any others. Disturbing. Witches were tough to deal with, even when alone.

'Move. *Now!*' he spoke in a tone he hoped would betray the urgency of the situation.

'One minute please?' Maya bleated.

'Maya, they're on to us. You want to live, don't you?' Adri spoke fast and low. He glanced at the pillar again. The witch was gone. He looked around, much more insecure, tightening the grip on his shooter. He started walking, fast. They could not risk a run now. The siblings followed, wrestling between their fear of the witches and God's implanted desire for air. They did not get far. It came out of the shadows, right before they were almost out of the construction yard; Adri's reaction time wasn't fast enough, as he glimpsed the fiery eyes and the silent, unfailing figure in mid-air. The Dyne sliced Adri's left shoulder and landed, on all fours, on a pile of rocks behind him. Ignoring the pain, Adri spun around in tandem with the creature and squeezed off a single shot. BLAM. White smoke. The witch was gone.

'Did you get her? Did you?' Gray asked, panting, as Maya stood frozen with horror.

'No, the shooter doesn't make them disappear,' Adri replied. Pain. Shooting up from his left shoulder. Everything was silent. The witch had survived. They needed to get out of here, and fast. Adri already knew why there was just a single witch after them— they were a competitive lot, and this one wanted all three of them for herself. She wouldn't call her sisters unless she was dying, and Adri knew he was in no condition to kill a witch. Not anymore.

Truth be told, he was clueless about how they'd found him. They mostly never hunted outside territory. Flight had been his first instinct, he hadn't really stopped to think about the reasons behind their appearance.

'You're hurt. I can see blood,' Maya exclaimed.

'I know. We need to get out,' Adri replied, forcing his attention back. He led the way again, hobbling. He had not looked down at his shoulder yet and he didn't intend to until they were out of here. Claws of a witch were honed to the maximum, always razor sharp. *You're getting careless, man. It's only a flesh wound, now move!*

Gray had picked up a metal pipe from somewhere and he held it tense as they walked. No one dared to walk fast now. A mud road led towards a railway crossing and beyond, and they looked everywhere, suspicious of all shadows. It was quiet again, and Adri held the shooter tightly in his good arm. With luck, the Dyne would have smelt mercury during the first discharge and would know what it was up against; it would be more cautious, even though it wouldn't give up. The railway crossing was unmanned, and they stepped over the tracks, crossing to the other side. The area was slowly becoming residential once more—walls ran along both sides of the mud road, trees grew every few yards, casting the path in darkness. Streetlights were visible in the distance, as were houses and a few scattered people. Adri knew that was where they would be comparatively safe, but it was still a good deal away.

The siblings were scared, even more so as they saw the red trickling down Adri's shirt. But he was still leading them, and the lights in the distance made them hopeful even in their fear. Maya felt a familiar fear grip her as they started walking beneath the trees. It had overcome her when the thing had attacked Adri; she had been frozen stiff like on the train, on the verge of tears. She had to focus, she had to keep her mind trained on making it to the lights.

A branch creaked. Maya looked up. Red eyes, gleaming. The loud gunfire came as a shock. Adri had seen the thing too and fired, and despite his good arm trembling, he hadn't missed this time. The witch screeched in what could only be agony and jumped off the tree into the depths of another, further away from them. It was gone in seconds, and looking around, it seemed to Maya that she had just imagined all this happening, as if it was all part of some magical dream and they were simply out on an undisturbed evening stroll. It was merely a touch of escapism. She hurried to Adri and examined his wound.

'No, we must get to safety first, we aren't out of the woods yet,' Adri muttered. He sounded weak. Gray offered to support his weight but Adri declined; the group slowly moved towards the buildings in the distance. There was no sign of the witches again as they reached a crowded street and walked through, unnoticed.

Adri's wound didn't catch too much attention among the other wounded on the street. Many people were bandaged. Everyone looked rough and struggling. Signs of a meagre survival. Many carried backpacks similar to Adri's. People walked together, but they walked fast—conversations were quick and to the point. No time for dallying. They weren't noticed much; though this suited them fine, the siblings did feel that the first real crowd of people in Old Kolkata felt rather cold to them. They were quite disturbed by the condition of the people. The streets were dirty, littered with all kinds of garbage—old newspapers, plastic bottles, empty cartons, everything tossed around by the evening wind as they walked, and they constantly stepped on something or the other, rarely finding the road itself. Some people seemed to be collecting all the trash into huge, boulder-sized mounds that they were tying up, and Maya guessed they would be sold—no one in a city struggling to survive would be bothered with civic duties. Somewhere, a man was screaming his lungs out in loud argument, and a baby bawled as they began to cross residential complexes. The buildings were all densely populated, candlelight burning inside every window. The gates were shut tight, padlocked. An occasional security guard. Without weapons.

'How're you doing?' Gray asked Adri, who had been hobbling along silently, without any audible protest; except for his sudden grunts of pain when he stumbled and lost his footing.

'We're close,' Adri replied.

Maya could see that it had taken Adri a lot of strength to just utter the words, and she did not ask any questions of her own. Adri moved off into a side street from the main road, then down an alley, into a web of buildings. They walked for about a quarter of an hour down narrow lanes, occasionally lit with lamp posts that burned with magical fire, taking sharp, sudden turns. Then Adri stopped all of a sudden, clambering up the few stairs leading to the front door of a house. It was a duplex, grey, wasted, squashed **in** the middle of two extremely tall apartment buildings—its windows boarded up. The front door, however, was a dark, rich wood; a touch of class, even in the semi-darkness. Even the pounding sounded rather nice as Adri knocked thrice, loud and impatient.

They waited.

'Anyone home?' Gray asked Adri.

'He's always home,' Adri grunted.

Right on cue, a loud sound was heard—a latch being pulled back—and the door opened a mere crack.

'Look who's here!' a booming voice spoke.

'I've got a couple of friends with me,' Adri replied.

9

The man who shut the door behind them didn't have a name so far; Adri was too informal with him to call him by one. Not that Adri was talking much. Clearly knowing his way around the house, he had disappeared right after they entered. Maya and Gray watched in silence as the man locked the door, latched an age-old latch in place, and then finally slid a heavy chain around the handle. He was quite tall and huge. As he turned, they caught a proper glimpse of his countenance—shiny bald head, a huge black beard covering most of his lower face, and a thick, stubby nose. His features coupled with his size would've made him look formidable if not for his eyes—they glimmered with a light of their own, almost immediately making him look livelier, like the owner of a sense of humour. From the looks of it, he seemed to be in his fifties.

When he spoke, his voice boomed. 'He already scarpered inside, did he?' His voice was loud, rather brash, but had an uncanny texture to it; the siblings knew they would never forget this voice again. 'No matter. Come this way.' He led them down a long, dark corridor at the end of which they could see light. They emerged into a living room which seemed surprisingly comfortable—there was a fireplace where a fire crackled, lit for the express purpose of illumination; Old Kolkata was rather hot throughout the year. Two well-padded sofas stood facing the fire. An enormous rug lay under their feet, which their muddy boots were leaving marks on—not that the man seemed to notice—and various paintings and photographs ornamented the walls that otherwise would look bleak with the peeling wallpaper and windows boarded up. Adri's bag lay near a sofa, but he was nowhere to be seen.

'You two get some rest, right? Can see that you've been running. I'll go see what Adri's up to.' The siblings nodded, and as they settled in the two sofas by the fire, the man spoke again. 'We haven't been introduced, I believe. You can call me Smith.'

'I'm Maya, and this is Gray.'

'Good to know. Well Maya, Gray, I'll be back with your friend soonest I can.'

Smith made his way up the stairs. He knew where Adri would be. He thought he had seen blood on Adri's shoulder as the young Necromancer had hurried by. Smith opened the door to his infirmary, and sure enough, there Adri was, shirtless, looking down at his shoulder, stitching a wound.

'Would it hurt you to stay out of trouble for at least a short while?' Smith asked, lighting another torch. Adri laughed harshly. Smith moved closer and peered at the wound. 'Witches? How serious is it?'

'The cut was deep, but she didn't release too much of the paralysing agent; she didn't consider me a threat until I made her taste mercury.' There was distaste and anger in Adri's voice as he continued stitching. 'Speaking of which, I have only three quicksilvers left. Which brings me to you.'

'Not a problem, you can stay here for as long as you see fit. But where did the Dynes get you? They never come this side.'

Adri paused mid-stitch. 'I have some rather *bad* news, Smith.'

'Tell me.'

'I was hoping *you* would know something about this, but now I see I was wrong. My house, here in Patuli, has been burned

128

down. Father is missing. The house Familiar is missing. There is no trace.'

Smith was grim. 'Did you perform a—'

'Yes I pyromanced, and the results are unsettling. I saw an Infernal.'

Smith was silent. 'I did not know anything about this,' he said finally.

Adri was silent.

'Have you eaten? I will make something for the three of you, then. It's late. Let your friends sleep off, then we will talk.' He left.

Adri continued with his wound. Minutes ticked away, and to help hide the pain, Adri thought about his next move. Stocking up on ammunition was the most important thing. Never again would he be at the mercy of witches; he needed to perform some protective enchantments too, call in some spirits for defensive purposes. He had forgotten, for one day, how dangerous and unpredictable the city could be; it had almost gotten him killed. If the shot he had fired hadn't connected with the Dyne, none of them would be here right now.

The door behind him opened again. Adri didn't turn around until he heard Maya's voice. 'Adri?'

'Yes,' he replied, continuing to stitch.

Maya crept into the room. Adri was facing the other way, sitting on what seemed to be an operating table, with a complete set of tools next to him. The walls, wooden, had only shelves and more shelves—the room reeked with the smell of medicine and blood. She looked at Adri, and in the guttering yellow light she saw the inscriptions—old writing that crawled over his arms, then continued down his bare back in perfect symmetry. Tattoos. Her eyes were lost in the black swirls, in the intrinsic movement of the designs—they seemed to be moving in the torchlight; all of a sudden she realised that Adri was shirtless, and that he might not want her to see him like this.

129

He didn't. Adri was quite uncomfortable, but he continued tending to the wound.

'I was slightly worried, and Smith, he told me the way here,' Maya said.

'I'm okay. It's not too deep. It could've been worse.'

Maya moved closer. Scars. Too many, for his age. Adri's skin was battle worn with scars, little and large, recent and old, on his back and on his arms.

'You have a lot of scars,' she said without thinking.

Not all of them physical. He said nothing.

'What did the Dyne use?'

'Claws. Sharp. But I'll tell you how I got lucky. If they want they can secrete a kind of venom from their claws, a paralysing agent. It was there in this slash, but not enough to work immediately.'

'Oh my god. So is it still at work?'

'No, it's worn off. I just have to finish with this,' Adri fiddled with the needle, tore the string with his teeth, and then dropped the needle next to him, into a pan full of hot water. The blood slowly left the needle and swirled in the water, as both of them watched.

'You need help with the bandage?'

Adri grunted. Bandaging was one part he could not manage alone; if he did, it would be terribly clumsy. Maya seemed glad to be able to contribute somehow—she took the bandage roll that he handed her and got to work. Adri watched her slowly bandage him, and tried not to feel awkward. It was.

'I don't like the effect they have on me, Adri,' she spoke all of a sudden. It had either been on her mind, or she was trying to make the bandaging less uneasy.

'The witches?'

'Yes, the witches.' Her eyes glittered in the firelight. Adri noticed for the first time that they were black. Not brown, not blue, not green. Black. What a strange thing to notice. 'They make me want to give up all hope,' Maya continued. 'I feel like I'm on the verge of tears.'

'The influence. It's terribly strong in the first few encounters.'

'How do you fight it?'

'I told you, I've had training.'

'Will we be seeing more witches in the future?'

Adri did not reply. He wanted to know what Maya was getting at without having to ask. Either she wanted to learn to fight the influence, or she wanted out. Should he be honest?

'We might be,' Adri said. 'I'll be better prepared for them from now. I wasn't really—'

'That's not what I want to know. Train me.'

'Took years.'

'You're so brutal,' Maya frowned.

'I'm honest,' Adri replied dispassionately.

'Doesn't matter. You learnt at an early age, I bet. Try me now, I think I'm older than you were.'

'Thus your consciousness is more developed. It will be tougher for you.'

'Why are you constantly dissuading me?'

Adri sighed. 'There's not much to it—ow!'

'Sorry.'

'—yes, not much to it, but fine, I will tell you what I know.'

Maya finished bandaging the shoulder and took a step back, inspecting her handiwork. 'How does it feel?'

Adri moved his left arm slowly. 'It's tight. But it will heal. Thanks.'

Maya smiled. 'You're welcome. Glad I could do *something*!'

Adri smiled back rather grudgingly.

'There's something else I've been meaning to ask you, since you do tend to leave a lot unexplained,' Maya continued.

'Yes, I tend to do that. Ask.' Adri hoped it wasn't going to be about the amulet she was sure to have spotted hanging from his neck.

'Witches,' she said, and Adri breathed once more. 'You told me they could *mark* someone.'

Adri nodded. 'Yes, when they do that, they gain a certain amount of power over that individual. What happens then is that the individual's smell gets recognised by the entire Coven. Think of it as a most wanted poster. All the witches will immediately recognise the marked person by smell and come after him as soon as he's in range of their abilities.'

'That sounds ghastly.'

'It *is* quite tiresome,' Adri said, and brought his left palm in the light, where a burn mark, scorched into the flesh, stood out black and circular.

Maya's jaw dropped. 'You're marked?'

Adri nodded, a grim smile playing on his lips.

Maya shook her head in disbelief. 'You are *so* full of surprises.'

Adri chose to not reply, again. *There are reasons why I do not tell you everything.*

'This house, for example,' Maya continued, 'and Smith. Who's he?'

'Have you heard of the Defenders of Old Kolkata?'

'Yes.'

'He's one of the surviving three. The Gunsmith.'

'I heard rumours about them being alive, but still, wow. How do you know him?'

'My father used to be a Defender as well. The Gunsmith, like my father, retired from an eventful life. The weapons he made are still the best though, and he still makes them for a very select clientele. I'm one of them.'

'So that gun you used against the witch—'

'Built by him, yes. He's dependable, and we needed to make

132

this stop. I need to stock up on ammunition and ingredients, maybe another gun. I also need to put some more protective enchantments in place before we leave. I can't afford to be taken by surprise again.'

'Which way are we going after this?'

'I haven't really decided yet. How about we all catch some dinner right now? You must be hungry.'

'Not really. But dinner seems okay.'

Dinner was an enormous affair. Smith was a good cook—the meat was delicious and everyone loved it. There was stiff, guarded conversation, and Smith asked about where they were from, but nothing about the purpose of their visit. After dinner, they gathered near the fireplace again and the siblings were reminded of how the fire was there only for the light it provided, though it was nice to watch the flames. Smith pulled a couple of armchairs out and all of them settled comfortably; the fire burned without fumes or smoke, magical in nature. Smith sat with a wooden box on his lap. It contained a pipe and tobacco. He started filling his pipe while everyone sat silently.

'Why do you guys smoke?' Maya asked.

Smith almost dropped his pipe. He looked at her incredulously. Adri, cigarette in his mouth and matchbox in his hands, froze.

'Excuse me?' Smith asked.

'Smoke. Why do you people smoke? I mean Adri here has smoked so many cigarettes since we met him! And now we see you smoking as well. Is it ritualistic?'

Adri and Smith exchanged glances.

'Sort of,' Adri replied finally. 'You see, fire keeps spirits away, acts as a natural guard against almost every kind of spirit. Because of this, all Necromancers are trained to carry a pack with them, just to ward off unnecessary spirits in public places. When the cigarette's burning, spirits in general tend to avoid you.' He didn't do a good job at sounding convincing.

'But what about cancer?' Maya asked. She wasn't accusing, but her questions had uncomfortable needles to them.

'The life expectancy of an average Tantric is about thirty years,' Smith said gruffly, not looking at Maya, filling his pipe once more.

'Thirty for a *good* Tantric,' Adri said, still not lighting his cigarette. 'It's a noted fact that smoking has saved several Necromancers on various occasions, thus *increasing* their life expectancy.'

'Yeah, that's a true word, that is,' Smith nodded.

'Aren't *so* many Tantrics all old and stuff?' Gray asked rather cautiously. 'I mean I'm not against the whole smoking thing, but I just want to know.' Maya gave him a poisonous look before she turned to the two.

'You see the few who make it there. Necromancers are the most killed lot. Quite a few are trained, and quite a few die during the training itself,' Smith replied. 'It's brutal, that's what it is. All it takes to kill a Necromancer is one tiny mistake, one slip up while calling upon a spirit, or a Demon. Seen too many go that way.'

Adri finally lit his cigarette. 'Dangerous profession,' he muttered.

'You were one of the Defenders of the Old City, no?' Gray asked Smith, who nodded slowly in reply. 'Aren't you a hero then?' Gray continued. 'I mean, why stay here in Old Kolkata?'

Adri understood where the question was coming from. Gray and Maya had walked their way through a wasted, dilapidated city that was now a mere ghost of its former self, fraught with danger and mysterious in every way. Not having ever seen the city in its full glory, how could they be expected to ever understand the Gunsmith's love for the city? Or his own love, for that matter?

Smith lit his pipe. 'You do not understand,' he said simply, his voice low. There was silence before Gray replied.

'Well, make me.'

'Old Kolkata has a beauty no other place has,' Adri stated.

'I understand the appeal of a place destroyed, of the fragments . . .' Gray began.

'No,' Smith said. 'What Adri means isn't that. Old Kolkata has *soul*.'

Gray looked blank.

'There's more than bricks and mortar keeping this city together. It's seen everything there is to see—from war to famine to political unrest to utter chaos—and it has survived. Something about the city keeps it together; it is that, that something that we find the charm in, despite everything dangerous that's inside and every building that's broken.'

'I still don't get it,' Gray muttered.

'And you won't,' Smith said. 'It's not something for you to get, you who just steps in from wherever it is you come from. It's something *we* know, we who have been with the city through the times it has faced, we who will be here. I am here because the Old City is here. I don't protect it any longer, yes, but I guard my memories. Oh, and no offense meant.'

'History makes the city breathe, Gray,' Adri said quietly. 'You will hopefully understand in time.'

'I wasn't born here,' Gray said. 'Most of my generation was born in New Kolkata, but I know this is where my ancestors were. No one stayed here because of its wretched condition.'

'No one? A lot of people chose to stay,' Smith replied with a touch of scorn. 'There were always the people who couldn't support their families here, and they left. They weren't the only ones. People who couldn't deal with change, even people who loved the city, people who could not witness it broken. Obviously, the hardships here are not for everyone. And it's not like MYTH let everyone enter New Kolkata.'

'Excuse me?' Maya exclaimed.

'MYTH does not let survivors inside New Kolkata,' Smith said. 'I'm not surprised you didn't know. MYTH is good at acting as the perfect government.'

'They don't let people in? But what about the train?'

'We *left* the city,' Adri said. 'I daresay you will find measures stricter when you try to get back in. Both of you are already citizens so you'll be let in, don't worry.'

'I thought New Kolkata was open to everyone!' Gray said.

'Yes, that's what they make it sound like.'

'But–but didn't *you* work for MYTH?' Maya asked.

Smith swore loudly.

'Ah,' Adri spoke.

'I would never work for those bloody bureaucrats!' Smith cursed. 'Don't you know the Defenders never worked for MYTH? They worked for the city!'

'Victor Sen was one—'

'My father left MYTH when he was a Defender,' Adri cut in. 'He was a rogue Necromancer for a long while and MYTH hunted him for years. It was much later that he came back to MYTH and the government applauded him, making him into what you know him as. Maya, you have to understand that people here in Old Kolkata do not take kindly to MYTH; or for that matter, knowing that you hail from New Kolkata. Most powerful figures here are anti-establishment, and it's best you remember that from now.'

'But why this antagonism? What has MYTH done?' Gray asked. 'Hasn't it protected people inside New Kolkata?'

'No,' Smith said. 'Don't flatter yourself, son. MYTH needs your taxes, your services. New Kolkata was built for a reason, and now the territory wars are happening for the same reason. As is the case with Old Kolkata. MYTH is looking for something.'

'For what?' Maya asked, hanging on to every word.

'We don't know,' Smith replied darkly. 'But there have been several instances to prove that MYTH works on an agenda which goes beyond the obvious *people-need-saving* and *evil-needs-punishment* mask. The other governments keep their peace. I wouldn't see the Faces of Moonless Dilhi, the Sea Lords of Frozen Bombay or even the Warlocks of Western Ahmedabad trying to interfere with MYTH's work.'

'What's happening with the territory wars these days, Smith?' Adri asked. 'We'll be heading in that direction soon, I think.'

Smith raised an eyebrow. *You've got one hell of an explanation pending.* Adri acknowledged him with the tiniest of nods.

'You know how it is,' Smith replied at last. 'Ba'al's troops are powerful, and MYTH's troops are numerous. The stalemate continues.'

Demon Commander Ba'al. Considered by many to be one of the strongest and cleverest, Maya remembered. A dangerous combination. She'd read a lot about him in her initial studies. She remembered Adri's diary, where even Victor Sen seemed to be in awe of Ba'al's power. It was obviously Ba'al who would be the leader of the Free Demons, none of the others really had the leadership to keep such a war running for ten years.

'What about the Coven?' Adri asked.

'Bloody hellspawn,' Smith swore. 'They're still around with their whole swooping act, coming in and interrupting battles, I've heard. The usual guerrilla tactics, obviously, those witches can't ever face a Demon, or an Angel head on.'

'I didn't even get a good look at her,' Gray said. 'Are they nocturnal?'

'They don't like the sun,' Adri replied. 'But they're not vampires or anything—they don't burn up. They simply prefer the night.'

'I remember some Commandos,' Smith said. 'Back some fifteen years or so, MYTH Commandos, thinking them witches to be creatures of the night, devising a trap. An entire pack of witches, say about seven or eight of them, were hoisted into the sunlight. Of course they didn't burn. They ripped through the nets and then ripped through the Commandos; they didn't even know about mercury in those days, poor devils. Magical firearms don't count for shit if they aren't shooting quicksilver.'

'We learn through the mistakes of others,' Adri said.

'Yes, and when *you* make a mistake you die.' Smith blew out smoke.

The mood was dark, and no one said anything. The fire burned, and two people smoked. It was not long before Gray excused himself.

'I think I'll get some sleep too,' Maya said, rising with Gray. 'Um, Smith? Do you have a map of this city I could borrow for now?'

'Yes, I've drawn several over the years,' the Gunsmith replied, rising from his armchair. 'I will show you to your rooms as well.'

Most convenient, Adri thought, that the siblings decided to leave. He needed the Gunsmith to know several things. He needed to ask questions and hope for answers. Smith had his questions as well, evidently, and being one of the people Adri trusted with his life, he also had the sense to ask nothing in front of the siblings. He looked around the room and sighed softly. He used to come here as a child, with his father, and every time, Smith would argue with his father about giving him a gun for protection. When he finally did get a firearm, it was one the Gunsmith had made especially for him, one that served him well and for years. Reaching into his bag, he took out his shooter and turned it over in his hands.

It was a beautiful thing and he admired it once more as he had on countless other occasions. Magic needed to be channelled, and unlike Sorcerers whose very art lay in the channelling of different kinds of magic directly from their modified gauntlets, Necromancers needed to rely on magically modified firearms. Tantrics needed to be crack shots, and were taught to shoot from an early age. The weaknesses of each enemy were imbibed in bullets modified by decent bullet alchemists, and the Tantrics used different rounds for different enemies accordingly. Damage that wasn't being done through the spirits or Demons they summoned had to be inflicted through these modified bullets. The silver gleamed in the light and shadow, and Adri was reminded of how old-school the weapon was. MYTH Commandos used automatic rifles that released magical ammo in a volley; but being mass manufactured, they lacked the power and the class of a personally crafted magical weapon. The Gunsmith remained one of the best weapon makers in the land; he took his time and made weapons only for a selective clientele, but the quality was always worth the wait. The last time Adri had seen the Gunsmith had been a year ago, and he hadn't changed much. The retired defender now lived a life of loneliness in the Old City, doing Adri didn't know what.

The Gunsmith came back soon and sat back in his armchair, puffing on his pipe quite fast. 'Okay then Adri, *where* are you taking those two?'

'The Lake of Fire,' Adri answered.

'Near the wars, great. No, you need to start from the beginning.'

And that's what Adri did. The Gunsmith listened patiently, though his eyes bulged with disbelief as the tale progressed.

'The Horsemen,' Smith said at last. 'No, I'm sorry lad, I don't know shit about them. Mostly legend, but I bet you've heard that before. Victor must have known something, but he's . . .'

'Did you know about Father's archives, Smith?'

'The books?'

'Yes. Extensive notes on almost everything he ever encountered,' Adri said. 'Hidden away in a secret basement that I never knew about in all my years in that house.'

'Victor always had his secrets. We learnt to respect them early, me and the others. I'm not surprised one bit, Adri. But what are you getting at?'

'If my father had ever encountered the Horsemen, he would have written it down.'

'Well, did he?'

'I don't know. The books are arranged alphabetically in that basement, Smith; and the letter H is missing.'

'Just H?'

'No. H, J, and C. Do you know anything about this?'

Smith nodded. 'I think so. You remember Professor Sural?'

'Vaguely. The man who used to teach in some university, right?'

Smith nodded. 'Jadavpur. He was a professor at Jadavpur. I believe Victor used to lend him books, and most personal ones.'

'Is he still here in the city?'

'I have no idea. Rumoured dead. Try calling his spirit.'

Adri shook his head. 'No good, I don't have any personal object belonging to the professor. And neither will you, I suppose?'

'No, never really even knew the professor. But there's a possibility.'

'Which is?'

'His office.In the university. He might just have Victor's books stored away in there.'

'The original Jadavpur University?'

'Yes. He was a professor of Demonology. If you can get to the department, you can verify.'

'You mean to say the books could still be there?'

'They should be. Every professor had some kind of a wall safe, if I'm not wrong.'

Adri sank into his thoughts. The original JU campus fell on his way to the Lake of Fire anyway, but his original plan had been to skirt around it—the place had always harboured ill. There were rumours of people disappearing within, of things long-forgotten living within the vine-infested walls. 'I suppose I could go through JU. Though I don't like that place.'

'None of us do. Might be the only way if you don't want to wait for the Fallen's report. Aurcoe is an old one, a sly old thing. He'll get the job done if you can get his blood. Who's the Angel?'

'Kaavsh. I don't know him.'

'I do. He's an interesting one. Takes his job here seriously. I met him years ago, he wasn't as powerful then as he's now.'

'Will he part with his blood?'

'No,' Smith said simply. 'There's no way someone like Kaavsh will give his blood for a Fallen. And I suspect he won't be happy about you using both his siblings either.'

'They're not his blood siblings,' Adri returned darkly.

'Kaavsh seemed to take the whole earth sibling thing quite seriously. I wouldn't be surprised if he's more than a little attached to these two here.'

'I'm worried now, Smith. I don't have a plan to make the Angel part with his blood yet.'

The Gunsmith waved the comment aside. 'You will figure out a way, I know that. I am yet to come across a Necromancer as resourceful as you. No, what I'm worried about is Victor.'

'You must realise, Smith, that I can't follow up on my father's kidnapping until I get this out of the way. But neither can I let it lie.'

'I know, lad, you don't need to defend yourself. Thing is, Victor could always take care of himself. I have seen him summoning Infernals in the past. He's quite capable of controlling them; this isn't a summoning gone wrong. He has been *taken*.' Smith leaned back. 'I don't know who it could be, or where to start looking. Victor always had too many enemies.' He looked at Adri. 'How were things between you and Victor?'

'The same. As always,' Adri replied drily.

'You two could have been the best father-son team to date,' Smith said. 'You two needed to talk it over, clear it out.'

'We had our talks, and I never got my answers.'

'You can't say Victor ever stopped you from growing, Adri. In fact, a lot of the power I see radiate within you is Victor's. You have learned a lot yourself, agreed, but he kind of *was* there to show you the way.'

'He's not someone capable of having a family, Smith. You know that.'

The Gunsmith did not reply. His face was in shadow, and all that came from those depths was the smoke of his pipe. 'I owe him,' he spoke at last. 'And I am responsible for you as well. Whatever your differences might be, I have allegiances to both of you and I still intend to see them through.' Adri nodded slowly, and the weapon maker continued, 'This is what I would suggest. Tomorrow, you go your own way to the Lake of Fire. I will go back to your house, see what I find, and then see if I can track the Infernal. At present, that Fire Demon is the only thing that can lead us to Victor.'

Adri knew Smith was an extremely skilled woodsman of the city. Victor had often ranted about how the Gunsmith knew not only the most secret, undiscovered places the Old City had to hide, but also all the possible routes that could be taken to get to these places. And there was no doubting either Smith's abilities or his intentions, he could most certainly handle himself in any fight that might come his way. Relief washed over Adri now that his father's disappearance was being looked into, that too by someone he trusted to this extent.

'Show me the firearm,' Smith said suddenly. Adri realised it had been in his hands all along. He handed it over. Smith turned it over in his expert hands, something that immediately reminded Adri of the way Death had inspected it; except it had been more of an oddity for Death, something it didn't encounter very often, while Smith's eye was a completely expert one. In the next twelve seconds, Smith had dissembled the revolver, its pieces, all separate, on his lap.

'You're still using this?' he asked. 'I would've expected you to come asking for a new one ages ago.'

'I don't really need to use a shooter while I'm in New Kolkata. What's wrong with it anyway?'

'How long has it been since I made you this? Five, six years?'

'Yes, something like that.'

'The artefact has almost faded away, there's very little magic left, and you're bloody lucky that you could give that witch even the two rounds you fired.'

Adri raised his eyebrows slowly. 'Well I'm glad you're here, then.'

'And the springs are gone. The trigger is kind of squeaky. You would've been murdered if this is all you were depending on.' Adri laughed. 'It's no joke, young idiot,' Smith said, gathering the pieces in his hands. 'I've got some work ahead of me tonight. You give that wound of yours some rest, I'll see you in the morning.' He got up. Adri lit another cigarette as Smith left for the staircase. Then he stopped midway, and turned around. For a moment Adri imagined him making some sort of remark about his smoking too much.

'Adri,' Smith said, 'you're manipulating these two to your own end. And you're lying to them about the Angel. If they've grown up seeing Kaavsh around, this realisation, it might shatter them.'

Adri said nothing.

'Watch where you tread, lad,' Smith said and walked up the stairs.

'They're not going to know,' Adri said aloud long after Smith was gone. He was standing now, the cigarette burning fast between his fingers. 'I'm not going to let them know.' His words echoed in the room, and except for the gentle crackling of fire, there was no other noise.

Every wall-mounted torch in the Gunsmith's house had the artefact clearly visible in the handle. A sliver of a gemstone, slightly warm, that kept the fire burning magically. When the artefact was removed, the torch would go out. Gray had done exactly that to get the darkness he needed for sleep. Maya, however, hadn't, and the torch near her bed burned bright as she poured over the map she had acquired. Her objective, she realised with the thrill of guilt, was not that far away. She could sneak out this very night if she chose to. There were complications though. She didn't know how she would protect herself, and she didn't want to leave the front door open and unguarded after she snuck out. Other than Adri and Smith, even Gray was sleeping inside, clueless about her hidden agenda. She could not risk witches creeping in through an unlocked door.

Her indecision caused her pain. She was betraying Adri's trust. Yes, there were things he was not telling her, his agendas were secretive as well. But he had stood by them, taken care of them, and protected them. Of course it was all because he needed them to get to Abriti, but there was still something decent about Adri, something human. He had done some terrible things, but she could see how misguided he had been in his childhood, how alone. His very words spoke of his loneliness, of how he always felt different, trained in an art he had not chosen for himself. Maya realised with a start that she was beginning to understand Adri a little for the first time. Then again, there was that feeling of hers, a certain *thing* about Adri that did not seem right. She could still not, however, try as she might, place it.

Maya looked at her bag. This was it. All she needed to do was grab it and sneak out, shut the front door as firmly as possible to make sure it looked shut. Then stick to the shadows and walk. She knew the way now, she had memorised it well enough and it was clearly marked in her mind. She had thought about requesting Adri to take her where she wanted to go, or even demand it in exchange of leading him to her brother. She had thought about this many times since they had started, but no. If he refused she could not even try to escape afterwards; duping Adri then would be tougher, almost impossible. She reminded herself to be strong. She needed to do this. Maya reached for the bag—and jerked back in surprise at a soft knock on the door. It was Adri.

'Hello! Was wondering if you two were still up,' he said. His usual confidence was missing, Maya noticed. It seemed to have been replaced with something more shaky, more vulnerable.

'Is something wrong?' she asked.

'No, it's fine, everything's fine. Just wanted to let you guys know that tomorrow we'll be going through the original Jadavpur University campus. That's where your university originated, thought you'd want to know.'

Maya froze for a couple of seconds. 'That's . . . that's great,' she managed to stammer. 'Why though?'

'I have a little work there. In and out. It won't take long.'

'It's fine then. It'll be nice, seeing the original JU. Thanks for the information, I guess.'

'Have a good night's sleep,' Adri said. Smiling weakly, he left.

Maya shut the door after him and stood there for a long while. *He's taking me right there. Adri is taking me exactly where I want to go.* Her plan would have to change a bit. Gray and Adri would now be around, she didn't know if it was a good thing. Why did Adri knock at this time anyway? Maya did not go to sleep. Instead, she picked up Adri's diary and began to read. She read all night, and when the first rays of the sun washed over the Old City, she had finished all the diaries. She kept the books back in her backpack, thinking about Adri in a new light. Cautious. Admiring. Compassionate. Perhaps even a little afraid. Overloaded with all the new information and forming her own opinions on them, she slowly lay down on her bed, and allowed sleep to claim her.

10

The Gunsmith awakened Adri early, barely an hour after Maya had gone to sleep. Adri sat up, his mind in a whirl. There were a lot of things to be done today, and he quickly summed up the events so far. The first thing he remembered was the conversation with Maya in the dead of the night; an attempted salve to his conscience. It didn't really make much sense to him now. He moved his shoulder. *Better.* He washed up, brushed, and then made his way down to the living room, where Smith was making tea.

'This is good. Thanks,' he said, sipping.

'Tea isn't all I made you,' Smith grinned. He picked up something from a table next to him and walking over to Adri, handed it to him—a pair of dual shoulder holsters from which the handles of something jet-black peeked out. Adri withdrew one. It was a large revolver, a hand cannon; supremely made, a perfect mix of matte and shine. The huge barrel gleamed black, while the handle remained dark. Inscriptions from the handle crept their way up the body, ending halfway up the barrel. Both the hammer and the trigger were beauteously curved and looked persevering. A dark red glow emanated from within; gentle, almost unseen. It had the look and feel of a panther ready to spring. A majestic weapon.

'This is . . . incredible,' Adri whispered, gazing at the weapon in awe.

'Glad you like it,' Smith was still grinning as he looked on proudly.

'You made this in *one night*?'

'Don't be an idiot. I worked on the pair for over a couple of months. These damned things need a lot of testing. Didn't want any to go kaput or blow up in your hand.'

'You were making them for me?'

'One for you and the other for Victor. But you can have both now, you'll need them.'

'You were trying to resolve our altercations.'

'Hmm. Know your gun. .50 calibre. Powerful bullets, they'll hold a lot more ingredients. You can maximise damage, deal out more in less.'

Adri turned his attention back to the gun. 'Five chambers, that's excellent. That's ten shots without reloading if I use both the guns.'

'Yes. It shouldn't need any servicing for a year or two. The magical artefact is a red *alagar*; extremely dominant yet doesn't give out too much light. I'll give you empty cartridges for these.'

'I'll need a lot of cartridges.'

'Yes, I know.'

The sudden sound of a loud yawn had both of them turning around and looking at the doorway where a sleepy Gray stood scratching his white hair.

'Morning, people,' he said wearily. 'I need coffee.'

Adri turned to the Gunsmith. 'I need yet another favour. I need you to give him a gun. Something he can use easily.'

Gray froze. 'Seriously?' he asked, his sleep gone.

'I'll have something for him,' Smith said, thoughtful.

'Holy yeah!' Gray exclaimed, grinning wide in excitement. 'Why the change of heart, Adri?'

Adri said nothing. He had thought about this. A very simple action had sparked off this decision—it was when Gray had picked

147

up the pipe during the attack of the Dynes. Simple self-defence. If Gray wanted to help, then he should be able to. The Old City refused to forgive mistakes.

Smith looked at Gray. 'You ever handled a real firearm?' he asked.

'No,' Gray said blankly.

Smith walked over and opened a door beneath the staircase, a door that Gray didn't know existed. Adri knew where it led. He had been to the Gunsmith's workshop many times in the past. Devices and instruments. Canisters and magical containers. Tools and apparatuses. A place the Gunsmith considered his own, something that couldn't be defiled with foreign presence. Adri had learned this at an older age and hadn't gone down there since. Smith hadn't invited him to.

Adri poured Gray some tea.

'You didn't answer me,' Gray asked him, constantly shifting his glance between Adri and the workshop door.

'Firing a gun is easy,' Adri said. 'Aim and pull the trigger, that's all. If you can help protect yourself and your sister while we're out there, it's a bonus.'

Gray nodded. 'I can help.'

'Where's Maya?' Adri asked after a moment. 'We don't have too much time. We've got to leave soon.'

'She's asleep like a log. Doesn't look like she'll be up unless shaken awake.'

'We'll need to.'

The Gunsmith emerged, and shut the door behind him. Cradled in his hands was a sawn-off double-barrelled shotgun, roughly the size of Gray's entire arm. The weapon looked old, worn out—there were no inscriptions or intricate embellishments of any kind on its surface, and it looked unimpressive. Adri, however, stared at it, and then at the Gunsmith.

'You're not giving him *this*,' he said.

'It's easy enough to use, and he doesn't have to be a good shot. I would say yes,' Smith replied, shrugging.

Gray had been looking at the weapon with a streak of disappointment, but was immediately curious after Adri's reaction to it. 'Why? Why?' he asked.

Adri ignored him. 'This is too . . . treacherous.'

'You need such kind of power against your enemies. This whole business isn't exactly small, Adri. It doesn't seem to me that this is about your *little* problem, or about your father alone. I think the right pieces are being removed from the board.'

'I have suspected a conspiracy from the beginning.'

'And if it is, you will need backup.' Smith turned to Gray. 'This is an ancient weapon, handed down to a few. Its immense power is carefully hidden within its innocuous appearances.' He handed the weapon to Gray, who was surprised at its weight. 'The Sadhu's Shotgun,' Smith said.

'What's the history of this weapon?' Gray asked, fascinated.

'Blood. Lots of it,' Smith said. He proceeded to familiarise Gray with the basic operations of the gun; using both triggers and the tricky reload among them. Adri looked darkly at the weapon, and then looked away. Smith knew what he was doing. Gray would be okay with the weapon; if Gray ignored it, it would, in all probability, stay just that—a magical shotgun; and with the right kind of ammunition created for it, would be a decent weapon to have by his side. Which reminded him, he needed to make bullets. Leaving Gray to Smith, he went up to his room to get his bullet alchemy case, and on the way, caught sight of Maya on her bed, still fast asleep.

When they finally did leave Smith's house, it was high noon. The sun was beaming down on the Old City with its usual merciless temperament. It hit them right as they left the house. They turned around to bid the Gunsmith farewell.

'Tread well,' Smith said. 'Adri, I will start for your house under the hour.'

Adri nodded. 'Do let me know if you find something.'

After Smith shut his door, they started off, and Adri soon realised it wasn't going to be easy, this trip in the sun. It irritated him, he sweated easily. He looked at the siblings and was surprised to see them hardly affected; Gray was wearing sunglasses now, looking even more like the musician he wasn't. *Bloody college students. Must be used to tramping around in the sun everywhere.*

Only a few people were out in the heat, walking with umbrellas. No one gave them a second glance as before, though Adri was now wearing his newly acquired weapons in a twin shoulder holster over his shirt and Gray had slung the Sadhu's Shotgun over his shoulder with a shotgun sling; it gently bumped against his backpack as he walked.

'Where are we?' Gray asked.

'A few kilometres from Santoshpur. Places here are a lot more spread out than in New Kolkata,' Adri added when Gray opened his mouth. New Kolkata had been modelled on the blueprints of the original city, but everything was much closer. The Old City was like a small country; the two could hardly be compared.

The roads were destroyed, long and prominent cracks running in any bit of tar that remained. Everything else, otherwise, was either dirt or pebbles, crunching under their feet as they walked. The lack of maintenance had resulted in a massive growth of the local flora in Old Kolkata, but this was not an area where trees were in abundance. They were few and far between and did not shade Adri as much as he had hoped.

The Old City was without movement. Old things looked at them as they passed, things that had been lying in wait for decades, things undisturbed. Water did not flow anywhere, and where it gathered, it was murky and dark. The skies were burning, yet there were distant clouds in the horizon, promising rain. The city was unpredictable with its rain, fickle, and only frequenters like Adri knew what the real chances of rain on a day like this were. They travelled for hours, slowly but steadily, Adri explaining as they walked that the area they were traversing through wasn't really considered dangerous; although danger chose not to restrict itself to fixed places in Old Kolkata. *Mostly* safe was probably a better word. Nevertheless, he was ready for anything, Adri reassured the two. He would not be caught off guard again. However, he cautioned, they would need to be extra vigilant inside Jadavpur University.

'It might seem oh-so-precious, this reunion with your college, the original institution from where yours originated,' Adri said. 'But do not wander off under *any* reason or circumstance. I mean it. Jadavpur is one of the oldest, and hence, most avoided places in Old Kolkata right now. There are *things* there that don't need to know we're taking a walk through.'

'What kind of things?' Maya spoke for the first time now. 'You're *always* so vague!' She had been strangely taciturn so far. Distant. Observant. Adri had felt her gaze burning into the back of his head often, but he'd thought it a little stupid to spin around and check. Her preoccupation had even gotten to Gray. Adri had heard him ask her what the matter was, but she hadn't answered.

'Isn't it better if we don't get to know what things?' Adri said, raising his arms in mock protest.

Gray looked nervously at the bandolier he was now wearing, at the shotgun shells lined neatly along its side. Adri had two, slung diagonally below his belt, and looked like a strange modern cowboy. Adri had made bullets for himself and shells for Gray's shotgun before they'd left the Gunsmith's house. Bullet Alchemy was another art Tantrics needed to know—an art that had been around for just as long as guns. The details were simple enough.

'Normal bullets don't hurt supernatural creatures. Not much of a help when practically *everything* in the Old City is pretty much supernatural,' Adri had said. Basically, the aura of any creature could be classified broadly into three types: holy, unholy, or neutral. Holy and unholy countered each other—all one had to do to hurt the creature was hit it with the opposite aura(neutral was affected by both). Here's where alchemy came in; not only did one have to fill the bullet's interior with holy or unholy ingredients, but there were formulas—specific ingredients which when applied in specific quantities, had certain specific effects. The art of bullet alchemy lay in knowing which ingredients to carry, which ingredients to find and how, which ingredients to put in bullets and how much, and in using the right bullet for the right enemy.

Like a lot of others things in Necromancy, this needed a lot of knowhow. There were books to be memorised, formulas to keep on one's fingertips, bullets to be colour-coded so as to remember what contained what—and of course, one had to keep a quick reloading hand in case bullet types had to be changed on the fly. Besides, it was pretty delicate work. Gray had watched with fascination as Adri had brought out his wooden alchemy case, opened it, and taken out all the different layers and tools. He worked fast and intuitively, Gray realised as he saw him at it. Within the hour, Adri had filled in over a hundred bullets of the different varieties that he would need. And that was before he had moved to shotgun shells for Gray.

Maya had not approved of Gray getting a weapon, even though she knew it would probably protect him more than anything else. She had been persuaded at last, mostly by Gray. She was not in the best of moods, as a result; already having too much to think about from the night before, now her JU plan was getting a lot more complicated than it was supposed to. And Adri talking about the dangers in JU didn't help.

'I'd rather know,' she said. 'So tell me. What things?'

Adri stopped walking. 'The mysteries about the Old City' — he spoke at length— 'are all connected to its *age*. Things happened here in this city, in every corner and every street. And the things that lurk here are all related to those incidents; unforgotten instances, unfulfilled vows, promises broken, incredible acts of humanity and insanity. What we do is always linked to what has happened. And it is where we fail to discern the reason that we begin to dread, to fear. No one really knows what happened in JU. There are creatures in there which are long forgotten, things whispered about in nightmares, between the yellowing pages of rare books. Those who have combated them have mostly not made it out to talk about them—those that have, consider themselves lucky, and have not dared to make a study of them. Thus there are no weaknesses that we know about in the few creatures that we do know exist. And then there are others that we haven't seen or heard of yet.'

'Are they Demons?' Maya asked.

'No. They are *other* things.'

'Like what?' Maya snapped.

Adri glared at her for the first time that day. 'Like an Alabagus,' he said shortly.

'The Heart-eaters? Impossible!'

'Believe what you want. I'm in no hurry to meet one either,' Adri said. He started walking, and Maya hurried after him.

'Wait! But the Alabagus is supernatural!'

'Bingo.'

'No! What I meant to say is—it's legend! Doesn't really exist! Like the Horsemen of Old Kolkata, for heaven's sake!'

Adri almost missed a step. The pendant swung as he walked, and he could feel its cold surface against his chest. He breathed in deeply. 'There is a grain of truth in every legend,' he said.

'Don't give me a stupid old saying as a justification,' Maya said.

'I'm lucky enough to have not met an Alabagus myself. But I have met people who have. Now, they could be lying. Or not. Me, I prefer to be a little more careful, that's all.'

153

'Why are we going through JU anyway?' Gray asked from behind; he'd been following the two, listening closely. 'I mean, if it's so dangerous? Can't we just go around it or something?'

There it is, the question. Matters were complicated enough with Maya having borrowed a map from Smith; he could not lie about JU being the only way through. And he did have work there, he couldn't hide that—they *would* see what he was up to. *Tread carefully, Adri.*

'No, I want to see the university,' Maya said.

'You do?' Gray asked wearily. He had not taken his camera out of his bag for a long time now.

'Yes, it's the very place that our ancestors studied in, jackass! You mean to tell me you have no interest in seeing what the old college was like?'

'I have no interest in seeing what an Alabagus looks like,' Gray muttered.

'Legend! Fairy tale!' Maya said, her voice shrill.

'Okay, okay.'

'Err, even I have some work in there,' Adri added casually, and the siblings did not react. *Excellent.* He had no clue why Maya would be so enthusiastic about wanting to see the old university, but it was fortunate enough for his needs. Who needed to understand why she was eager when this need of hers could be used to shield his guilt?

Do not feel guilty. You have led them to a dangerous place just for your own needs, yes, but you need to live, and it is because of the only letter your mother wrote for you. All you need to do is make sure Maya and Gray are safe when you lead them, either back to the train or to the Angel. That's all. They can hate you forever when they find out. It doesn't matter. You have always been hated. You could never even meet the only person who loved you.

The heat of the day receded as late afternoon came upon them. The sun began adopting a more golden glow and shadows began to lengthen. They mostly walked through narrow alleys, cutting through the occasional wide roads as quickly as possible. People lived along the alleys—they could hear distant voices like before; clothes were hung out to dry; dogs sunned themselves lazily outside locked doors; an occasional strain of music, but mostly people talking. Often far away. Often nearby. Gray imagined eyes watching them and every time he would look up to confirm, he would find his intuition mostly correct as curtains behind windows fell back into place and footsteps hurriedly exited balconies. They ran into the occasional traveller who crossed them without a word. A couple of these people, Gray noticed, were carrying rifles slung over their shoulders.

The city seemed alien to him. It wasn't clean in the least; all sorts of filth lay in the back alleys they were walking through. Some areas stank so bad he had to hold his nose. He didn't like it and had no idea why people raved about the greatness of the city. Was it some sort of delusion employed deliberately to make the residents feel better? But there was no question about it, the city could not compare to its new counterpart in terms of either safety, cleanliness or living standards. People seemed much, much happier in the utopia of New Kolkata, and somewhere inside, Gray was glad that when all this was over, he would be going back there.

He hadn't photographed anything in the Old City after the witch incident. But he shouldn't have let it get to him, he now decided. He had come to the Old City fantasising about the photographic opportunities it presented. And maybe his photographs could actually dissolve the urban raving about the Old City. Why obsess over something so desolate and dead? Gray reached into his bag and withdrew his camera, and from then on, he busied himself with taking pictures when he could, jogging lightly to catch up with the other two every time he fell behind—Adri and Maya never waited for him.

Some more conversation-less travelling later, they stopped. Up ahead in the distance, across the completely deserted road, they could see the twin gates of Jadavpur University. They stood there for a minute, not talking. The road was completely deserted. The wall running around the campus was visible as well, a long brown line in the horizon, the buildings beyond silent, uninhabited. It seemed like a giant trap, the lack of life almost deliberate.

Then Adri began to walk up the road, and they followed. They walked past broken-down cars that were permanent landmarks, scattered not just along the roadside but also, occasionally, bang in the centre of the road; past broken-down shops and remnants of what must've once been busy newspaper stalls; past broken-down ATM machines with their shutters pulled down and padlocked. The place sang of quiet desolation and no witnesses.

A crow cawed loudly in the distance. Adri gently eased one of his hand cannons out of its holster and held it by his side as he walked. He turned back and nodded at Gray.

'What?' Gray asked.

Adri sighed. 'Keep that goddamned camera in and carry the shotgun.'

Gray nodded. Maya offered to carry the shotgun so Gray could continue taking his pictures. Gray wasn't willing to relinquish his newly found weapon so easily, but Maya insisted with sibling finality. Grudgingly, Gray gave in.

The sense of bleak increased as they stepped past the twin black gates of the university which, once proud, were now rusty and decaying, vines choking every inch of space. Beyond the gates was the empty university campus, nursed only by the elements, its buildings, though they still stood, all weak and crumbling. It looked unvisited for years. A road went down as far as the eye could see, diverging into various different directions. Old weathered buildings everywhere. Maya and Gray immediately realised that like most of New Kolkata, even their college had been modelled after the original one; they could recognise the buildings and the turns. Adri confirmed this.

'Your college in New Kolkata is built according to this design. So tell me where the Demonology department is.'

'This way,' Gray said, glancing at Maya, who silently followed, taciturn again, just barely being able to lift the heavy shotgun.

They passed a series of buildings, took a short cut through a huge field, and then walked on a cobblestone path, passing more abandoned, broken-down cars and an old tank model. There was no sign of any life around as they walked.

'This place is too silent,' Maya spoke suddenly.

'Yeah, and it's pretty much freaking me out,' Gray muttered.

Even the trees—there were quite a lot of them—were silent to the passing wind. They grew incredibly tall and thick with no gardeners around to control their growth, often crashing into buildings and weaving their branches through windows and collapsed ceilings, emerging out of roofs. Vegetation had almost entirely taken over the campus. Wild grass grew high in what had earlier been a manicured lawn and even the smallest of cobblestones they walked on was lined with moss. Adri had told the siblings to expect this sort of a plant infestation—the Old City had gone through drastic changes in its isolation, with parts of it being transformed into complete forests, while others got submerged under water.

Maya was beginning to understand why people avoided JU. Dread. An inexplicable feeling of being watched. Thoughts of sudden and brutal ends. She could never have come here alone and unarmed. She understood Adri a lot better now, but she realised he was taking them through here because of something he wanted to see, a selfish personal interest. The location coincided, and that made things easier for her; she did not speak out. Her apprehension was mounting high, and it had made her sullen and silent the entire day.

When the Demonology Wing finally came in sight—a lone building at the end of the path—Adri slowed down, and half raising his weapon, he led the way, cautiously and slowly. His eyes darted everywhere, every window with a broken glass pane, every place that was in shadow, every place that he couldn't see. The building itself was a dark motley green-grey, covered entirely as it was with moss and vines. The tall, wooden front doors were ajar, and nothing could be seen except for the yawning darkness within. Adri approached the doors with his weapon completely raised—one hand supported by the other—and pushed the door open. Gently. It swung inward with a loud creak, and everything was silent once more.

Adri peeped inside. Ahead of him lay a dark corridor, the darkness occasionally broken by dim sunlight trickling in through an open window, or a crack in the wall. He looked at the light and realised the sun would set soon; they could not, under any circumstance, linger around the university after dark. He needed to hurry. He took a step inside. Splash. Looking down, Adri saw water running all over the black and white chequered floor. Moving inside as quietly as he could, Adri made his way to an old, faded notice board on the wall right opposite the door and found exactly what he was looking for—a list of all the professors in the department and their offices. Professor Sural. Third floor.

'Third floor,' Adri whispered. Maya pointed towards a staircase on their right and they began to move. When they reached the staircase, Adri noticed that it went down as well—this place had a basement then, he noted. He started walking up the stairs, gun raised. It took them about ten minutes to find the professor's office; their watchfulness slowed them down. When Adri entered the professor's room, the first thing he noticed was a setting sun, beyond a broken window. He swore softly, holstered his hand cannon, and looked around the small office.

It was as forsaken as the rest of the building. A small table lay next to the window. Three chairs, barely standing. A bookshelf. The weather had not spared any of them; every paper that lay about had been washed in muddy water and dried in harsh sunlight. The books crumbled in Adri's hand as he thumbed through them. He slowly let go of his backpack, dropping it to the floor, and began scanning the bookshelf with greater care for anything that might resemble his father's books. Nothing familiar. He hoped the professor had not kept them on the bookshelf; nothing on it was readable any longer. He carefully studied the spines. Nothing. He turned and began to look around the room.

'What are you looking for?' Gray asked.

'A book,' Adri said.

Then he saw it. A portrait of the professor mounted on the wall behind his desk. Adri took a moment to look at Professor Sural's face, to look at the shining eyes, firm jaw, the hint of a smile playing around his lips, before yanking it off the wall rudely. There, behind it. The safe Smith had talked about. It was built into the wall—comparatively untouched by the elements—with a crude handle and a keyhole. Adri wondered if it was magical.

'Open,' he spoke in the Old Tongue. Nothing happened. Mechanical, then. He took a step back. 'Appear, Sh'aar,' he spoke softly in the Old Tongue once more. In about exactly a second, he felt its presence in the room.

'On this charge I get my freedom,' a voice spoke from nowhere. It sounded bored.

'Oh my God!' Gray exclaimed.

'Open the lock,' Adri said, 'and have your freedom.'

The safe lock clicked open, and simultaneously Adri felt Sh'aar's presence leave for the higher place.

'One of the protector spirits I had commissioned to defend us. Don't worry about it,' Adri said without turning around, his hand on the handle.

'You let it go?' Gray asked.

'Yes.'

'You still have more, right?'

'Yes.'

Adri opened the safe and the books caught his eye immediately. The Gunsmith had been right. They were here—three books, clad in black. Adri picked up the one with the letter H on its spine and opened it in the dying sunlight. *Heretic, Hoensach, Hoggath,* and finally, *Horsemen*.

Death is by far the most interesting of the four. There have been few victims of Death, however. Over the years, Death has reportedly taken three known people: Aniket Das, Kinsheal Naidu, Roland Thomas.

That was all. Three names he had never heard before. Nothing else. Adri read and re-read the short passage, the shortest of all the descriptions in the fat book. Vexation gripped him and he threw the book against the wall with a scream; it hit the wall and fell heavily, a couple of pages floating to the floor. Adri scratched his head, sweeping back his hair repeatedly without realising it. Dead end. Three names. Maybe links. But he had no clue where he could find out more about these people. No clue at all.

Focus, Adri. First things first. You need to get out of here, along with the siblings. The sun has gone, and you need to go.

He took a deep breath and looked up. Gray was staring at him. And Maya, Maya was not in the room.

'Where's Maya?' he exclaimed in shock.

Gray looked around him, surprised. 'She was here just now!'

'Bloody hell,' Adri muttered, and drawing a shooter, strode past Gray out into the corridor. Gray followed him hurriedly.

'She has the shotgun,' Gray said.

They would've heard it go off. Adri looked up and down the darkening corridor. There was no sign of her, no trace suggesting where she could have gone. Or been taken.

'MAYA!'Gray shouted, panic in his voice.

Adri looked around sharply for a reaction. Nothing. His problems were increasing. The sun had set and the last dredges of light were leaving the sky. Visibility in the small corridor was declining rapidly. Adri didn't want to use the second spirit so soon, but he was at a disadvantage. 'Arrive, Masir,' he commanded. 'Fireball. Show me the way.'

The spirit materialised as a translucent orb suspended in mid-air, a few feet from Adri's head. As Adri and Gray looked at it, it caught fire and began to burn. Light returned to the corridor. Adri moved and the fireball moved with him, keeping a distance. Removing the other shooter from its holster, Adri wordlessly handed it to Gray. Gray was momentarily thrilled to hold the majestic weapon, but it did not show on his face. He shouted his sister's name again. They walked down the corridor, opening door after door, peering into offices, classrooms, broom closets, all empty and dilapidated.

'We-we can search faster if we split up,' Gray muttered.

Adri shook his head. 'Stick to me. Like glue.'

They checked the whole of the third floor, but found no one. Whatever it was that had carried Maya off, it had made no noise at all, and it had left no traces; Adri wondered what it could be. He had heard tales and speculations, but had encountered very few beings in these grounds to be sure. Unless—

'Gray,' Adri said, turning to a very worried Gray staring into the darkness. 'Gray, tell me, did Maya have any work here in the Demonology building? Any agenda? Anything she could want to find out?'

Gray was taken aback. 'Maya would have told me if she wanted something from here.'

'But supposing she didn't,' Adri pursued. 'Supposing she wanted to find out something about some professor, or some course, where would she get that information?'

161

'Um, that would be Records and Research. Basement. Always the basement.'

Adri turned and ran, the fireball whooshing along. Gray ran after him, overtaking him and shooting down the stairs. When he reached the ground floor, Adri found Gray staring at the darkness beyond the steps leading down to the basement.

'Adri, there is something down there,' he spoke softly.

'What did you see?'

'Something moved in there. I'm sure.' For just a second, his voice trembled.

'I know you don't like the dark,' Adri said. 'But you have to come with me. You're not safe anywhere else.'

Gray shook his head. 'If Maya's in there, I have to go.'

Adri led the way. Darkness had descended in entirety now. The sun was gone, and along with it all sunlight. They were descending into the subterranean in Jadavpur University at night. Sheer madness. But Maya was in danger, owing to his carelessness, his distraction with the book. He would pull her out—or find her body. He bit his lip and furiously hoped it wouldn't come to that. The fireball floated a little ahead of them, lighting up peeling walls and thick, dirty spider webs, and footprints—someone had been through here recently.

'Footprints,' Adri said.

'Maya?' Gray asked immediately.

'Not sure. Stay close to me and the fireball.'

'These spirits, they obey you?' Gray asked, looking at the floating fire.

'Not yet,' Adri replied. 'I give trapped spirits freedom in exchange of a certain task.'

'Oh.'

'Be on your toes. I don't like this.' Adri considered the possibilities, none of them pretty. Silently, he removed some bullets from his shooter and added other ones in their place. The darkness increased as they headed deeper down; it tried to envelop them, but was held at bay by the lone fireball. Gray looked behind him and saw complete darkness. There was no way back. Everything was dead silent except for their footsteps which rang loud, echoing for long spaces.

Something came into view at last, right at the end of the stairs, something that sprung out of the darkness almost magically—a door, wooden, with a faded glass sign on it that said RECORDS.

They opened the door—the creaking resonating for ages—and walked through. Neither the walls nor the ceiling were visible in the light of the fireball—all they could feel was a void, a complete lack of anything solid within their reach, save for the ground beneath their feet. Adri looked down. The ground wasn't wood or cement, it was raw rock, dirty and unpolished. He inspected the complete darkness on every side; he realised Gray must be terrified.

'I saw something move earlier, I'm sure of it,' Gray whispered, right on cue. 'Oh God.'

'Easy, now. Just wait for my signal before you go trigger-happy on anything.'

Gray nodded solemnly. His eyes were wide, fearful, looking for activity. It came soon. They walked a little bit in that dark when they heard it. The movement. Soft snapping noises in rapid succession. First to their right, then to their left. Surrounding them. The fireball rose above Adri's head automatically, as if sensing the danger. The noises gradually stopped. Nothing happened for the longest time. They were being watched.

Adri spoke first. 'Come on out, now. We know all too well you're there.' No riposte; everything stayed quiet. 'Come on,' Adri said again, lowering his hand cannon. Silence once more. Then the soft snapping noises began again.

Adri had recognised the creature the first time he had heard the noise. An Ancient. He charted possible outcomes. Adri had no experience in fighting Ancients at all; in fact, he knew of Tantrics

163

who had died at their hands. But he was skilled at negotiating with all manners of creatures, and he tried to think of how to approach the problem. For the first time he noticed how frantic Gray was with the gun he'd given him.

'Give me that,' Adri whispered, snatching the revolver from Gray and holstering it. 'There is an Ancient here. Both my guns are useless.'

'What is an—' Gray began and stuttered to a stop as a shape slowly slithered into the light. A human skeleton waist up. Bones old, dry, and yellowing with scraps of cloth hanging on to some of them. Waist down, the backbone widened out—sharp needle-like ribs jutting out—and continued downwards, curling serpentine to support the creature's entire weight. Its face was exactly like a human skull, except for the prominent canines gleaming in the torchlight. Its fingers ended in sharp claw-like points, dancing gently; whenever it moved, its entire bony structure stirred, making the soft snapping noise that had first alerted them to its presence. Its meandering end moved into the darkness and out of sight.

Adri looked at it. Horror. He realised he was facing all of this just to get the Horseman off his back. Here was a different death, but death nevertheless.

The Ancient observed him and Gray silently, continuously moving in the same place, the edges of its sharp tail shifting, slithering.

'The girl, is she dead?' Adri asked.

Darkness, in eyes hollow. Silence. The Ancient stayed where it was, looking at them, swaying gently.

Gray, scared out of his mind and frozen in his place, wondered dimly if what stood in front of him was going to reply to Adri. Did he really expect this monstrosity to have a voice?

'No,' the creature whispered back and a shiver ran through Gray. The whisper was nothing more than wind channelled hrough a dead bone throat, given a certain shape, through a ertain utterance. A rush of cold, and the words stayed longer han any echo. He looked at it despite himself, still frozen. Its ntire body was just bones, yet it stood, it talked. At the same ime, there was a pounding sense of relief.

'Well, prove it!' Gray whispered.

The Ancient turned its neck to look at Gray. Then, slowly, nother Ancient entered the circle of light, holding Maya's limp ody tight in its hands. She was unconscious, and it held her up rom her shoulders; her legs dangled loosely. A ragged doll. The Ancient's hideous face was inches from hers. Its fangs old, sharp.

'Did you guys take a bite out of her yet?' Adri asked, his hands lowly going behind his back. Gray noticed, but the Ancients lidn't.

'No,' it replied again in the same hoarse whisper. 'Not yet.'

The corner of Gray's eye strained to see what Adri was doing. He realised that behind his back, Adri was turning the chamber of his revolver. Once. Twice. Thrice.

'Well then, clearly you intend to make a deal, Ancient,' Adri poke again, slowly bringing his hands to his sides again, the novement almost imperceptible.

'You are a Tantric,' the Ancient moaned. 'You can enter places lenied to us, places cursed. There is one such place you must enter.'

'What do you want from there?'

'A crypt guards the body of one of our enemies, Mazumder ais name is. He is long dead, this vampire hunter, but we must ip his body to shreds, to little pieces!' Here the Ancient's voice ose, high in its tiredness, its age. 'His skin needs to adorn our valls, his eyeballs need to roll around for our amusement! Get us he body, and we will give you back this human.' It finished and lrew backwards, gently moving its long fingers.

'How far is this crypt?'

'Park Street,' the Ancient rasped. 'Surely you know the way? It is a day's walk to the graveyard, Tantric, so I shall expect you back by tomorrow night. If you are not back by then. . .' It looked at Maya, and the Ancient holding her opened its mouth, revealing its canines, inches from her bare neck.

'Don't you dare!' Gray roared. Both the Ancients turned to look at him, and in that instant, Adri lifted his weapon and fired once, the gunshot echoing loudly in the room. Gray eagerly looked past the smoking barrel of the gun and saw both the Ancients standing perfect and unharmed. Horrified, he looked at Maya and saw a gaping bullet hole in her stomach. 'You shot-you shot-' he started, turning to look at Adri with horrified amazement.

The Ancient seemed disturbed as well. It looked at Maya, and then at Adri with distrust. 'What did you shoot her with, human?' it asked.

'A corruption,' Adri replied calmly, as Gray saw the bullet hole close itself up. 'Her blood will be so toxic under the minute that your biting her will prove most—*unhealthy*.'

Both the Ancients hissed angrily. The one holding her drew its finger along her cheek, and a thin red line appeared. 'She still bleeds,' it breathed. 'Maybe we won't feed on her, human. But if you're late, you will find us playing skittles with her pretty little head.'

'We'll need the gun she was carrying. Park Street isn't close,' Adri said.

The Ancient holding Maya retreated back into the darkness. It came back soon, holding the Sadhu's Shotgun. It threw the gun to Adri who caught it and wordlessly handed it to Gray, who took it in a state of shock.

'The deal is on then, Tantric,' the first Ancient spoke. 'Tomorrow night.' Both the Ancients backed away into the darkness and were gone. The soft snapping noises faded away.

166

'We can't leave without her, Adri,' Gray whispered, holding the shotgun tight.

Adri looked at the shotgun quietly and shook his head. 'We have to return with the body. That's our only chance.' He turned around and holstering his weapon, started walking back. The fireball took the lead immediately.

Gray stood where he was, the darkness closing in fast around him. Then he turned around, strode up to Adri and pushed him with a cry of anger. The push was hard, and Adri fell on his face. The fireball froze in place.

'Damn you, Adri!' Gray screamed. 'Damn you to hell! Why did you have to do this?'

Adri coughed, sending dirt flying. Slowly, he put his hands to the rocky floor and sat up, examining his cuts. 'Maya knew the risks when she agreed to come to Old Kolkata,' he said softly.

'Why did you have to come to JU?' Gray shouted. 'What bloody book was that? What are you after, Adri Sen?'

'Look,' Adri replied, his guilt keeping his anger in check. 'Right now, all I'm doing is trying to save Maya. I've got to get that body here before they kill her. Does that make sense to you? Or do you still want to play the blame game until it's too late?'

'I know you're hiding your agenda,' Gray said after a few seconds. His voice was calmer now, threatening to break. 'I know this is all about what *you* want. But now you listen and listen good to what *I* want. I want my sister safe and I want to get out of this godforsaken city. Do we understand each other?'

Adri nodded silently, getting back on his feet. His clothes were dusty, there was dirt on his face, sticking to the stubble; and with that came the realisation that he hadn't shaved for a while now. His shoulder stung. The fall had hurt his wound. He cursed silently and started hobbling back.

Gray followed him, conflicted. He felt stabs of guilt for pushing Adri down—without the Tantric he would be lost—but

167

it was also true that without the Tantric they wouldn't be in this mess in the first place. Adri was selfish and secretive, and he had reasons of his own that had led them to this place of horror, not that he wanted to know what Adri's reasons were. He just wanted Maya safe and he wanted to get back on the train. And he would make sure Adri got them back, no matter what.

'How come they made a deal with you?' Gray asked a few moments later. They were climbing up the basement steps once more.

'They needed a Necromancer. They saw I'm one and took their chance. They didn't harm Maya, she was bait; if none of us were Necromancers we'd have been dinner.'

'What are they? These confounded Ancients?'

'What do you think? Vampires of bone, held together by curses and spells. My weapons were useless, I hadn't created any bullets to handle them. And there were well over ten to fifteen of them in the shadows.'

'You saw them in the darkness?'

'I heard them all around us. They can't hide that noise they make when they move. Too many of them down there. One wrong move and they would've been on us; my gunshot almost made them pounce.'

'Speaking of which, what the heck did you shoot Maya with? What is a *corruption*? And where are you going?'

Adri was on his way up the stairs past the ground floor. 'I've got to get my bag,' he said. 'It's still in the professor's office.' Gray nodded and followed.

'About the corruption, it's the only thing not letting the Ancients drink Maya's blood. Thus, it's keeping her alive, as well as killing her slowly, as it's a corruption. It will not kill her as fast as the Ancients would have. We'll deal with it once we get her back.'

'I guess I owe you a thanks,' Gray said slowly. 'And an apology. I mean, Maya did go off on her own, right?'

168

They reached the floor and Adri, revolver in hand, headed towards Professor Sural's office. 'She did have an agenda of her own, yes. I don't think she was prone to random curiosities,' Adri said. They reached the office, and it was still empty. Adri picked up the black book he had cast away earlier, opened the correct page, and memorised the four names. It took him two readings to do it. Casting the book away, reminded again of its uselessness, Adri picked up his bag and wore it. Gray stood at the door, wondering about how best to apologise.

'Save it,' Adri said, crossing him and entering the corridor. 'Long night ahead, and the journey isn't really easy.'

Gray was slightly angered again, but he swallowed it and followed Adri, the Sadhu's Shotgun in his hands.

11

Gray looked at Adri. The young Tantric seemed preoccupied with his own thoughts, and looking at him, Gray understood for the first time that thing Maya had mentioned. That something about Adri, something which she couldn't understand, that he felt *different* somehow. Gray felt it too right now, only Maya wasn't around for him to tell. He felt alone, he felt cold. He didn't really know the Tantric and had been brash with him sometime back; Adri had sort of withdrawn since then, and even though Gray knew it was valid, his reaction as well as Adri's withdrawal, he still felt alienated and lonely. The surroundings were partly responsible.

They were resting in what had once been a children's playground. Broken swings, abandoned see-saws, a picture of desolation. There would be no children found here; Gray hadn't seen a single child in the Old City as of yet, and this place served as a stark reminder to the same. Old Kolkata had many ghosts, and among them was rumoured to be a mother searching for her children, long gone. She was said to wear white, and held a lamp as she walked through broken buildings and dark places, softly calling out their names. Gray had been told of this as a child, and it made him sad even then; when they had entered this place of the children who once were, Gray found that mellow sorrow once more.

Adri had cleared some space and made a fire in the centre using the same spirit, and was now heating some canned food on it. Everything around them was pitch black, and the tall dark buildings surrounding the playground gave it an even more ominous feel. Gray's stomach gave a low growl as he looked at the food, they hadn't eaten since leaving the Gunsmith's house earlier in the day. Turning his face away, he looked around some more to get his mind off the food. The desolation depressed him. Adri had already told him this wasn't a residential area any more. In fact, from now on, he had said, and all the way to the Lake of Fire, they were only going to find lesser and lesser residential areas. And closer to the dangerous areas, the people lived together in huddled and guarded colonies called Settlements. They would soon be encountering these, Adri had warned. Gray had heard about the Settlements of Old Kolkata, and he had also heard that most of them were quick and brutal with outsiders—they trusted no one.

Gray looked up at the night sky, and thought he saw something move on one of the neighbouring roofs. He peered into the darkness. Nothing. He mentioned it to Adri, who in turn looked long and hard, but saw nothing. Nevertheless, Adri kept one of his revolvers ready, and Gray cradled the Sadhu's Shotgun in his lap, his fingers running along the weapon's surface repeatedly. The fire burned as their food got heated. They ate soon. It was vegetarian food, canned, but to a hungry Gray it was heavenly.

A dog. Strutting into the playground. Attracted by the smell of food. It stood at a distance, watching them, eyes glittering in the firelight.

'Is that just a dog?' Gray asked.

Adri had already seen it. 'Yes.'

Gray whistled to it and the dog promptly trotted over, wolfing down the scraps Gray offered. It was the first living thing they had come across in a long time that belonged to a normal place,

to a Kolkata that once was. The sight of Gray feeding the dog
fascinated Adri; it reminded him of things he had long forgotten,
of things he cherished. Gray was an animal lover, and he wasn't
to know what he had sparked off, but Adri revelled in nostalgia
for a blissfully long time before he realised they needed to get
moving. Embarrassingly enough, it was Gray who roused him
from his near stupor; he got up and packed everything back into
his backpack hastily. The bag was heavy, Adri realised as he wore
it once more. It would have been easier to not be a Tantric. He
would have been able to enter Settlements and buy necessary
supplies. Yes, not being a Tantric would really have made his life
so much easier. Adri shook his head and lit a cigarette as they
moved out of the playground. The dog followed them.

'The dog's coming with us. Not a problem, is it?' Gray asked.

'Hardly. If it has survived for this long, it's probably used to
smelling danger a long way off. I would call it useful.'

They walked on. Gray wanted to move faster, worried that
they weren't covering enough ground. It took Adri most of his
patience trying to convince him of the need to move slowly. 'It's
night. There are things out here,' Adri said, impatience creeping
into his voice. 'We have to move slowly, that way we can stay
alive, and get to Park Street and back.'

The fireball was no longer with them. Adri had it put itself
out for fear of detection. They walked for a long time, and the
dog followed them to a certain point, beyond which it just stood
watching them go, wagging its tail. They walked on through a
labyrinth of crashed cars and bent street lamps—a part of the road
where everything seemed chaotic and devastated even in the quiet
of the sparse moonlight.

'What happened here?' Gray asked in a whisper.

'A massacre,' Adri replied.

They were weaving their way through a tangle of parked
cars, when all of a sudden something blocked out the moon. For

a second there was darkness, then the shadow passed, gigantic and black as it flew over their heads. Gray's eyes shot up as he saw the edge of something disappear over the edge of the tallest building. He did not ask any questions then; whatever that creature of the night was, it was completely soundless, and that scared him. He stole after Adri as fast as he could, casting nervous glances behind.

It was surreal, and for a time Gray tried to forget it all—all the pain, all the anxiety, all the weight of responsibility tugging at him. He followed Adri mechanically, and they were nearing the end of the road when he heard voices that brought him back to the present. Adri slowly came to a stop and sat down on the road against a crashed car, signalling him to do the same. The voices were very coarse, harsh and deep, accompanied by grunts and heavy breathing. Not too far away. Whoever it was, they were only a little ahead of them. Adri silently raised a finger to his lips, and it was probably all in his imagination, but Gray thought Adri's face seemed to be a little drained of colour. In any case, he looked extremely nervous; more than Gray had ever seen him be. Not a good sign.

Adri was opening both his revolvers as quietly as he could, changing ammunition. The voices were conversing in the Old Tongue. Gray didn't fully understand it, all but snatches—*blood, blade, chop.* It did not sound optimistic to him; he clutched the shotgun tightly to his chest. Then he saw them, reflected in the side mirror of the car in front of him. Two of them, walking slowly.

Humanoid. Mostly. About ten to eleven feet in height. In the moonlight one could see they were wearing armour and clothing, all black, gleaming. They were heavy, hulking, hard-bodied; they moved slowly, with weight in every footstep. Though he couldn't see much in the small mirror, Gray saw the one thing that confirmed what they were: the horns. Both of them had a pair each—long, curving, rising high above their heads, and then cutting a wicked arc right back down, coal black in the white light of a pale moon. A chill went up Gray's spine. *Demons.*

He saw Adri's lips move in what he thought was a prayer—Adri was actually performing a small and immediate incantation, but Gray didn't know that—and to see a Tantric pray scared him even more; all Necromancers were atheists.

Adri ignored Gray's shudders and reaching into his bag, did some frantic groping before withdrawing a couple of vials. He felt the weight of the pentacle against his neck. *I have a lot more to do. I cannot let this be the end.*

The Demons walked slowly, their steps heavy, their weapons sheathed. No MYTH troops had been seen in this area of late, but there had been sightings of an unknown creature that they needed to keep a watch over, according to the Commander's orders. But it was their third night of patrol and they hadn't noticed anything so far. Seemed like another peaceful night.

'Then he crushed him with one foot. One! That's all it took,' one of them spoke loudly. 'He split open like a ripe pumpkin, the dog. Demon-killer, *ha*!'

The other one was smoking an enormous cigar. It nodded viciously, breathing out smoke.

'Hraathar always had a temper problem with the Tantrics. Never really worked for them. Everyone thought him useless until he killed that Demon-killer. He was a dangerous one, he was. He made me think before I went to war, and that's something, that is.'

'They were nothing but trouble, they were,' the first one agreed. 'Give me some of that cigar.'

The second one handed it over and the first one took a long drag. 'Bloody human Plane. I got such a cold, I can barely taste this thing.'

'Plane got its advantages, Garth,' the second Demon said. 'I support the decision to stay here. Compare this to where we come from, eh?' It began to laugh, and so did the Demon named Garth, until the second one stopped all of a sudden. It sniffed the air. Twice, thrice. Then it turned its head in the direction of the open street they had just crossed.

'What is it?' Garth asked, puffing on the cigar.

'Humans,' the Demon replied, baring its fangs in a grin. Hideous. It sniffed again. 'No wait—there's more. There's something else.' It sniffed again. 'Two humans and a half-breed, I think. Can't say what, I'm not so sure.'

'I'm hungry,' Garth said. 'But I can't smell shit.' The other one laughed in response.

Adri peered over the hood of the car and then sat back down, looking at Gray very seriously. 'Okay, look. I'm going to make this very clear,' he whispered. 'We cannot possibly take on both the Demons right now, not in this light. However, they will smell us any second now and we can't help that.'

'So what do we do?' Gray asked.

'I will try and take them down one at a time. You have to keep one busy so that they don't attack me together.'

'*What?* I have to *what?*'

Adri lit a cigarette. 'Distract! Talk to it, shoot at it a couple of times. Basically run from it, but keep taunting it. They're warrior Demons, they're slow. Keep your distance and you should be fine. Oh, and if they throw something just dodge it. Jump out of the way, they can be pretty nasty at times.'

'Can't we run away?'

'No chance, they're almost always hungry and they'll track us down. In other words, it was too late the moment we saw them—they were too close to not have smelt us already. And I don't think we have the luxury of time anymore—they're coming!'

Adri shoved his bag aside and stood up straight, a revolver in each hand and a lit cigarette in his mouth.

'Ah, maggot!' one of the Demons roared. Its voice was hoarse and cracked, yet it radiated with power, with might beyond human or animal. Both the Demons changed course and made a beeline towards Adri.

Adri chose the one on the right, the one without the cigar. He lifted his guns and fired two rounds together. Holy water infused with the essence of tulsi and the ashes of holy men stirred in it for greater effect—one extremely strong holy bullet. Both the bullets hit the Demon's head and stopped it in its tracks. It roared in agony, clutching its head. The other Demon paused as well to see what his partner had been hit with. He found out the next instant as Adri plugged him with two rounds as well.

As both the Demons bellowed and howled, Gray got a good, clear look at them, and he watched them in awe. They were gigantic, one of them over eleven feet tall. Their skin was a dark, muddy brown and it reminded him of elephant skin with all its wrinkles and cracks, but it seemed hardier, like rock. Their faces were a bit warped; they had started out with human features, but somewhere in the middle someone had decided to play around and expand the eyebrows, make the nose almost disappear but for a slit-like breathing hole, and shrink the eyes deep into the face where they glittered like marbles. They had hair though, facial hair as well; the one called Garth was bald with a huge beard, and the other one had long dark hair, which it had tied in a ponytail. Their ears were sharp and pointed, and they had tails—Garth's was short and unimpressive, whereas the other one's was thick and large like a crocodile's. Their torsos were much bigger than their lower abdomens, though their feet were strong and muscular and supported them well, but it didn't look like they could run.

Their horns, however, remained the most majestic thing about them, bloodthirsty as they were.

'Vile weapons!' Garth roared in anger and pain. 'He's a Necromancer! I will drink your blood, Tantric!'

They removed their hands from their heads and Gray saw that Adri's bullets had acted like acid, burning their very skin and hair. Both the Demons started walking again towards Adri. When they were a mere hundred metres away from him, Adri fired again, and though Garth got hit again, the other Demon deflected the bullet with an armour plate on the side of its hand.

'He's mine, he's mine!' Garth rumbled, recovering from the bullet.

'I don't think so, Garth,' the other Demon replied, striding towards Adri. 'I will crush this fool.'

Adri waited for the Demon to close in before he began to back away. The Demon ignored the fact that Gray was standing a few feet away, open-mouthed; its anger was directed at Adri and Adri alone, at this little Tantric who needed to be shown what the Free Demons were capable of. It moved vehicles aside with a casual swipe of its claws as it approached—cars went flying, a bus was shoved aside with the ease of a paper model—nothing was going to stand between him and this Tantric. Adri was running away, frequently glancing back as the Demon cleared a path, rapidly gaining on him.

Garth had recovered, and started walking after the other Demon as fast as it could. It was near Gray when Gray remembered his duties.

'Oi!' he shouted, clambering on top of a sedan. The Demon stopped, a few feet away and then turned to stare at Gray. It hadn't smelt him because of its cold.

'I will eat you after I eat your Tantric friend,' it growled.

'Eat this,' Gray said, and lifting his shotgun, squeezed both triggers together. Tulsi coupled with hundreds of small, blessed iron beads and bent iron shards, packed together with gunpowder. A powerful holy package, containing an incredible punch; it threw the Demon off balance as some of it pierced through its armour and bit into the skin. Garth had known enough pain, and now it knew even more. It did the only obvious thing. It roared in anger as it tried to regain balance. Gray hurriedly emptied out the shells; his hands trembled as he slid new ones into the now warm firing chamber.

Adri saw Gray's fight at a distance. Provided he could keep the other Demon distracted, he would probably live for about another two minutes; these were Warrior Demons, insanely strong and tough, but not that fast. Or bright. And that was what Adri was counting on more than anything else. He had taken a stand, turning around to face the Demon approaching him. The creature snarled, tossing another car aside carelessly in a show of power as it strode towards Adri. Now that Adri had stopped running, and had actually turned around to face it, its gait had slowed down. It bore down on Adri in a slow, heavy manner, its lower jaw slowly twisting itself in a bare-fanged grin.

'Masir, Bhuto,' Adri said in the Old Tongue. 'Now would be a good time.'

'Then on this charge we get our freedom,' two voices replied in perfect unison.

'No! I have need of your services.'

There was silence. The Demon approached steadily.

'I command you!' Adri shouted.

No replies again.

'All right, goddammit,' Adri snapped. 'Have your freedom after this charge, you bloody opportunists.'

A car rose in the air, supported by an invisible force. It hovered for a second. The Demon looked at Adri. He was only a few meters away. 'I hate your kind,' it said. The car flew into the Demon with a sudden, incredible speed, sending it flying into a nearby wall which erupted with dust, smoke, and debris. Adri raised an arm to shield his face, and then ran towards the wall, coughing from the dust.

Gray fired again, and the shots glanced off the Demon's armour, though he saw it wince. While Gray hurriedly ejected the empty shells again, the Demon stood its ground, smoking the cigar. A fireball erupted into existence in its open claw, and Gray stared at it in mid-reload. Then he dropped the gun and ran. The Demon gave him perhaps a half second heads-up before it flung the fireball as one might fling a baseball; it narrowly missed Gray and shattered into an abandoned shop's window display, setting mannequins on fire instantly.

Gray stopped and stared in terror at his near escape. The Demon stood where it was. Another fireball exploded into actuality in its hand while it stared at Gray with hatred, breathing out cigar smoke.

'Don't you want to *eat* me?' Gray shouted at it in desperation.

'I don't mind fried,' the Demon growled. It threw the second fireball.

Gray flung himself away from the projectile, at the cost of a painful recovery on the footpath. He watched the fire burn away on a solid wall this time. Suddenly, he realised that the Demon had not been speaking in the Old Tongue. It knew his language. He forced himself to get up. The Demon hadn't lit another fireball so far—it was watching him. With mild interest.

'How come you're talking in my tongue?' Gray shouted, supporting himself to his feet with an enormous effort. *Keep it talking.* His brain wasn't working straight anymore, but if there was one thing he realised, it was that he didn't know shit about Demons. That, and that if even one fireball found its mark, he was history. If only Maya was here, more than anything, she would know its weaknesses. Adri, curse him, had severely under-informed him. He risked a glance at the Necromancer and saw a huge cloud of dust in the distance. Whatever it was, he hoped Adri had survived it. Without Adri he was gone.

He looked back and realised the Demon was almost upon him. It had crept up to him in *less than five seconds*. That wasn't slow! He stumbled back and fell hard, bumping his head against the footpath. His head spun. Colours. Spinning fast. Dissolving into an image. The grinning face of a Demon. And then he was in the air—he felt heavy and weightless. He kicked, but all he felt was air. He was dangling. He realised that the Demon was lifting him up with a vice-like grip on the back of his neck and all it was using were its thumb and forefinger. His vision cleared a little; he saw he was several feet off the ground, facing the monster.

'Yes, human, I speak your language. I have been trained,' Garth said.

'Let me go, let me go,' Gray muttered.

'So that you can pick up your toy and shoot me again? I think not. You think me dumb just because I like violence, just because you are food to me? I am educated in seven languages, human filth.'

'Do you have family?' Gray shouted, struggling fiercely. 'I've got a sister I need to save from the Ancients in Jadavpur. She's counting on us!'

'I do have family,' the Demon replied. 'Family young and old—but if that was a stab at me letting you go, then you have to try better.' It laughed brutally, spraying Gray with spit.

'What do you want?' Gray asked, and stopped struggling. It wasn't helping anyway.

'Ah, good question. I will first snap your neck gently. You will stop feeling a lot of things right then; I will proceed to go and kill that little Tantric, then come back to you, and eat you slowly. I will chew your bones, not the head though—I don't eat heads, that's brutish—but all this will obviously happen after de-clothing you. I won't munch on your clothes either. Then I will eat the Tantric, I don't like their taste much, but you're my main course anyway.'

'Why do you want to kill me?'

'I don't want to kill you, I want to *eat* you. Two different things. If you can tell me a way I can have all your flesh and bones and you can still be alive, then I'd love to—HOLD IT!'

The Demon spun around in its place, Gray loosely dangling from its outstretched hand. Adri skidded to a stop a small distance away; he had been running at Garth. The Demon looked at Adri and gave off an angry puff of smoke.

'One step and I snap this moron's neck,' it threatened. 'Drop them weapons.'

'God, this is like some gangster film,' Gray complained loudly, embarrassed.

'Shut up, human,' Garth drawled.

Adri was thinking. He really didn't have much of a choice here. If only the Demon hadn't seen him, if only he hadn't been cornered into dismissing all three of his spirits already, if only. He slowly lowered his weapons to the ground—they were too beautifully crafted for him to drop—and stood back up, glaring at the Demon. He still had two vials of holy water, but that was nowhere enough to do more than just sting the Demon. Gray's shotgun lay a few meters away on the road, but as long as the Demon had Gray's neck between his fingers, nothing could be done. And with all probability, the Demon would kill Gray any second now.

SLISH.

The noise came out of the blue. Adri had expected a SNAP or a CRICK. He looked at the Demon and saw something buried in its right wrist, something bright red. It gave one of its loudest howls of pain yet. Both Gray and the cigar dropped as the Demon examined its wrist, still bellowing in a voice of pure power. Gray lay in his place, stunned, until he felt Adri's firm hands pulling him away from the creature.

'Pick yourself up,' Adri panted. 'It's far from dead.' He ran back to get his guns from the road.

The Demon could not smell the newcomer, but knew it was the third person his partner had smelt before. Instinctively it looked up and saw him, standing high up on one of the balconies of the buildings surrounding them. His body was completely in shadow; his eyes glinted.

'GRAAAA!' the Demon roared and threw two fireballs at him. Its arms were well practiced at lobbing these weapons of death—both the fireballs set the balcony on hellfire, but the figure was no longer there. He had jumped, and was making his way down to the street, springing off windowsills and drainage pipes like an acrobat. The Demon threw fireballs again. And again. The figure dodged and in a leap, landed on the road. Holy bullets dug into the Demon's back—it cringed in momentary pain before turning around to launch fireballs at Adri, who ran fast to dodge them.

The Demon picked up a car without any apparent strain and flung it after a fleeing Adri. Adri dived to the road, bruising himself, just as the car flew over him, crashing into another. Gray's hands trembled as he hid behind a pillar with his shotgun, trying to reload it. He tried and tried, but his hands would not stop trembling; the roars of the Demon did not help. The mysterious figure was gone—the Demon could not see him as it looked around, the bullets eating into the flesh on its nape. It was angry.

Adri's hands were bloody, he had grazed them badly. They trembled as he reached for his bandolier and reloaded his revolvers, still lying down where he had dodged the car. Gray peeked out from behind the pillar and unloaded both shells into the Demon; it was more infuriated at Gray revealing himself than the wounds he inflicted—it rushed at him. Gray fled and the Demon punched through the pillar. Cement shattered as its clenched claw missed Gray by inches. It saw him run towards Adri and fireballs came to life in both its claws. Before it could throw them though, the Demon felt fresh pain in the back of its knee joints. Loud, immediate pain. It looked down and saw sharp, bright red objects sticking out of its kneecaps.

Adri got up and approached the Demon, as Gray ran past him. He lifted both hand cannons and let loose a volley of bullets, aiming at its head and chest. The Demon took the punishment—blocks of its cracked skin exploded as the bullets hit, but it still stood. It sent a couple of fireballs at Adri in return, and Adri ducked behind an SUV for cover.

The Demon spun around just in time to catch the third figure sneaking up on it with something red and glowing in his hand. Garth whacked him with a fist and he went flying into a car, denting it, and falling to the road. Then he was up again—something the Demon didn't believe possible—and began throwing sharp glowing things at it that sank into its flesh. They hurt incredibly. It wanted this newcomer gone; it could easily take care of the other two. It broke off a nearby lamp post and threw it. The figure danced out of the way and silently threw more of his weapons at the Demon. Garth retaliated with fireballs, but dodging them seemed almost too easy for this stranger.

Shotgun shells bit into its back again and the Demon regretted not snapping Gray's neck when it had the chance. It sighed. Too late for that now. It half spun, igniting yet more fireballs in its claws when Adri's bullets joined the fray once more. Adri threw his vials of holy water next. The bottles smashed when they hit the Demon and the water ran down its body like acid. The pain was slowly beginning to numb itself out. The Demon's fireballs went out, its legs gave way. It fell on its knees with a downcast head, praying for one of the humans to come within its arm's reach, perhaps in sympathy or whatever. No such luck. More shrapnel penetrated its neck; the burning slowly faded out. The Demon shut its eyes and did not open them again, its giant body still in a kneel.

Gray collapsed to the ground, his shotgun clattering beside him, his breathing slow and heavy. Adri put a hand on his shoulder; Gray nodded slowly, not making any move to remove it. The dozen or so missed fireballs were burning elsewhere, forming a rough ring of light around them. Light and shadow played on the face of the dead Demon, and on the figure now closely observing it.

He was tall, the stranger, tall and very well built; one could tell that by the way his muscles coiled even when he was still. It indicated he could move any split second and do exactly what he wanted to do. His arms were bare and muscular with small rings inscribed along the sides. He wore black robes, the upper part tight and fitting his frame perfectly, the lower trousers loose, whipping around in the wind. His face was possibly the most interesting thing about him. He wore a mask that covered everything tightly, but his hair—long and black—playing around in the wind like his robes. The mask was simple—it had absolutely no detail except two round glass eyepieces, like a gas mask. His feet were bare, except for black bandages wrapping up the arch, leaving the toes and the heel visible.

He turned to look at Adri, who looked back at the glass eyepieces reflecting everything but the man inside. Adri holstered his weapon in what he hoped was a sign of good faith.

'Thanks for the assist,' Adri said.

The man in the mask shook his head. '*Rashkor.* I merely came in when I saw you in a catch 22. I am not concerned with either of you.' He had a gravelly voice which was further muffled because of his mask.

'Right,' Adri said. 'We'll just carry on, then.'

The man nodded.

Gray slowly got to his feet. 'What was that?' he muttered softly.

'I don't like their kind myself, Gray,' Adri said, helping him stand.

Gray looked at Adri. 'How did you take care of the other one so fast?'

Adri had almost forgotten. He let Gray go, withdrew a revolver, and jogged towards where the other Demon lay. He approached the pile of rubble gingerly, weapon raised. He inspected the debris closely, then looked around, holstering the weapon again. The masked man stood a few feet away.

'It's gone?' he asked.

'Yes,' Adri said. 'I had drawn a negative circle around its body, though,' he murmured in a lower voice, mostly to himself. The man heard.

'Curious. It must have scraped off a part of the circle with a brick or stone,' he said.

Adri looked at Gray, still standing where he had been left; presently looking at the Demon's dead body with great repulsion. Adri turned to the masked man.

'Who are you?' he asked.

The masked man did not hesitate. The reply was natural and came with a practiced ease. 'I am called Fayne of Ahzad,' he said.

'Fayne,' Adri said, his eyebrows narrowing. 'You are a long way from home, assassin.'

'It is not coincidence which brings me here,' Fayne said calmly. 'I am on a charge: to protect the one called Maya Ghosh from any kind of harm until the charge is lifted from me.'

'*Maya?*' Adri could not hide his surprise. 'Who put you on this charge?'

'It is forbidden to reveal the owner of the contract,' Fayne said.

Adri had already anticipated this reply. 'Well, you're a bit late. She's a captive, and dying as we speak,' Adri said.

'I have been following both of you since Jadavpur,' Fayne replied. 'I know there is a chance of saving her. I am not concerned with either of you, but I will help you get the body back to the Ancients.'

The assassin had eavesdropped on them surely, or else had slight telepathic abilities—Adri wasn't sure which. He knew that he couldn't have taken the Demon down without Fayne's help, and he knew that if Fayne *did* hail from Ahzad as he claimed, then he would be a powerful companion and certainly a useful one to have. The infamous Assassins of Ahzad needed no elucidation; their names were whispered with fear across lands. They were masterfully trained, extremely capable, and were incredibly expensive to hire; Adri had absolutely no clue as to who would pay that much for Maya's protection and why. Who even knew she was here in the Old City? Adri brushed his questions aside for the moment. They did not matter. What mattered was not getting in the assassin's way deliberately, or by error—the assassins of Ahzad were patient enough when needed, but otherwise they were cold and brutal. If shedding of blood was needed to save Maya, it would be shed. If he and Gray were to slow Fayne down—

'So will you travel with us?' Adri asked.

'Normally I wouldn't. The two of you were quite erratic in the fight with the Demon, proving yourselves amateurs of true combat. But since you are the only one equipped to enter the crypt and get the body of the vampire hunter out, I will.' Fayne turned around. 'The fires will attract undue attention, not to mention the Demon which got away. We should leave. *Ghawaziya.*'

True. Adri walked towards where his backpack lay, occasionally glancing behind his shoulder at the unmoving assassin, now gazing into the distance.

12

Adri wasn't all that sure if Gray was hiding something. Gray had said that he had no clue when asked who would pay money to protect Maya, but there was something too quick about his answer that put Adri on his guard. Something was not being revealed, some details were not being talked about. Fair enough, seeing that he himself had hidden as much as he could from the siblings; but there was something he wanted an answer to.

'What was Maya looking for in the basement? What was she after?' he asked Gray.

'I've been thinking about that myself, and I really don't have the faintest idea,' Gray replied.

'What do they keep down there? Records of what?'

'Well since it was Demonology, I would presume Demons. Encounters, sightings, heritage.'

'Hmm.'

'Adri?'

'Yeah?'

'You think you can save Maya? From the Ancients?'

They had been walking for quite a long time, and it was almost dawn. They had not met with any encounters since the Demons, and it had been mostly walking and talking. Fayne did not talk much unless spoken to; he scouted ahead or brought up the rear, making sure no one was following them and there were no ambushes in store. They had moved from the main road to side streets. It had gotten increasingly quiet as well, and apart from the odd loud call of some nocturnal bird, their footsteps resounded loudly as they walked down the streets. Fayne's bare feet, however, refused to make any noise.

'Yes, I think I can, Gray. It's partly my fault she's in that mess and I intend to see her out of it. While in Old Kolkata, she's my responsibility,' Adri said without looking at Gray.

'And mine,' Fayne spoke quietly. He was a long way off ahead of them, and he spoke without turning back.

'Yes, your sister's got a new boyfriend it seems,' Adri muttered.

It was madness, breaking into a protected crypt. If there was a curse on it, it was only going to be all the tougher for Adri. Being a Tantric did not grant him any natural immunity against the curse. It merely meant that he was supposed to have been educated in the ways around the curse, or in creating an anti-curse to neutralise its effects. Adri had been in expeditions which had broken into tombs, and he knew there was safety in numbers. He had never attempted something like this before, nor was he eager to. He had never heard of this particular vampire-hunter in his studies or travels, and thus he hoped the curse wouldn't be something too deadly. Certainly deadly enough to scare the Ancients though; that alone worried him.

Maya's fate hung heavy in his mind too, and try as his conscience might to convince him that it was Maya's fault she had run off, his guilt still stabbed at him a little too often for comfort. He had brought her here and she had trusted him to keep her safe, although he now suspected she had come along for this very errand; that would explain the change in her behaviour after he'd first laid down his proposal, and her interest in seeing the Old City; but Adri had been her protector, and he had failed. Holding back a sigh, he patted his pockets for a cigarette.

Park Street, once the greatest social hub of Old Kolkata, was still somewhat of a hub, but with all the wrong kind of people.

As the rumours went, it was mostly the looters who had control over Park Street; people who, before the fall of the Old City, had amassed a collection of whatever they could get their hands on from all kinds of shops, warehouses, and even homes—a great variety of things they now sold to survivors for large amounts of money or food. The looters were not gangsters as much as they were opportunists; some of them were just simple people with a fear of the supernatural, trying to make a living amidst desolation. There were, of course, others who were always striving for leadership and superiority, for recognition. Adri had been here before, he used to buy a lot of his ingredients for his rites from here. Once a shooter had also caught his fancy, but it had jammed in less than a week and the Gunsmith had stubbornly refused to repair it.

As they entered the main street, Adri realised that the population had dwindled even more than before. Not surprising, considering the territory wars had moved even closer, but still a visual shock, seeing the place so empty. And empty it was, like the landscape they had traversed so far.

Skyscrapers surrounded them, uncared for. Bits of buildings were breaking off; traffic lights burned with fire. Giant beacons. Enormous shadows. They occasionally saw movement. People went by; some hawkers closed up their roadside stalls. A group of people smoking cigarettes with confidence stared at them from a corner. They had guns on their laps, Gray noticed, but Adri did not seem to be worried about them. Gray found himself wondering yet again what the deal was with Old Kolkata. He had been taking pictures of the Old City and thinking about it as they walked. He had even remembered to take quick pictures of the dead Demon before they had left, though Adri warned him that possession of those pictures would be illegal once he was back in New Kolkata. Gray wasn't really thinking about later. He was trying to breathe in the moment, this moment in which he had no clue as to what lay in store for his sister or for him; what kind of trouble they would face in the future, and whether they would even live to get back to the new city. Little mysteries knocked against his head, little questions that formed themselves in queues without him even realising it. Questions about Adri. Questions about Fayne. Questions about the old, unforgiving city.

The Park Street Cemetery was behind high walls and they could see nothing of it, except for all the foliage that rose above. Now that they were standing at the black gates—locked with chains and padlocked—they could see through the iron bars a narrow cement path that led into the graveyard. There was no one around, either to open the gate or question them. Adri looked up and saw that dawn was approaching. A few birds flew, and the sky was slowly turning into its usual red.

'Is this it?' Gray asked. He looked up and saw the curving metal above the gate. *Park Street Cemetery.* 'Oh right, this is it. What are we waiting for, then?'

'Sunlight,' Adri said.

'Sunlight?'

It was Fayne who replied. 'In the Old City, you do not enter a graveyard until the sun is up, not unless you are asking for trouble. Of course, someone like me could manage that, but this is more than a tourist warning.'

Adri nodded slowly. That Fayne was someone with experience was quite evident to him, and it kept getting reinforced with Fayne's composure and the things he chose to say. Adri never liked working with inexperienced people; they were a liability, a burden of all sorts, and he regretted, yet again, having to bring the siblings to the Old City, though momentarily, but yes. He didn't know what he was going to do next. He was out of all supernatural defences at the moment. He needed to perform his rituals, and they would take time, something he did not have. He dreaded the thought of having to enter the crypt alone, without any spirits backing him up; but then again there was the problem with using spirits—no matter how powerful or useful they would prove themselves to be, they always had to be let go after their charge was complete.

The three of them sat down with their backs against the gate, looking at the empty street in front. Time had to be killed, the sun was not fast enough. Fayne withdrew a hip flask from a pocket and took a swig. He had pulled his mask back to his upper lip as he drank, and Adri caught sight of a fair, clean-shaven jawline. Fayne did not offer to share the contents of the flask, he merely pocketed it again.

Gray turned to Adri, who absolutely did not want to entertain questions. 'The Ancients, tell me about them,' he said.

'Didn't I already—' a weary Adri began.

'I will tell you about the Ancients if you want to know,' Fayne spoke. 'Did you see them, or did they talk from the darkness?'

'Saw them,' Gray replied, shifting in interest.

'They live in darkness as they need no light to see. Vampires as they are, the blood they suck is circulated through the centre of all their bones. That is the essence of the Ancients—they need no organs as their bones have become the organs, the hollow within forming their regenerative system. They move like snakes, except for the human torso at the end, making them fast and vicious in combat. They're exceedingly strong and equally swift.'

'What's their history?' Gray asked, drinking in everything.

'A storyteller would be able to tell you more about legends,' Fayne replied.

Storytellers. The men who roamed the land, the walking compendiums of legend and lore alike, Gray had heard about them, but never met one. It was said they could hold one captive for as long as they pleased, simply through their tales.

191

'How do you kill them?' Gray asked.

'Not an easy task. They attack with their bone claws and their fangs, and if you do cut off a part of their bodies, they tend to regenerate it within hours. To kill an Ancient, one will have to first sever their connection with their bone tails, effectively severing the spine. Once this is done, the creature will writhe and twist, but it will still be just as deadly in this stage and killing it properly and entirely will involve destroying its brain inside its skull, for even the undead body continues to receive commands from the brain. Once there is a bullet or blade through the head, the Ancient will still find time to land one or two killing blows if it finds the prey in its range, and then it shall proceed to be silent forever.'

'That was a tad more information than I bargained for,' Gray said.

'If you happen to be squeamish, I suggest you take that quality of yours and burn it. The Old City is not for those who cringe at the sight of blood.'

'I *know* the Old City is not for me,' Gray snapped. 'Ever since I've come here, I've had creatures stalk me, had my sister kidnapped, and have been thrown around by Demons. I don't like it here, and I refuse to see its charm. Do you see it?'

'It is impossible to understand a place without living there long enough,' Fayne replied. 'For me, the only place in the world where I find peace is Ahzad.'

'Good memories of growing up?'

'Hardly. I was tortured there.'

Gray stared.

'But that exactly is my point, *ta yeregee*,' Fayne said. 'Feeling a connection with a place, understanding the *soul* of a place, it's not about how good it's been to you. It's about how you connect your memories, both good and bad, to the place. It's not just about the virtues, but also about the vices. Today, if I was fortunate enough

192

to reach Ahzad, I would remove my mask for a moment and take in the freezing air, and it would feel like home.'

'I guess New Kolkata is home for me then.'

'That place is an abomination, a home of puppets forged as an experiment. Your generation grew up as a part of it, thus you will never know what Kolkata actually is and what it was meant to be. The Old City still has all the pieces, but one must pick them up and arrange them to see the whole picture.'

Gray stared at Fayne. He didn't know what to say. Fayne spoke without regret or fear. Here was a man who spoke his mind completely, and spoke it like fact. Gray didn't know if that was a good thing, if he preferred things so simply, so directly. Where Adri had been largely reticent, Fayne was giving him a chance to know more about New Kolkata, about why MYTH had created the new city in the first place. Gray opened his mouth, but it was Adri who asked Fayne a question. A different one.

'So how is it that you're *protecting* someone? Isn't your kind hired to do the exact opposite?'

If there was a touch of sarcasm or spite in the question, Fayne completely ignored it. 'The assassins of Ahzad will do whatever the charge dictates; we do not hold boundaries, only the amount of time involved. I have killed countless women and children, babes in arms. There are no ethics. I could befriend you over a decade and kill you in a moment, without a single impulse of hesitation.' He turned to look at Adri. 'Do not toy with me, Tantric. I will slit your throat before you realise you need a spirit for your protection.'

Adri lit a cigarette. 'No offence meant, assassin. It was, by all means, an honest question.'

'Your questions are welcome as long as they do not turn and pierce my back. If you have something to say, say it to my face. That is what I would prefer, *pashlin*,' Fayne said.

'Not all of you assassins are like this. I once knew an assassin from your place, he had a jolly good sense of humour,' Adri said.

'Of course, what I mean by that is that I could not have anticipated your taking offence,' he added hurriedly.

'Who did you know?'

'Kahn of Ahzad.'

'How did you know him?'

'I would like to think he is my friend. We had worked together on a series of . . . err . . . *charges*. You know him?'

Fayne nodded. Then all was silent. Gray lost his nerve to ask Fayne anything after his reaction to Adri's question. He realised Fayne was deadly and remorseless, something Adri had already warned him about. His curiosity could wait, he decided. Who knew what it took to piss the assassin off?

Sunlight crawled down their clothes. A dagger emerged in the assassin's hand and Gray glimpsed its red blade briefly as it sliced through the chains; the gates swung open and the dagger was gone. Fayne led the way and they followed.

The graveyard was vast and they immediately felt a sense of being enveloped as they entered. It was the last place to be maintained here in the Old City, and like Jadavpur, vegetation had taken over the graveyard as well. The pathways were covered with moss, trees spiralled and grew out of normal proportions, and vines crept all over the tombs, covering their existence. They walked softly and as silently as they could, for it was dead silent, and even Gray knew that one didn't talk too loudly in a graveyard—it was wise to not interfere with the sleep of the dead. A fog that had been there all night was lifting as the sun came up; it swirled and moved out of the way, near their feet, as they approached. They passed grave after grave and Gray finally whispered, 'Which one is it?'

'The church,' Adri replied.

They moved onward, weaving their way in and out through the cracked, silent stones and the grass that had grown up to their knees. The church's spire was visible between the branches of a tree ahead of them. When it came into view, they saw it was old, like the graves. The stone was cracking and moss lined the walls. A part of the roof had caved in, the windows dark, desolate, glassless. It was a black, black picture, and did not look like a church at all. Gray looked at it and realised that he was scared of going into the building.

'How come it's in the church?' Gray asked.

'The Ancients mentioned that the body's in a crypt. More chances of finding it in the catacombs than elsewhere. Plus, if he was a vampire hunter then the odds are he'd want himself buried in there,' Adri replied, silently selecting an assortment of bullets from his bandolier.

Fayne was looking pointedly at Adri's holsters.

'I'm hoping the underground will muffle the shots,' Adri replied, defensive. 'Then again, what is a man to do? I don't have knives like you.'

Fayne nodded. 'If you wake the dead,' he said, 'I will make sure they go back to *Zahanem,* where they came from.'

'Am I coming with you?' Gray asked, as they neared the church.

'No,' Adri said.

'Good.'

The front doors were wood and iron, rusted, rotting; vines spiralled through the carvings and hollows. One door was slightly ajar; Fayne pushed it with a strong arm, and it opened. They crept in. Everything was devastated—the benches had all crumbled and given way to time; one of the support beams of the roof had angled and dropped to the floor. A part of the roof had gutted in, allowing sunlight which lit the hall. Dust swirled lazily in the beam of light. There was no movement anywhere inside the church as they stood near the door, Adri and Fayne checking for any signs of life while Gray took in the moment, the scene in front of him, eyes wide. Then Adri moved towards the fallen support beam, slowly, a revolver in his right hand. He crossed it and saw the slab he was looking for on the floor. He signalled the other two to make their way over to him.

The three of them caught the slab by its handles, picked it up, and put it out of the way. It was carved out of pure granite and was a good three feet long on each side. It was heavy too, as the trio found out; Fayne did not seem to have much trouble with his side though, and he was the first one to look down at what they had uncovered as the other two recovered, wheezing. A small room, right below them, with a door on one side, cut into the stone. With the slab gone, sunlight fell directly into the little room; things were visible clearly. Fayne dropped in gently.

'Is this the one?' Adri asked from above, still panting. Gray looked at his palms, red from the lifting.

'I think yes,' Fayne's voice came up from below.

Adri joined him. Recovering from the light drop, Adri looked around the room. There were no plants down here, only stillness. Nothing moved, and it felt like they were already in the tomb. The entrance to the crypt lay a few steps ahead of him. A door as old as the church, if not older, made of stone, with old writing on it, preyed on by time, but Adri could distinguish the endings of the word *Mazumder*. It was, as he had thought, the final resting place of this unheard of vampire hunter. The door bore no other signs, no art, no protective symbols. It was bare, noticeably so, something which gave it a look of immeasurability, of pure strength. A round fixture curved its way out of one side; a handle.

Adri would have wanted Fayne to come along—his weapons had harsh effects on all kinds of supernatural, Adri was sure. But even the Assassins of Ahzad were not taught the mystics of the Necromancer; the dead-talkers had since long protected their art within their inner circles, whispering it in closed classrooms under supervision of the government which they were a part of. No one else knew, and it had to remain that way; and it was for this reason that today Adri Sen would have to walk in alone through

196

a protected crypt. It also was the reason, Adri mused, that Fayne had let them live and was travelling at their pace.

'Adios, Adri. Hopefully, I will see you soon, *with* the body,' Gray spoke. He still hadn't stepped into the pit.

'I'm off, then,' Adri said. His stomach felt a bit queasy. He had no spirits, and summoning them would take a while, a luxury they did not have. But then again, maybe he should summon spirits before he entered. He did not know of a single Tantric who had braved a protected tomb without a spirit's shield; except, of course, his father. Yes, his father had done it. There was no reason why he shouldn't be able to. Adri walked up to the door. The handle was the first trap and the easiest one to avoid. He pressed a flat hand on the door. *A vampire hunter, eh? Maybe nord.* He moved his fingers on the surface of the door, drawing a certain invisible pattern. Nothing happened when he finished. *Glesh, then.* Adri's fingers moved again, and nothing happened again. Wait, he thought. Why was he thinking defensive? The most powerful offensive sign against vampires was what he needed to try here. The cross. Quickly he drew it, imbibing it in a circle, and as soon as he finished, a low rumble started. Adri stepped back as the door began to shake, bits of dust and dirt dislodging themselves. Finally the hinges found life, and the door swung open. And then all was still.

Fayne's eyes darted in every direction, trying to catch sounds of movement, any evidence of anything which might have heard the rumbling. But nothing else was heard, the stillness was back. Adri did not look back, but at the darkness before him. He dropped his backpack, and withdrew his hip flask with the flammable liquid. Fayne understood his purpose and quietly climbed out of the pit. By the time Adri had decided which shirt to sacrifice, Fayne was back with a large dead branch. Adri wrapped the shirt around the dead branch, soaked it with the liquid, and set his makeshift torch on flame. Then, not picking up his bag, he entered the darkness of the crypt.

This whole torch business was so much easier with a spirit around, Adri thought. He walked softly and slowly, being extremely careful before he would plant a step. He was walking through a tunnel which led *down*, into the earth; the sides of the tunnel were cut straight out of rock, roughly, and without detail or workmanship. Adri's torch burnt fiercely as he burned down old, gigantic cobwebs, but he knew the torch wouldn't last too long, he had to hurry up. Yet one false step could be his last, and he checked for trapdoors and switches the best he could as he walked gingerly down the tunnel.

Physical traps weren't the deadliest of things in crypts; magic was. Protectors and protective charms, blood curses and enchantments, these were what he was looking out for. Most crypts, however, weren't designed keeping Tantrics in mind. It would be the occasional grave robber that the traps were actually meant for. Adri was counting on his ability to sense magic to keep him out of harm's way as far as magical things were concerned. But one never knew, a lot of buried folk had a fancy for giant spikes, lethal sharp blades and big boulders rolling downhill; Adri would certainly have to be on his toes.

He was slowly getting nervous. For some time he'd been hearing a low grating noise somewhere in the darkness behind him. He suspected the presence of a golem, but as he made his way further and further down into the tunnel, he faced nothing. The queasy feeling in his stomach, however, only increased. Even though he didn't want to admit it, the absence of any noise, the dead quiet coupled with the apparent absence of any resistance was getting to him. He looked behind him many times, but nothing appeared to be following him. What also plagued him was the thought of how he was going to get the dead body all the way back up. But that was something to worry about later. He was here for the owner of the crypt, and he would not leave without him.

His mental state did not improve as he continued walking

downward for the next twenty minutes. The corridor was endless; it stretched, took turns, had slight drops and climbs, all as it headed steadily downwards. The air got thinner, and Adri was beginning to have breathing trouble. He began to wonder if there was even a crypt here. Perhaps that door was simply a decoy of sorts. But he could not go back up, not without the body, not until he could walk no more and Fayne and Gray had to come down to check on him. Adri began to tire as he descended, and slowly his mind began to offer explanations.

An endless tunnel. Couldn't be. Nothing was really endless, unless this was some Demon's illusion on him. He would've been able to sense the magic faintly if that was the case though. He closed his eyes and stopped for a moment, concentrating. There was nothing. No magic. He continued walking. The branch had begun to tremble in his hand, ever so slightly, but he could feel it. It worried him. He realised then that he was hungry. He hadn't eaten in a long time now, completely ignoring all the warning signs from his stomach because they couldn't have afforded to stop and eat. Now that nothing was really happening, his attention began to come back to his own self, to his tired physical and mental state. Yet he walked on. It was too late to stop—he could not possibly climb all the way back.

And then, the burial chamber.

His mind was still in a limbo, as it had been for most of the last part of his walk. He had to force his mind to focus back on the things in front of him, to make it face what his body was facing now. His mind, however, refused to budge, and stayed on in that space he had created for it, comfortable. A small part of his mind talked to him.

This was the trap of the crypt; it wasn't physical danger, it wasn't even magical. It was something else, something which was playing with his mind—that's what the whole walk down the length of the tunnel had been about—it had simply set his mind up for this trap. But his younger days in Old Kolkata were so much more pleasant to think about. The time he spent alone. The relationships were not worth remembering at this point They had made him face many problems many things he was rather happier without But the time he had spent alone. there were pleasant moments, very pleasant moments. The afternoon sunSomething else was happening here; hismindwasrefusingtomovewhenheaskeditto. It was as if his mind was getting a mind of its own, thinking what it wanted to, even protecting itself through pleasant thoughts onlyLike the hammocks and the books a few days again lonely but yes well spent And it was right here. in his mind that was all he needed. Ah the sunTHE BIRDS the sight of the fishermen catching fish early in the morning while Father made coffee in the kitchen. The fish the fish the fishwould go wild WILD in their attempts to escape?but the fishermen were strict and clever—the net would be pulled from one end of the pond to the other. The fish had no chance, no chance, a chosen few who were too small could pass through the net, other energetic onestried to jumpthenet as it came for them. Adri would love watching a successful jump, a successful escape. Escape, he needed to. What did he need to escape from? MYTH castle? No, he had done that already. fishermen. fish. er. men. There was something that he wasn't realising. he didn't need to realise.His mind was happy, was content; he could just sit here thinking thinking—but something was wrong. NO. Something was wrong somewhere. If only he could put a finger on it. If only he could know; there was a word he needed to get back to. get back to. Get back. Escape, yes that was it. Escape. He needed to escape. He needed to escape from this; from his mind. He needed to push away, he needed to break free. He needed to JUMP over the net asitcameforhim—

'Yaargh!' Adri screamed and fell on all fours, panting. Gingerly, he reached into his mind with a simple thought—and it responded as it should. Panting, he slowly sat upright and looked down at himself. His right hand was still firm around the torch, but his left—he had needed to burn himself in order to help his mind snap out of whatever it was caught in. He looked at his left palm and saw angry red burns. Nothing to be done now; he looked around and for the first time saw where he was.

The burial chamber was circular. It was a simple construction, without any fancy carvings or statues guarding the coffin, as tombs usually had. This one, like the tunnel, was roughly cut, purely out of the rock, with a high, domelike ceiling and rough pillars in a circle supporting the roof. In the centre of the chamber, on a raised pedestal, was the coffin. Adri's eyes went to the sides of the room, to the skeletons there—roughly seven to eight of them, who, by the looks of it, had simply starved to death, wrestlingwiththeirminds. They lay decomposed and dried, cobwebs amidst their bones and insects running in and out of their eyes, weapons lying useless near them, supply bags ignored in dusty piles. They didn't bother Adri as much as the one other skeleton—this one was impaled against a pillar with a spear in its heart.

Hunger didn't do that. Adri's hand instinctively went for the shooter by his side. Almost immediately the lid of the coffin began to shift. A horrible grating noise filled the chamber as the lid shifted to one side, and then fell to the stone floor with a deafening thud. As the echoes gradually faded away, Adri stood where he was, shooter pointed at the open coffin. The coffin was only a few meters away from him, yet Adri could not see within it. He could, however, immediately smell the fetid odour that began to fill the room—something rotting, something vile. It reminded him of something; almost like a revenant's smell, only they smelled much worse, he knew. No, this wasn't that.

Perfect silence brewed. Adri did not dare to breathe or talk as he stood, revolver raised, clutching it with a hand, the other holding the torch pointed towards the coffin. He stared at the dark, open coffin, not blinking, not moving. Nothing happened, but Adri could sense a slow change in the chamber—the light was dying, softly. Shadows were increasing and the fire was flickering more and more. He risked a glance at the torch and saw that the cloth had almost burnt itself out. Though he was carrying the flammable liquid with him, there was no time to make a new torch. *Something* had moved the lid.

He took a step towards the coffin, slowly. Then another. Then one more. The torch flickered more and more. It began wavering wildly now, crying out in pain and protest, living out its final few moments of flame. Adri's brain was threatening to shut down; he had no clue what was in there inside the coffin, but it lay still and unmoving as he approached. Another step. One more to the coffin. The smell, stronger than ever. The torchlight dimmed rapidly. He had no more time. In rising panic he took a last hurried step towards the stone pedestal and gun raised, looked down into the open coffin.

The torch gave out then.

Complete darkness. Adri looked down at complete darkness. Then two eyes opened beneath him, two eyes—bright blue and burning with inner fury. The creature laughed, a symphony of three different voices laughing together. Something hit Adri. A bright blue flash. He flew from the mouth of the coffin to a wall across the room, landing painfully on his back. The creature rose from the coffin and climbed down. It was the body of a human being, male, now pulsing with a paranormal energy; blue fire burned in his eyes and open mouth, and invisible waves seemed to dance around him. As the creature stood, dressed in a spoilt tuxedo, Adri could see that unlike his clothes, his skin was unblemished, fresh as the day he was buried.

Adri rose to his feet, realising several things. One, his shirt had been charred instantly and he was now bare-chested, his tattoos glowing a bright electric. Two, he had just been hit by a spirit bolt, and the mystical protection woven into the tattoos

202

had saved him. Three, the creature was a Wraith and his ballistic weapons were, thus, useless. Four, the Wraith, surveying him with a smile lingering on its face, had obviously expected the spirit bolt to wipe him out. Adri looked at the Wraith and raised his hands. 'Not fighting. And I haven't come here to steal anything.'

'Oh, I don't know,' the Wraith replied in its collection of voices. 'Grave-robbers come in all shapes and sizes.'

'Oh come on, Mazumder,' Adri snapped. 'You used to hunt vampires once, and now you're so desperate in your undead bloodlust that you kill anyone who walks in?'

The Wraith was taken aback. It stared at Adri. Its aura could not harm Tantrics who, after their tattoo ceremonies, were immune to spirit energy. Only physical damage could harm them. But then again, no one had talked directly to it for a while now. Come to think of it, this was the second Tantric who had ever visited. 'What do you even know of me, Necromancer?' it asked. 'Look at you, big talk and no weapons. I sense no other spirits, who I would have scattered like dust, by the way, but still, you walk in without armour, like the fool that you are. You pose me no harm.'

'I *mean* you no harm,' Adri said. 'I know Wraiths cannot be exorcised without the place of release; and this isn't your place of release, is it? This is your place of entombment.'

'An exorcist too, I see. My, my, you know quite the lot for your age.'

'I know enough, yes.'

'So why do you walk into my crypt?'

Adri was silent. 'The Ancients,' he said finally.

Blue fires erupted from the Wraith's eyes and mouth. It flared as it roared, 'WHAT about the Ancients?'

'They are holding my friend hostage,' Adri said grimly. 'And they want your past body in exchange of her life.'

'And you think I will part with my body, Necromancer? Or did you perhaps leave your brains behind as mortgage to pay for those fancy tattoos?' The Wraith's reply was mocking, yet it held a serious note of finality.

'You are done with your body, Mazumder,' Adri replied, unaffected. 'There is a young girl who will die unless you let her live.'

'Like I give a damn.' The Wraith shook its head and started walking back to its coffin. 'You disturbed my rest for this?! I can't believe it. Go back, Necromancer, today, I let you live.'

'Life is not yours anymore!' Adri spoke loudly.

'Your stabs won't get me. You want to see a magic trick?' the Wraith asked, turning to Adri again.

Adri paused, his mind working furiously.

The blue fire was gone. The human body stood on its own and darkness took over. 'I care,' a lone voice spoke. Then the Wraith was back in the body. 'Now I don't care!' it shouted gleefully, waving its arms. 'Voila!!'

Adri stared. 'You fond of that body so much?' he asked.

'I've preserved it with my magic. What could that possibly be for?' the Wraith cried. 'Now, honestly? Stop fooling around. I'm not helping you. Get lost.'

'I don't get it, Mazumder,' Adri said softly.

The Wraith listened with interest, which it tried hard to conceal. Adri did not speak. 'Don't get what?' the Wraith blurted out finally.

'I thought you were a vampire hunter, I thought that's what's keeping you here on earth as a Wraith, that burning hatred. Wraiths are empty shells devoid of their former selves, sure, but I thought some of that vampire-hate would still remain, some of that desire for a chance to payback the vermin who did this to you, and all the vampires you couldn't kill. But what I find instead is a Wraith who's concerned with repairing its human body with magic, with killing inexperienced grave robbers. Strange how this all works out, eh?'

'Clever, Tantric. Quite clever, you playing on my hate for the Ancients. But tell you what—honestly, I don't feel the need to stay here anymore. This crypt bores me, and the eternal sleep is even more drab. I'm refusing you on two counts.'

'Which are?'

'One, the Ancients will destroy my body which I'm not agreeable to. I'm sure you're aware that I cannot exist independent of a body; my very nature is symbiotic. And two, I don't know if you've ever dealt with Ancients before, Tantric, but let me tell you that your pretty little thing is already dead, probably *turned* by now.'

'I shot her with a corruption,' Adri replied calmly. 'Whoever bites her bites the dust. That's one problem solved right there.'

'Clever,' the Wraith said. 'Then you must be clever enough to also know what I'm leading towards, and what I will want from you if you do take my dead body back to those vampires.'

Adri knew. One was perhaps the death of the Ancients, the Wraith would not stand for anything less. The second, though, was the tougher one, the tricky one. According to his father, and a million other books, it should never be done. Being symbiotic in nature, the Wraith always needed a host. 'You want possession of my body,' Adri said.

'Possession *and* control,' the Wraith grinned.

'You're not getting control, you piece of filth,' Adri swore.

'Was worth a shot. Fine, only possession, then.'

'Only till your place of release,' Adri said. 'Where is it?'

The Wraith looked at Adri with calculative eyes, burning blue. 'Howrah. There is a small place there where I killed my first vampire. It is there that I want my release.'

Adri raised a hand. 'I will bind you to these words, spirit'
—'Please don't insult me,' the Wraith spoke— 'so that when we

visit this place that you mentioned, you shall leave the carrier that is my body and take your place in the higher Plane.'

'I doubt it's up there that I'm going,' the Wraith laughed.

'Fine. The next Plane or across the River, wherever. Are you okay with the binding of the words?' Adri asked irritably.

'Yes, whatever it takes for you to get over your tiddly little human insecurities.'

Adri performed the hand gestures and murmured a spell. The Wraith was bound to its word within ten minutes, throughout which it kept distracting him with a string of comments and remarks. Adri knew the risks of what he was doing, yet he did it anyway. There were too many things already spiralling out of control, and here he was making a deal with a Wraith and offering partial possession. Bodies were not cabs—they couldn't just ferry souls here and there. There were always repercussions and problems; the body functions changed and health issues always cropped up because of the presence of another soul. It also required a tremendous amount of willpower to keep the spirit in check; a strong spirit could very easily take over a weak body—a phenomenon popularly known as possession, dealt with by Tantrics who also carried a degree in exorcism. What was very simple Tantric law was to *never* wilfully allow a possession; Adri knew the law, and Mazumder knew Adri knew the law. What's more was that the Wraith didn't strike Adri as being the particularly righteous kind or the kind that stuck to its word honourably. With all due respect, Adri thought the creature was slimy and seemed treacherous. And powerful. Which didn't add up to a very good combination.

'My body cannot leave the crypt as long as I'm in it,' Mazumder spoke.

'You planned this crypt yourself right?' Adri asked.

'I was a different person back then. I have—*improved* over the years in the eternal sleep.'

'Sure.'

'So what I was getting to, putting aside your direct criticism of my foolishness in trapping myself in, was that I will need to make the switch right now so that my body may be carried up.'

'It's a long walk,' Adri said.

'We'll manage,' Mazumder replied.

'I don't like the way you said "we".'

'Fool, you better get used to it.'

Adri readied himself. His body was trained to resist possession, it would not be ready to accept the Wraith; he would have to override his subconscious defence systems.

'Having second thoughts, are we now?' the Wraith smirked.

'Merely trying not to kick you right out of my mind,' Adri said.

'Anytime you're ready, sweetheart. I've got all day!'

'I haven't got all day,' Adri breathed, sweating slightly from all the focusing. 'Okay, I'm ready.'

The Wraith did not waste any time. It left its older body with a liquid like spin, erupting as a mass of black, a murky form covered with shadows and tentacles, radiating blue energy from cracks within itself. It spun in the air, and lightning fast, manoeuvred itself and shot straight into Adri's body.

For a few scattered moments, Adri's mind experienced a loss of control, like he had upon initially entering the chamber. The feeling stayed until Adri fought it and calmed it down. It was simpler this time and put up lesser resistance; probably because of the Wraith controlling its magic, Adri thought. The turmoil was lessening and his vision, blurred and bleary until now, was clearing. But there was no more spirit energy around to act as a light source. He could see nothing.

Cosy. A voice inside his head. *Not bad, Adri. Not bad at all.*

'You found out my name?' Adri asked incredulously.

That's not all.

'Mazumder. You have to stop looking into my head,' Adri said.

Make me, the Wraith smirked.

Adri sighed, then concentrated. Hiding information was simple enough if you had the right training for it. The Wraith realised what Adri was doing.

No fun! All right, I lay off your stuff. Was just curious. It's like entering someone's house, you know—you see all their things and feel like snooping around a little.

'Respect my privacy, Wraith. There are things I don't want people to see.'

I know. I caught glimpses. Most . . . interesting. But then again, how would I possibly tell someone? I cannot reach out to others while I'm in your body. And when I finally do leave, it will be to enter the next Plane. Your secrets are safe with me, even if you do choose to reveal them.

'Ha!' Adri gave a bark-like laugh. 'I don't trust you.'

Well met. Was still worth a try, though.

They were silent for a moment. Then Adri spoke, 'We should go.'

But you can't see. Easily remedied.

Adri felt something like water flow into his eyes, cold and liquid-like. He blinked, and immediately the liquid heated up. He could see in the dark. His eyes burned with blue flame and it took him a moment to get used to it.

This is how spirits see the world, Tantric.

There was a blue tint to the world and everything was blurry except what he immediately focused on. But the lack of light did not matter now, he could see everything in the small chamber, though whatever he did not focus on seemed to visually merge, ingrain, combine, expand, and contract like a slow kaleidoscope. It was weird, and he did not prefer it over his normal eyesight, then again, he would prefer anything over the darkness. He walked towards Mazumder's now lifeless body on the floor.

Handsome devil, the Wraith said.

The vampire hunter had been handsome, yes. He must have been in his mid-years when he died. The man's head was bald; the eye sockets had sunk back in with the eyes mercifully shut. A sharp, prominent jawline and a muscled neck lead to a well-built body, trained and maintained.

'How do I get him to the top?' Adri asked.

There is a separate exit. That way.

Adri tried to lift the body and couldn't. Grabbing a leg, he started dragging the body in the direction the Wraith motioned to. If the Wraith was offended by the dragging of its past body, it refused to show it. He saw one of his revolvers on the floor and picked it up. There was a secret switch built into the wall; and once the new passageway opened up, the exit was a few minutes away. Adri watched the door open with surprised anguish—he walked out, dragging the body behind him, into bright sunlight. He wished he had known about this route instead. He looked up and saw the silhouette of an Angel against the sun; the exit was built on the base of a giant Angel statue, right outside the church. He left the body there and walked inside to inform his companions that he was back. The Wraith remained quiet, but removed its energy from Adri's eyes.

He found them where he had left them. Fayne was watching the entrance, while Gray was lolling around lazily, carrying Adri's bag with him. He had been exploring the church, apparently.

'I'm glad you made it. You were beginning to take some serious time down there; we have to get back to JU before nightfall, remember?'

'I haven't forgotten, Gray,' Adri said.

'You look like hell. What happened to the shirt?' Gray asked, looking at the scraps Adri was wearing.

Fayne was facing Adri. 'I can smell a Wraith on you, *pashlin*,' he said before Adri could react.

'I had an encounter with one,' Adri replied.

There was a red blade in Fayne's hand, Adri noticed. A dagger, something red and translucent; Fayne was toying with it as he faced Adri.

'Are you sure you are still the same person who walked inside the crypt?'

'There's no way to confirm that, is there? If I were possessed, the creature would have access to all my memories. Thus it would answer any question you put to it. Enough of this, assassin. We should move, I've already have had a hard time inside the crypt.'

'If you are a Wraith you will have access to Adri's memories,' Fayne said, unmoving, 'but not his skills.'

Adri looked at him with a mixture of exasperation and anger.

Fayne pointed at a mural on the wall. 'The black knight—you see the black knight? Fire a shot and hit his helm.'

The target wasn't near. It was quite a shot with the free hand and though Adri knew why Fayne was doing this, he couldn't help but be annoyed at this lack of trust after his ordeal. Fayne had seen him shoot though, and he would be able to easily see if the same person was firing the shot. Adri did not dally; he roughly yanked a revolver out of its holster and taking aim, fired the shot. Without even waiting to see if it hit, Adri turned around and walked out of the church.

Fayne and Gray stood, watching the black bullet hole exactly in the centre of the knight's helm.

'It's Adri,' Gray said.

'The Wraith was a vampire hunter, bound to have been an equally good shot,' Fayne said.

'Then now what?'

'I was watching the way he *drew* the weapon, not the shot. He's used to it. It seems it is indeed Adri. *Khayer,* I will still keep a watch on him,' Fayne said. They turned around and followed Adri out of the abandoned, silent church.

13

Interesting how you didn't mention little old me in front of your friends. Scared, Adri? Scared they'll stop trusting you?

'Shut up,' Adri murmured. 'Don't make me talk to myself.'

You could always open up your mind to me. Then you'd merely have to think it.

'I said shut up.'

The Wraith obeyed. Adri looked around to see if either of the other two had been watching him. Thankfully, Gray was checking the open road for Demons, and Fayne had gone scouting ahead. The vampire killer's body lay in front of him, wrapped up in a sheet. They were almost back at the university—Adri could see its gates in the distance.

The young Tantric was having troubles of his own. Having to cope with another creature living in his mind, for example. It was very distracting; the Wraith talked all of a sudden and would always take him by surprise, mostly being its usual sarcastic self, an entity Adri could not learn to trust. It observed a lot, seeing through his eyes and hearing through his ears. It did not share any of Adri's physical pains or mental pressures though—and he always had to consciously hide his secrets from the creature, though he would know immediately if the Wraith tried to dig around for them. He didn't know yet what would happen when he slept; he was sure the Wraith needed no sleep.

He slapped his forehead without realising it. He was getting himself into more and more trouble. Not something he needed.

'There's a problem, Mazumder,' he said.

Yes?

'We can't possibly take on the Ancients. You know how powerful they are; and there are perhaps fifteen or more of them waiting in there.'

Fifteen?

'Yes.'

You walk in there and you are not walking out. Getting the girl is out of the question.

'What would you suggest?'

Leave the girl. She's clearly a liability. And, you have already hit her with a corruption. She's not going to turn, she will just die and have her peace afterwards.

'Not possible. I have made my oaths.'

And I have made mine, human. If you die, your body is useless to me, and I cannot wander free like other spirits. I will be trapped in your loathsome body without a foreseeable future. That's not possible either.

'There's a word called *compromise*, Mazumder. I can stay alive *and* get Maya out of there.'

So what's the catch, fool?

'The catch is the assassin. He must not know of your presence. That will make me a threat to him, and he will kill me. Immediately.'

So that is why. Your survival is my survival. I shall show no signs.

'Which also means that I can't count on your help in taking care of the Ancients. You must be invisible. I can use no help you give me, not even the sight of spirits.'

Or you could convince the assassin to not come along.

'His charge is to protect the girl. He'll come. We'll have to think of something else.'

I love the way you are already saying 'we'.

Fayne was back soon. 'The road is clear. I thought I had seen something, but it was a dog, hiding among corpses,' he said to Gray and Adri.

'No wait,' Adri said. 'Before we go on, I think we should talk about this.'

'Indeed,' Fayne nodded.

'You're not expecting a fair handover, are you now?' Adri asked.

'Hold on,' Gray spoke. 'Yes, I was.'

'There's going to be none. We hand over the dead body, they slaughter us *and* Maya.'

Gray's eyebrows climbed.

'How many Ancients are in there, Tantric?' Fayne asked.

'Fifteen, maybe more.'

Fayne did not reply. The eyes of his mask shone without expression; yet it was clear what his silence indicated.

'You could take them out if you were fortunate and fast enough,' Adri continued. 'But you will *not* be able to save the girl.'

'You didn't tell me about this!' Gray protested.

Adri stared at him. 'Shut up. There is much I did not tell you about. There are more complications after I save Maya.'

'What complications?'

'I have had to choose the lesser evil,' Adri replied.

'Don't talk in riddles man!' Gray shouted.

Fayne interrupted. 'The sun is almost gone and the *fatiya's* life hangs in the middle. You speak the truth, Tantric' —he turned towards Adri— 'I cannot take out all of them and yet fulfil my charge. So what is it that you suggest we do?'

Adri looked at the setting sun, casting the usual red sky in more red.

'I need to call upon a spirit,' he said.

They entered Jadavpur University on a run and headed straight towards the Demonology building. There was no time to be lost; it would be too late once the sun had set. *And after all I've done,* Adri thought, *I cannot allow Maya's life to be lost in the balance.* They settled near the building. Adri quickly cleared the ground and fishing out his silver knife from his bag, started the lengthy process of scratching the call-sign on the ground. It was complicated, but he remembered it like the clearest picture he had seen, his hand having a life of its own as he remembered and etched the sacred runes in the soil.

'Candles. From my bag, now!' he hissed. Gray hurried over to his side and started groping around in his bag. Fayne stood by them, his gaze moving from the sign to the sun and back. Once the candles were arranged according to Adri's instructions, Gray lit them, all in the specific order they were supposed to be. Adri placed a tiny red mask, as big as his thumb, in the centre. Then, one of the Lost Pages. And finally, the silver knife between two runes. Then Adri started the incantations, slowly and softly.

'The sun,' Fayne said. 'She sets.'

Adri kept chanting, and long moments later, he felt a gust of wind pass through his very bones, a wind that did not bother the candles. Something was here.

'Reveal yourself,' Adri said.

'Blood,' a voice said out of nowhere. 'I need blood.'

'So we've got ourselves a practical joker here,' Adri sighed. 'Why do your types always have to receive my call?'

Of course spirits didn't need blood. He would have called a spirit he knew, but that would take much more time, something he didn't have.

'You seem to be in a hurry, Necromancer,' the spirit replied, its voice now sharper, in control.

'I give you the chance to move to your next; complete a charge for me in return,' Adri said.

'I obey your terms. What kind of charge?' the spirit asked to Adri's immense relief.

'Reanimation. Of the simple kind,' Adri replied.

The sun had just set when Adri opened the door and moved into the darkness, another makeshift torch burning in his hand. He walked in silence, his boots crushing tiny rock, the noise echoing loudly in the caverns beyond. Adri knew where he was, and it unnerved him. This was someplace no one dared, no citizen of Old Kolkata, no matter how experienced or powerful. Heck, his own father had warned him of this. Along with warnings against Wraith possession.

'Ancients!' he screamed, waving the torch around.

He knew he was being watched from the moment he had entered. He heard the soft snapping noise start in droves as bodies unwounded from around stalagmites and rocks, making their way towards him. He could only see the empty, airy darkness all around him, and though he could hear the Ancients approaching, not being able to see them made him very, very uneasy. He was not used to them; his work had never let him deal much with vampires. He had dealt with Wraiths before, but that was a long time back; Adri cursed himself for not remembering the sharp smell of the Wraith. Not that any damage had happened, but he would have been able to plan things out a bit earlier. Planning was always where it was at. Planning had saved his life on countless occasions.

One of the undead vampires slowly emerged out of the darkness, the black hollows of its eye sockets glaring at Adri. It looked at the flame in his hand with great distaste before turning to face Adri once more.

'Where is the body, human?' it rasped angrily. 'It's not with you!'

'The girl,' Adri shouted. 'Let me see the girl.'

This time the other Ancient entered from behind him, bringing Maya's limp body in its hands. Adri turned around and found Maya's face incredibly close to his own, mere inches away. He looked at her and it seemed it had been a long time since he had last seen her. Here she was, right in front of him, but she was not with him. Yet. Her eyes were shut, and her skin was paler now, a bluish tint creeping up her face; her hair seemed to be losing its lustre and looked dry, hanging as if it were not a part of her. Adri slowly extended his free hand and first felt her neck for puncture marks and then checked her pulse. She was alive and unbitten; a rare feat for the Ancients.

'Let me hold her and you will have your body,' he said.

The Ancient did not speak. It considered.

'Either way, I cannot walk out alive without your leave. Let me hold her,' Adri said.

The Ancient remained silent. Then, slowly, it nodded. Maya was handed over to Adri roughly, and her sudden weight overcame him for a few moments. But then, he was standing, supporting her limp frame with his shoulders, careful to keep the burning torch away from her. He pointed at the door from which he had come. 'There's Mazumder. I got him, but with a bonus.'

The door opened and the dead body of Mazumder walked in, slowly but surely. The Ancient's heads whipped towards this spectacle, staring without reaction, unable to believe what they saw. There stood their hated vampire hunter, dressed in a torn tuxedo, standing tall and defiant and looking at them with his usual unusual hatred; his skin unexpectedly fresh when the Ancients were expecting a creature of bone and dust.

That's supposed to be me? An insult. I do not stand like that.

Adri ignored Mazumder's complaint in his head. 'A gift for the Ancients; this gutless worm who was hiding away, still very much alive,' he spoke.

The Ancients were hypnotised. They did not react, did not speak; they only stared at the dead body of Mazumder which stood watching all of them. Soft snapping broke the silence as more and more Ancients slowly gathered around Adri. Three emerged softly from the darkness to his left. Adri could hear one more right behind him. Then another one next to the first one, and another one to his right. Everyone stood transfixed; until Mazumder's body broke into a sudden run and disappeared into the darkness of the cavern in the other direction.

Screeches broke loose. 'The hunt is on!' several Ancients rasped as they slid forward at an incredible speed on their snakelike bodies, disappearing after the mobile cadaver. It was a rush, a mass of writhing, speeding Ancients, of old and powerful predators, and then they were all gone. Adri looked at them, puzzled and unable to believe that his idea had worked so well. Slowly, he started to move towards the door. Maya wasn't very light; moving her wasn't as easy as he had hoped.

He had taken a few steps when he heard the soft snapping in the darkness behind him. He froze. The sound circled around him and came to a stop in front of him, slowly, with leisure, and then the Ancient appeared from the darkness.

'Going somewhere, human?' it asked, coiling its bones beneath it.

If it was smiling, Adri again, couldn't tell. He could still hear the cries of the other Ancients echoing in the caverns. They seemed far away by now. The dead body was a fast runner.

'You are a dead-talker,' the Ancient whispered. 'There is obviously another spirit in the hated one's body.'

'It is his body, the one you asked for. I have fulfilled my part of the deal,' Adri spoke.

'Idiot,' it replied with relish. 'With vampires, there *is* no deal.'

Many things happened. The Ancient lunged forward, raising its claws, baring its fangs with a deadly predatory hiss—a move that would send shivers up Adri's spine whenever he would think about it in the future. In that instant, Fayne burst from the shadows behind the creature, his eyeglasses reflecting the torchlight. With one muscled arm he grabbed the Ancient's bony neck, pulling it back. In the other arm, his red bladed dagger gleamed; the next moment, the Ancient had been cut from its spine. Blood, dark and silent, sprayed from the open bone wounds all over Adri, Maya, and Fayne. The Ancient would have screeched in agony had it not been for Fayne's dagger buried in its skull. It was over in seconds. Fayne's strong arms easily lifted Maya over his shoulders, and they ran towards the door, Adri abandoning the makeshift torch at the doorway as they ran up the stairs. They did not stop until they were out of the Demonology building and near the tree where Gray waited anxiously.

Fayne put Maya down in the grass and turned to Adri. 'Well played, *pashlin*,' the assassin said.

Adri shook his head. 'Complications,' he said quietly.

Gray had been relieved to see Maya, but Adri did a good job at sounding ominous; and Gray realised if he kept this up, the Tantric's company wouldn't be something to keep. All Adri seemed to do was attract trouble, he thought silently, cursing. He knelt near Maya and tried to look at her, but there was no light. 'Before you do anything else, take the corruption out,' Gray said.

'That is what the problem is,' Adri said. 'I have no idea how.'

Gray's shotgun was a few feet away, but had it been in his hands, Gray might have fired it. He was livid—he could not believe his ears, could not believe what this Tantric was saying and what he had done. The blinding rage converted itself, midway, to sorrow; hot angry tears surfaced in his eyes, try as he did to control them. He fought to keep his voice steady. 'What do you mean you *don't know how*?' he asked.

'A corruption is not an easy thing to control. It is not something to give and later take away. It's a venom, ultimately fatal,' Adri looked at Fayne. 'An assassin's weapon.'

'What kind of corruption did you give the *fatiya*?' Fayne asked, his voice still expressionless.

'The Whisper of Dread,' Adri said. 'It was the only one powerful enough to affect the Ancients. And the only one I had at that moment.'

'Well, so what do we do?' Gray asked, looking from one to the other.

'There should be an antidote for every poison, every venom,' Fayne said.

'So make one!' Gray exclaimed, not daring to breathe. 'Make one.'

'I am an assassin, not a healer. Antidotes are best found with them. However, the Whisper of Dread, I'm sorry to say, is one of the most masterful, dependable poisons. I have used it on countless occasions myself when I have needed to be far away when it does take effect. Not immediate, but deadly in time.'

Adri turned to Gray, not meeting his eyes. 'I think there is an antidote, but I'm afraid I do not know the ingredients required to fashion it.'

'How long does she have?'

'Till sunrise, if she's lucky,' Fayne said.

Gray forced his head to stop spinning; he forced that nauseating feeling in his gut to go away. Now was not the time. He needed to help figure things out. 'So what can be done? Who knows the cure?' he asked desperately.

'The Lake of Fire. MYTH will have the antidote for sure,' Adri said, looking at Fayne.

'We cannot reach there by sunrise,' Fayne spoke. 'It seems I shall fail in my charge.'

'There must be a place closer!' Gray yelled. 'Are you giving up already?'

'No,' Adri said. 'Recollecting.'

I would have helped this lass, she's not half bad, the Wraith crooned. *But this bloody city changes every time I close my eyes.*

Adri moved off to a side. 'It also retains its old,' he whispered. 'Do you know a place?'

Do you know of Nagina? The cinema hall with the tragic incident?

'Yes. The fire which had burnt everything down,' Adri whispered. Behind him, Gray was engaged in furious conversation with a completely calm Fayne.

Yes. But the cinema never shut down, it seems. It still runs.

'How's that possible?'

The dead are still trapped in that hall, Adri.

Adri waited, thinking.

I had a friend among the victims. A healer, one of the best. This was long back, but even the Whisper of Dread is among the venoms of old.

'Will he know the cure?'

He is our best shot, at any rate.

'Can't I summon him here?'

Do you have something that belongs to him, fool?

'Oh, right. It's not very far from here, is it?'

Couple of hours.

Gray tapped Adri's shoulder. 'And who are you talking to?' he asked sharply.

'Myself,' Adri said. 'It calms me down. Any agreement?'

'The assassin is short of ideas when it doesn't involve killing,' Gray spat.

'I might have a lead. It's narrow, but there's a chance.'

'What is it?'

220

Gray's mind told him that Adri was not at fault. Like the Necromancer had said earlier, he had chosen the lesser of two evils. In a twisted way, the corruption had saved Maya's life, and was now threatening to claim her for itself. But even though nothing was sure and everything was at stake, there was one thing that gave Gray relief—the fact that Adri had not backed away. Adri made countless mistakes and choices that made Gray angry, but he knew they were the right ones, at least under the given circumstances they were. Adri could have backed out at any given moment; he could've said sorry and left Gray with Maya out here. He did not hold any responsibility towards them. There was no written word, no contract binding him to them. The commitment Adri was honouring was purely verbal, and he was doing his best to put up with it in spite of everything that was happening. And that meant that either Adri was a greater being, capable of giant feats, or whatever he wanted from Abriti was of immense value. Gray could not decide which one was more plausible an explanation. Adri puzzled him. There were streaks of selfishness and cold that he saw in the young Tantric, but he also saw selflessness and heroism;there was something about Adri that made Gray want to trust him. Something Fayne did not have. Gray knew though, that Fayne was capable of extremely deadly acts, and he was glad he was on their side, even if it was only for the moment.

The assassin of Ahzad was the one who carried Maya as they walked through the Old City towards the cinema hall. Fayne's training must have been quite something, Gray thought as he shot a quick look at the assassin walking behind him, strong as a horse, carrying his sister's limp body over his shoulders without any sign of fatigue. Gray kept checking on Maya; though she did not move, she breathed, and the fact that she was physically with them was a matter of reassurance to Gray, somehow. It wasn't much, but she was within arm's reach, and that mattered.

As he turned back again, Gray heard Adri, who was leading them, whisper to himself again. He'd been doing that occasionally, and wondered if Adri was cracking under all the pressure. He hadn't heard the Necromancer do this before, but then, they hadn't been under this kind of a constraint before.

Adri was having a disturbing conversation with the Wraith as they walked.

'Tell me something, Mazumder. You were a vampire hunter. You must have dealt with corruptions.'

Quite often. I oiled most of my blades with them.

'Didn't you use the Whisper of Dread?'

Yes. Not often, but yes.

'Don't *you* know the damned antidote?'

The Wraith replied in time. *I did not want to say this, but unless my memory fails me, the Whisper of Dread is among the three incurables.*

Adri stopped walking.

There is no antidote for it, not in my knowledge.

'Then–then why?' Adri asked softly.

Because the eternal sleep often makes you mix up your facts. But Mishrah will know for sure. He did not forget before his death; I doubt he will have forgotten after.

'Fayne should know this,' Adri started walking again, waving aside Gray's questions.

He already does. Either he believes something else will come to light and is playing along, or there is actually an antidote and my memory is worse than I could ever realise.

'I hope it's the latter, Wraith. I really hope that's the case.'

This girl. You have sworn to protect her, have you not?

Adri was silent again.

That puts you in the same shoes as the assassin.

Every road in Old Kolkata was at a perfect right angle with every other road. If they could fly like eagles did, Adri mused, they'd see a great circuit of squares that made up the city. Of course there were exceptions, but this simple rule had helped Adri gain most of his knowledge of the layout of the Old Town. Abandoned cars were parked all over the roads, most of them looted clean of all parts that could run. They used the vehicles as cover as they walked, even though the roads were deserted as usual. After an hour of slow travel, however, they chanced upon some traders heading in another direction. They had bodyguards, mercenaries with their cheap makeshift rifles, who stared at them with suspicion. Adri's holsters were clearly visible and Gray carried his shotgun openly. They were a threat, but they weren't stopped or spoken to. Adri was in no mood for conversation, nor did he need to learn anything. They needed to get to the Lake of Fire eventually; they would have an antidote if there was one to be found.

They made their way through the roads without anything eventful happening. They stopped once to eat. Though they were short of time, they needed to eat and Adri, for one, was tremendously hungry. They ate cold, canned food. Nothing tasted good, and nothing was nourishing, but it gave them energy and they ate. Fayne, once again, refused to eat. He sat down and watched them eat, drinking from his hip flask.

When the cinema hall finally came into sight, they stopped and watched it from a corner; it seemed as deserted as everything else.

'Any traps we should worry about?' Adri murmured.

I haven't been around here for a long time. In case you didn't notice, I'm dead, fool.

'Yet you knew about this theatre, something I didn't know.'

Well, you can't know everything, you pompous—

'Why do you keep murmuring?' Gray asked. 'It makes me very uneasy.'

'Good, you'll be on your toes then,' Adri said.

Fayne changed the subject. 'I think I will stay here with Maya. Whatever you need to do, do it and come back.'

Gray believed the assassin most capable of guarding his sister. 'I'm coming with you, Adri.'

Adri waited for the Wraith to give him a reason why not, but it did not object. Adri made up an excuse, something very vague about Tantrics getting exclusive entry. Gray complained before finally agreeing to stay back, muttering about it being just a movie hall and Adri being a shameless liar. Adri gave him his bag for safekeeping and moved off.

The fire had been a very unfortunate event. It had happened a long time ago, much before Adri had been born. How the fire had started had never been discovered, but speculations ran from a faulty electric line, to a careless smoker. The sad part was that over two hundred people had perished, making it one of Old Kolkata's biggest tragedies.

Adri lit a cigarette and walked silently towards the building in the darkness. He stopped beneath the huge signboard. *NAGINA*, it said, in broad half-burnt letters. The cinema hall itself was still standing, dark and silent. The silent part was getting to him. Not a sound came from within, nothing moved. He looked around and saw no one. He was at a crossroad with four completely deserted streets running in all four directions, the theatre looming in front of him. Breathing smoke, he slowly made his way through the ruined entrance to the cinema hall and into the building.

There is something else you should know.

'I'm listening.'

There is a film which plays in the theatre. It has been playing ever since the hall burned down. That is the film the dead watch, and they

224

watch it over and over again. Do not be caught inside when the film ends. If you do, the curse will have you and you will never leave.

'Places like this often have a curse like this. Maybe I should work on freeing the spirits sometime.'

Hah! A curse as old and as powerful as this one will need an army of Tantrics.

'You're right,' Adri said, walking through the corridors. 'I can feel it.'

Empty and lonely, the corridors were pitch black and charred. Ash everywhere. The ceiling was cracked, all the lamps broken. A lone light burned in the distance, at the end of a corridor, and Adri walked towards it. On reaching it he saw a ticket counter built into the wall. A weak torch smouldered outside the counter, and there was a hole in the wall with TICKETS written above, nothing but darkness beyond. Adri approached the hole with caution, slowly.

'Hello?' he said.

Do not talk. Do you have the payment?

'How much is it?'

One.

Adri reached inside his pocket and withdrew his wallet, a leather pouch bound at the top with sharp black rope. *The dead only accept silver,* he recalled as he put the coin on the counter. A hand emerged from the darkness. It was a burnt hand, black and bony with scraps of charred flesh hanging on to it like old paper. It covered the coin and dragged it into the shadows. Then it emerged again, soundlessly, and left a ticket on the counter. Adri picked up the small, faded piece of paper and looked at the entrance. A wooden door.

'This is it, then,' he said.

Stop wasting time, the Wraith retorted.

Adri crushed his cigarette with the heel of his boot and entered the hall.

14

The film was an old blockbuster he had seen before. Adri realised this as soon as he entered—a cult film that had survived the years and was appreciated to this day. He also saw that the film was nearing its end. He better hurry. The projector was very loud, the whirring even louder than the sound of the film itself. It was projecting on a ragged, half devastated screen, not watchable by any standards. But a curse was a curse.

He walked down the aisle to the screen and turned around so he could see the entire hall. It was full. Dead men, women, and children watched the movie silently. They had burned to their deaths; their scars had not gone; they were disfigured, some of them burnt to the bone; their clothes charred and black, indistinct from whatever was left of their skin; their eyes glittered like cold jewels, the screen reflecting in them, blank. Everyone was silent, their eyes glued to the film. They would've been like statues if not for the slight movements and occasional shuffling.

'Am I in any danger?'

You've been in similar places before. You tell me.

Curse-bound places mostly did not have vindictive dead, not unless they met their killer. Or if the dead people had been killers themselves when they had been alive. *These had been innocent people*, Adri thought. 'I'll take my chances. Find your friend.'

Allow me, maestro.

Adri's eyes burned with spirit vision. He blinked and adjusted. He could now see everyone clearly, in much more detail as the darkness melted away. He didn't like what he saw; his immediate repulsion was not based on the physical appearances of the dead people. No, it was rather their condition, the curse that held them, which made Adri pity them and instinctively not want to go near them.

There he is in the fifth row, the Wraith announced.

Adri did not hesitate. This had to be done. Mercifully, there was an empty seat next to the man; Adri muttered apologies as he brushed against a few dead knees and took the seat. Then he looked around. The dead paid him no heed. As far as they were concerned, he did not exist.

Oh, and don't mention me. He hated me.

'Hello, err, Mishrah,' Adri said, recalling the name just in time.

The dead man to his right slowly turned his head to look at him. His face was horribly defaced; there was no flesh beneath his nose where skeletal teeth and gums grinned at him. Flames had claimed the man's hair as well, leaving a burnt raw scalp. His eyes, probably the only things intact, stared at Adri sharply. Adri saw they were bright blue, though that might have been the spirit vision.

'Yes?' he asked.

'I need your help,' Adri said. Perhaps this was going to turn out easier than usual.

'After the film,' Mishrah said, turning back to watch the film.

'That isn't an option, Mishrah,' Adri said darkly. 'It will start again.'

Mishrah did not look at Adri. He spoke, sounding slightly unsure. 'Again?'

'Yes, again. And again. You have seen this film before. Remember.'

'There is a vague—something,' Mishrah spoke slowly. He looked at the film. Whatever was left of his eyebrows was starting to frown. There was something wrong here, something wrong with the film. He couldn't put his finger on it, but there was a bit of truth in what this young man was saying. Somehow.

'I need your help, and I need it now,' Adri said. 'There isn't too much time.'

It was coming back to Mishrah, gradually, but yes. He dwelt on it, pulling facts out and hiding other things he did not want to see. He heard the young man's voice next to him, but he did not hear the words; he was someplace else, playing his thoughts like a piano. The film was everything; that was all there was to it. That was the purpose, but then, it wasn't—he was *supposed* to think it was the purpose. He was trapped. Somewhere.

'I'm . . . dead,' he said after a while.

Adri gazed at him, at how hideous he was. 'Yes,' he said finally.

'I'm not supposed to be here. Why am I here? Wait, there is something here. Something binds me here.'

Adri let Mishrah continue. The dead man was in a daze.

'There is a pull. It forces me to stay here. It whispers in my ear and tells me to watch the film.'

It was useless to tell Mishrah to fight it. He would not succeed. Adri remained silent, but sneaked a glance at the film. There was still time.

'And now you come here. You ask me to help you,' Mishrah said. 'You confuse me.'

'I need your help with a corruption,' Adri said.

Mishrah's eyes focused immediately and Adri knew he would know about this. The Wraith had been correct.

'Which corruption?'

228

'Whisper of Dread,' Adri said, his heart beating faster. 'Does it have an antidote?'

The reply came almost instantaneously. 'Tricky, tricky corruption. No antidote. Never has been. You can slow it down with the Dreamer's Brew, but no cure, no.'

Adri stared at the man. He had come here hoping for not just knowledge about the antidote, but also for a list of its ingredients. He had thought that he could, perhaps, reconstruct the antidote. Maybe visit some hidden street vendors Mishrah could tell him about. And everything, every single thing had just been dashed to the ground. He remembered the first time he had been handed over the recipe of the corruption. He had always wanted the most powerful corruption and had come across a mention of the Whisper of Dread. His father, Victor Sen, used to call it 'undeniable'. And now Adri realised why. He felt stupid, cheated. Everything had failed. Everything was lost. His father had been kidnapped; Death was after him; and now his responsibility would die because of his personal choice of venom; and her brother would not only hate Adri for life, but would probably put the Angels on his tail—if Kaavsh got to know about this, which he inevitably would. He might as well give up right now. But then again, there was something else. Something new. The dead man hadn't stopped talking.

'You are asking for a cure because someone is afflicted, eh?' Mishrah asked for the second time.

'Yes.'

'Someone you care for?' Mishrah asked further.

Adri hesitated for a second. But there was no time to ask himself questions. 'Yes, I do,' he said.

'Then you must weigh your love in ounces.'

'Meaning?'

'Meaning yes, there might just be a way to save her; but sometimes being dead is better than being alive—like *that*.'

'Come to the point, healer.'

'Something was here, among us dead. But now it walks among the living. It is spreading, and spreading fast. And it might just be the key to saving the one you care for— if you can call that saving. What I'm referring to, of course, is a Devil Mask.'

Adri's eyebrows narrowed. 'A Devil Mask has escaped?'

'From our side, yes. And it's on the loose, if I'm not wrong.'

'I would not call that a solution. But thank you.'

Mishrah's eyes glinted in the light. 'We will soon walk the earth. Perhaps we shall meet again.'

Adri was about to get up, but he paused.

'The Apocalypse is on its way,' Mishrah continued. 'The dead hear it coming closer and closer. Like drums. We wait for our summons.'

Adri took one last look at Mishrah, then he turned around and walked back down the aisle and out of the hall. The last fight sequence in the film was underway; he had made it out in time.

Well that was informative, the Wraith said.

'This Doomsday business is also getting to me,' Adri said as he walked back down the corridors. 'I'm hearing about it more and more, from the living as well as the dead.'

Load of crap if you ask me. We've always been fascinated by the idea of our own deaths. It's romanticism, nothing more. And you are a bloody idiot if you're concentrating on this rather than what Mishrah had to say about the corruption.

'You can stop with the spirit vision now.'

A plan was already forming in Adri's mind. Something devious yet exciting, something that involved risks, and if everything went absolutely, absolutely right, then maybe Maya could be saved. Everything hinged on the bloody Devil Mask; it had chosen a good time to cross the River. The last one had entered about a hundred years ago. He had read stories about that one. If Mishrah's information was correct—and the healer did not really have any reason to lie—then yes, Maya could be saved. And he was doing it again, he realised—endangering too many lives to save one. Adri waved these thoughts aside. Useless, come to obstruct the present. First things first, he needed to explain things to Gray. It all depended on Gray's decision now.

'So what? So there's no cure?' Gray asked ten minutes later. Adri had just begun to explain.

'No antidote. But there's something else,' Adri said.

'What? What something else? What can we do?'

Fayne was sitting behind Gray, looking at Adri silently. The assassin's charge was more important to the assassin than his life; such had constantly been the teachings of Ahzad. Nothing had changed. The assassin was deciding his next move. Adri looked at Fayne and then at Gray. 'Have you heard of something called a Devil Mask?'

Fayne sat back, leaning against a wall. He had understood Adri's entire plan.

'My grandmother,' Gray said after a moment of silence. 'She used to tell me stories when I was a child, because I was a little Demon who refused to sleep. She had a tale in which there was this word. Devil Mask.'

'It is a dead-puppeteer. It raises revenant, controls them, spreads them like an infection. It is a Necrotic, a being from the other side, a vicious devourer of life. Yes, it exists for real; but rarely do they cross the River. Yet one has, and is loose in Old Kolkata, if I'm not wrong.'

Gray nodded, waiting for Adri to continue, unsettled by the description of the creature.

'But every Devil Mask needs a host. Like every other parasitic entity, it cannot survive without one. And my point is' —Adri looked into Gray's eyes— 'that the host is *always* kept alive by the Necrotic. Always, no matter what condition the host might be in.'

Gray nodded slowly. 'Even a host under the influence of the Whisper of Dread?'

'Yes. Even that.'

'Then what?'

'The Devil Mask heals the host and keeps it in a perfect condition; the irony being that this undead creature needs a living thing to survive, a *heart* if you will. And then, if we can remove the host from the Necrotic—'

'Then we will kill it and Maya will live,' Gray said, a new light starting to dawn in his eyes.

'But there's something else,' Adri said.

'What?'

It was Fayne who continued. 'Killing a Devil Mask,' the assassin said, his voice dead calm. 'The damn thing can only be killed by penetrating it and killing the host, thus forcing the creature to die. And men have been lost on it, good men. Lots of men. As for killing the Mask *and* getting the host back alive, it has never been done.'

'Doesn't mean it can't be done,' Gray said. 'Right?'

'If you walk down this path I will go with you. I go with Maya Ghosh, you know that,' Fayne said. 'But you should also consider the alternative, brother of Maya.'

'Do you mean—' Gray started.

'Once she is inside the mask, it is a tortured existence, a damned thing. Each breath is a little more not worth taking than the one before. And the pain, it is supposed to be unbelievable. If we do not succeed in freeing her, it is the greatest injustice we could ever be doing to her,' Adri said. 'The choice between such an existence, Gray, and a painless death is up to *you*. You are her family and thus you alone will decide.'

'There is a chance, right?' Gray said, shaking his head gently.

'It has never been done before, as Fayne said,' Adri replied.

'But do you think you can do it, Adri?'

232

Adri looked down the road. 'Yes, I think so,' he said.

'That is good enough for me. Do you not understand, Adri? If there is even a sliver of hope, a mere sliver, then I will see this to the end before I let my sister die.'

Adri looked at the unconscious Maya. 'We're not going to let her die, Gray,' he said firmly. 'If we need to find the Devil Mask, we need to find MYTH. If it's really on the loose, then they will know where it is. But before that, we have to stabilise Maya. The healer told me of a brew that could do it. I'll make it. Shouldn't take me too much time.'

'This is just getting so complicated,' Gray mumbled. 'I should've just stayed back in New Kolkata.'

'Your sister had an agenda,' Adri said, starting to rummage around in his bag.

'I don't know what she could have been looking for,' Gray said. 'I already told you that.'

'The assassin could put light on that,' Adri spoke. 'But he's got his code to think about.'

'Apologies,' Fayne said.

The Dreamer's Brew wasn't hard to make, but it involved some rare ingredients. Adri was sure he had most of them, but there was always the highly elusive Aujour that needed worrying about. Adri hoped he would have it, but a quick search revealed he did not. He decided to search more thoroughly.

Gray walked up to where Fayne was sitting, close to the unconscious body of his sister. 'Can she hear us?' he asked.

'No,' Fayne replied. 'The corruption forces one into a coma. She will remain trapped within her recent thoughts, she will be reliving them in a loop.'

'Does it hurt?'

'*Rashkor*. It is painless right up to the last breath,' Fayne replied. 'Do not be concerned.'

'You have a strange way of saying things,' Gray said, shaking his head.

'You have said that before. I am direct. But some people, they prefer this quality in a contract killer. If I were to be sarcastic and rude, I doubt I would have access to the clientele that I do now.'

'You could make a lot of my doubts go away if you just told me who you're working for now. It would really help, man.'

'Apologies, again.'

Gray looked at Fayne. 'Can I take a photograph of you?'

'No,' Fayne said.

'Why do you wear that mask?' Gray asked.

'Stop asking questions,' Fayne said.

Adri swore loudly.

'I do not have Aujour!' he exclaimed angrily when they looked at him.

'Wait, so my sister is going to die because you shot her with something that has no cure, and now you don't have some ingredient which could've at least slowed down the effect of the poison?' Gray exclaimed, incredulous.

Adri looked at his watch. 'There's still time. I'll have to go and find a dealer. It won't take long.'

'I'll come along this time,' Gray said. Adri knew he couldn't refuse, not after having put himself in another false position. They hurried off towards where Adri knew a few dealers lived; Fayne remained behind to guard Maya.

15

A map of Old Kolkata lay open on the table, a burning candle next to it. Small, carefully modelled wooden pieces lay strewn all over the yellowed parchment, giving it the semblance of a board game, except for the goblet playing paperweight at the edge, filled with a dark red liquid that suspiciously resembled blood. There were markings on the map, infinitely spread notes and arrow marks and circles. The table also supported dozens of books, all thickly bound. The candle was not the only source of light in the room. There were a few glowing crystals in a corner, where they had been disregarded. Near this heap of crystals was a human skull. It had been cleaned and the top had been sliced off; something now burned in the brain cavity amidst hot coals, releasing veils of thin reddish smoke that filled the room. The walls were cold stone, bare, apart for a couple of magnificent shields, mounted rather occasionally. In another corner stood a mannequin. It had once been a human, but now he was long dead, and his body had been stuffed and impaled on a stand. It wore a suit of armour that looked rare and rather frightening, but it obviously wasn't the owner.

No, the owner sat silently on a small wooden stool, between two large windows, their curtains billowing against the assault of the wind. His eyes were closed, and yet he did not seem relaxed; his body was taut, ready.

'Commander!' came a cry.

Demon Commander Ba'al's eyes fluttered open. His red irises pierced through the semi-darkness of the room, and he looked at the messenger.

'Speak,' he said in a voice hard with experience.

The messenger was a gargoyle, an ugly creature made completely of stone, with huge bat wings protruding behind him. However, it chose to wear its inner skin in front of Ba'al, as a gesture of respect. Not that it made the gargoyle any less ugly. 'A Demon has come from Hazra, Commander, bearing certain *news*.'

The Demon Commander nodded, and the gargoyle continued, 'There were two Demons—warriors—patrolling one of the roads there when they were attacked. One of them was killed; the other one managed to escape his negative circle and has just reached us.'

'Necromancers?' Ba'al asked, an involuntary growl starting to build within his throat.

'Yes, Commander. But just one. He had allies. The Demon who escaped, however, he has something to tell you in person. He requests an audience.'

'Send him in.'

'Forgive me, Commander, but I doubt he will fit.'

'Ah yes. I will meet him in the courtyard then.'

The gargoyle bowed and exited the room. Ba'al got to his feet and turned around. He walked up to one of the large windows in the room and stepped off. Five floors down, he landed on his feet. Recovering from the drop, he looked around. The inner courtyard was empty as it should've been—the guards on the battlements were vigilant. Torches burned in brackets along the walls, casting light on the Demon before him. The Demon was evidently nervous; its tail was between its legs and it hung its head low in respect and anxiety. It towered over the Demon Commander with its size, but refused to impress. Ba'al surveyed it closely.

'What is your name?' he asked.

'Gnu Shi'l Un Aishth, Commander,' the Demon replied.

'And your deceased partner?'

'Garth Ol Eshan.'

'Do not mourn him. He will be prayed for, if not remembered,' Ba'al said. 'What did you have to tell me, Gnu?'

The Demon lifted its eyes ever so slightly to look into the eyes of the Demon Commander. Meeting his burning gaze, it dropped its eyes again, immediately. 'They were not MYTH. Of this I am certain, Commander.'

'Not MYTH? Then who could they be, wandering around Old Kolkata with the power to end Demons?' Ba'al mused.

'I do not know, Commander. There were three of them. I took on the Tantric, but before my escape, I saw Garth under siege by three assailants. Magical arms by the sounds of them. I also saw some red blades fly, of the kind I haven't seen before.'

'Your escape let Garth die, incidentally. The power of two warrior Demons isn't something they could have withstood easily. There is, after all, a reason why you are *paired* whence patrolling,' Ba'al said, a rumble of anger in his deep voice.

'Forgive me, Commander. I thought it best to live with the information of this enemy.'

'Nothing you have said has been of any help so far. Unless—'

Ba'al approached Gnu, who immediately shrank back a little, looking tremendously scared. The Demon Commander stopped right in front of the Demon, however, and sniffed. His eyes opened ever so slightly as he sniffed again, and then again.

'I do not have many Demons, Gnu. My forces are hardly as vast as MYTH's,' Ba'al said. 'This war must be fought though, and the Old City cannot fall to the hands of the Necromancers. It is for this reason that I will let you live. Go and rest.'

Gnu trembled and sniffed as he slowly bowed before the Demon Commander before walking away as commanded, the ground moving under the weight of his footsteps. Ba'al stood, watching him go. After the giant creature had passed out of sight, he turned around and walked, but not back towards his tower. Instead, Ba'al chose to walk towards the hall he called the *Septaranium*, where his great collection of books was herded by the old man Hermlock. The great doors of the hall swung open as he approached, and they shut after he had passed through. Even though he was preoccupied, Ba'al remembered to tread lightly; he was barefoot and his claws could easily damage the Septaranium's carpets. Hermlock saw him coming and shuffled towards him, but Ba'al waved him away as he passed. The old man understood; the master was going to his secret chamber.

It was behind a bookshelf. Ba'al was one to uphold certain clichés he felt were amusing, and secret passages behind bookshelves had existed since time immemorial. Nothing was amusing, however, about the passages beyond—all the richness and grandeur of the great library melted away into darkness and a tunnel made of dirty stone. A flame burst into existence in Ba'al's open palm as he walked into the darkness. He could see in the dark; the fire was meant for things lurking in the darkness, so they would not think him for some treasure hunter.

And they did recognise him. It was Ba'al! Thus they did not even dare face him, they slithered and crawled away and hid as he approached. Everyone knew what the Demon Commander was capable of, no one wanted to test his patience, or ignite his wrath. Ba'al saw the entrance of the first room soon, but that was not where he was headed. The Demon Knights that stood guard at the first door saluted briefly as he passed by and then resumed their posts.

Ba'al immediately wished he had more Demon Knights in his army. They were, aside from a few special Demons he kept for special purposes, the most hardy and versatile soldiers he had ever had the honour of commanding. Once every now and then, a Tantric would decide he was powerful enough to summon a

Demon Knight; in most cases this was not the situation and the Knight ended up killing the Tantric and finding its way to Ba'al to join the Free Demons. The Demon Commander could not summon Demons himself, and he dearly hated this restriction.

Doors went by and Ba'al did not stop. When he finally did, it was in front of a crude wooden door, unguarded. He opened it and the stench of blood washed over him immediately. Ba'al had already eaten so it did not affect him. He entered the room and spoke, 'Chhaya.'

'Master,' replied a hiss that seemed to come from a corner.

Ba'al moved the fireball around and looked at all the corpses. 'You've been rather busy, I see,' he said. 'Something has come up.'

'You but have to ask,' the creature replied, still in the darkness. Sounds of soft tearing of flesh reached Ba'al's ears. Chhaya was still eating.

'Adri Sen is in Old Kolkata,' Ba'al said, and the sounds stopped. Liquid shadow swirled, soundlessly, immediately, and the creature formed itself in front of Ba'al, kneeling on one knee, its wings folded.

'I remember him *quite* well, Master,' Chhaya said, white fangs glinting in the semi-darkness.

'I know, and thus you will be the one to recognise him the easiest,' Ba'al said. 'I have a task for you.'

16

'I'm going to kill you, Adri Sen,' Gray spoke.

Adri sat and thought. There wasn't much time left.

'I'm regretting the fact that I ever met you,' Gray continued.

'If that shotgun tells you to pull the trigger on me, don't,' Adri said, eyeing the Sadhu's Shotgun with an amount of casual caution.

'Yes, my shotgun talks to me all the time!' Gray yelled. 'What's wrong with you? You're going to kill my sister!'

'Let me think,' Adri said. 'Shut up and let me think, Gray.'

'I don't believe this guy,' Gray said, walking away from Adri, tearing at his white hair.

Adri lit a cigarette and thought about possible options. The dealers didn't have Aujour. In fact, it would be pretty impossible to get it from anywhere at this time of the night. The Settlements would shoot them if they went knocking, and any stash he knew about was too far away to reach by sunrise. He needed people who brewed, who would use ingredients—

He stood up. An idea again. Reckless, but yes, would get the job done. Which was becoming his modus operandi ever so fast.

And what, pray, is your idea? the Wraith asked.

'The Hive. They will have Aujour.'

Pfft. They also have death, which they serve by the droves, and for free!

'It's the only shot left right now. It's everything left in *me* right now,' Adri spoke true. His strength was failing for lack of sleep, and yet his guilt kept him up. But it was also wearing him down and he knew he would not last for long now. He needed to do something about it before he had Maya's blood on his hands.

Adri walked over to Fayne and had a talk with him. Fayne was okay with his idea, even though he said they wouldn't live to pull it off. 'We are not an army,' were his exact words.

'There are many entrances to the Hive. We aren't going to take the main one. We'll be sneaking in,' Adri said.

'You bear the mark on your wrist,' Fayne said. 'They will smell you. The hive is a network, they will come from everywhere.'

'I'm prepared to take that chance. They have a range. How good are you at killing witches?'

'I know them well. I was born of one,' Fayne replied.

'What?' Adri exclaimed, thrown off guard.

'Stories can wait, *pashlin*,' Fayne said calmly. 'Yes, I can kill them well.'

'Gray will have to carry his sister then,' Adri said, looking at Gray, who in the distance, was throwing stones at windows.

Imagine an area with twenty to thirty skyscrapers, and now imagine half of them collapsing into each other, merging within themselves and destroying each other partially, even penetrating the ground at places, breaking the roads, going underground. Now imagine a lack of light in such an area, turning it into a dark labyrinth of broken walls and collapsed passageways, some opening to the surface and some leading deeper into the subterranean. And finally, imagine a pack of predators taking over such an area for

241

their lair, their home-ground, and one could probably come close to knowing what the Hive was. This was how Adri told Gray to imagine it, and Gray did not like it.

'Wild goose chases, Adri. That's all you're leading us on while the clock is ticking on Maya.'

'So far nothing has been irrelevant. I have gotten information at every single stop that we've made,' Adri replied, now irritated. 'If your sister hadn't run off, I wouldn't have had to resort to the corruption, which, by the way, is the reason she's not sucking blood right now. Everything's got another side to it, Gray. Grow up.'

'You are being unreasonable,' Fayne told Gray, who could not believe his ears.

'I'm just concerned, okay?' he protested vehemently. 'My sister's dying!'

'You can help instead of complaining,' Adri said. 'For example, you can show an interest in where we are headed right now.'

It took Gray some time to swallow his anger and pride. He knew he was being a little unreasonable, but he didn't want to stop; he was feeling increasingly helpless and he needed someone to blame. But he was curious; they had been travelling for the longest time now. Sunrise was not too far away and Adri seemed to have a plan up his sleeve once more. Better to let go of the anger and hear it out.

'Where are we headed then?' he asked. 'Take a deep breath, Gray. Anger never gets you anywhere,' Adri said.

Gray nodded, biting back an urge to start shouting again.

'Good. We're headed to the Hive, the place I just told you to imagine. It's the lair of the Dynes, the witches. When in human form, they are fantastic brewers, which means they will have entire assortments of ingredients there. Aujour should easily be found. What is not easy is getting there.'

'Wasn't it *one* witch that gave you the shoulder wound?' Gray asked incredulously. 'How many will the Hive have?'

'A little less than a thousand, if my estimates are correct.'

'A thousand? A thousand witches?' Gray squeaked.

The very chance of their survival lay in the less populated routes, the ones the witches avoided. The tunnels were numerous, and travellers usually stuck to a route until the witches discovered their travelling with nasty ambushes; then the routes were changed. Adri had been through the Hive many times without harm. But tonight they needed to go where he had never gone before—to the very heart of the place where the elder Dynes lived. There was almost no chance, Adri knew, of reaching and leaving the place alive with the amount of Aujour needed—but caution was for the winds now. The clock was ticking; any chance would have to be taken if it served the purpose at hand.

'We will need to be dead silent. And you will have to carry Maya,' Adri said.

'Me?' Gray exclaimed, still not able to believe where they were headed.

'Fayne will need both hands free, as will I. We need to take her with us, because we won't have the time to go in, get the Aujour, come back, and make the brew. I will have to do it in the Hive itself.'

'A thousand witches,' Gray mumbled.

Maya was in space. Everything seemed unreal and though she saw things around her she could not believe them. A vortex of swirling visions surrounded her, things which glowed brightly and whispered amidst the darkness, things of different colours. Some protected her, some mocked her. She tried not to look at them, but her eyes would just not shut. Her body refused to listen to her; it was as if she had no control over anything, and was just a spectator. Thoughts morphed into visions, and she re-imagined past happenings and events, with strange, new entities making their way in and out, familiarly. Something lingered on in her memory, something she had read recently—words, which she was now visualising, clear as day. It was a painting. A portrait, an exact replication, painted beautifully, masterfully. Adri, clearly in his late teens, stood looking at it.

His clothes looked worn and used—his face dirty, his hair cut short. His frame suggested he was tired; he looked ready to drop, and yet he stood and gazed at the painting. Maya did not get to measure how long he looked at it; her dreamlike state was confusing her, and time was something she found herself unable to keep track of. However, when Adri did move, it was not soon.

'She was beautiful,' Victor said. Adri did not turn as Victor entered the room, dressed in a housecoat over loose pyjamas. Adri continued to look at the portrait. Maya noticed then the bag he had dropped by his side. The bag not only looked just as dusty and tattered as his clothes, but also had the occasional dark stain Maya suspected to be blood.

'You never got to meet her,' Victor said slowly, looking at Adri.

'I know,' Adri replied.

Victor turned to look at the painting, and there was silence as the woman looked down at them calmly, smiling. Adri turned to Victor. 'How did she die?'

'Well,' Victor replied.

'You know what I mean,' Adri was serious and smile-less.

'We have talked about this before, Adri.'

'And I have never been satisfied with either your answers, or the one note she left me,' Adri was talking fast. Maya got the distinct impression that he had been through this before, as though he had the lines ready.

Victor was unaffected. 'My answers will remain the same.' He turned and started walking back into the corridors from which he had emerged. 'Come.'

Adri picked up the bag and followed. So did Maya.

It was the same house that they had been in, once grand. Maya saw that several heavy curtains lined the corridors, and one had to part them as one proceeded. A security measure, of course. Demons got confused by curtains.

Maya got to see the now ruined library in all its glory, for that is where they went. Victor sat down on a chaise-lounge next to a reading desk. A half finished drink and an open book suggested he had been reading. Adri collapsed into a chair opposite his father and leaned back, reaching into his jeans pocket.

'I loved your mother,' Victor said. 'I do not need to say that anymore and I won't. I've told you this before, and we will not go through this again.'

Adri lit a cigarette and took a long, lazy drag. 'We will go through this again and again, Father,' he said, 'until you will answer *all* my questions.'

Silence brewed.

'You are a Tantric under the employ of MYTH. Currently your status is black and you are answerable to me,' Victor said, grim. 'We will now discuss your mission, and nothing else.'

Adri breathed out smoke. 'All right, then. But I'm not letting this slide, Father.' There was a twist of the lip in the way he said the last word.

Victor did not react. 'How many have returned?' he asked.

'Just me,' Adri replied.

'I will expect detailed reports about all of the rest on my table later.'

'They were good. They knew their stuff.'

'Not good enough, apparently. Any of them MIA?'

'All of them were killed. Bad deaths, but had to happen if we were to bag the *thing*.'

'Which you did, I presume?'

In reply, Adri unzipped his bag and reached within. Maya saw hair. Adri was grabbing *hair*—and then she winced as Adri withdrew a severed head from the inside. It was a Demon's head, much larger than a normal human head, black-skinned and black-haired, and much, much more animalistic than humanoid. It was a Feral, Maya realised, and even from where she stood, she could make out the abnormally large fangs. Adri let the head hang and sway; he looked at it without expression, smoking his cigarette.

'Not bad,' Victor said, looking at the head with a half smile. 'You went quite overboard with the evidence though.'

'This bastard deserved it,' Adri said.

Maya had been here before. She knew about this. In some time Adri was going to retire to his room and then scribble in his diary, a diary she had already read. Right now, however, she could *see* it all, vivid and detailed. She did not know if it was merely her imagination filling in all the blanks for her or something else at work, but it was something she could get used to. The Demon's head, for example, she could see the wretched thing for exactly what it was—from the dull red eyes to the leathery skin—and it was not something she had ever seen, for her fat books never had illustrations.

Adri let the head drop onto the carpet. The blood had dried up already—it landed like a heavy piece of wood wrapped in dry paper, and rolled onto one side. Victor looked down at the carpet, at the brink of what could be called objection, but did not say anything. Adri smoked lazily, but it was evident that Victor could see what he was—a string stretched taut. All Adri needed, or seemed to need, was an excuse.

'You've come from a long way off,' Victor said. 'Get some rest. We'll discuss the mission later.'

'I'm fine with now, in case that's what you mean.'

'No. Later,' Victor said.

Adri looked at his father expressionlessly for a moment before he got up. The conversation was over. Ignoring the severed head, he grabbed his bag and trudged off into the corridor and upstairs, parting curtains with his face. Maya decided to follow him. Her last glance at Victor found him grim, staring at the Demon's head with dark, serious eyes. Adri entered his room and shut the door behind him; Maya realised she was merely a link to his memory and not in some time machine as she passed through the solid door. Adri stubbed the cigarette out in an ashtray and smoothly lit another one, pausing briefly before a drawer. His hand halfway to the drawer, he stopped, and then with a tired and resigned yawn, he entered an open bathroom, and turned on the shower. Then he started to unbutton.

Adri looked at the structure through eyes that remembered. A place of death, a maze to beat all mazes, a lair hiding a dangerous kind of predator. He lit a cigarette and looked at the Hive silently. It was dark, but fires burned occasionally, throwing certain parts of the building into light. He saw silhouettes crawling about for mere seconds before they would disappear. There was an eerie sense of quiet in and around the Hive, and even beyond the demolished wall behind which they crouched, they could feel it. Nothing really moved much; even the night winds chose to stay still.

'Why would you want Maya and me to enter that thing?' Gray whispered urgently.

'You will die a grisly death if you stay here,' Fayne replied.

'Quiet,' Adri whispered.

Witches. I see them. Mazumder spoke.

Adri smoked silently, taking cover behind the wall every time its burning end flared in the night.

'They will smell your cigarette, Tantric,' Fayne said.

He was right. Adri was so used to smoking to just reduce his stress, if not to continually maintain the natural armour that the flames were, that he hadn't thought about this. He stubbed out the cigarette without showing any apparent hurry. Then he checked his revolvers in the dim light of a faraway fire—all ten chambers held mercury rounds. Witches. How he hated them.

One of them is heading this way, the Wraith cursed softly.

'One coming this way,' Fayne said. Adri saw that he was already holding a couple of his red daggers ready. Where did they all come from anyway? Gray was supporting Maya's limp body, as their agreement had been. They ducked deeper and slumped behind the wall, resting their backs on the approaching witch. She made no noise as she came closer.

'You have the mark,' Fayne said.

Adri nodded.

'Then she will have already smelt you. She knows who you are,' he continued. 'We cannot allow her to alert more Dynes.'

Adri nodded again.

This was the moment she chose to leap above them. In a perfect aerial one-eighty degree turn, she landed on all fours, facing them. They barely got seconds to look at the withered but powerful figure, the flying, dirty hair and the burning eyes, before she sprung. The intended target was Gray, but a mercury round caught her in mid-air, as Adri's gun erupted in white smoke. The witch screeched as she hit the dirt. Within a moment, Fayne had slit her throat, cutting her shriek in half. He got up from the corpse and looked around quickly.

'Lucky,' he said.

No one said anything as the group moved slowly towards the Hive, checking the area for witches. Gray took a last glance at the unmoving Dyne. *There had been no possible choice,* he told himself.

In the semi-darkness there was no way to distinguish one fallen building from another—it all seemed like one solid structure designed by some drunk architect. Fayne, as always, could see just as well in the darkness as the average werecat—he led the way. They moved towards a small window, partially buried beneath rubble. Fayne kicked it in and cleared the glass away effortlessly, and through it, they entered the Hive.

Darkness became black. The silence bothered Gray even more than the darkness. With everything dark and quiet, their breathing seemed loudest; Gray himself was practically panting from Maya's weight.

'You cannot see,' Fayne said softly. 'We cannot risk fire here. You must follow me to the best of your ability.'

Adri did not argue and stamped out Gray's squeaks of protest. What followed was not something to be remembered fondly— Fayne led in complete darkness, Gray carrying Maya in the middle, and Adri bringing up the rear, guiding Gray the best he could based on the Wraith's whispered directions. Nothing was smooth though—Gray and Adri bumped into pillars and walls, tripped and stumbled and tried to mask their cries of pain the best they could, for every word they spoke would echo in the darkness for minutes altogether. They moved through flats and garages, down horizontal lift shafts, through destroyed art galleries and dry swimming pools, all fused together underground in an unnerving swirl. Gray could not carry Maya for the entire way, and Adri took over whenever Gray could not take it anymore. They heard nothing, except for the scurrying of rats in the darkness around them. Surprisingly enough, they did not run into any more witches even though Fayne was leading them into the very Heart of the Hive.

All I have to do is give you spirit vision and you will be able to see everything.

The Wraith did keep talking throughout their journey. It told Adri how he should have come clean about its presence, and how its capabilities were being wasted. It also kept telling Adri about

249

its past; the complete silence in the Hive did not let Adri shut him up and the Wraith took full advantage of that.

Maya had turned away, and now when Adri came out wearing just his jeans, she saw the recent cuts and all the dried blood crisscrossing his frame—all of which would become scars. He lit a cigarette as she looked on, and although she realised she was getting used to Adri smoking all the time, it troubled her to think that he had started so early. This wasn't really a good habit, although people around him seemed to have gotten accustomed to it. Victor evidently had, and Maya did not like that. She did not know what to think about Victor anymore; her opinions had changed drastically over the last few days as she read the diaries, realising that he wasn't that perfect a hero when it came to taking care of a family, raising a son. She had seen, however, in Victor's eyes, that he had tried—she had seen the tired resignation that can only come after a lot of trials, after regret and attempts without fruit towards making good on one's mistakes. She had caught a glimpse of the father in Victor when he told Adri to go and rest, moments ago. Victor was also conflicted, and terribly so. His face though, would remain a mask to her—stealing diaries was not one of her hobbies, and thus everything she would gather about Victor would be from Adri's memories, distant and scattered as they were. It was dysfunctional, this father and son relationship. It was lost, disintegrated, fraught with friction. Both of them suffered in their own way. In silence. Maya realised that the only thing that had united them, or would ever unite them was the portrait of Adri's mother in the hall. When they had stood looking at it, Adri and Victor were father and son. They had not needed words. There had been an understanding, one Adri broke when he attacked his father for information. Victor resisted firmly, like a stone.

Adri was clearly a loner. There were no signs of a lover, or even a friend, in his room. Yes, there was angst. His clothes. His scars. Maya, however, could not sense an outlet, a release. Anger and confusion, and no listener. No one to share Adri's pain. Even with all his power and his immense capabilities as a Tantric, Adri was alone.

Maya could not blame him. If Adri kept secrets from his diaries, it was a different thing, but going by what she had read, and was presently seeing, Maya wished she could have been there for him. As a friend. As a listener. As someone who could've helped him. Adri was very strong, something she had realised a long time back. None of his entries had ever spoken of him crying or breaking down; nor had she ever come across dried tears on the pages. And now that he was alone, and the door behind him was locked, he still did not break. His face was impassive, cut out of stone, bearing a constant expressionless expression as he made his way to his bag and withdrew a leather satchel.

Maya inched closer. This was a memory, she reminded herself. *There is no way he will be able to sense you. Or harm you.* Maya knew she was scared of Adri. She was only just beginning to realise what Adri was actually capable of, and how little of his true self he guardedly displayed. However, she did not want to forget him. She did not want to leave him to his confusions and flee. No, Adri still intrigued her, and if nothing else, a mixture of sympathy and curiosity would keep her at the young Tantric's side.

Adri had withdrawn a small piece of parchment and was scribbling on it furiously with a black fountain pen. Maya leaned forward to read what he was writing but he was already done; he rolled up the parchment into a small tube and Maya caught the word *Keeper*, before Adri withdrew something more interesting from his bag. She recognised the object instantly—a small metal dragonfly powered by a sliver of a magical artefact. Adri put the parchment into a hollow on its tail and let it fly. Its tiny metal wings whirred into sudden motion in mid-air and cutting a deep arc, it swished out of an open window. Adri had just sent a message. But to whom? And about what? Maya did not know. It was not something he had mentioned in his diaries, nor had the word *Keeper* ever been mentioned in what she had read so far. But how could she see it if this was just a part of his diary memory? As Maya dealt with her revelation, Adri took out a small black book—something Maya was all too familiar with—and started to write.

Maya watched, fascinated. Adri was writing his diary, describing everything she had just been through—he was making her present happen in the past. But her new doubts about what had just happened assailed her, and she sat on Adri's bed wearily and watched him write.

'Light,' Fayne spoke under his breath.

Adri had seen it too, in the distance. Flickering light, reflecting off puddles of water and pieces of broken glass. Silent light; they could still be heard, their whispers still shouts.

'Where are we?' Adri whispered.

'We are where you wanted to be,' Fayne said. 'At the Heart of the Hive.'

'Impossible,' Adri breathed. 'Not one witch so far.'

'I chose a route that made this possible. Do not doubt my abilities, Necromancer.'

'How many times have you been here?'

Fayne paused. 'I was born here,' he replied at length. 'These passages have not seen me for ages, but I have not forgotten them.'

No one said anything as they looked at the assassin standing silently facing them. The eyepieces of his mask reflecting the faraway light. His long hair still against his shoulders.

'Son of a witch,' Gray spoke softly.

'So your sight in complete darkness, it's a gift,' Adri said.

'I am not proud of my parentage,' Fayne said. 'It is something to be discussed later, if at all.'

He turned around and started moving towards the light. 'Up ahead,' he continued, 'there will be witches, and lots of them.'

'Don't they, err, cut you some slack?' Gray asked.

'After the hundreds I have killed? *Khabashud*. I think not.'

As they got closer, the silence began to leave. Voices crept into their ears now. Old voices. Withered voices. Chanting.

'I led us around the back. They will not be guarding this entrance,' Fayne said as they found the source of the light: a circular door at the end of a dirt tunnel. An entrance. The Heart of the Hive. They were overlooking a cavern, a giant underground hollow, brightly illuminated by torches. Witches, of course, did not need light to see, and hence the fire was being used for—

'Cooking? Are they cooking?' Gray asked incredulously.

'Yes,' Adri replied.

There was a gigantic stone cauldron in the middle of the cavern, a cauldron about fifteen feet tall and around the same size across. A stew bubbled within. The door they were crouching at was at a height, and they had a vantage point of almost the entire cavern before them; it also meant, unfortunately, that they could see what was cooking in the cauldron—apart from the occasional human limb and head that floated and submerged, crows and bats, snakes still alive, wiggling, strange and peculiar vegetables and other unrecognisables. Unmentionables. The brew was a thick and murky yellow. Red. Green. A circle of smaller cauldrons surrounded the big one, all with something cooking in them. After these visions, the smell that had been there seemed to hit them with new force—partly nauseating, a thick stench of blood along with various different smells.

'They are in human form . . .' Adri said absently to himself, his mind working furiously.

There were about thirty Dynes in the cavern. Old women who looked very, very old and hopelessly out of place; their clothing was strictly in various shades of grey and black, and their skin, old, wrinkled, and scabby, seemed unclean and weathered even from a distance. They cackled and laughed and talked loudly, their dirty hair moving about as they went around stirring the brews, adding more and more ingredients. The big cauldron had a ladder that led to a wooden platform above it. No one seemed to bother with stirring—it was simply too big.

There were other exits to the cavern, Adri noticed. Since this was the Heart of the Hive, it was connected to every other area of the Hive. Which practically meant that if alerted, Dynes could come out of everywhere. He counted four ground routes, seven in the walls, one in the ceiling.

'So, what now?' Gray asked. He was apprehensive. Watching old women, clad in dark hues and laughing in unearthly voices gave him the chills. It wasn't tough to believe these women could transform into the merciless creatures that witches were.

The assassin looked around keenly. 'Place hasn't changed,' he grunted.

'If you are a Tantric, why the hell are you always travelling without spirits?' Gray asked Adri.

Adri made a face. 'Let's see—perhaps because the time involved in summoning could be better used for saving your sister, yes?'

'You are the one who took your so-called *responsibility*!' Gray spat.

The eternal debate, the Wraith hissed. *I've heard this so many times it's not even funny anymore.*

'We need to figure out a way to procure the Aujour,' Fayne said. 'Where can we find it?'

'I've already spotted the damn thing,' Adri said. He pointed into the distance, amidst the smaller cauldrons and the witches, to a small wooden trunk stuffed to the brim with every kind of ingredient one could imagine. 'Behind the lobster claws, poking out. The red herb.'

Fayne looked at it and nodded.

'I heard assassins make great thieves,' Gray said.

'You heard wrong,' Fayne replied. 'Tantric, what's the plan?'

'Is there one?' Gray asked. Adri looked at Gray in a way that Gray didn't like.

'Have you ever done any sneaking, Gray?' Adri asked.

'No.'

'Good. First time for everything, then. You're going to leave Maya here and sneak all the way to the Aujour and bring it back. While you do that' —Adri groped in his bag, while Gray's eyes widened in horror— 'I will create a smell distraction.'

'It's a barren cavern! How am I supposed to *sneak* past the witches?' Gray protested.

'They're *Bahzeeradynes*,' Fayne replied, looking down at the cavern. 'Only the elders are allowed in the Heart of the Hive.'

'Elder witches are blind,' Adri added.

Gray looked. It was true. The Dynes did not have eyes, just hollow, sunken sockets. They seemed to know the area extremely well though, and not once did they stumble while going around. They knew every ingredient by touch, and did not need to examine anything closely while they cooked. It was tough to believe that they could not see. Gray did not find much solace in this newfound revelation.

Adri held a glass orb in each hand. 'I will give you about ten minutes of smell which will keep them busy. Get to the chest, grab the red herb, and get out of there.'

'Why me?' Gray asked.

'Both Fayne and me are marked,' Adri said. 'We don't want the entire Coven rushing in here, do we?'

'But what if I get marked?'

'Elder witches don't do the marking. They do the cooking; you'll probably end up as an ingredient.'

Gray Kebab, the Wraith suggested.

Adri didn't say it. Gray looked nervous enough.

You had planned this, hadn't you? You were planning to use her brother here. For this, the Wraith whispered as Gray took his bag off, glancing nervously at the cavern below him. Adri did not reply, busying himself instead with taking out a length of rope from his bag.

Quite the manipulator you are.

'The last thing I want is you to be my conscience. All right?' Adri snapped softly. Gray strung the Sadhu's Shotgun over his shoulder and looked at Fayne and Adri.

An innocent lamb, headed for the—

'Let's do this, then,' Gray said, looking at Maya's still frame.

Fayne took the rope. 'I'll lower you down to the floor,' he said. After tying the rope securely around Gray's stomach, Fayne started to lower him down. Gray had barely descended an inch into the cavern when the assassin stopped. '*Myrkho.* Gray,' Fayne said.

'Yes?' a curious Gray asked, looking up.

'No matter what, do *not* eat the cookies.'

'The what?'

'The cookies. Do not eat them.'

'Umm, all right.'

Fayne continued to lower Gray down.

17

Adri threw the orbs. He aimed them away from where Gray was, as far as he could possibly manage. They shattered as they hit the floor, releasing an immediate, pungent odour. Gray hit the ground and watched the witches as they reacted. It was fast. Their heads whipped around, one after the other, towards where the orbs had landed. They did not, however, move.

Everything was silent. 'Why aren't they moving?' Adri whispered.

'Quiet,' Fayne said.

Gray was beginning to sweat. There was absolutely no sound, and he was right near the witches, flat on the hard, cold ground, half-hidden in the shadows. Not that the shadows would help.

'Who's there?' a Dyne asked, in a high voice that trembled.

'Who disturbs the brewing of poor blind women?' asked another.

No one spoke. 'Something is wrong,' a witch whispered.

'The smell keeps changing too rapidly,' another complained.

'Sisters?' a witch cried. 'Maybe it is someone with honour. Someone who can free our souls from the curse.'

'You're right. Are you an adventurer, a brave adventurer?' another witch started. 'You can help us. You can help us helpless old hags.'

Silence again. Gray's heart raced.

'No one falls for that one, Uskula,' a witch said with a sudden savage snicker.

'Not true. That time that young boy offered to help, remember? He was hiding. And then he emerged and asked us how to break the curse,' Uskula said.

'He tasted funny,' a witch murmured.

'Yes, but he still counts, doesn't he?' Uskula screeched. 'And you, Veela, your fat mouth just gave it away in case someone *is* hidding here!'

'Bah,' Veela dismissed. 'Let's just go and see what the smell is.'

All the witches moved together and started walking towards the smashed orbs. The distance wasn't too great, and Gray, even from his position, knew he would have to move fast, which he did, scuttling towards the trunk as fast as he could. He could see the damn thing clearly now, just a short distance away. He went from cauldron to cauldron, using them as cover, keeping a wary eye on the witches. Then the witches went beyond his sight, disappearing along the big cauldron in the centre, and Gray hurried to the trunk as fast as he could.

Fayne watched the witches moving past the big cauldron; they had almost reached the shattered glass. 'How long does the smell last?' he asked.

'Long enough. Gray has more than enough time to grab the Aujour and sneak back to the rope,' Adri replied, his eyes roving from the witches to Gray. Gray, however, was not moving. He was standing in front of the trunk. Standing perfectly still.

'What is he doing?' Adri hissed.

'It's the cookies,' Fayne replied.

'What? What cookies?'

Fayne looked at Adri. 'You haven't been in the Heart before, have you?'

They looked at Gray, looking down at the trunk motionlessly.

'I didn't spend my childhood playing hide-and-seek among these cauldrons, no,' Adri said.

Fayne ignored the crack. 'Cookies are the Coven's mantraps. They've been using them for a long time now, the elders.'

A loud murmur went up among the witches just then, drawing their attention.

'Trouble,' Adri said quietly.

'Broken glass, my sisters,' a witch exclaimed. 'Broken glass and a changing smell.'

'Toys of a Tantric,' Uskula grunted.

'So is there a Tantric here?'

'A filthy dead-talker?'

'The glass could not have arrived by itself.'

'Perhaps a sister brought it here, perhaps it's a little joke?'

'A joke by Tantrics, then! No one of the Coven would dare do this to the elders!'

'But Ailiya was rather mad the last time she did not get her share. Would she resort to such devilry?'

'Ailiya is not like this, sister! No, I sense trickery here. Tantrics!'

'This just might be something else, my sisters. This might be a simple ploy.'

'A distraction, perhaps?'

All the thirty witches turned their heads together. 'I would say a Tantric hides in these shadows,' one rasped. 'Separate the smells, sisters. We will find him.'

Gray was on his knees now. He was reaching towards the trunk.

'Too late. They're going to turn,' Adri cursed, going for his revolvers.

Ooh. Fun.

Fayne, saying nothing, stood up from his crouched stance.

It wasn't Gray's fault. Adri had never known about the cookies. A casual last-minute warning from Fayne had not been enough. They were right there, the cookies, in a small basket amidst the ingredients. Right in front of him. The cookies. Various colours, from a rare light shade of brown to the darkest dark chocolate. Looking right at him. Begging to be eaten. They smelt warm and heavenly, and Gray could see each individual crumb. He stared at them for a long time, taking in the sight, the beauty, the overpowering, thick smell. He picked one up and ate it.

The witches began to scream, all of them. Together. They screamed and screeched as if in torture. They threw their heads back and writhed in agony. Transformation. Their old papery skin ripped apart, as did their clothes. Old shaky limbs gave way to strong, bony ones underneath. Fangs emerged from under broken and rotting teeth; claws slid into place where there had once been dirty fingernails. It was as if the human body had been but a cocoon, hiding the monster underneath. The real witch was out now—lean, immediately falling to all fours like the predator it was. No burning eyes; a blank patch of tight, rotting skin where the eyes should've been. They were larger than normal witches, and looked stronger. They would have sniffed across the cavern looking for intruders if Gray had not chosen that very moment to bite the cookie. It was like an alarm siren that the thirty Dynes could perceive at the same time. They ran, they scampered, they charged in a beeline for Gray.

The spell broke when Gray took the bite; he realised he had done exactly what he shouldn't have.

He looked up and everything seemed to freeze in time for him. A witch was running straight at him, saliva dripping from her fangs—his death in person. He stared at the witch, not able o believe what a magnificent and terrifying hunter she was, not being able to believe that this creature was the end of everything for him. Something caught his eye above. A figure, hanging in mid-air, directly above the witch. An assassin, poised with both arms raised, red blades gleaming in gloved hands, tied hair flying round his suspended body like a lean whip, glassy eyepieces reflecting Gray's amazed face.

Then reality kicked in. Fayne landed on the witch when she was mere inches from Gray, and simultaneously sank two daggers into her throat. He used the witch as a cushion for his landing; literally bouncing off the bleeding creature he plunged straight into the pack of oncoming witches. His hands held blades again, which he swept in exact arcs, catching one witch in the throat and another in the face. Each time, he left the blades in the wounds; when he faced a new enemy, his hands, almost magically, held fresh daggers. Parrying claws with the flat sides of his blades, Fayne used the momentum of the oncoming horde as a matador might to strike deadly and exact blows in lightning flashes of speed.

Gray was frozen stiff, until a mercury round whistled past his ear and into a witch. He recovered and found his legs. Staggering, he hastily unhooked the shotgun from his back and looked around. Adri was walking towards him, firing away from both guns. His face was grim. He knew the odds. None of them were getting out of here alive. It was a sacrifice; their plan had never been good enough. Living by the edge could only take one so far. The alarm had already been sounded throughout the Hive. The screeches of war, the screeches of death were loud, echoing into the other caverns, as was the gunfire. They were up against thirty elder witches, not counting the hundreds that were probably on their way by now. This wasn't the way to die, to pull three others to the grave with him. It hadn't been his intention, no, it hadn't been what he had started out for. There was nothing to do now, nothing to do with his guilt but face it, face it like the witches, riddle it full of holes. His teeth were grit. Bloody hell. Everything done so far, useless, fruitless, bloody hell. Die, die, die. Die, cursed creatures. Die. He did not want to die far from home, but here there was no escape, no measures he could take, no twenty-four hour time limit, no pentacle to shield any aura. Here there was only death, and by lord, he would take some with him. At least the soil was of Kolkata, Old Kolkata, the Old City, *his* Old City.

Gray was confused. Cauldrons were overturning. Screeches and death knells. Shadows and the light. Chaos. Terror. And in the midst of it all was the assassin of Ahzad, who wasn't letting a single witch pass him by alive. The witches that skirted him were being picked off by Adri. Gray raised his shotgun nervously, looking for a possible target. There were too many and Gray shifted targets like a madman, unable to decide who to pull the trigger on.

Fayne stopped in the middle of a fatal thrust for a fraction of a second. 'Watch your fire,' he said and continued.

'Close range only, Gray!' Adri yelled. 'You might hit Fayne, those bullets will spread!'

A witch leapt for Gray that very instant, but he somehow managed to pick her off in mid-air. A couple of full-blown mercury shotgun rounds—the Dyne wasn't getting up again. The witches were still too many, Adri realised as he saw four Dynes running for him. He backed away, firing with both hands. Gray reloaded as fast as he could. For a second he looked up, and for the first time saw Fayne covered in blood, still fighting. He did not know whose blood it was, and before he had time to think a claw swiped his back.

'Yaargh!' Gray screamed, dropping the shotgun. The witch clawed him again and then leapt onto his back, dropping him to the floor. She was heavy, Gray realised. He found himself unable to move. Knowing he had seconds, he struggled madly, but he could not overturn the witch. His shotgun was a few feet away, and he reached out in a futile attempt.

Fayne was killing witch after witch. The Dynes came at him from every side and he did not care. It was almost as if he had eyes on all sides of his head; even with the restrictive vision of the mask, he kept countering their attacks with smooth moves. Bodies were piling up incredibly fast.

Adri saw the witch on Gray's back; instinctively, his last two rounds were fired between the oncoming witches, right on mark. The witch collapsed on top of Gray and Adri heard him cry out in pain. Good, that was one problem solved. Now he had to deal with the witches that were almost on him. His guns were empty and there was no time to reload. Adri turned around and started to run—he knew he could not outrun a Dyne, but still he ran—and then, right in front of him, he saw a sight that made him stop. Witches. Dynes. Hundreds of them. Pouring in, from every hole in the wall, from every passage, from every exit. Like a scourge, like a plague, like so many ants. A swarm. A wave. Scuttling on the walls, on the ceiling, on the floor in front of him, headed at him. At the three of them.

He realised he had stopped. He turned and saw the three elder witches right behind him, panting, ready to pounce. They hadn't because they wanted to give him that last moment of awe, that satisfaction of gazing upon the might of the witches, not something to be trifled with. Something for which he was about to pay with his life. He turned and saw Fayne standing similarly still, witches surrounding him in a circle.

He was observing the coming horde as well, dealing with the unsuccessful fulfilment of his charge.

And for the first time since the fight had begun, the Wraith spoke.

Let me through.

Adri did.

His eyes burst into blue flames. His shirt burned in a blue blaze and exposed the tattoos within, which were afire. 'Aargh!' Adri screamed and swept his hand in a wide arc, releasing pure spirit flame. It stung the elder witches around him and they burned and backed away. Adri ran towards Fayne, who had moved to where Gray had fallen. He burned his way through the circle of Dynes, surrounding them, and stopped in front of them, hands raised, blue fire burning in both palms. Adri spun the fires around like a giant blue whip, keeping the witches at bay while the assassin watched silently and Gray looked on with unbelieving eyes.

'Are you a God or something?' Gray gasped.

'*Zimakh*. Rubbish. The *pashlin* has harboured a Wraith,' Fayne replied.

Adri knew he could not keep this up. Spirit fire was not something that killed witches; he could only keep them away for now, but he knew the cost of this transformation. He was being drained of energy at a phenomenal rate, and he probably wouldn't be able to even stand once he was done. Not that it mattered. He had no plan whatsoever—the Wraith had suggested something and he had done it. The Wraith, however, had not taken control of him, merely lent him its power. Adri found it curious, but now was not the time to ponder over this.

'Mazumder! What now?' Adri shouted, spinning the fire.

Fayne was examining his wounds.

'So, the guy from the tomb?' Gray murmured, still trapped beneath the dead witch. 'Hey Fayne, how about a hand here?'

'Pointless,' Fayne said, but he stooped and pulled the witch off. Gray stood, dusting himself.

I do not know. Vampires were my thing, to be honest.

'Beautiful,' Adri said darkly.

It will be my end as well, Adri. Pity you do not have the energy to make my powers last longer.

Adri did not reply. His mind raced. Think. A possible way out, any single possible thing that could be done. Nothing came to him. He drew a complete blank, and he felt tired and stupid. His energy was running out. Gaps started appearing in the fire. Adri gritted his teeth and kept burning. The witches were observing them hungrily. Apart from the elder witches, normal Dynes were also there by the droves—they were surrounded by hundreds of witches on every side. And with his spirit vision Adri could see them all, every single detail about every single witch. They had no chance. They would be ripped apart. Adri kept on pushing, but now he was weak, weak in the knees. Maybe it was time to accept the end.

'Stop,' Fayne said quietly. 'There's nothing we can do.'

'Gray,' Adri said, 'I'm sorry.'

His fire flickered, and so did the other fires in the cavern. Adri noticed it because of his spirit vision, but did not understand. The fires under all the cauldrons, some of them raging, flickered again. There was no wind down here, no sudden draught that could whisk away a burning flame. The witches too, had begun to notice something was amiss—the entire army of witches was shifting in its place, and uncomfortably so. They were looking around, at the ceiling and the walls. The next moment, every flame in the cavern, except the one burning in Adri's hands, went out.

The witches screeched, and screeched together. The sound was deafening, and caught everybody off guard. All hands went to ears except for Adri's, who heard even the Wraith cry out in pain. They recoiled to an amazing, unbelievable sight: the witches were retreating. All the witches were heading out of the cavern—scampering, running, growling in low voices, shrieking in high ones. Within minutes they were alone in the cavern. The witches had left without looking back.

'No,' Adri said.

'What-what the hell was that? What's happening?' Gray asked, looking at the empty cavern bathed in blue light.

'Light a fire *now*,' Adri said. Urgency.

Gray looked around for anything that could be used. Nothing.

'Matches in my pocket,' Adri said.

Gray walked to Adri and took the matches out. Spotting a wooden plank close to him, he struck the match obediently, trying to burn the wood. 'Need paper or something,' he said, his voice shaking. 'But Adri, what was that?'

Fayne looked at the surroundings. 'Something witches fear,' he said. 'Something that would scare a witch, something you know, Tantric.'

No one said anything, and silence reigned. Then Fayne spoke again. 'It's in here with us.'

Gray managed to light the fire at last. The flame started small, but gradually caught; Adri let the Wraith's powers go. His eyes turned normal and were hit by darkness, and as he had expected, his body collapsed. He was awake and conscious, but he could not move, and he lay on the ground, panting. Fayne looked at him, then at Gray—hunched over the wooden plank, trying to increase the size of the fire—and then at the vicinity. He could sense the creature. It was watching them.

'Can-can you see it, Fayne?' Gray asked.

'No,' Fayne said.

Fayne spoke true. Even with his eyes, the creature was not something he could see. That disturbed him. He did not need to know how dangerous it was; the witches had done all the explaining.

The fire had begun to crackle louder now, and Gray headed over to Adri to make sure he was okay. He found Adri still panting and trying to breathe, not able to say a single word. But he could also see that Adri was recovering.

Adri sat up soon. Everything was quiet and Fayne had still not sighted the creature. Then Adri spoke.

'I can see you, you know?'

It laughed. The laugh was high and had an underlying screech, a hiss to it, like nails grating across a blackboard. Adri recognised it immediately. A laugh from his nightmares. A laugh he had heard time and again, a laugh in whose mortal fear he had lived for years. A laugh which had haunted him in the past. A laugh which still did.

The Demon formed itself slowly, drawing shadow from everywhere. Like liquid. It formed itself a small distance away from Adri. In the semi-darkness, they saw that it was like a gargoyle—a strong bestial entity standing on two legs, with gigantic wings folded behind it. There was no beginning and no end to it, nor were there any details in the smooth, flawless shadow that was the Demon's skin. It stood there, facing them, not moving.

'Chhaya,' Adri said slowly.

The Demon of shadow snickered loudly, and Adri caught a glimpse of white fangs. 'Not a name you can forget, eh, boy?' it hissed. 'Remember.'

'What do you want?'

'The smell of your flesh. Same as before.' The Demon's voice reflected a savage longing.

Adri got impatient in spite of his weakness. '*Al Mashith!*' he shouted, and the word hit the Demon and burned its existence for a brief second. It hissed in pain and recoiled, taking a half step back. 'Come to the damn point, Demon,' Adri growled.

'So the rat claws at the kite,' Chhaya said in an amused tone. 'Does it not realise that at the end of the day, blinded by the sun, all it sees—as it scurries desperately across the open field, towards its lair—is a *shadow*?'

'I have seen the shadow of death,' Adri said, 'and it does not have anything to do with you. So, why are you here?'

'I work for the great one now, the Demon Commander,' Chhaya said. 'He wants to meet you, boy.'

'Ba'al will have to wait,' Adri said. He tried to keep his voice from shaking.

The Demon shook its head. 'He is not used to waiting,' it said.

'Ba'al knows me,' Adri said. 'Tell him that while the life of an innocent is at stake, we cannot meet.'

'You think I'm a messenger?' Chhaya laughed in the same scratchy voice. 'I'm here to take you to him.'

'I am not helpless here, Chhaya. If Ba'al gets to know about anything *you* have forced me to do, you know he will not react most-ah-*graciously*. After all, it's *me* he will be meeting.'

'You cannot threaten me,' the Demon said, all laughter gone.

'No. *You* cannot push me into a corner. I am here for a reason. I will finish what I have started.'

'So what—'

'You will go back to Ba'al,' Adri cut the Demon short, 'and offer him my apologies and tell him he will have to wait for a while. I will have the audience with him. I know what it's about.'

The Demon looked thoughtful. 'I don't know, boy. You do not have any power over me. All that has ever stood between us has been that stone pillar. Perhaps it is time to come out from behind the pillar, boy, and face me.'

Adri was sweating.

'I have been ordered to *take* you to the great one,' Chhaya drawled. 'Writhing, struggling. If I do choose to follow my orders, I will not be blamed. I couldn't care less about the innocent life. Screams. They will haunt you some more. Besides, you collect nightmares, don't you?'

Adri's mind raced. 'Ba'al will care. You know that.'

'For a *human*?'

Adri withdrew his revolver from its holster.

Chhaya looked at it curiously. 'Ah, don't tell me. Fire and light, is that it? Are you going to amuse me by shooting at me? Feed me some metal?' Chhaya laughed again.

Adri stuck the barrel under his chin. 'Mercury, but a bullet nonetheless,' he said, talking fast.

'You won't kill yourself, you love yourself too much for that,' the Demon said.

'If I pull this trigger I'm useless to Ba'al and only you are responsible.'

There was silence.

'You're bluffing!' Chhaya hissed.

'I've been pushed to the edge,' Adri sniped back, breathing very fast.

Silence. Only Adri's breaths, rapid. And his mounting heartbeat.

'Fine!' the Demon exclaimed at length, sitting down on the ground. 'I will tell the great one what you told me. He will not be pleased.'

Adri slowly lowered the empty gun. Of course he had been bluffing, but that was a chance the Demon couldn't have taken. Not when Ba'al was involved. He looked at the creature of shadow sitting in the distance and tried to keep calm. He felt stabs of fear whenever the creature looked at him, an old fear, resurfaced, which he had to fight all the time. He turned to the others who had been silent witnesses. Gray was holding a bunch of Aujour in his hand. He wordlessly handed to it Adri.

Ooh, time for the Tantric to get cooking, the Wraith said.

'Chhaya,' Adri said. 'I have to brew something, a draught. Your presence would keep the witches away while we are here.'

'Witches!' Chhaya rasped. 'Excellent, I was rather hungry. This hunger, it pains me. Insatiable, she is.' It laughed. 'I'll be around.' The Demon melted back amidst the shadows.

Adri started brewing the draught, while Fayne and Gray brought Maya down to the ground level. Goatskin bags held clear water that the Dynes used in their cooking, and emptying a cauldron was all Adri had to do. He kept a careful watch on the brew, adding certain measured amounts of ingredients at exact times. He stole a glance at Maya when he could afford it and knew she was dying. Her skin was a pale blue, the poison having reached her very lips, draining them of colour. She lay as lifeless as always.

'Her breathing is getting shorter! Adri!' Gray shouted.

'A little more time . . .' Adri murmured.

'You should hurry,' Fayne said calmly.

'There had been absolutely no pressure by the poison so far,' Adri complained as he stirred. 'This isn't fair.'

Maya's body, however, was really giving signs. The corruption was taking effect, something had to be done soon if she was to be saved. Cursing and complaining, Adri prepared the Dreamer's Brew using all his brewing skills, all the shortcuts he knew. Risky things had to be done, like substituting ingredients and not waiting long enough for a certain section to stew properly—there was no time to make the brew the way it was supposed to be. And then it was over and he was pouring the boiling concoction into a crude wooden bowl. Gray looked at the grey, swirling mass for a second before emptying it directly down his sister's throat. Adri slumped down with his back against the cauldron, extremely tired, but watching Maya, as did the others. Extremely slowly, her irregular breathing returned to normal.

Gray and Adri breathed out deep sighs of relief.

'*Paakhiyaad*. That was as close as I've seen it go,' Fayne said. He sat down as well, a rare sight. The other two were dead tired; they hadn't been sleeping well on their travels, and after this particular rush of events, Adri and Gray felt quite dead themselves. However, they were quite interested in what the assassin had to say, in spite of their fatigue.

'Nostalgic,' Fayne said, looking at all the cuts and slashes across his chest and arms. 'This place brings too many old memories. I was brought up here until my *padar* took me away. He was human.'

'Then?' Gray asked.

Fayne remained silent.

'Well, wasn't that a lot of information,' Gray said.

He's funny, the white haired one.

'Yes,' Adri said.

'You agree?' Gray said, surprised. 'You actually *agree* with what I have to say? Well isn't that a—'

'He wasn't talking to you, *myrkho*,' Fayne said.

Gray stared at Fayne, and then at Adri. Adri looked at him, then looked at Fayne.

'It was the only way I could get the vampire hunter's body,' Adri said. 'There was no other way for me to get Maya back.'

'You gave him control,' Fayne said. 'During the fight.'

'No!' Adri protested. 'I just *used* his powers. We would have been dead anyway.'

'Wait, wait!' Gray exclaimed, his eyes bulging. 'There's another guy inside of you? Like inside you? *Who's* talking right now?'

'He can't talk,' Adri said.

Oh really now? What is this supposed to be then, the little Angel on your left shoulder?

'I mean he can't talk to *you*,' Adri corrected himself.

'But he talks to *you*?' Gray asked, horrified. 'You two keep having little conversations all day?'

'He's helped me out at times,' Adri said defensively.

'Wraiths are dangerous, and you of all people should know that, *pashlin*,' Fayne said. 'I was afraid of this and now it has happened. I would kill you here and now, but it seems we need you to find the Devil Mask.'

'What *are* you after, Adri?' Gray asked, unmoved by the assassin's words. His eyes were narrow, his tone accusatory. 'I mean, I've been watching you, man. You are facing death again and again. You're going to any lengths to save my sister, but that's not it. You want something from my brother, and you want it really *bad*. That's why you're going through with all of this. *What* is it? *What* are you after?'

271

Fayne and Gray were both looking at Adri. Fayne had his mask, but Adri could imagine the assassin's expression within. Gray wore his expressions of distrust pretty openly. It was an ugly sight to see. Adri took a long breath. He could not manipulate any more. He was tired, and perhaps, just perhaps, these two deserved to know.

'A Horseman is after me,' Adri spoke.

Fayne did not move. Gray's face changed to confusion.

'An ancient, powerful entity,' Adri explained.

'Which one?' Fayne asked.

'Death.'

'So–so this Death,' Gray asked, raising his hands, trying to slow the pace of the conversation. 'What does Death want from you?' He paused. 'Okay, stupid question. But why is Death after you?'

'The Horseman wants my soul. I do not know why.'

'Something does not add up, Adri,' Gray said. 'Death wants your soul. Okay, so basically Death wants to kill you, right? If you're going to my brother because he has a way out, isn't it a little extreme? As in, you've already faced death—literally—too many times during our journey!'

'It's bigger than just me. It's something else. Death used some specific words when it met me, and I think someone is setting me up. But it's not me I'm really worried about; this conspiracy is moving towards a direction I don't like. There is something *more* to this whole business, something I don't know. And I am not going to die without understanding why my death is needed.'

'And that is why you wear the *Ai'nDuisht,*' Fayne said all of a sudden. 'It was evident that you were hiding from a *dorelshelaha-urkhaayen,* a being of great power. But now it is clear.'

'Yes,' Adri said. 'I *am* on the run.'

'So if I stick with you, I have chances of meeting Death himself,' Gray said drily. 'Aren't you quite the exciting person, Adri? You personally *know* a Demon of shadow who just appears,

272

not to mention that the leader of the Free Demons wants you over for coffee.'

'Ba'al is another story,' Adri said. 'But Chhaya, he was the first Demon I ever saw in my life. I was a boy then.'

'Yes, sidestep the Demon Commander,' Gray said. 'He's only the most powerful Demon in Old Kolkata.'

'I am not apologising here,' Adri said, grim. 'This is not a confession. This could've been within me all my life without you knowing. You—both of you—have been through a lot because of me, and Maya is battling it out because of me. Saving her is my responsibility, Fayne's job, and your duty—and if this unites us then maybe you deserve to know what I have been going through, and why I am here.'

Gray nodded slowly. 'How can my brother help you?'

'He has something I need.'

'What thing?'

'Something that will grant me an inside view to whatever is happening to me, and why the Horseman is after me.'

'What *is* the thing?'

Adri paused. 'Your brother wouldn't want you to know,' he said at length. 'And without asking him I can't tell you anything.'

Gray slumped back against another cauldron, and no one spoke for a while.

How truly interesting, the Wraith spoke slyly. *It seems I have quite the gift for choosing the right bodies. Adventures galore!*

'This isn't a game, Wraith,' Adri mumbled.

'Hey Wraith,' Fayne said, looking at Adri. 'I know you can hear me. You even *think* about taking over the Tantric, and I will gut you.'

Oooh. I'm scared, the Wraith crooned.

'You know what my blades are made of, vampire hunter,' Fayne said further. 'You keep your end of the deal you made with the *pashlin*, and you keep it well.'

273

Yes, eternal peace is so much preferable than rotting forever in a carcass, which your future would definitely seem to be.

'He said yes,' Adri said.

'He better have,' Fayne said.

'What *are* your blades made of?' Gray asked Fayne. 'I mean, how many of them do you carry? I can never see a single one either on your person, or hanging from your belt—and yet they seem to jump to your hands—'

Fayne's hands held the customary red dagger and Gray stopped mid-sentence.

'A dark ritual,' the assassin said. 'In Ahzad, before we are trained, we are assigned to certain disciplines. Call them *fiditeii*, classes if you will. Specialisations. These define the *alkhatamish*, the assassin, his path, and his modus operandi.' He looked down at the metal rings all over his arms and chest. 'These are not rings. They are hilts.' He pulled at one of the rings, and to the others' horror and fascination, a handle followed, after which the familiar red blade came into view as he pulled it out.

'I am an *alkhatamish* of the human sheath,' Fayne said.

'All of those are daggers?' Adri asked, unable to contain himself.

'The sheaths have been burnt and welded beneath my skin which has regrown after. I carry the longer daggers on my back and chest, and the shorter ones in my arms and legs. The human sheaths are never separated from their weapons.'

'How does your body take it?' Gray asked, eyes wide.

'It hurts all the time. But you forget I am a half-breed. I can take pain better than most. My body does not reject it because of a blood curse performed on me at Ahzad—the essence of my daggers runs in my blood.'

'Which means you can actually create the daggers from your bloodstream,' Adri said.

Fayne nodded.

'His body makes the daggers?' Gray asked, incredulous.

'My daggers are of anti-life essence, something which now runs in my blood. If I replace a thrown dagger with an empty hilt, my blood solidifies on it and forms a new weapon. That's what my daggers are made of. Solidified blood.'

Powered with anti-life, the Wraith hissed. *Not good at all.*

'And thus the same daggers take down witches and Demons alike,' Adri said. 'Interesting.'

'This was not a secret,' Fayne said. 'Anyone with a keen eye and a good knowledge could have known this.'

'No, but you still said something about yourself. That's a start!' Gray said.

'Don't get used to it, *myrkho*,' Fayne growled.

Adri thought about it as Gray and Fayne kept bickering. Fayne had revealed a lot about himself in a short time. Was it because he was spending more time with them? It was easy to get fooled by a professional such as the assassin, and obviously he could not be trusted beyond a certain point. But Adri noticed how Fayne had talked about his weapons only after Adri had revealed his true motives the best he could. Maybe Fayne would only give his trust if he could trust in return. Adri had no intentions, however, of being friends with Fayne—the manipulative side of him, however, was kicking in and telling him what a good fighter Fayne was—but, they were going to journey together for a while now and he could not have the assassin think he was not to be trusted because of the Wraith inside. Not only was it a question of being mistrusted, something Adri was used to, it was also a question of when the assassin might decide that Adri was no longer needed.

You are thinking a lot, aren't you? I can feel it, but I can't quite hear you. Frustrating.

'You're not meant to hear this,' Adri said.

But I'm SO sure it's interesting!

Adri ignored the Wraith. He looked around, fascinated by the fact that they were actually resting in the Heart of the Hive. 'We should start moving,' he told the other two. 'This is hardly the safest place around, and I don't know how long that Demon will actually stick around.'

No one disagreed. They were all extremely tired, but that could easily be overlooked for now.

'There were paralysing agents in the witches' cuts,' Fayne said, standing up. 'Not enough to knock me out, but I am slowing down. I suggest we not meet any Dynes on the way back.'

Adri nodded and reached for his bandoliers, starting to reload his gun.

You might want to change into a new shirt. Your tattoos keep amplifying my energy too much for your shirts to survive. Call it my little joke, if you will.

Adri grunted and groped around in his bag for another shirt. Fayne bent down and picked up Maya, slinging her over his shoulder as he usually did. Gray had a flesh wound in the back where the witch had clawed him. He hadn't said anything about it so far, but Adri called him over and bandaged the wound. Then Gray went looking for his shotgun, which was lying somewhere in the darkness. It was not long before they were ready to move out. Chhaya was not back yet, and they started to retrace their steps.

18

The journey to the Lake of Fire took another day, but they were a little more relaxed now that the effects of the Whisper of Dread had been delayed. Even the assassin seemed more casual with the others, although his alertness never slackened. He was a machine, an instrument merely meant to be wielded, Adri came to think over the next few days that they travelled together. Fayne's personal opinions and desires would never conflict with his missions; in that way he was a mercenary, a soldier of fortune. He was deadly, yes, and Adri knew without him they could not have survived so far. He had respect for the assassin's skill, but it ended there. Ahzad had done things to him that could not be done to mere people—apart from the killing machine he had been sculpted into, there were other things that disturbed him about Fayne. He slept standing up, for example. The assassins of Ahzad were trained to sleep vertically so they could be ready for a fight the second their eyes opened; even their sleep was a cursed one as the assassin would be up at the drop of a hat. Almost anything woke Fayne up—things like the wind changing its course. It was a weird sight, Fayne leaning against a wall or a tree all night, straight as a pole. Asleep. The mask too, was tough to get used to initially, but now Adri had begun to imagine that as Fayne's face—plain and bug-eyed. Fayne did open up a bit more over the journey, and his stories were fascinating even for Adri who had known another assassin from Ahzad.

'There were eight of us. Eight. And he was alone, right there,' Fayne pointed to a tree in the distance.

'He was a whipmaster,' he continued. 'We saw his weapon from a long way off, but we didn't know how expertly he could use it. Sawwrat lost an eye from that whip and the six others lost their lives. Six assassins of Ahzad killed by a young village boy.'

'How's that possible?' Gray asked.

'Angel. That *mieserkha* was an Angel. We didn't know; the contract-giver had not revealed this, and perhaps did not know it herself.'

'What happened to him?'

'Am I not alive here, *myrkho*?' Fayne asked, irritation in his voice. 'What do you think happened to him?'

'Ah. I know so little about Angels,' Gray said.

'What's there to not know? They are political beings who will only work for a certain selfish reason, which they will conveniently mask under the greater good excuse. They joined the territory wars some time ago on MYTH's side because I'm sure the government is offering them something big in return. And they don't like Demons. A Demon is an Angel's natural nemesis.'

'What do they look like? I mean, how did all you assassins see just a village boy with a whip while he was actually an Angel?'

'They are protected,' Fayne replied. 'There is a certain magical formula built to guard them on earth. It doesn't allow anyone to find them, except their siblings.'

Gray frowned. 'Explain.'

Adri eavesdropped on them shamelessly. Gray was being given information; vital information that Adri wanted to keep hidden, information that might lead to unpleasant revelations and the complete destruction of his plan. He tried to keep himself as nonchalant as he could.

Their journey was a rather long one. The Hive was in what had earlier been central Ballygunge—they had to go northeast to reach the Lake of Fire. It was safest to approach from the south, which was where MYTH fought from. The Free Demons fought from the north, beyond the Lake. The nearest northeast route, Broad Street leading to Rifle Road, took them to Park Circus.

They passed through an intersection, deserted like all the rest. Gray recognised it; in New Kolkata this very intersection was always clogged with traffic, overcrowded, busy. For a second, this connection affected Gray.

'Is all of Old Kolkata this empty?' Gray asked, looking around. 'Where is everyone?'

'Hiding,' Adri said. 'The few people who still live in these parts, are hiding. Most have left this area. There'll be even fewer people near the Lake. The Settlements are all down south, or out of the main city's perimeter, that's where people go to survive.'

'I wouldn't want to live here,' Gray said.

'It's war. Does bad things to a place,' Adri mumbled, lighting a cigarette.

'Who's right? In this war?' Gray asked.

'Beg your pardon?' Adri said.

'Who do you support?'

'Me?' Adri asked, taken aback.

'Yes, you. You're not with MYTH anymore and now the Demon Commander wants to meet you. Are you with the Free—'

'Childish. I am on neither side. Both the parties are destroying the city in an attempt to destroy each other. The city has taken a lot already, the last thing someone should do is try and claim ownership. MYTH has a city of its own, it should be happy with that. If it has to expand, expand southwards, for heaven's sake. But no, the government eyes the Old City and brings in the Angels as allies to boot. The Free Demons are no less—damaging half the city in the name of protection. They should not even be claiming territories in the first place—the city has always been generous with space. There is enough space for everyone, they can always roam free like their ancestor Demons did.'

'I've been hearing a lot about Angels lately,' Gray said.

Adri cursed himself. 'Yes?'

'You think I could meet one?'

'They are quite well-hidden.'

'Always wanted to meet an Angel.'

Hahaha, the Wraith chuckled.

'What's so funny?' Adri mumbled.

His innocence. He's like a child. I would love to see his coming of age, and reality's bite along with it.

Adri was having a problem along the journey. The ring finger of his right hand was beginning to itch, and frightfully so. He spent half his time itching away, until the finger had become too swollen and raw to itch anymore. Even then it bothered him, but he could not find a reason why it was happening. The Wraith blamed it on the weather when he wasn't laughing about it, and Gray and Fayne had nothing helpful to say. Fayne did act all knowledgeable once when he ground up a mixture from leaves to help stop the itching, but it did not help.

Adri was having other problems as well. He found himself looking at Maya during their pit stops. He gazed at her for long times, at her olive skin and dark hair, at her sharp features. Most of the time no perverted thoughts crossed his mind; he would simply look at all the way they had come, would think of Maya as he knew her before the Ancients took her. That always got him thinking about Maya's secret agenda—he knew Fayne could clear some doubts, but it was useless asking the assassin. At other times, he had thoughts about Maya that he knew he shouldn't be having. He banished them as soon as he thought of them—he did not give them time to fester in his mind. They didn't bother him up to a point, they were natural; the Wraith, however, saw through his eyes and began to give him hell about it soon enough. It was amazing how Gray did not catch Adri gazing at his sister.

Gray was the one who had to change Maya's bandages, and he acted very, very reluctant about it whenever he had to do it. He would comply in the end, but his reluctance became well known. Adri occasionally thought he heard Fayne snicker at Gray, but he couldn't be sure. The assassin was always dead serious when he talked.

They started avoiding the main roads as they neared the Lake. They stuck to small alleyways and shortcuts like they had before. It took more time because of all the winding and occasional blocked path, but they were comparatively safer. The most eventful thing that happened to them was at Tangra, about eight hours away from Beleghata, which was at the outskirts of the Lake of Fire. Having travelled the whole day, they retired for the night by breaking into a boarded up house.

Fayne kicked the door open and moved inside, disappearing into the darkness. Maya was with Gray and Adri, who moved just within the front porch and waited for the assassin to return. Adri readied a revolver just in case, but he didn't think he would need it; the area was silent and still, not a sign of life anywhere. No one wanted to live this near the war zone, and quite naturally so.

The familiar glint of the bug-eyed visor was visible soon. 'Empty,' Fayne said. They entered and Fayne put the door back in its place roughly. They spent some time barricading the door with furniture, before settling in their own separate places, doing their own separate things. Maya was put down on an old dusty sofa. Adri busied himself with making new bullets, Fayne sat down in a meditative posture, and Gray brandished his violin, something he hadn't had the chance to play in quite a while.

Adri walked up to him and snatched the violin immediately. 'Risky, the noise,' he said, tempted to smash the unholy instrument.

'Give that back!' Gray shouted, angry. 'There's nobody listening!'

Adri did not agree, but eventually he gave in to Gray's nagging. They were all tired and testy. They would have to be careful, but he could afford to let this one thing be. It wasn't really necessary to take this one little thing away from Gray. It could be the only thing he had left.

Gray polished the violin for a while and cleaned the dust carefully, before he took his bow with the grace of a master and started to play. A long, thin screech.

Adri dropped a bullet. 'What the—' he started.

After the initial cacophony in which Gray claimed he was rusty and Fayne did not react at all, remaining in his meditative pose, Gray continued to play.

Death, Gray thought as he played, a curious happening, rather a curious state, something one could slip towards any moment, any second. Yet, there was life. Bloody idiot, had he ever cared that his sister breathed, that she talked? There could have been more happiness, perhaps. Fewer doors slammed. Fewer angry words exchanged. Goddamn it all, all the memories, forcing themselves out now that he was weak. Now that he needed her forgiveness. For every single mistake.

They had been walking all day. All the buildings they passed, desolate, the candle burning behind curtains, one in a hundred. So desolate. Ghosts murmuring, eyes watching them go, they who would make no difference. He wished he could be there, among those people, with Maya, with nothing to do with the Tantric and the assassin. Nothing at all, living out their lives, in a seemingly immense struggle, perhaps, but a life lived out, with Death waiting only at the very end. Wishful thinking. Here, there was movement. They had been moving, and moving. There was nothing else, nothing but the next mission; he did not want to take another photograph in his entire life. He wanted Maya back, he wanted out. He was forgetting what they had set out to do, that somewhere, Abriti was walking on the soil of this very city. How would he face *Dada*? Would they even make it to the Lake of Fire?

He needed to focus. Adri seemed focused. The Tantric was managing somehow, he was holding on to his promise, to his word. He had not cracked yet, and Gray could not afford to crack either. Must hold on. Must hold on. Prioritise. Maya would be saved. Of course. She had to be saved. He would see to that.

Gray played slowly and mournfully, agonisingly so, with many imperfections. Adri loved western classical music, and Gray's attempts were murder to his ears. Still, he chose not to protest anymore. Gray played for another full hour, until the first dead man broke in through a window.

Adri and Fayne were up immediately. They looked at the spectacle before them—the walking corpse, the zombie that had broken in through the window.

'What-What-' Gray exclaimed.

The creature was disgusting. It had been dead for quite a while now—its rotten skin hung loose, its hair had dried up, eyeballs sunken deep within the sockets. It still wore its old clothes, but they were faded and dirty and tattered. It was moving, slowly, but with extreme ferocity. It opened and closed its mouth to emit noises, but its dead throat did not function.

Adri closed his revolver's chamber and unleashed three holy rounds into the revenant; it collapsed noisily. Fayne walked over to the window it had broken in through and peeped out.

'More,' he said.

Adri, who was reloading, asked how many.

'About fifty to sixty,' Fayne said.

The building did not have a back exit, but Fayne made one and they exited through, beating a hasty retreat from the dim-witted revenant. Gray did muster up the courage to apologise to the other two, saying he had no clue his music would wake the dead. Adri knew, however, that revenant were woken up only at graveyards—and there were no graveyards nearby to his knowledge. Where then had the living-dead come from? He decided to think about it later; either way, they were too close to the Lake of Fire, and he needed a plan. They ran across other revenant on their way to the Lake, and if there weren't too many, Fayne summarily finished them off.

'Tortured souls,' Adri told Gray as Fayne hacked away at revenant who were trying unsuccessfully to surround and take bites of the assassin. 'They cannot depart as they're very attached to their bodies; thus they reanimate, often helped by a festering curse or a Tantric—but often just the magic in the air along with the will to live again is enough.'

'Wasn't that Mazumder's thing as well? Attached to his body, wanting to live on?' Gray asked.

Why that little—

'Yes. But revenant are mostly everyday people without the magical training needed to go down the road of the Wraith.'

'Sounds like a horrible fate. They're zombies!'

'Yes. And there's lots of revenant out there.'

19

'Okay. Take it easy,' Adri shouted. 'We're not drawing any weapons.'

'You better not,' the Commando shouted back.

The first sign of reaching the Lake of Fire would, of course, be the Commandos, MYTH's army of mass-produced soldiers, equipped with increasingly sophisticated armour according to rank. It was tough, almost impossible to sneak past these guys. The most logical way, Adri figured, to meet Kaavsh was to let oneself get caught by the Commandos. One didn't want a bullet through the head from some Commando sharpshooter who caught one sneaking.

The one they were facing right now was a sharpshooter. He was sitting on the fourth floor of an abandoned four-floor building. Adri and the others were in the street next to the adjacent building, standing still.

'Stand still,' Adri said. 'He's packing a modified Sharps carbine. One false move and he'll blow our heads off. Commando snipers are good.'

'Hey, tell me something, Fayne,' Gray said. 'How do you face such an enemy? As in a sniper or something similar? Your blades can't reach him in this scenario.'

'He has to see me before he hits me,' Fayne grunted.

'Okay, supposing he's seen you,' Gray said.

'I'm too fast for a sniper, *myrkho*,' Fayne said. 'He cannot possibly take me out while I'm moving.'

285

'Supposing you're still,' Gray said blankly.

'Why would I be still?' Fayne asked. He sounded insulted.

'Supposing you are,'

'I wouldn't be.'

'Say it's a hypothetical situation. You're still and a sniper has you in such a standoff. What do you do then?'

'*Khabashud*. Such a situation is against my training,' Fayne said stubbornly.

'And why do you call me *myrkho*? What does it mean? Would you like it if I call you Aladdin?'

'Here they come,' Adri interrupted.

A group of Commandos, about ten of them, were on their way. Gray looked at them and realised, almost immediately, that he had seen them before, in New Kolkata. Dressed in military green suits with protective jackets and helmets, they cautiously made their way towards the four of them, rifles raised.

'Identify yourselves!' a Commando shouted as they neared.

'I am a banished Tantric,' Adri said. 'This here, is an Assassin of Ahzad, and this is a citizen of New Kolkata. The girl with us is in urgent need of medical attention.'

'This is not a hospital, it's a freaking war zone! You got the wrong address, Necromancer!' the Commando replied.

Adri had hoped the Commandos would be more charitable; evidently not. Fine, he would have to take the chance of naming the Angel. They would obviously not recognise his false name, nor would they care for Gray's possible revelation.

'We have work with Kaavsh. He will know us by face,' Adri said.

The Commandos froze. 'Kaavsh?' one of them asked.

'Are you sure? If this is a ruse—'

'Just take us to him,' Adri said.

'Who the hell is Kaavsh? They will know Dada—' Gray began.

'Quiet,' Adri hissed.

Now the Commandos seemed massively unsure; all they did was stare. The leader snapped them out of it all of a sudden. Search them and confiscate their weapons!' he barked. The other Commandos nodded and started moving closer.

Fayne, who had been carrying Maya, tried to put her down.

'Watch it!' a Commando roared.

'Oh no, no. He's just keeping her down. She's in a coma, man,' Adri explained hurriedly.

Adri's revolvers and Gray's shotgun were the most visible weapons and were taken by the Commandos immediately. They ran into a snag when they told Fayne to empty out his weapons. Fayne had scores of daggers in his body and there was no point in emptying them out anyway—they would simply grow back. The Commandos panicked, however, and they made him empty out his daggers nevertheless. It took the better part of a quarter of an hour, and by the end of it, everyone except Maya was staring at the huge pile of red daggers, knives, and a couple of red short swords on the floor. Fayne was taking long, deep breaths. His patience was being tested. Obviously, he could not lose focus; but these Commandos were irritating him. Normally, he would not put up with such trivial issues, but being with Gray had helped him deal better with irritation. Finally, when the Commandos were done searching them, they were escorted down the road towards the MYTH camp.

A change from the usual silence that Old Kolkata had got them used to—distant gunfire, frequent, along with muffled explosions. The buildings were not too high this side of the city; apart from the few skyscrapers which were choked with snipers, all structures were partially or wholly destroyed by magical damage. They walked down a road, then through alleyways and more roads. They ran into yet more Commando patrols as they walked towards the camp, the place was filled with them. Everyone looked tired and grim, though they did not see any wounded—then again, this was just the outer circle of the Lake of Fire. This was where the MYTH camp was. This was where Kaavsh would most likely be found.

It had initially been a small football field, Adri realised when they reached the place; he could still see the goalposts on either end. Now it was crowded with a sea of tents, large and small, soldiers moving and sitting in large groups in and around. It reminded him of a typical war camp in the medieval times; how a besieging army would lay camp in an area while they whittled down a castle in the attempts of breaking through. They were still trying to do the same thing, and this *was* war.

The buildings surrounding the field were mostly empty, though they saw movements on certain floors, where the other troops were stationed. The field was evidently well watched and guarded. Groups of Commandos were already watching them; new arrivals attracted interest here. As they were taken near the field, Adri saw a man walking towards them, his black robes billowing in the hot afternoon winds. Adri recognised him. The smooth black hair and clean-cut goatee were unmistakable.

'We have guests, it seems!' the man shouted from afar as he made his way towards them. His tone was gleeful and there seemed to be a bounce in his step. His smile though, spoke of sadism.

'Arshamm,' Adri sighed, looking at him and pulling off a forced half smile.

'Don't smile,' Arshamm replied, still grinning widely. 'You don't get to smile. You are banished and you are here, I have you now. You don't get to smile.'

'You know what happened was an accident,' Adri said, still trying to maintain the smile, sounding dreadfully like someone pressing a lie forward.

'Not an accident, Adri Sen. A lot of things it was, yes, but not an accident,' Arshamm replied.

'Does Adri do this to everyone?' Gray whispered.

'Shut up,' Fayne said.

'And you've brought guests!' Arshamm exclaimed cheerily, looking at the Gray and Fayne. 'Guests who, no doubt, have been fully convinced by you of the hospitable welcome they will get here!'

'Our business is not with you,' Adri said, the smile finally leaving his face.

'And neither is mine. Lock them up, boys. And chain them while you're at it,' Arshamm said, still smiling.

'Sir, they have come here to meet—' a Commando started.

'I do not care. They are outlaws and for their own *protection,* we should do what we do,' Arshamm replied, talking fast. 'You will now proceed to the red building and lock them up in the basement.'

'Yes, sir,' the Commando replied. The entire group changed its direction, moving away from the field and towards the adjacent buildings.

'This is ANGEL business, Arshamm!' Adri shouted at the top of his voice, all of a sudden. 'You don't know what you're obstructing!'

'Hardly,' Arshamm said. He looked unsure for a moment, but then the expression was gone. 'I don't see how *you* would have anything of interest for *them.*'

Adri was the only one in the group protesting violently; the others had simply turned and started to walk. Adri struggled, refusing to walk and was pushed roughly with quick threats from the Commandos. Then a loud, deep voice broke the fray and everyone stopped.

'You, Arshamm, are not the judge of our business,' the voice said, clear and deep.

Everyone turned and saw a figure approach from the direction of the tents. Dressed in pure and complete black, the figure was tall and well-built—he walked with imposition, a long cloak wrapped around his shoulders, covering his entire back and front. One could catch a tiny glimpse of his boots beneath, coal black like the rest of him. He was fair-skinned and his face stood out in all the black that covered him; he had wild hair and black tattoos circling his piercing eyes, beneath which was a black cloth that went all around his face and trailed down, hiding his nose, mouth and neck. Adri, with his Second Sight saw the wings. They were undoubtedly one of the largest pair of wings he had ever seen; they were folded neatly behind him—but that wasn't what made him stare in awe. No, he stared because the wings were black, unblended black—each and every feather.

An easy enough description. This was the Dark Angel.

Arshamm turned around and froze. 'I merely assumed—' he began.

'Know your place, Sorcerer,' the Angel spoke without looking at Arshamm who stopped immediately. The Angel then, amidst the perfect silence, walked up to Adri.

'And this better not be an excuse to escape our prisons,' he continued, his bold voice echoing in the silence, his eyes transfixing Adri.

'Our business is with Kaavsh,' Adri said, trying not to stammer.

The Dark Angel stared at Adri and then at the others. Adri saw his gaze pause as he looked at Gray, and then at Maya. The siblings were here, and Adri knew that the Angel would have to honour the magical contract of their kind. Now he had permission to see Kaavsh, he had permission to see his wings in Second Sight.

'Let them go,' he told the Commandos, and then turned to Adri again. 'Follow me.'

Wordlessly they complied. Adri winked at a sullen Arshamm as they walked past him and into the field. The Angel led them without looking back, and they followed through lanes of tents and busy men shuffling around with papers and maps and food and weapons; civilians as well as Commandos, and also the occasional Sorcerer or Tantric.

'I don't know where you're going with this Angel thing, Adri,' Gray hissed as they walked. 'We should've just named my brother.'

Adri knew that in all probability, Gray was in for a very nasty revelation. This was exactly what he had been afraid of, the exact thing the Gunsmith had warned him not to do. It did not bode well with his conscience, and nor did it bode well with the fact that Kaavsh would be angry as hell with him. But there had been no other way, had there? Adri had seen this coming the moment he realised that they would have to give themselves up to the Commandos; he knew the eventuality of the fact that Gray would know his elder brother's secret. He had known it all along.

They reached a tent larger than the others and the Angel paused for a moment. 'One of you, with me,' he said and entered, sweeping the curtain on the entrance aside.

'Wait here,' Adri said needlessly, and entered.

There was a man inside, hunched over a table, writing something. He looked up as they entered the tent, first at the Dark Angel and then at Adri. He was clearly not prepared for battle or anything of the like—he was dressed in his pyjamas.

'Kaavsh,' the Dark Angel said.

'Raven,' Kaavsh acknowledged. The Dark Angel's first name, not something many knew.

'Intruders. Outlaws,' Raven said, gesturing lightly at Adri. 'Two more stand outside. Claims he has business with you. He has gained a right to meet you, hence I bring him to you.'

Kaavsh looked at Adri. The Angel was as majestic as Angels were despite what he currently wore; he was good-looking, with prominent features and an impressive built. His huge white wings were currently folded behind him. There was the slightest of resemblances in his face to Maya and Gray; but then that was how the Angels were assigned to families in the first place.

'I've never seen you before,' Kaavsh said in his clear, crystal-like voice, but Adri could sense the mounting alarm in him. 'And how have you gained the right to see me in my form? Surely . . . surely not—'

'Gray Ghosh is standing right outside this tent,' Adri hissed.

It took a second to sink in.

'What?' Kaavsh asked, stunned.

'Your earth brother is outside. He does not know your real identity. I suggest Raven take us somewhere else where you meet us as Abriti,' Adri continued, speaking fast.

'Gray is here? How?' Kaavsh asked, lowering his voice immediately.

'Does it matter?' Raven said. 'We will do as he says. The stone ring is empty, be there in a few minutes.'

Kaavsh nodded, looking sharply at Adri. Raven swept out of the tent and Adri followed. The Angel led the way once again, and the three of them followed, Adri explaining on the way how Kaavsh wasn't in his tent and thus, how he explained himself out of his situation using Abriti's name. The stone ring, an amphitheatre, was by and large empty when they reached it a few minutes later, except for a couple of Commandos who were sitting in the rear, smoking. They got flustered when they saw the Dark Angel and left quietly and wordlessly, making as little noise as possible. Everyone sat down on the stone seats, except for Raven.

Kaavsh did not waste time; they saw him walking towards them soon enough; he was dressed in a shirt and a pair of trousers. Adri spied a pen in the shirt pocket; clearly, this was the exact disguise the Angel lived by. Gray got up as soon as he saw Kaavsh approach. Kaavsh looked back at him seriously. Then his gaze moved to Fayne, and then Maya.

'Maya?' Kaavsh exclaimed in disbelief. 'Gray, is that *Maya?*'

'Dada,' Gray said quietly.

Kaavsh came to a stop in front of Gray. 'Tell me what has happened,' he demanded.

'Maya was bringing Adri here, to meet you,' Gray said, eyes low.

'Adri?'

'Adri Sen, him. He's a Tantric. He needed to meet you.'

Kaavsh looked at Adri for a moment, his eyes calculative. Adri knew that he knew the purpose of bringing Maya.

'He's Victor Sen's boy,' Raven commented loudly.

'I came along to keep an eye on Maya,' Gray continued. 'But—'

'What happened to her?' Kaavsh asked seriously.

'A corruption,' Adri spoke for the first time. 'The Whisper of Dread. She's currently under the Dreamer's Brew so she's stable.'

'Incurable,' Raven said, frowning.

'Yes,' Adri agreed. 'But I have a plan.'

Kaavsh looked at the man sitting beside his sister. 'Who's the masked man?'

'I am Fayne of Ahzad,' Fayne said without moving. 'I have been charged with protecting Maya Ghosh.'

'An assassin. Quite the group,' Raven said.

'Take them away, Raven. Anywhere, but here. I need to talk to the Tantric. Alone.'

Raven shrugged. 'Figure this out,' he said. He walked out, gesturing the others to follow. Gray seemed too afraid of Kaavsh to question him; he obeyed meekly. Fayne left Maya lying down and got up. Kaavsh waited for them to get out of earshot, all the while looking at Adri.

'I am going to cut you up, Tantric,' Kaavsh finally said when he did.

'It was not in my intention to have Maya come to harm,' Adri said, looking Kaavsh in the eye.

'I'm not afraid of your father, or what he will try and do to me if I end you right here,' Kaavsh said, his face slowly starting to betray his anger.

'My father has been kidnapped and if not already dead, is certainly facing death. In his current situation, I don't think he would be much of a threat to you.'

Kaavsh paused for a moment.'Tell me why you were tracking me down,' he said.

'I wouldn't have needed Maya's help if you didn't have that magic protecting your identity,' Adri said. 'I need your blood, and that's why I'm here.'

Kaavsh shook his head in distaste. 'A Fallen's errand. That's what has landed my sister in this state.'

'She landed herself in that state,' Adri said, knowing the Angel would not believe him. 'She ran off inside Jadavpur University, away from me. I could not reach her in time, and Ancients had her. Rescuing her from the vampires was another thing; but in the end, she ended up with a corruption in her veins. It was the best I could do under the circumstances.'

The Angel did not negate his story. Kaavsh looked at Maya lying motionless on the steps near him. Slowly, he walked and sat down beside her. There was silence and Adri did not break it. Kaavsh gently put his hand on Maya's forehead. 'Foolish girl,' he said softly. 'This was meant to happen.'

'What was she after, Kaavsh?' Adri asked slowly.

'Nothing you need to bother with,' Kaavsh said sharply. 'You are not getting away with this, Tantric.'

'You do not understand,' Adri said. 'This isn't about me or her or you. There is something else that is happening. There is a disturbance in the entire universe, in the land and the air. And I know you have felt it, Angel.'

Kaavsh exhaled. 'I am angry,' he said. 'I want to see you punished, I want to see you suffer for what you have done to my innocent earth siblings, playing on their curiosity for your own ends, for the ends of some Fallen. But you're not lying. I can sense that. Yes, I have sensed the change, the pollution. It is everywhere. I have felt it in the very fabric of existence; all the Angels have. But how do you know of this?'

'It's a conspiracy, Kaavsh. Something is about to happen, and as a part of it, a Horseman has been unleashed to collect my soul.'

Kaavsh could not hide his surprise. 'A Horseman?'

'Death,' Adri spoke.

'How are you still here?'

Adri lifted the pendant around his neck slightly so that the Angel could catch a glimpse of it before letting it fall. 'A Fallen has been helping me get to the bottom of this,' Adri spoke. 'And you know how every Fallen has his price.'

'Then it is true,' Kaavsh said, falling into deep thought. 'Then the universe is indeed rearranging. If the Horsemen are riding again—' The Angel looked troubled and doubtful, his anger gone. 'What about my sister?'

'A Devil Mask is loose,' Adri said. 'Making it accept her, then extracting her is the plan.'

The Angel shook his head. 'It's never been done before. There is no guarantee you can do it.'

'Is there an alternative?' Adri asked roughly.

'There are MYTH Necromancers, well-versed, experienced, more in number,' Kaavsh said. 'They would have a greater chance at what you said.'

'Someone has paid for your sister's protection, Kaavsh, and it's not you,' Adri said. 'She is involved in this machination. Like it or not, she is already a player on the board. Fayne is here on the orders of someone who knows much more about this than we do. And we sure as hell need to know more. It is me who has to try and save Maya's life; she is a part of the puzzle, don't you see?'

'I do not want to see,' Kaavsh replied suddenly, standing up. 'I do not want to entrust her life to you.'

'You are making a huge mistake, Angel,' Adri said, coming closer. 'Whatever is about to change in this world needs to be known beforehand and stopped if necessary.'

'I cannot give you my blood,' Kaavsh said, looking straight at Adri, grim.

'I have respected your secret. Gray and Maya will never know,' Adri replied.

'Are you *blackmailing*—' Kaavsh began in anger, but Adri cut him off.

'No. I'm not. I'm trying to *not* be like my father for once,' Adri said, looking at the Angel, keeping direct eye contact. 'For once in my life I'm trying to do what is *right*. They will never know regardless of whether you give me your blood or not, because that would not be right otherwise. But you, Angel, are you doing the right thing here?'

There was a pause. Kaavsh stared at Adri, who stared back.

'Fallen are filthy,' Kaavsh said. 'They are cursed and banished, and their wings have always been ripped off as punishment for their sins. A Fallen cannot gain such easy entrance back into our ranks, Tantric. It will be the greatest dishonour there is to our order.'

'You talk about dishonour?' Adri asked incredulously. 'Your order is strictly political right now; the idealism you're telling me about is dead and you know it. Who are you ashamed of—your three brothers in hell, or the rest of your brothers who are in Old Kolkata strictly for their own agendas? You used to be saviours, guardians, now look at you. Look at you, look at the government you side with!'

Silence loomed.

'There are still many left, Tantric,' Kaavsh said. 'Many who are not influenced.'

'You can count them on your fingertips, Angel,' Adri said.

Kaavsh looked at Adri, troubled as before.

'There will be no order left to worry about!' Adri snarled. 'You feel the change coming, goddammit! You have the gift to connect to the entire fabric and yet you are so blind!'

'Truth always hurts, Tantric,' Kaavsh said softly.

'You are one of the few good ones,' Adri spoke after a moment. 'No one cares about their earth siblings anymore.'

'I do not want Maya to stay in the Devil Mask, do you understand?' Kaavsh asked calmly. 'If you cannot pull her out then kill her. Kill her, no matter what Gray says. She must not go through that kind of existence.'

Adri looked down at the ground. 'You have my word, Angel,' he said slowly.

'She was looking for proof,' Kaavsh continued. 'She wanted to work for the government, to study magic and become a Tantric or a Sorcerer. The government denied her the chance based on her ancestry; she was a little girl then, but it stung her. She had always wanted to know why she was denied—she suspected that someone in her lineage had magic in their blood, and had been involved in something the government was trying to hide. The records were all abandoned at JU and she knew that too.'

'And what about her ancestry made MYTH deny her?'

'I would not know. I never went looking in JU despite her pleading. In the Old City, some things are always better unearthed.'

Adri nodded.

'Do you have a vial?' Kaavsh asked.

Adri had kept one aside for this exact purpose. An empty vial had not been removed by the Commandos when they frisked him. He produced it, handing it to the Angel. Kaavsh looked at it long and hard, then threw out his right hand. The Angel's Blade had been summoned. It shimmered into existence in his right hand, a long, magnificent sword fashioned out of pure crystal. After rolling back a sleeve, Kaavsh used an edge on his left arm. Blood

297

fell, bright red. The Angel was careful about it—he caught every drop delicately in the vial, careful not to spill a single drop. When the vial was full, he ran a healing hand on the wound, which closed up. Corking the vial, he gave it to Adri.

Adri held it up in the light, hardly able to believe what he was holding: one of the hardest things to procure, one of the rarest sights seen by mortals—and one of the most powerful magical sources ever created. The blood of Angels. And he finally had it.

'Don't wave it around,' Kaavsh growled. 'This is between us, Tantric.'

'Right,' Adri said, pocketing the vial carefully. 'Kaavsh, I was hoping you could inform me of the most recent sightings of the Devil Mask.'

'A task force has already been dispatched,' Kaavsh said. 'The thing was last seen near Howrah, that's the best we know.'

'Good enough. We'll need our stuff back from the Commandos.'

'It will be done. Tantric—I don't know how what just happened did. But don't prove me wrong. You have kept Gray safe so far. Don't fail my trust.'

'You will have both your siblings back,' Adri said. 'You have my word.'

20

The metal dragonfly buzzed as it landed on Adri's shoulder. Adri removed it gently and unscrewed the tip of the tail, removing the parchment within. He read the message and knew where to go. Aurcoe was waiting for him.

That was well played, the Wraith said.

'Funny,' Adri said. 'I was honest.'

Nevertheless. The plot is quite exquisite though. Dirty secrets you keep.

'You stay out of this, Mazumder.'

Goodbyes with Kaavsh hadn't been very long drawn. He told Gray he couldn't accompany them as he was needed at the Lake for Fire, that it was up to him to see to the safety of their sister. Gray accepted the responsibility ceremoniously, it was clear that Kaavsh was a role model and his word was law. 'Your informant—how will he help?' Gray asked Adri as they walked.

Adri lit a cigarette. 'There are things afoot, Gray,' he said. 'Things that have to do with my father's kidnapping, with Maya, with something big which is about to happen. I need to know what I'm getting into before I do.'

'We are saving Maya no matter what, right?'

'Yes, we are.'

'Then let's go and meet this informant of yours. Who is he?'

'You saw him after the train ride. A Fallen, now about to become an Angel.'

'How far is he?' Fayne asked, speaking after a long time.

'West. A little west of here.'

Their walk wasn't long. They saw the tree Aurcoe had described soon—it was a giant, one of the largest trees they had ever seen. It stood in the centre of a large semi-devastated park. Two figures were sitting beneath its shade. Aurcoe stood up as they approached. Adri could sense his restlessness, his excitement, like a child eager for his newest toy. He hadn't changed at all, and if he had had to go through a lot to find the information Adri needed, he wasn't exactly worse for wear.

'Calm down, Fallen,' Adri said, ignoring Aurcoe's outstretched hand. 'I get my information and *then* you get your blood. You know I have it.'

Disappointment streaked across the Fallen's boyish face, only to be replaced a second later by a grin. 'Yes, I can feel its power. The raw power,' he said, his voice trembling slightly.

Adri looked at the other man. An old man, with pearl-white hair and a beard. He sat simply, wearing a simple cotton dhoti and kurta. A rough wooden stick lay at his side. He appeared harmless, looking at them with a friendly smile. Adri glanced at Aurcoe for an explanation.

'He's one of the wandering storytellers of Old Kolkata,' Aurcoe said, adjusting his glasses. 'I consulted a number of sources, went to dangerous places and read forbidden tomes, but nothing is more reliable than a storyteller's tale. These guys know a lot. Lore is what they are. And this storyteller in particular helped me put it all together and make sense out of what I had been reading and finding out.'

Adri nodded. There was no doubting the exaction of legend the storytellers churned out. He marvelled at the fact that he was standing in front of one of their kind right now, most were dead and the remaining ones were extremely hard to find; someone none but a Fallen could have found.

'I am Adri, a Tantric,' Adri said, stretching out his hand. The old man took it, still smiling.

'I am nameless, I'm afraid,' he said. 'Children call me Dadu.'

Adri nodded slowly and sat down in front of him. 'Even I shall call you Dadu then.'

'I sense great power within you,' the old man said, looking at Adri. 'I wish I had found you earlier, when the Devil Mask crossed the River.'

'You know about—'

Adri raised his eyebrows as he heard Gray react as well.

'I was there when the creature manifested,' the old man said sadly. 'I tried to get help, I went looking for Tantrics. Unfortunately, when I got back with some MYTH Tantrics it was too late—the Settlement of Barasat had been devoured. The creature went into the Shongar Ruins, and through to the Ondhokaar. It could have moved anywhere from there by now.'

'I am hunting the Devil Mask,' Adri said. 'It has been sighted near Howrah and MYTH has dispatched forces already.'

'Dear boy,' the old man said, 'you are being hunted yourself. Death is hunting you for a reason, and to know the reason you must know more about the Horsemen first.'

'Yes,' Adri nodded, settling into a more comfortable position. A story was on its way, perhaps one he would not like.

'The Keeper sits in his Library, doing his task well,' the old man began. 'He keeps souls of the departed and of the unborn; he keeps them well and guards them with all of his terrifying skill. It is a job he has been doing since the beginning of time, since life itself manifested on this Plane. But among all of these souls, the Keeper found a certain soul he could not risk keeping with him. He found it eons ago, when men had not learnt to speak and were afraid of thunder; and even back then he knew of its power, for it whispered to him and told him of things he had not seen, of secrets he had not heard. The Keeper is an ancient creature with no mortal desire or want; he is endless, and he is chronos itself; but even then he was afraid of the dark presence he knew the soul would attract.

'For the soul was a unique one—it was the soul of a *God*. The only God who ever had a mortal soul had siphoned it off on a mere whim and sent it to the Keeper, and had then forgotten about it. But a soul is not a piece of clothing to be simply removed and thrown away. For a mortal it is everything—the very existence, but bodiless—for the God concerned, however, he had no problem surviving without it as they were mighty beings of a time long past; they created the rules and were not bound by anything. The *soul* in question, however, carried a lot more with it than the God could have ever suspected. It held the very secret of *creation* within itself, and when it whispered this fact to the Keeper, he arranged for the soul to be taken away from his Library.'

No one breathed in the pleasant afternoon under the tree's shade. Everyone hung on to the storyteller's words, even Aurcoe who knew the story well.

'Inside a large unknown mountain, deeper than where the liquid fires of the earth run, a fortress was carved. The best metal, the best wood, the best magic, and the best architects were used for this purpose, none of them of mortal origin. This fortress was called *Ashil Heob*, the fabled impenetrable place—and once every single kind of magic was used to cement its foundations, its protectors were chosen. The protectors had to be perfect—they would not need to sleep or eat, they would be alert every moment of the day and the night, of the month and the year. They would be unconquerable, and they would carry weapons and wear armours forged in the armoury of *Nedrashish* itself, the forge of Dominion.

'Four brothers were chosen for this role. They were not of mortal origin and their father had offered them for service willingly.

302

They had been trained and trained well. The brothers were first outfitted with armours and steel as they saw fit; then, out of the best stables in the Plane they selected four steeds of varying degrees of power and skill. And then, they retreated into the heart of *Ashil Heob,* to start their blood-bound duty of guarding the soul which had been locked in the deepest vault that the fortress had to offer. The vault was controlled by the four brothers, and could only be unlocked by all four together, as each brother knew a separate phrase that needed to be whispered into each of the four locks for them to open. Each brother hid his own phrase from the other brothers; and since this was considered duty, it did not lead to any disagreements or conflict. They loved one another and lived well for hundreds of years, serving as the most capable guardians of all time.

'But just as the Keeper had feared, the dark presence did sense the soul in time. He was a vicious creature—a fiend, a murderer, a trickster and a thief who had many names. He was *Abaddon,* the Father of lies and the Angel of the Bottomless Pit; he was *Belial,* the accuser and the tempter, the Prince of Darkness and the Serpent of Old. He sensed this power, this power he now realised he must have. He knew of the fortress too, and knew it had no weaknesses. He tried forsaking this treasure, but he could not; it ruled his thoughts, the possibilities of what could be his robbed him of sleep and hunger and lust. And he sat in the shadows and hatched a plan that would get him this object he so coveted.

'The four brothers did not leave the fortress except when they went horse riding, for they loved their steeds and they loved the open air. They were true to responsibility, however, and only one would go riding while the other three would stand guard, and this was always the rule they followed.

'Abaddon observed them and soon became wise to their habits; and one day, while a brother was out riding he called out to him in the voice of a small girl. The brother was a warrior by nature and hearing an innocent in danger he rushed thoughtlessly into the forest from which the voice came. In the darkness of the woods, Abaddon overpowered the brother and made him his prisoner. When the brother did not come back, the other brothers waited for a week before another brother rode out to find the first. The deceiver called out to him as someone robbed of everything; being a guardian of peace with a strong sense of justice and right, the second brother rode into the woods as well, and was taken prisoner. The third brother rode out after another week, and this time the voice that lured him was a diseased one. Being a healer and a holy knight, he sped to help the voice he heard and was unwittingly trapped in Abaddon's trap.

'Abaddon was happy that his plans had almost succeeded. All he had to do now was wait for the fourth brother to show up. But the final brother never rode out. Abaddon waited for days, which then turned into weeks and then years, but the last brother did not leave his guarding post. The dark one was angered, but he still did not dare face the brother head on, and so, he guided cries for help towards the fortress, cries in the voices of the other three brothers.

'The last brother had the gift of granting life; he had been troubled by the disappearance of his brothers, but he stood firm by his duty, ignoring all else for years. His will, however, was curbed when he heard the voices of his dying brothers who he knew he alone held the power to save. The voices seemed close and perhaps a quick rescue was possible. The last brother rode out, the voices guiding him into the woods, where he fell for the sinner's deception and was trapped like his brothers.

'Abaddon rejoiced and sped into the now unguarded fortress to claim what he so ardently sought, only to find four locks guarding it, locks such as he had never seen before. He tried for a year and a day to break the locks with physical and magical force, but they would not give way. Knowing that only his four prisoners knew the secret of opening them, he whisked them away to the Abyss where he imprisoned them, on four sides of one hall, and tortured them. He tortured them for millennia, it is said, but they would not yield. The brothers had a grim sense of satisfaction from Belial's torture; they had been fooled once and they considered this pain their redemption. They accepted the pain as a part of their lives; they would be tortured forever but they would not be fooled again. They kept their mouths shut, and their minds were better fortresses than the *Ashil Heob*, and the sinner could not breach their thoughts.

'Abaddon was bereft of ideas. He did not know what to do; he was so close and yet so far. He could not kill them for their secret would die with them, and no amount of the most extreme torture would work on the brothers. He felt the power of the object every day, tempting him, luring him in, and he realised he could not give up.

'The vile idea of how to break the brothers came to him one day after eons, while he was bathing in blood. He *separated* them. The brothers were not kept in the Abyss anymore. They were moved to vile tombs of torture—one in the deserts, one in the mountains, one in the islands, and the last in the moors. And then the torture began again. It went on for hundreds of years, and finally the brothers broke, not being able to take strength from each other as they had. Each whispered his secret word to Abaddon, who combined the four and opened the lock. The soul, at last, was his, and the power of creation along with it.

'He did not sit idle. He started creating—he created evil thoughts and emotions, vile mindsets, and spread his dark teachings through these. He shaped his own personal universe far underground, and then created creatures to fill the space and do his biddings. All sorts of sins were embodied into these creatures, who were then let loose in a dark, cruel universe where Belial played his twisted games with everyone. His gaze moved to the mortal Plane soon enough, but before he could break through, the

Gods blocked him, placing seven seals between him and the mortal Plane—seven seals that protected mortals from all that was unholy. The dark one, however, figured out a way to break these seals.

'He realised in his amusement and his drunkenness over his newfound powers he had forgotten the four brothers completely. He visited their prisons and found, to his delight, that their failure in their duty had cost them heavily—millions of years of torture coupled with the collapse of their blood-bound duty had transformed them into living corruptions, horrors that were still bound in their unbreakable chains, time eating away into their bodies and minds. Belial washed them in his dark power, cruelly giving them lordship over the very thing they had fought against when they had been fair and noble; turning them into darker shadows of their former selves. Then he bound them in the greatest of curses—one that did not allow the four brothers to find each other. There was always a way to break the curse though, Belial assured them; and for that, all they had to do was to break the first four of the seven seals in his path. He was confident about breaking the last three.

'The four Horsemen follow the curse. It is said that every seal has four souls, four specific souls that will unlock it. They forever hunt for these souls, for the brothers want to ride together once more. And it is said that when the Horsemen do ride, the end of the world shall come along with the sound of their hooves. The Serpent will rise and usher in a new era of blood and darkness.'

The old man ended quietly and looked into the distance, his eyes soft and brimming with expression.

'The Apocalypse,' Adri said gently. 'The end of all things. I have read three names Death has taken. My soul is the last soul it needs.'

Gray looked stunned. He leaned back against the tree wordlessly. Fayne said nothing, his eyepieces occasionally reflecting sunlight.

'How are these four souls chosen?' Adri asked the storyteller. 'Is it random, or is it something else?'

'I do not know,' the old man said. 'This is all of the legend of the Horsemen and their origin.'

'The Apocalypse is real, then,' Adri said. 'If the Horsemen are real—and if Death wants my soul—then everything is real. Then I might be the only thing standing between Death and the Apocalypse.' He got up and looked into the distance.

'That might just be the case, assuming the other Horsemen have broken their seals,' Aurcoe said. Adri started to walk out into the park, his steps slow.

'Your father was removed because he might have known this,' Gray said slowly. 'Or perhaps he may have been able to help you to a massive extent.'

Adri continued walking away from the tree saying nothing.

'The Apocalypse is not the end of all things,' Fayne said. 'It is a new order. Things will change. The government will fall and almost all living creatures will either be enslaved, or hunted down and killed. We call it the Age of Suffering—it has always been hypothetical and a part of legend, of course.'

'Like he said,' Aurcoe spoke, 'if the Horseman is real, chances are the Apocalypse is too. And it makes sense. There has been a strange vibe in the air, a strange feeling. Something is about to change and now we know what.'

Adri had walked a bit away from the group.

'I'm glad this came to light,' he said. He was perfectly audible in the afternoon silence. 'Now I know what exactly it is I have to do.'

He turned around and faced them, the destroyed, burned park behind him, collapsed buildings and a broken over-bridge beyond, looming in the distance—everything empty and quiet, devoid of life.

'I'm going to have to kill Death,' Adri said.

Part II

The Madman's Song

21

'You made it sound like you were going through something actually dangerous,' Adri said. 'You just found an old man and solved this.'

'Don't even *think* of going there, Sen,' Aurcoe smirked. 'The forbidden texts of *Quish'iar* resemble no newspaper to be read over a hot cup of coffee. It's one of the best guarded text pieces in the world, and little old me had to get past all those marvellous death-traps and things that guard that place just to go through that damn document as it had a reference, a mere passing reference to the Horsemen. This was a *process*, Sen. Rome wasn't built in a day, and Old Kolkata sure as hell wasn't.'

'Is our deal at an end, then?' Adri asked. 'Or do Angels still make deals?'

'You have tortured me long enough, Sen,' Aurcoe said, beginning to frown. 'I have upheld my part of the bargain.'

'Not quite. You still don't know *who* is behind this,' Adri said.

'What do you mean, who?' the Fallen barked. 'You know the Horseman is after you because your soul is the last one he needs to break his seal.'

'My father has been removed from the board for a purpose, Fallen. And someone is paying for Maya's protection to counter the same. We are pawns, a part of something bigger here. Someone is watching me, and I want to find out who that is.'

'Wasn't part of the deal. I don't know if you're imagining the whole conspiracy thing here, Sen, this does sound a bit farfetched. But regardless, all this has happened and I'm still willing to look into it after my transformation. For a price, of course.'

'You're quite the slippery bastard, aren't you?' Adri said, smiling grimly. 'What will this price of yours be?'

Aurcoe grinned. 'Depends on what you can offer, Tantric.'

'How about this?' Adri said. 'I will not give away your source of return to the Angel Order. They will not know that the blood came from a fellow Angel; you can lie about doing your great deeds of good and noble self-sacrifice that are usually the path to growing back those wings.'

Aurcoe's grin faded. 'You play dirty, Sen,' he said. 'And it's a hard bargain, but you have the knowledge of how the Angel Order works and the fact that you brought the blood does tell me you are capable of what you claim. Fine. I will find the players of this game and bring them to your attention; do not expect me to help you in any fights, of course.'

'I wouldn't. But I will need to hang on to the pendant until I figure this out.'

'Yes, fine. Now the blood!' the Fallen snarled.

He was desperate, and Adri thought he had squeezed all he could out of the situation. He reached into his pocket and brought out the vial; even in his hand he felt it pulse with raw power. Temptation seized him for a wild second, a crazy second. The thought of all that power being given away, it was not fair. Then he snapped out of it and handed the vial to Aurcoe.

Aurcoe almost leapt as he grabbed it and in doing so dropped his human guise. Gray stared in horror at the entity before him— at the white and blue shredded, burnt skin; at the sunken grey eyes; at the stumps with scars where the wings had once been; at the odd angles the feet were placed in; at the overall damnation the creature was. Aurcoe did not care about anyone watching him. He stared at the vial and at the blood within. His hands shook.

'You have done the impossible, Adri Sen,' he whispered, looking at the blood with pure desire, with ambition and the desperation of happiness. He did not waste time; he uncorked the lid and drank the blood immediately, not leaving a drop in the vial. Then he threw it away and waited, looking first at the others and then at his own arms and legs. Everyone waited with baited breath for something to happen, but nothing did. The Fallen was nervous, and he began to lose his patience. Breathing faster, he looked over his back again and again to check for feathers, but saw none; he palmed his raw head for hair, but felt nothing.

He looked questioningly at Adri. 'This was supposed to—' he began, and then it happened. His skin started changing. At first it was colour, but then his muscle fibres started transforming; everything was developing, changing. His complexion was becoming creamier from white. His shoulders were starting to expand. While everyone watched, fascinated, his chest widened and bones rearranged themselves—his legs grew more muscular and taller than they had been. Hair sprouted magically from his head and his eyes changed colour as his face changed structure. A nose grew out of nowhere. His clothes were a tighter fit now. Finally, the wings. At first, mere feathers. Then suddenly, the process sped and the entire wing cartilage spread wide in opposite directions with swift promptitude. Two giant, powerful Angel wings, raining wispy feathers everywhere.

Adri looked at him. Aurcoe now looked like the human guise he used to keep, except that his body was now better built than before. Angels were created ready for war.

'You still have a paunch,' Adri said.

'I am beautiful,' Aurcoe said. 'I am everything I wanted to be and your cheap comments cannot possibly take that away.' His wings flapped and he rose into the air, effortlessly.

'Find out,' Adri said with finality.

'Yes. And if you are still alive after your little escapade, I will find you,' the newborn Angel replied, and then flew up, skirting around the tree branches. They watched him fly away and out of the park and towards the MYTH camp.

'That is the way to travel, huh?' Gray said, fascinated.

'Well, he's an Angel now,' Adri replied.

'You gave him an easy way out,' the old man said.

Adri turned to him. 'He has done as he had promised.'

'He did not rightfully earn the wings he now wears,' the old man replied. 'And you know it well.'

'I would keep my word even with filth like that,' Adri said.

'You *did* blackmail him though,' Gray shrugged.

'Aurcoe is dangerous. He's best kept under weight than let free,' Adri observed.

'Your wisdom guides you well, I can see that,' the storyteller said. 'The path ahead is not easy for you. Your rewards will be much harsher earned than Aurcoe's.'

Adri looked seriously at the old man. 'What are you trying to tell me, Dadu?'

'The legends say that the Horsemen are not mortal,' the old man said.

'That doesn't mean they are immortal.'

'But the way you choose is foolish. There is no sense in confronting Death without the knowledge to end him.'

'Do you know how I must confront Death then?' Adri asked.

'No. But I can do something else, I can guide you to someone who might know.'

'Who?'

'There is a banished Tantric who is now a sadhu. No doubt you have heard tales of him; he is called Kali. His specialty, when it comes to open combat, is always weakness—he studied weaknesses to the core even when he was with the government.'

'I have heard rumours about him, yes,' Adri said.

'They say he is mad,' Gray spoke, his eyes wide.

'And that MYTH banished him because the Seven got afraid of him and his capabilities,' Adri continued, 'and, the only Necromancer my father never talked about.'

'He was greatly gifted,' the old man said. 'And there are many who consider him more powerful than your father, though that is an eternal debate among young trainee Tantrics and old veteran Tantrics alike.'

'But are you suggesting we go to him?' Gray asked. 'He doesn't sound friendly.'

'He is quite, ah, *disturbed*. But his mind is still as brilliant as it once was. You might get your answers and get them well. *Getting* to him might be a little tougher than usual though.'

'Where is he?'

'His temple is somewhere in the centre of the *Bishakto Jongol*, the venomous forest. Be careful, but then I do not need to tell you that, do I?' The old man smiled at Adri. 'You have been there before, young one. I can see it in your eyes.'

'Not much, but yes,' Adri said softly.

'Why does that not sound good?' Gray asked Fayne. 'I mean, it's called a bloody venomous forest! Why do we have to go through such places?'

'My skills are not getting rusty, *myrkho*. You will not find me complaining,' Fayne said. 'I thought protection of the *fatiya* would be a dull job until I met this Tantric.'

Gray almost choked. 'Why am I not surprised? Who am I talking to anyway—an assassin! Both of you—you and this damned Tantric—you get off on all this! You *like* staying on the

315

edge! Why am I the only one who wants to take the longer way around?'

'You could get really good with that shotgun if you took an interest in it,' Fayne said calmly. 'It is a noble weapon, not deserving the likes of you.'

Gray seemed to be swelling with rage and disbelief. Adri turned to him. 'There is no way around—even if we were only tracking the Devil Mask, we would have to go through the forest to Howrah if we were to beat the MYTH forces to it. They will doubtlessly not risk it.'

A large part of Old Kolkata had been dominated by flora, but unlike Jadavpur University, there were entire parts of the city that the trees engulfed completely. Most of the buildings were destroyed, but few still stood; there were many trees and little sunlight in these areas, making them humid and swampy—thick with venoms and all kinds of wildlife. These were the nature ruled areas of the city; even the Demons would not tread into the *Bishakto Jongol* unless it was completely necessary. The government, after losing a tremendous amount of men to the forest decided to name it an officially out-of-bounds area. The forest covered a large stretch west of Narkeldanga and frayed out near Howrah.

'It will rain,' the old man said, looking at the cloudless sky. 'I'm saying it again, by no means will your journey be an easy one.'

Adri had respect for the old man's judgment and did not question him. He was grateful for the knowledge and the help the old man had provided, and he thanked him the best he could.

'It hasn't been easy so far either, though,' Gray muttered. 'I mean, I wouldn't call this easy.'

It hadn't been, Adri thought. But then, this was really what was expected from the Old City. It tested you and threw quite a lot your way, but if you could take it, then it would let you through.

There was a lot more they had to see now. A lot more. Adri had now found the main reason as to why he was being hunted, and its implications. There were people who did not believe in the Apocalypse and he had been one among them. But that was earlier. Now he had witnessed things, discovered the existence of the Horsemen, seen the Old City change and behave differently, had his father disappear, and listened to whispers of the end and songs of Doomsday that only confirmed what he had previously thought lore. He could feel it in the air of the city, what the Angels were feeling.

Something was coming.

'We should move out, then,' Adri told Gray and Fayne.

'Adri,' Gray said. 'What about Maya?'

'I shall make sure we find the Devil Mask before I find Death,' Adri replied.

'How do we force her out of the creature without killing it?'

'I will discuss my idea when the time comes.'

You're planning to kill her, aren't you? the Wraith spoke gleefully. *You're one clever bastard. You needed her and her sibling to just point out the way to the Angel. And now that you have the Angel's permission to not let her live if an extraction isn't possible, you're simply going to kill her once she's in the Devil Mask. Gray cannot blame you, you will simply point at Kaavsh. Hence you cannot discuss your idea now.*

'Know your place, Wraith,' Adri said quietly.

I'm starting to know you better, Adri Sen. And I actually like what I see. We could have been friends if I had met you in my lifetime.

'I do what is necessary,' Adri said.

Quite the statement. The protector of peace, are you, now?

Adri ignored the Wraith.

'Let us eat here,' Fayne said.

Adri, who was stooping to pick up his backpack, stopped. 'All right,' he said in agreement. 'Will you eat with us, Dadu?'

'If you offer me food, I will not decline,' the storyteller replied.

They had their food cold and directly out of cans. Gray, chewing beans, looked at Fayne. 'You do not eat. I have never seen you eat. You just keep drinking from that hip flask of yours.'

Fayne, who had just taken a few sips from the flask, kept it back within his robe and pulled his mask back down. He said nothing.

'What do you keep drinking?' Gray persisted.

'Blood,' Fayne said.

'*Blood*? *Human* blood? Why?'

'Because he's half witch,' Adri said. 'It is a necessary sacrifice on his part.'

'It has everything I need for my nourishment. I can survive only on this,' Fayne said.

'But you're a damn *vampire*!' Gray squealed.

'It is human blood, correct. But it is treated in a certain brew; drinking raw blood would be too *overwhelming*.'

'So you can't eat food?'

'He can, Gray,' Adri said. 'It will just take a *lot* of food to keep his reflexes up, to keep him in shape, and give him the energy he needs. One drink of treated blood can do the same.'

'What he said,' Fayne said, nodding.

'How do you get the human blood?' Gray asked, curious.

'Let's not go there, *myrkho*,' Fayne said.

'Have you been in the venomous forest, Fayne?' Adri asked.

'*Rashkor*. I was never assigned to that forest. Those of my comrades who survived the forest claim they saw unbelievable things, things that are beyond what the supernatural presence in Old Kolkata is like. My fellow assassin, Monore Drassia, returned insane from there. That made him a more efficient killer in the years to come, but clients were rather *afraid* of his unpredictability and his obsession with the colour red. No, Tantric, bad things have happened in that forest.'

'Can you take care of Maya well while we cross it?'

318

'To the best of my ability, *pashlin*. I might be wary of the forest, but there is no fear involved.'

Silence returned to the group. Adri ate fast. The forest wasn't far away, but "somewhere around the centre" wasn't a good enough description for him, which meant they would have to do some searching. Kali did not make him optimistic. He would have to call some spirits. He told the others to eat slowly and take their time, and grabbing some ingredients, he hurried out of the park and onto the road where he drew a pentacle and started off a series of summonings.

22

It was raining. The clouds had appeared almost magically as they had drawn closer to the entrance of the forest. Not only had the clouds made the sun disappear, but now they were getting wet as they walked. Adri was annoyed, but he knew there was no other way. One could see where exactly the forest started—an ominous line of foliage in the distance, thick and unfathomable.

Adri held out his right hand as he walked; the raindrops, he found, soothed the itching that had developed a while back. The hand felt better, even though its condition was much worse. Something strange was happening to his ring finger—a scaly infection was slowly enveloping it. He could feel real scales growing on his skin and could not fathom why. The scales were dark in colour and tough to the touch. Initially, he had panicked, wanting to get rid of whatever it was as soon as possible. He had seen nothing like it before, and he was more than a little scared inside. But Tantric training was made of sterner stuff and he soon found a certain peace, even as he watched the infection grow. Weird things were known to happen in the Old City. There were diseases and ailments beyond control, beyond explanation. And this was just one of them. Sometimes things would get better, sometimes a healer would have to be visited. Either way, it did not hurt and it did not restrict his movements. As for a healer, Adri did not have time for healers. He did not have time. Period. The *Ai'n Duisht* weighed heavy and cold against his chest, and at times like this it drew attention to itself, to how it was all that stood between him and the Horseman. Adri knew that he was treading a thin line and that his luck was bound to run out soon. But there were things to do. If only the weather, at the very least, would be a little more forgiving.

The rain trickled off the scales on his hand and the water that seeped in to his skin felt good.

He was walking ahead with Gray and Fayne following him, Fayne carrying Maya. Gray walked faster and caught up with Adri.

'Err, how's the Wraith doing?' he asked a bit nervously.

'You can tell the assassin it is nowhere near taking control,' Adri replied.

'Oh, okay. Horrible weather, huh?'

'Yes,' Adri said.

They were getting closer to the first line of trees. The rain wasn't heavy, and though it did not really drench them, it was a bother. Adri was glad most of his ingredients were in waterproof containers and pouches. His guns were probably waterproof, knowing the Gunsmith had made them.

Gray drew back to Fayne.

'What did he say?' the assassin asked.

'He knew you had sent me,' Gray said guiltily. 'He says the Wraith is nowhere near controlling him.'

'There is no shame in our distrust, *myrkho*,' Fayne said calmly. 'You must understand that we have to be wary of the Tantric. He has already given control to the Wraith once—and even if that saved us back there, the Wraith will have left some of its essence in his mind. Unless we can reach the place where the Wraith will depart, it might take control of him, in which case I will have to put him down.'

Gray nodded. 'This feels horrible. He has done a lot for us,

321

and he is going through a great deal himself. The last thing we should think about is killing him.'

'The Wraith is the one I shall be killing,' Fayne said. 'If he loses control he will but be a prisoner in his own mind.'

'But he seems fine to me,' Gray protested. 'Why are you always thinking about the Wraith?'

'I do not take chances with anything. And besides,' the assassin said, looking at Adri's outstretched right hand, 'the process has already begun.'

Adri stopped just as they were about to enter the forest, and turned around. 'The most important thing is to stay together,' he said. 'The forest is known to play tricks on one's senses. Do not believe what you see, just what you can touch. Get me?'

Fayne and Gray nodded quietly. Adri drew a revolver and led the way into the thicket. Gray held his shotgun as he followed, while Fayne took the rear with Maya.

'So tell me Mazumder,' Adri whispered a few moments later. 'You ever been here before?'

I must confess that I have. There was this camp of runaway vampires— mostly women and children who I had been hunting for the longest time. To elude me, they finally decided to run into this forest for their protection. You see, those blighted things were terrified of me! The Wraith laughed.

'Brave job, hunting women and children,' Adri said.

I do not pretend to be a saint, Tantric. I have killed hundreds of vampire children in my time before they could age and be more of a threat than they already were. Yes, I have done things frowned upon, but back then I was their bane. I was the one they would see in their daymares! It is unfortunate that my earth time was limited. I would love to hunt them again.

'You are leaving for the next Plane soon enough, Mazumder.'

Unfortunately, yes.

'Where is this graveyard of yours?'

Incidentally, right across this bloody forest, near Howrah like I said. We are close.

'Excellent. I believe you were in the middle of a story though.'

Ah, yes. Though I cannot really tell tales like that old man, curse his soul. Yes, I was hunting this group of bloodsuckers in this very forest when I realised that something was hunting ME. My senses, you see, were quite keen when I was human. I heard it for hours, creeping behind me, following me, and sensing my movements. Though I was tempted to, I dared not face it. I knew the damned thing, whatever it was, wasn't a vampire.

'Then?'

Then I chanced upon the group I had been tracking. Turns out there wasn't much left to kill. They were dead. Eaten, scattered.

'What did you do?'

What do you THINK I did? I got the hell out of there as soon as I could. Didn't meet whatever had been stalking me.

The stories were similar and yet different, Adri realised. He had given a lot of thought about what did live in the *Bishakto Jongol*, but he never got his reply. He had gone through a similar experience in the forest, and had survived without getting to know what had killed the others. He knew of creatures that lived here, dangerous creatures—but there was something else, something he did not know about.

The forest was dark and depressing. They were walking on marshy ground and the rain did not help. They had to constantly search for good and solid footholds, and wade through mucky water quite often; this made their progress very slow. The forest wasn't quiet either. Along with the calls of birds and the occasional forest creature, the rain and the wind were creating a symphony of their very own. It was tough to be alert and wary; their field of vision was always terribly limited by the thick undergrowth which did not allow whatever little sun there was to come through. Shadows dominated heavily. 'Darkness,' Gray said loudly an hour later. 'Not good.' Evening was descending.

'Arrive, Aina,' Adri commanded in the Old Tongue. 'Spirit glow. Show me the way.'

A translucent orb materialised in mid-air near them, and slowly filled up with a deep blue glow.

'Not as much light as a fireball, but it'll have to do,' Adri said, frowning and looking at it. 'Fireball's no use in this rain.'

The spirit hovered around them as they walked. With the setting of the sun the forest had been plunged into complete darkness, and apart from the eerie blue glow of the spirit, everything was pitch black. Adri checked his compass at regular intervals; Gray complained a lot and loudly so, while Fayne carried Maya, silent as ever. The sounds of the forest increased as night fell; a thousand crickets started a sonata around them. Frogs croaked and things slithered and crawled away as they walked through the muddy ground, their steps heavy and wary. Gray was extremely jumpy; he pointed his shotgun at any branch that moved, any splashing noise that they heard in any direction. He was the only one with a weapon out as Adri had holstered his weapon long back.

'Need more light, Adri,' Gray said nervously after they had travelled for a while. 'I don't like this place.'

'Ashthir. Spirit glow. With Gray,' Adri spoke in the Old Tongue again.

Another spirit appeared and lit up near Gray.

'Thank you,' Gray said—and collapsed.

He had taken a false step. The ground completely gave way beneath him. He was falling, free-falling for a couple of seconds before hitting a muddy slope. He rolled down, shouting, trying to hold on to anything that he could find, but everything that he could grab—mostly plants and roots—was either too slippery, or broke in his hand. He fell into complete darkness, slipping and sliding and rolling down a long way until finally he was in a free-fall again, landing on soft ground in the end.

'Aaaah,' Gray moaned slowly without moving. He lay there as he had landed, breathing heavily, trying to recuperate, his eyes tightly closed. Then he opened them, blinking mud out, and realised he wasn't in darkness like he had expected. The spirit had followed him and was bathing him in blue light. Slowly, Gray moved, and pain immediately shot up his body. He cried out, and his voice echoed before silence returned to wherever he was.

'Adri? Fayne?' he cried out wearily. No replies. Nothing at all. There was a noise, water falling somewhere in the distance. It was an echo of the actual noise, Gray realised. He tried to move again and slowly twisted around and sat up. The effort induced pain, but not otherworldly—in all probability nothing was broken. He tried to see from where he had fallen and noticed fresh soil scattered around him—the landslide had occurred behind him, maybe he could still crawl up the slant. He got up slowly and realised he was still wearing his bag. His shotgun was gone, he could not see it on the ground around him.

Gray approached the slant behind him and tried to climb, but it was impossible; the slant was wet and slippery, and water was still pouring down softly. He turned around. In the dim blue light he could see that the soft soil on which he had fallen ended after a while, giving way to rocks. He was underground. He peered up one last time and saw nothing, no one. He called out again. Nothing. He would have to find a way out, then.

He began to walk, and the orb went with him. His shoes stepped on hard rock as he walked forward. The ground gradually narrowed into a passage. CRUNCH. He had stepped on something and broken it. Looking down, Gray realised, with a sudden burst of apprehension, that it was a bone. A bone that looked too long to be anything but human. The orb hovered lower as he bent down and started to walk slower and soon the other bones came into sight. The rocks were strewn with bones of all kinds; Gray had never been one to study the human skeleton, but he recognised parts of a spine, a broken rib cage among others. Human bones then, he thought. This did not look like a burial ground—something was here. He felt chills go up his spine; he felt insecure and vulnerable.

'Gray!' He heard Adri call behind him.

'Oh thank God!' Gray exclaimed, and turning, walked into the darkness faster than the orb could keep up with. Then he tripped and fell. What he tripped over was the Sadhu's Shotgun and in doing so he set it off. In the brief flash of gunfire the entire space was illuminated just for a moment, and in that moment Gray saw something white not far from him. It seemed like a humanoid figure and it disappeared the instant Gray saw it, and then he hit the ground hard.

'Ow, twice,' he groaned painfully and at that moment, firm hands grabbed his shoulders from behind, pulling him up.

'You okay?' Adri asked.

'Huh? You were right ahead of me—' Gray mumbled as Adri pulled him to his feet, and then slung the shotgun around his own shoulder.

'Fast. Lets' go,' Adri said, urgency in his voice.

Gray did not protest. They walked down a couple of corridors and then came to a wider space like the one before. Gray saw a crevasse above him, and Fayne's dark silhouette standing above with the other orb next to him. A rope was hanging in front of them. Gray grabbed it and Fayne pulled him up to the surface, then Adri. Once out, Fayne sat in the wet grass, resting his arms calmly on his lap. Adri and Gray sat as well, catching their breath, getting wet in the rain. Maya lay next to them, oblivious.

'The hole that you tumbled through closed up with mud immediately,' Adri panted. 'There was no way we could have followed you. We rushed and looked for another way and found this crevasse; I retraced steps once beneath and found you. Luckily.'

'There were bones,' Gray said. 'Bones down there, human bones.'

Something rustled loudly near them and all of them turned sharply. Fayne had a dagger in his hand already as he peered into the darkness.

'Anything, Fayne?' Adri asked slowly.

'My vision does not help,' Fayne said. 'There are plants everywhere.'

Another plant rustled away from the first one. They turned again immediately, gazing into the darkness. But nothing happened and there was silence again, other than the rain.

'You were saying something when I found you,' Adri turned back to Gray, looking at him seriously.

'I heard you call,' Gray said, 'from the other direction. And then you were behind me.'

Adri paused for a fraction of a second before he got to his feet in one move. He rushed to his bag and pulled it to where they were sitting, and then wordlessly started groping about like a madman until he found his bullet alchemy case. Moving the bag aside, he kept the open box on the grass, in the rain, and started crumbling and putting ingredients into a series of bullets. The bullets were aligned neatly with their heads unscrewed and he filled them quickly and decisively, taking only a moment to think and find the ingredient he needed. Fayne and Gray watched him just as silently, knowing he would not respond if they asked him questions right now. And then he was done. Calmer, he emptied out the bullets in his revolvers and started loading the new ones.

Another rustle made itself heard, from a new direction. Adri stopped loading and looked in the direction of the sound. The rustling stopped and there was silence. And then from the darkness, amidst the sound of the rain and the night, came a voice. One that Adri knew too well.

'Adri, help!' Victor Sen cried.

Adri looked down silently and fitted the last two bullets in his shooter.

'Who was that?' Gray asked incredulously.

'That,' Adri said, standing up, 'was a Nishi.'

'A Nishi?' Gray asked.

'An extremely dangerous spirit that can imitate voices.'

'What? Does that mean—'

'My voice you heard below, yes. Narrow escape. Now listen to me and fast. Nishis do not attack a group. They will try and single you out. Do not trust any voice you hear; they can imitate mothers, fathers, old lovers, siblings, *anyone* you know. Do not trust any voice, not even mine. Either wait for a visual confirmation, or make it call your name. It cannot call you more than twice.'

'Okay, but why do you sound like you're going somewhere?'

'I'm going after them,' Adri said. 'Both of you stay here until I get back. Your weapons will not affect the Nishi.'

'Point accepted,' Fayne said quietly.

'You're going *after* them?' Gray repeated unbelievably.

In response, Adri moved off into the forest, taking one of the orbs with him. The rain got heavier and came down with greater ferocity than before. Fayne and Gray sat quiet and unmoving, getting drenched. Gray realised he was scared.

'Gray!' Adri's voice hissed from the darkness suddenly.

'Oh my God,' Gray murmured, shutting his eyes.

Adri's voice laughed and Gray felt it moving around them in a circle, keeping to the darkness.

This was it, then. Nishis. I did not know of their existence, the Wraith told Adri.

'They are not vampires. You would not know,' Adri said grimly, walking unhesitatingly into the foliage.

True.

Adri heard a rustle to his right. He drew his gun and walked into the plants on his right. 'Nishi! Nishi! Nishi!' he shouted in the rain, walking into the darkness.

'Put the light out, Adri,' Maya's voice spoke behind his ear.

He spun around and saw no one. He knew where the creature was now—in the direction where he had initially been walking, ready to pounce. He spun again and fired. He saw the salivating fangs in mid-air as his gun roared, right on mark. The creature erupted in fire and Adri deftly stepped aside. The creature crashed into the mud, but its fire did not go out even in the rain. It turned and twisted in complete silence, without a single gasp of pain escaping its throat. Adri left it burning and walked into the forest again.

Voices were whispering all around Gray and Fayne. The assassin heard everything with mild curiosity, occasionally replying, while Gray sat as quietly as he could, hands on his ears and eyes shut. He was terrified.

'We did not finish what we started, Fayne,' a female's voice breathed through the woods.

'Do you mean I should have pushed that dagger further through your lungs?' Fayne asked aloud.

'You cannot refuse a good fight. Are you a coward?' the voice hissed further.

'You're the one talking from the shadows,' Fayne said calmly.

The voice hissed in anger and left; it came back on the other side and continued circling them. Both Fayne and Gray could feel the voices travelling like bodiless entities, moving freely and with speed all around. Then in the distance they heard Adri shout out loud, again and again.

'I think that was really Adri,' Gray said. 'Means he's still alive.'

'Oh, the *pashlin* can take good care of himself,' Fayne waved Gray's comment aside. 'I think he sounded *angry*.'

You're angry, Mazumder said.

'Shut up, Wraith!' Adri spat. 'And you, any more of you Nishi bastards out there?'

He was standing in a small clearing and four Nishis lay aflame on the ground all around him. Adri had a flesh wound on his side and it was bleeding. He holstered his gun and kept a hand on the wound. He winced.

'Well, any more of you cowards out there?' he roared.

He sensed something move behind him. He spun around and drew his weapon in a flash—a couple of rounds later another existence was in flames.

'Burn, you cruel maggots. Burn well,' Adri said, looking at the thing.

You hate them a bit too much, a bit too suddenly. Has it something to do with the one which just impersonated your mother's voice?

'I haven't heard my mother's voice!' Adri shouted. 'This vile creature—this bloody spirit has the audacity to call me *son* in what it supposes was my mother's voice! I do not believe it, that is not what my mother sounded like! I will summon my mother myself someday and talk to her, not listen to her voice through some cheap Nishi!'

Ooh. They touched a raw nerve, I see.

'You bloody bastards!' Adri yelled, firing again at the already burning Nishis.

Good thing you're making sure.

'Don't you get all smart-mouthed on me now,' Adri snarled. He looked around in the rain, shouted out some more challenges into the darkness, then retraced his steps with all the grace of an angry bull. Now that he had been around a few, he was beginning to feel their presence more clearly; he felt their vibes near where he had left the others. He approached the clearing and saw a flash of white; he fired unhesitatingly and missed. He dived to a side and the Nishi whizzed past him with a predatory hiss. He recovered with a roll; getting up on his knees and leaning against a tree, he waited. It was coming at him again—Adri dived out of the way again, firing—the Nishi incinerated amidst the heavy rain.

Adri reloaded a shooter and then moved towards the clearing where the others were. He burst into it, startling Gray, and walked across and into the forest again.

'Nishi!' he roared with hate.

Just so that you know, Tantric, I am completely enjoying myself.

Adri returned more than an hour later. The rain was slowing down and the sounds of the forest were beginning to take over once more. Adri emerged from the forest then; he looked tired and beat, and he had blood all over his shirt. He looked at Gray and Fayne, and finally at Maya. Then he collapsed on the ground next to her.

23

When Adri did open his eyes, it was morning and the rain had stopped. He was in a sitting position, his back propped against a tree. He was sore, his body hurt all over; he looked down and saw he had been bandaged. His hand slowly rose to his face and he felt a bandage around his forehead as well. Suddenly he realised he hadn't had a good bath for days. He reached in his pocket and withdrew his cigarette packet. To his disgust, all the cigarettes were wet. He looked around. He had more cigarettes in his bag, but it was on the other side of the clearing and he did not know if he should try and get to it.

Fayne sat in the centre of the clearing, cooking something in a small pot. Gray and Maya were not in sight; in all probability he was changing her.

'Anything happen?' Adri asked. It took him a surprising amount of effort to speak.

'Nothing since last night. We decided to wait here, wasn't possible to carry two,' Fayne said.

Adri squinted in the sunlight and saw a couple of pale blue orbs floating in air still; with a hand gesture he dismissed the spirits. Fayne looked at him.

'Your anger makes you careless, *pashlin*,' he said.

'Yeah well, those things were dangerous,' Adri said.

'But you could have easily dealt with them without getting a scratch. Your training shows. You are still alive, which is not what many can say after a night with Nishis.'

'They're inherently cruel,' Adri said. 'Vicious. The trick to fighting them is to not give them a chance to play their tricks.'

'And the flammable bullets you used,' Fayne said. 'There are not many creatures who can survive my blade, Tantric. Since Nishis can, I'm glad you were here.'

Gray entered the clearing, carrying Maya. He put her down and turned to the other two. 'God, I'm constantly afraid of a Nishi,' he said.

'They cannot exist in the light,' Adri said. 'It is impossible for them to come out during the day.'

'I wish I knew that,' Gray complained. 'I was constantly looking over my shoulder. But that's a relief to hear.'

'I killed a lot of them yesterday. They should get the message, they're not really the revenge type, Nishis,' Adri said.

'So they live in this forest?'

'Nishis are never self-existing. They are slaves, servants of Tantrics.'

'What? How come *you* don't have a couple of Nishis polishing your shoes?'

'It isn't right. They are evil things, and live to kill and destroy. I have never needed such creatures. I don't even prefer summoning Demons, for that matter.'

'These Nishis might have been servants of Kali,' Fayne said.

'Exactly,' Adri said. 'With luck, he's close. We shouldn't waste any more time.'

'We should eat,' Gray said, looking at the pot.

'And you should look at your hand,' Fayne said, starting to stir.

Adri did, and gasped silently. The scales had spread all over his right hand, making it look like he was wearing some sort of dark glove. He contracted and moved his fingers; there was a kind of snap to the movement, but he wasn't being restricted. He tapped the scales with his left hand. Hard, almost metallic.

'What is this?' Adri asked, disturbed.

'Something to be worried about,' Fayne replied without delay. 'Your body is not meant to harbour two souls. The Wraith is causing this.'

'Mazumder. What the hell is this?' Adri asked.

It is unfortunate.

'Come to the damn point.'

It is a side effect of carrying me. It will leave when I do.

'But what *is* it?' Adri asked, not being able to tear his eyes off his hand.

'A *bakheeyal*. An infection,' Fayne said. 'It will continue to spread.'

'Is that true, Wraith?' Adri asked.

There are, of course, ramifications of choosing to let another spirit reside in your body.

'I'm surprised you did not know about this, Tantric,' Fayne said.

'I don't know everything! The Wraith is saying it will leave when he does. Is that true?'

Fayne snorted loudly, the closest he had ever come to a laugh. 'It can go away right now if the Wraith wishes it. It is trying to take over, Tantric. It is consciously transforming your body.'

Nonsense, the Wraith spoke immediately. *Utter nonsense. This assassin is not learned in the way of spirits.*

'Of course the *mieserkha* will deny it right now,' Fayne continued, stirring the food. 'But know what's happening, Tantric. Getting rid of that Wraith is not going to be as easy as you think.'

'Mazumder,' Adri said, 'if there's even a grain of truth in what Fayne is saying, know that you're not going to get away with it.'

'He knows that. Why else do you think he's armouring you?' Fayne said.

Believe me, Tantric. I have not caused you any harm so far. I have helped you, rather, when you let me through, in the midst of battle when you gave me control. I could have taken over right then if I wanted to, yet all I did was lend you my powers. That should tell you something, not this assassin uneducated in the arts.

'Even Fayne has proved his worth, Mazumder,' Adri said. 'We will visit this graveyard sooner than you think, and you better stick to your word then.'

Rest assured.

Adri did not know what to think. Things were beginning to confuse him now: the assassin's bank of knowledge had not been unreliable so far, but even the Wraith had made no mental attack, or stab at control. It had been peaceful, in fact. He regretted not knowing more about this. He needed to get back to the books when he found time again. There was always so much more to learn. His father would know, he was sure.

He asked Gray to get him his bag. He extracted a cigarette packet which was dry and replaced the soggy one. Lighting a cigarette, he thought about their next course of action while Gray served him his meal in a bowl. After they had eaten and packed the bowls and put out the small fire, Adri finally made an attempt at getting up. It hurt his wounds immediately, and he cursed himself for his carelessness the night before. They had somehow hit a very personal nerve and he had exploded. His training demanded better from him. He shook his head and swore to himself that it would not happen again. He needed to keep a calm head under the circumstances.

Fayne cut a walking stick for him out of a branch in minutes. His pride told him he did not need it, but a few steps proved otherwise. Slowly, they began walking deeper into the forest.

'This is not good,' Gray told Adri. 'You can't afford to be this stupid, not in a place like this. We need both you and Fayne to protect Maya.'

'It was a mistake,' Adri muttered. 'And I'm the one with the wounds anyway.'

'You know what I mean,' Gray said, and Adri did not reply.

335

They travelled on, the forest getting marshier than ever after the rains, slowing their progress terribly and forcing them to wade through waist-deep water at times. Snakes crossed their path almost continuously and Fayne kept grabbing and throwing them aside with his free hand. When they finally got to higher ground, everyone was happier. A sudden rise in the height of the ground, which led to a more rocky landscape, greeted them. They climbed and then continued, on hard, dry ground after a long time.

They saw the first stone pillar soon. It was a block of stone slabs one above the other, chains connecting the entire structure. It was old, the chains having rusted ages ago; vines and moss had laid claim on the pillar completely, making it look like a tree amongst all the others. It was the first time they were seeing something like that though, and Adri took it as a sign that they were not far from their goal. Other pillars followed soon, and the narrow jungle path widened out after a while, leaving a stone arch in their way. The arch was just like the pillar in appearance, except it seemed to have a message inscribed across it in the Old Tongue.

'What's written on it?' Gray asked.

'It's intricate,' Adri replied slowly. 'And some of the writing has rubbed off. But the gist of it would be "Glory to the Dark Goddess".'

'The Dark Goddess? I haven't seen her around for a while,' Fayne said.

'You mean she's a living goddess?' Gray asked nervously.

'No, there were these cults that used to worship her seriously. Her idol, I mean,' Fayne said. 'We used to see her around often. I'm seeing a reference to her after quite some time.'

'Her offerings were always sacrificial in nature,' Adri said, looking at the arch intently. 'Led to a lot of religious fanaticism.'

They walked under the arch and almost immediately, Adri felt the level of magical activity increase in the area, and immensely so.

'We tripped some kind of magical alarm,' Adri said, drawing a shooter with his free hand. 'We have to be careful now. Gray, carry Maya.'

Fayne handed Maya over to Gray, who struggled with her weight yet again. Adri felt more relieved. He was hurting a lot, and because of his wounds, felt slower. His reaction time had evidently come down. Bad.

Stones soon appeared under their feet; they were walking down a stone road in silence. It was a long walk as the path twisted and turned. Gray was slow with Maya and needed to rest frequently, and though they expected hidden dangers at each turn, nothing disrupted their progress. After walking for a little more than two hours, they saw ruins in the distance. Huge pillars, made of the same stone, looking at them from beyond the trees and even higher. As they walked closer, they realised that the pillars had been part of some structure which had once existed here. Only ruins remained now, collapsed walls and exposed rooms, burned staircases and broken roofs, all in the centre of a very large clearing. The forest seemed to shy away from the ruins somehow; only grass and occasional creepers had laid claim on the ruins. It was evidently the remains of what had once been a fort, or a castle.

'Does this look like a temple to you?' Adri asked.

'We should be near the centre of the forest right now,' Fayne said. 'If we don't find Kali here I will be surprised.'

They entered the ruins. There was no other way, but to go through the remains of the structure, through passages and half-demolished hallways that seemed to go on and on. Everything was silent as they entered and continued through. The sun was high, and the ruins cast shadows everywhere. The stones were strangely dry though, as if it hadn't rained here at all. Gray pointed this out as he struggled and panted under Maya's weight; no one answered him. Fayne walked slowly, like a leopard on the prowl. Adri could sense just how tense the assassin's muscles were. Perhaps Fayne, too, was sensing something here. The Wraith spoke suddenly and made Adri jump.

I don't like it here, there is something quite powerful resting. Be quiet, it wouldn't be wise to disturb its afternoon siesta.

Adri was sure their arrival had already been announced by changes in the magic vibes in the air. With a place as thick with magic as this, even the slightest of changes resounded like echoes in every single corner. No, if Kali was here, he definitely knew of their presence.

Then they noticed the things on display.

'What's that?' Gray gasped.

'It's a skeleton nailed into a wall,' Fayne replied.

'I know,' Gray said, a touch of irritation among all the horror. 'But I mean—why are the bones *red* in colour?'

'A ritual,' Adri said quietly.

'What kind of—'

'It would help our case if you did not talk right now.'

They ran into other skeletons soon, propped up against walls with chains and nails, bones bloody red. They observed these with distaste and moved on, though the Wraith was clearly pleased.

My respect for Kali goes up, Tantric. I must confess, this is what I had done to my resting place as well. It does an excellent job of scaring intruders, grave-robbers and the like.

'I *saw* your resting place. There's nothing right with displaying your kills like this,' Adri hissed.

You are not like me, Tantric. You have potential though.

They broke into a huge courtyard in the middle of the ruins. The pillars stopped; all that lay ahead of them was a huge circular platform of stones, with the ruins continuing on the other side. They froze in their tracks and stared at what faced them—in the centre of the courtyard was an enormous statue, about twenty feet in height. It looked down upon them, glaring.

'The Dark Goddess,' Fayne said.

She was made completely of dark stone, but her tongue was painted crimson; it hung out as she glared at them, dressed in the skin of a leopard, her hair wild and untamed. Her gaze was terrifying to behold; it was cruel and devastating; her eyes, though made of stone, seemed to be alive. She had ten arms all about her and apart from an assortment of sabres and scimitars, she held carved corpses of dead men hanging from four arms. A necklace of skulls hung around her neck.

She was beautiful, she was petrifying. She was a horror. She was a slayer, wild and unstoppable, someone rising from the dark depths below, someone with unholy blood in her veins yet holy in herself, in her presence, and in her lineage. Terrible. She was fear itself and she made all three of them uneasy, even though she was a stone statue standing in the sunlight.

None of them could say anything else. They stood there, at the edge of the courtyard, gazing at the idol in wonder and in fear. They could not move, they felt transfixed in her stare.

'Move,' a man's voice rang across the courtyard. 'Approach me.'

The voice was old and harsh, like one that had been through a lot. They were jerked out of the trance by this voice, and they realised only then that beneath the idol sat a man. He was old. Dressed in a black dhoti and nothing else, he sat beneath the goddess on a stone pedestal, his eyes shut. His body had been left untended for years—his beard went down to his waist and his hair was tied in a million braids that spread behind him in an immense matted, dirty-looking clump. His face was aged and wrinkled, and black ceremonial marks covered most of his face and body. Apart from the Tantric tattoos on his arms, he had intricate black tattoos around his eyes. Like the goddess behind him, he too wore a necklace of skulls around his neck. Kali.

Slowly, Adri began to walk towards him. Gray kept Maya down on the stone floor and withdrew his shotgun as silently as he could. Fayne walked towards the Tantric with Adri, but stopped midway. Adri kept walking slowly until finally he stood before Kali. No one spoke, and Kali breathed heavily.

'You have your father's aura,' Kali said finally.

Adri was taken aback. He could sense small surges of power, but the Tantric was hiding the extent of his power from Adri. He did not reply.

'You have a good hold on your abilities,' Kali continued, still breathing heavily. 'But you still have a lot to learn. You must not be overconfident. No. Careful is what you must be. If you are careful, you can defeat any foe who needs to be defeated.'

Adri did not react once more. Then slowly, he nodded.

'You will be tested, and it will be much harder than what you expect or what you can deal with,' Kali said in his old, cracked voice. 'Your weakness is your parentage. Any foe who has knowledge of the secrets your mother or your father had, can defeat you, because you will let them. Your confusion leads you astray, Adri Sen, and until you resolve them you cannot be a focused Necromancer. Greatness will always shy from your grasp until then.'

'I need your help in dealing with my confusions,' Adri said.

'Ask, and I will answer,' Kali replied.

'I need to know how to kill a Horseman, one in particular. Death.'

Kali breathed for a while before he answered. 'The eldest brother,' he said. 'Understand, Tantric, that the Horsemen are not regular magical creatures. They are not entities summoned by our kind or ones that are seen, even rarely. No, they are among the oldest creatures that ever existed—created by the Serpent, fed raw power, power the likes of which has never been seen anywhere in the Old City or outside. The Horsemen are not immortal, but they are a foe beyond you or me, they are greater than any Demon or mortal. They are not entities you can vanquish in this mortal skin of yours.'

'You just said they are not immortal, and if not so, they can be killed,' Adri said.

Kali laughed loudly, an aged, hoarse laugh, nonetheless powerful. 'Yes, I'm certain they can, but I do not know of their weaknesses.'

'Then who does?'

Kali paused. 'The best person to know the secrets of a Horseman,' he said finally, 'would be another Horseman.'

Adri's eyes went wide. 'Why would another Horseman help me? They are brothers.'

'You disappoint me, young Tantric,' Kali said. 'I thought you would know more than this.'

'Know what?'

'That everything is not black and white. There are greys, and a lot of them.'

'Which Horseman can I approach?'

'The cave of Pestilence is beneath the Howrah Bridge,' Kali said. 'The Horseman should still be in there, waiting for its brother to break the last seal.'

'That is very close from here,' Adri said. 'Thank you.'

'There is something else you want to ask, I can sense it.'

'Yes, there is. I want to know how one can extract a living host from a Devil Mask,' Adri said.

Kali laughed again. 'Tricky,' he said. 'But it can be done. The Mask must be distracted.'

'The Devil Mask is a Necrotic,' Adri responded. 'It's *never* distracted.'

'Then you will have to find a way, isn't it? The devourer of life will have to be distracted when you strike. A perfect cut across the centre of the carrying cage, and you can safely cut away the host.'

'Distracting it is impossible,' Adri said, shaking his head.

'This is the only way.'

They stood in silence for a while, Adri's mind in turmoil.

'Thank you,' he said finally. 'I'm very grateful to you for your help.'

He started backing away gently. He reached as far as where Fayne stood when Kali opened his eyes. They were bloodshot, and he gazed at Adri with intention.

'You have your answers,' the Tantric said. 'Now, I must have my remuneration.'

Adri felt his heart sink. 'Kali,' he said, 'you did not talk about any remuneration.'

'You did not ask,' Kali said. 'Whatever made you think that what I know is for free?'

Fayne was completely taut, waiting for the right moment.

'What is your payment?' Adri asked.

'Leave me the girl,' Kali said. 'She will be sacrificed to the Mother.'

'No!' Gray shouted. Kali ignored him. His blood-red eyes were fixed on Adri.

'She has many cuts and bruises. The Dark Goddess will not accept your sacrifice,' Adri said.

'I will heal her for as long as necessary,' Kali replied.

'She is not conscious, and has been polluted by the Dreamer's Brew. A corruption runs in her blood.'

'If she is destined to die, then it should be easier for you. Do not question my methods or my sacrifices to the Mother. Leave me the girl and I shall let you walk out of here.'

Adri sighed. Here it was, the very thing he had been afraid of. 'I can't give you the girl, old man,' he said. 'You should look at yourself, asking for a girl the assassin here and me have sworn to protect. You let us walk out of here, or this doesn't go well.'

'You're right about this not going well, young fool,' Kali said. 'All of you will now die.'

Fayne's arms moved in a blur as he threw four daggers at the Tantric. They were thrown well, but Kali deflected them with a wave of his hand. The daggers flew off harmlessly and Kali waved his hand again.

'Possess those two,' he spoke in the Old Tongue.

Gray felt something hit him like a wall. He had been standing, and he toppled over, motionless. Fayne stood his ground, and nothing happened.

Adri waved his hand, whispering in the Old Tongue. Kali was thrown off the pedestal and onto the courtyard. In a flash, Adri withdrew a revolver and emptied a barrage of holy bullets at Kali. The fallen Tantric somehow raised a hand and the bullets vaporised as they reached him. He waved his hand again, casually, carelessly. Adri lost his footing as he flew across the courtyard, crashing painfully into a stone pillar. He crumbled at the foot of the pillar in extreme pain.

Fayne walked towards Kali. Spirits hindered him and formed walls, but the assassin broke through them, continuing his slow relentless walk towards the Tantric. Kali had sat up where he had fallen, and watched Fayne curiously.

'Not human,' he mumbled. 'And trained to resist spirits. You are not completely human.'

Fayne said nothing and continued to approach Kali.

'The assassins of Ahzad have always been most difficult to dispose of,' Kali continued. 'I am but an old man, incapable of physical combat. But there is someone who can test your abilities well, *alkhatamish*.'

He moved his hand in a series of arcane gestures. The Old Tongue poured out of his mouth unceasingly. Next to him, a small flame erupted in the stone and started tracing a path. Then a shape. Kali continued the chanting and the flame continued drawing.

Fayne came nearer and nearer. Kali was not far from him now. The Tantric's spirits created stronger and stronger resistances for Fayne, which just served to slow him down. Fayne watched the flame draw on the ground as he walked. He knew what was coming.

A pentacle of flame burned next to Kali. He looked at it and smiled. 'Arrive, Rudra,' he commanded in the Old Tongue.

Fire rose from the pentacle as the creature erupted from the ground below, raining fireballs in a circle. It looked around, then stood facing Kali, head bowed. It was a Demon; not a very large one, just a little taller than Fayne, but it stood hunched in its solid muscular frame. Its skin was dark red, and it wore armour. It had a shiny helmet and breastplate, and held a huge shield in one hand and an equally large morning star in the other. It was a Minotaur Demon—the head beneath the helmet was that of a bull; wild red eyes flickered and saw everything through the eyepieces in the helmet, and huge horns protruded from its forehead and through the helmet. Its arms and body were humanoid, hulking and well-built; instead of feet it had huge hooves.

'Kill this assassin,' Kali said calmly. 'He's bothering me.'

Adri looked up amidst his pain and saw the Demon, recognising it immediately. Rudra, one of the warlords. Its height was misleading; it was much stronger than the typical warrior Demons, a true threat even to Fayne. Adri wanted to shout a warning, but he realised that he needed to save his strength. Kali was going to be gunning for him now that Fayne was occupied. He shot a quick glance at Gray, still lying motionless beside his sister, and tried to get to his feet, ignoring protests from his entire body.

Rudra moved towards Fayne with surprising agility. Fayne reached into his back and withdrew two greater blades, the size of short swords. He said nothing. Rudra rushed at Fayne and swung the giant morning star. Fayne hopped back as the great spiked ball crashed into the ground, and lunged forward with his blades. He leapt into the air and came thundering down with his blood red swords; the Demon was quick and stopped Fayne's attack with its shield. It was quick to counter with its weapon.

Kali looked at Adri as he tried to somehow get to his feet using the stone pillar he had crashed into. 'Both of them don't have much use for words!' he shouted across to Adri. 'Even Rudra does not prefer to talk much. This is going to be interesting.'

Adri was still trying to stand. His energy was slipping away before he could collect it. Perhaps, he thought, Kali was responsible. Kali did not seem to be interested in Adri for the moment. He was busy watching the fight.

Rudra and Fayne fought fiercely and silently. Except for grunts and gasps as they struck and dodged and blocked, nothing else escaped their lips. Rudra's weapon looked old and menacing while Fayne's newly revealed blades were shiny and translucent, like larger versions of his daggers. Both had reliable weapons, and neither gave way as they met again and again. Sparks flew all over as the two fought. Rudra's shield became increasingly scratched and dented as the battle progressed, while Fayne narrowly dodged the morning star every time the Demon swung—he suspected one blow from the chained weapon would end him.

Adri leaned heavily on the pillar, one hand wrapped around it clumsily. With the other, he drew his other revolver, which he knew to be loaded. All he needed was one bullet to hit the Tantric's head. He aimed the weapon at Kali who was watching the battle. Adri closed one eye and aimed carefully, but his hand was shaking because of his injuries and the pain. Before he could take the shot, Kali gestured lightly and the gun flew out of Adri's hand to clatter to the ground several feet away.

'Either take the shot or don't!' Kali shouted again. 'Do not wait so long.'

Adri did not bother to retort. His weapon was gone. He felt a spirit repressing the revolver on the ground. He could not take it back, not right now. He leaned against the pillar, collecting his strength.

Fayne spun his swords like fabric. His rapid assault of moves was blocked by the Demon. Rudra moved towards Fayne, swinging the morning star in the air. Fayne backed away, swinging his own swords backwards, his eyes never leaving the Demon. It was impossible to say who would win the battle. This would end with a sudden blow, Adri thought.

Adri shouted in the Old Tongue all of a sudden, gesturing towards Rudra. Nothing happened. The battle remained uninterrupted.

'Your spirits,' Adri told Kali weakly. 'They are protecting the Demon.'

'He has his own immunity to spirits,' Kali said. 'Rudra does not need my help.' Kali gestured towards Adri in turn, who was thrown across the courtyard once more. As he flew towards another pillar, Adri whispered in the Old Tongue and his progress was halted in mid-air. He crashed directly down to the ground, painfully yet again. He tried to lift himself and failed.

I wish I could help, Tantric, the Wraith said. *But he will be immune to spirit fire, and you will be more easily killed if you take on my powers.* It sounded worried.

'I can't die here,' Adri gasped, trying to get up, grunting as pain shot up his body. 'Not-when-I'm-so-close!'

Supporting himself with one hand, Adri lashed out with the other, still lying fallen on the ground. Gesture was met with gesture. A spirit deadlock. Both forces collided in mid-air and fought a battle of spirits.

'Now you have my attention, Adri Sen,' Kali said, gritting his teeth. 'You could never have made it out of here alive either way. I could smell the death of my Nishis on you.'

Adri gasped for air and fought to sit up. He managed, after an enormous amount of strain. 'They deserve to die, Nishis,' he said.

'I will kill you and then make *you* a Nishi,' Kali said, laughing suddenly. 'I wonder what Victor would have to say about his son serving me?' He unleashed more spirits on Adri. Adri gestured back, deadlocking them yet again, knowing that he was going to run out of spirits before the other Tantric did.

Fayne received a tremendous kick from a hoofed foot. He was thrown across the courtyard and into a wall. He took half a second to recover, and rolled away just as the morning star smashed down, destroying the wall he had landed on. He danced away, throwing daggers; Rudra caught them on its shield, one landing on its breastplate. Nothing had even scratched it yet, but Fayne was not worried. He played his battles well, and impatience was the last thing on the perfect warrior's mind. Fayne knew he could not tire the Demon out; but he could, perhaps, force it to make a mistake by persisting. One mistake was all he needed.

Fayne sensed Adri was not doing well. Even if he wanted to help the Tantric, he would not be able to. The Demon gave no breathing room. And besides, he would always be more concerned about Maya's inert body lying where it was. But Fayne did not dislike Adri. In fact, he was having fun after a long time; journeys with Adri Sen were eventful, if nothing else. Fayne held no desire to stop Death from breaking the seal. The Apocalypse was not something he dreaded; he would deal with it if it did happen. For now, he was happy that the young Tantric always faced danger. It let Fayne keep his skills sharp, and he was grateful. In fights, he felt alive.

He somersaulted to where he had dropped his swords upon receiving the kick and picked them up. Rudra charged again, and Fayne retaliated, dodging the huge morning star as he went. The assassin marvelled at the Demon's ability to move so fast and use such a heavy weapon with such speed and accuracy. He also liked that the Demon did not speak. He knew though, that Rudra was not skilled enough to kill him, and that sooner or later, it would die by his blade. If the Demon warlord had sensed this, it did not show it. Rudra fought on with increasing speed.

Get up, Adri. Pull yourself together.

Adri unleashed another spirit at Kali, and tried to stand up. He failed. His strength had deserted him. There was nothing he could possibly do.

'I can't!' he cried.

You cannot give up now, you idiot! the Wraith hissed.

'He's too powerful,' Adri mumbled.

'Yes, acknowledge my power,' Kali shouted. 'Admit it to yourself, you will die here. There is no other truth.'

'Why did you answer my questions if you were going to kill me anyway?' Adri groaned. He reached in his pocket and, fingers fumbling, put a cigarette to his mouth.

'I may have let you go if you hadn't killed my Nishis and had given me the girl.'

Adri's fingers trembled as he smoked. He was holding something tightly inside his left fist, and Kali saw it.

'Hiding something, Tantric?' Kali laughed. 'A secret weapon?' With a wave of his hand, he sent more spirits at Adri.

Fayne realised that Rudra was using techniques. His swinging the morning star was not as random as it might appear; every time before he brought it down, the Demon would swing it in a set fashion. Every technique had its weakness, but identifying the technique inside a fast fight wasn't easy. Fayne looked for clues, and found them. In a corner of the Demon's shield, was etched a small horse, its hooves on fire. This was bounty armour, a gift for having completed training at the hands of a sensei.

'Adri!' Fayne shouted as he dodged a swing. 'What is the sigil that has a horse with burning hooves?'

'What?' Adri asked, not able to catch it.

348

A horse with burning hooves, the Wraith said. *The assassin wants to know what sigil it is.*

'Narcasra!' Adri shouted in seconds.

Spirits attacked him at that very moment. His own spirits were weakening and beginning to die; Adri knew he would have to resort to personal defence techniques now. His left hand still clenched, he put his right hand in his pocket and withdrew a piece of chalk. Then he drew a circle around where he sat, and started to scrawl runes around it.

'A positive circle isn't going to help you,' Kali laughed loudly. 'Not for long, anyway.'

Narcasra had three teachers, Fayne recollected as he danced about, striking Rudra's shield relentlessly. Two taught the art of shield and weapon. That made it simpler—Rudra was either using the long forgotten dual-hold technique, or the more recent fang-repeat technique. Fayne, of course, knew both—both were very similar, and thus it took him another minute to be sure of which one it was. If he were to be wrong, the result would be a very messy death. But then again, Fayne knew he could not be wrong.

Fayne followed a textbook breakdown of the *fang-repeat-flail.* He attacked Rudra, forcing the Demon to bring up the shield and throw its other arm back to begin swinging the morning star. Fayne backed away slightly, and Rudra swung; but Fayne ran in low and with the hilts of both swords, hit under the shield with just the right amount of force and the perfect angle. It flew upwards and in the way of the spiked ball, deflecting it directly back into Rudra's own helmet. The Demon was knocked over, the weapon having crushed its helmet and face. Fayne silently walked up to the fallen Demon and slit its throat. Then he looked at Kali and Adri.

'Take Maya and Gray and run,' Adri shouted with a sense of urgency. 'Into the ruins, now!'

Fayne was beginning to approach Kali, but he read the note of urgency in Adri's voice. Something was about to happen. He silently turned towards where Gray and Maya lay, and sheathing the swords into his back, he started to run.

Kali looked at Adri, a bit confused. He gestured with both hands, and two flames appeared on the ground, drawing two pentacles of their own.

'You have many Demons, Kali,' Adri said. 'But like you said' —he opened his left palm and let hang by the string the pendant of the crescent moon, and wore it— 'there are some foes beyond Demons.'

Kali could not believe his eyes. He started nodding slowly. 'How long had you taken it off?'

'Long enough,' Adri said, looking up at the skyline.

'But what makes you think I will let you run?' Kali asked, incredulously.

'That,' Adri said.

Kali turned and stopped the dagger aimed for him in mid-air. Fayne picked up Maya and Gray and disappeared into the ruins at almost the same time as Adri got up and made a run for it, out of the courtyard. Kali roared and lashed out with his spirits, but Adri had saved some of his own, and they deadlocked. Adri, Fayne and the other two were gone, gone among the ruins.

Kali did not get much time to react. Before he knew it, he heard them. Hooves. Coming closer and closer, getting thunderously loud. He waved his hands and two more pentacles formed themselves on the ground around him.

Kali looked at the skyline and saw birds dropping dead towards the east. It was coming, it was almost here.

'Arrive, Gosheel, Ashmm, Chhal, Sheyak,' he said in the Old Tongue.

Four Demons rose in their pentacles and awaited orders. Kali was silent. He looked at the forest towards the east. The hooves grew louder and louder. Ideally he should send the Demons after Adri, to drag him back. That would be his best way out here; but then again, the Tantric preferred to feel better protected. Perhaps the Horseman could be reasoned with to give chase. Perhaps at the end of whatever was to come, he could still heal and then offer the girl to the Mother. He would see.

Before the arrival of the Horseman, the hooves got unnaturally loud; and in the distance Kali saw trees shrivel up and die as it moved towards the clearing, towards the courtyard.

Death burst into the clearing, and Kali stared for the first time in his life at the ancient rider and its steed. Death's horse was a pale, almost-white mount; it was dead. Its skin had rotted in places, and its entire rib cage hung out, as did parts of the neck bones. Bits and pieces of broken armour hung on to its decaying body almost reluctantly, and it had two huge wings sprouting from behind the front legs—the wings were long gone though, just the winged bones remained, folded gracefully on either side. Its eyes were a menacing red, and it neighed angrily as Death pulled the reins. The grass beneath its hooves dried up and died as it trotted to a stop inside the courtyard.

Death screamed in anger. It was a tormenting, terrifying scream, the likes of which had never been heard in the forest before. It was complete and utter anger; it made one shiver in fright, it made one simply want to give up. It screamed and then looked at Kali.

'Horseman. Haven't seen any of your kind here in my forest,' Kali said.

'I sensed him here!' Death hissed in reply, ignoring Kali. 'He was here!'

'If you're looking for Adri Sen,' Kali said, 'I know where he is.'
Death was silent.

'He went that way,' Kali said, pointing a finger truthfully towards the ruins.

Death stared at Kali. 'You'll have to do better than that,' it rasped.

Adri was running. Ahead of him he saw Fayne lope heavily with both Maya and Gray slung across his shoulders. The assassin was still faster than Adri.

I thought you could not stand up, the Wraith said.

Adri, silent, continued running among the ruins, trying to keep up with Fayne.

Oh I see. An act, for Kali. Make him believe he's got you. Until the right moment.

'Only way to beat him,' Adri panted.

They ran through a path they had not taken before. They ran and ran until they reached a small tunnel leading inside a half devastated hall. Adri paused in the tunnel to catch his breath, as did Fayne.

'What now?' Fayne said, in between gasps.

'The Horseman is here,' Adri panted back. 'We have to hide somewhere secure.'

Fayne nodded and darted into the hall. Adri followed him.

'I cannot bring him to you. He's already escaped my grasp,' Kali said. He was slowly beginning to get nervous. This was not how he had hoped it would be.

Liquid darkness swirled around Death, and Kali found his gaze wandering off, mesmerised by the darkness, again and again.

'You would not bring him to me either way, human,' Death said. 'I think you are hiding him.'

'Rot! I just tried to kill him!' Kali shouted.

'Or so you would want me to think,' Death growled. 'You are a Necromancer like him. I think—you protect him.'

'You are wrong!' Kali spat.

'Why is he not here then?' Death asked.

'He *just* ran.'

'And you allowed it?'

'He distracted me.'

'Convenient. But it doesn't work for me, I'm afraid. I sensed his presence here a while back, and now I can't sense him anymore. It has something to do with *you,* Tantric.'

'He's wearing a moon pendant, that's why you can't sense him. You are a fool, you are running after the wrong prey.'

Death's steed neighed angrily. Death calmed it with a stroke on the half-melted neck.

'Curious,' Death said. 'If he is hiding from me with a moon artefact, how does he lose possession of it and then gain it again?'

'Bait,' Kali said. 'I would have killed him. He did it himself to distract me.'

Death laughed, a laugh that froze Kali's blood.

'He will know better than to bait me. He does not stand a chance if he stands up to me and he knows that. Why does my coming here distract *you* anyway, human?'

Kali looked at the Demons. His hands tightened, his fingers beginning protective gestures. 'He thinks you will kill me.'

Death looked straight at Kali, his gaze boring into the Tantric's eyes. 'I think,' the Horseman spoke, 'I shall oblige him.'

'There is a vault here,' Fayne spoke.

'That means only one way in or out,' Adri said. 'But we might be able to temporarily seal it off from the inside.'

'If the vault was meant to hold magic, it will hide our vibes well,' Fayne said.

'Worth a shot. I don't see many options anyway, and this is much better than playing hide-and-seek among the pillars.'

They entered the small door inside an ancient fireplace; most lords hid their vaults behind fireplaces, where a magical fire burned around the clock. There was no magic in the fireplace now, but hopefully the vault would still work. They entered a narrow tunnel, constructed out of rock, and light diminished rapidly as they progressed through it. At the other end of the tunnel was a spiral staircase, leading down.

'Well, down then,' Adri said.

They began making their way down, but the stairs seemed to go on and on. The darkness grew steadily, but Adri was too afraid of using magic with the Horseman so near. He trusted Fayne's vision, who was leading the way.

'Whaa—?' Adri gasped when all of a sudden, he felt a stone beneath his foot give way. It wasn't the only one. With a roaring scream, all the stones gave way as the staircase beneath their feet collapsed. There was nothing to hang on to; Adri's hands clawed only air as the four of them fell into darkness.

'I have no argument with you, Horseman,' Kali said, backing away slowly.

'I believe you do,' Death said. 'Your confidence that I was summoned here by Adri Sen to kill you will in no way arouse my sympathy. And I feel you think you are well prepared for me, with these Demons and these spells you conjure under your breath as we talk.'

354

Death held its steed lightly and dismounted. The chains around him rattled noisily. Turning to Kali, it took a step towards him.

'I am only defending myself,' Kali said, now beginning to feel fear. 'I do not need this, Horseman.'

'Of course you don't. You already know how it will end,' Death said.

'No! Keep away!' Kali shouted with anger, backing away steadily.

'Where is Adri Sen?' Death rasped.

'Keep away from me! He went that way, I told you! He's hiding in the ruins.'

Death stood for a moment in silence, extending his senses.

'You lie,' it hissed at length. 'No moon pendant can hide him if he is as close as you claim. No, this is an artifice. One that will not end well for you.'

'Kill the damn Horseman!' Kali roared at the Demons, jabbering in the Old Tongue, weaving protective enchantments of all kinds around him, calling more and more spirits to his aid from the other side.

The Demons dutifully rushed at Death with their swords and maces. Death extended a gauntleted hand from beneath his black shawl. A weapon materialised in his grasp—an enormous scythe. It was a beautiful and terrifying weapon, fashioned out of metal and rotten wood, a chain circling its entire length, two mammoth blades at one end, one above the other, both rusted beyond time. At the other end were a series of gems embedded in the wood. It seemed heavy, but Death wielded it easily and carelessly, spinning it like a toy.

'I was calm before, human,' Death whispered audibly. 'I was very calm, and happy. I had found the means to my salvation. I had found the key.'

The Demons came at him together. He sank his scythe into one, killing it instantly. Turning around in a spin, he beheaded the other. A Demon struck with a giant sword, and the Horseman melted into darkness as the blade went through, only to materialise a second later behind the hapless Demon. Raising his scythe, Death sliced the Demon into two from the centre. It was a clean blow, and the two bloody pieces separated and hit the already blood-splattered ground. The last Demon came thundering down with a mace. Death caught the mace with its left hand and snatched it from the Demon; the Demon gaped in bewilderment as Death's right hand swung the scythe, the last thing the Demon was ever to see.

Death turned to Kali. 'But he escaped, this young human. He has been avoiding my gaze well. It has been *angering* me. This one human has infuriated me, frustrated me, and I have been hunting for him all over the Old City. Sometimes I think I sense his presence, or the vibes he leaves behind somewhere. His journey has been *eventful,* I think, and yet I do not find him.'

'The ruins,' Kali said, terrified, as the Horseman approached him. 'For the last time, you *will* find him hiding there.'

Death stood before Kali. 'Protective magic,' he breathed. 'How—*quaint.*' He extended an open palm, and for a moment Kali thought something had exploded. It was the death knell of a hundred spirits that cried out before being ended from their state. His shields were gone.

'Tell me, why do you wear a necklace of skulls?' Death asked, breathing on Kali.

Kali felt the breath taking away his essence, his life force. He could not reply.

'It is funny,' Death continued. 'You do it to terrify your victims, to strike fear in their hearts. You imitate the Dark Goddess whose power and grace you could never dream of touching. But right now, *you* are afraid. I can smell it.'

Kali was losing touch with consciousness, an invisible hand was beginning to choke him. What was he even thinking? There was no way he could have defeated this creature. He had known it from the start.

'There is some truth in what you say, human. Before you die, die knowing that Adri Sen's soul is mine, and mine alone. I will hunt him down no matter where he is, and if he has indeed tricked you as you say, you will have your revenge through me. After your end, I am headed for the ruins you pointed at.'

Something moved within the dark eyeholes in the Horseman's mask. Kali screamed.

24

'Now I am truly wounded,' Adri said.

'I cannot carry all three of you, *pashlin,*' Fayne replied.

The stones had stopped falling. Now it was sand and loose cement and dirt raining down soundlessly from the broken staircase high above them somewhere. Even though Adri was flat on the ground, looking up, he couldn't see it. He slowly turned his neck and realised he could not see anything at all. They were in pitch black. He would have gotten up, but something was holding him down.

'Fayne, where are we?' he asked.

'In a tunnel,' Fayne replied in the dark. 'This is no vault.'

'I don't think I can move,' Adri said slowly. 'Are you okay?'

'I landed on my feet. I'm fine, but it is not me you should be concerned about.'

'Yes, yes, you're right. Well there-argh-is one thing good about this. I think we're too far down for the Horseman to be able to sense us.'

'I hope you are correct,' Fayne said. 'But we should get moving as soon as we can.'

'How's Maya? And Gray?'

'They are fine, for the moment. Unconscious as before.'

Adri slowly called upon his spirits in the Old Tongue. None answered.

'My spirits are all destroyed,' he said, straining to talk. 'Mazumder, I need eyes.'

Done.

Adri's eyes burned blue and he slowly looked around. Two stone blocks pressed down on him, preventing him from moving. Something might have broken inside his body. The dark tunnel they found themselves in seemed to give off a fairly strong magical vibe. It was unpleasant and dank; water leaked from the mossy walls and a pungent smell filled the air. It was not somewhere he wanted to be. Fayne walked to him and heaved the heavy stones off his body, one at a time, grunting as he lifted them.

Adri tried to get up and to his immense relief, succeeded. Fayne was silently looking at Gray and Maya. Adri moved towards them and crouching beside them, he checked for injuries—nothing appeared wrong other than some cuts and scratches from all the running and falling.

'Gray is not unconscious. He's been possessed by a spirit which has kept him from moving or responding,' Adri said, looking at Gray, opening his eyelids and checking his eyes within.

'So what now?' Fayne asked.

'Have you been trained to resist spirits, like Kali said?'

'Yes.'

'Hmm. And spirits find it tough to possess other beings which are not human-like in nature. Your witch blood saved you. With Gray, I will have to perform an exorcism.' Adri paused. 'It will not take long. Where's my bag?'

'Up in the courtyard,' Fayne said.

'No food, no ingredients, no medical supplies,' Adri thought aloud. 'We will need to hurry our trip into Howrah.' He took out a chalk, dragged Gray to a side, and propped him in a sitting position against a wall. He then drew a semicircle on the floor against the wall, sealing Gray within. Then Adri sat in front of Gray and slapped him. Hard.

'Spirit!' he shouted in the Old Tongue. 'Spirit!'

'Quiet,' Fayne said behind him. 'The Horseman may be searching for us.'

Adri nodded. A good call. He slapped Gray harder, but his voice was soft. He hissed now in an urgent tone. 'Spirit!' he hissed, slapping Gray the hardest he had ever.

Gray's eyes flung open, the insides a murky white.

'All right all right! You don't have to keep slapping me, you know,' Gray spoke in a voice that was not his. It was younger, but belonged to a male.

'Shut up, spirit, and listen to me,' Adri said.

'Oh God, what is this? A negative circle?' the spirit yelped when it saw the chalk line. 'The others have told me about this, though it's the first time I'm seeing one for myself.'

Exorcism was tricky business, and part and parcel of a Tantric's learning. Banishing spirits was delicate in itself, but making them step out of a body was always tougher. It could be forced out with certain tools and ingredients Adri almost always travelled with, but for now, he would have to do with talk.

'You're trapped in the negative circle,' Adri said to the spirit. 'And you can't leave until I let you.'

'Does it have thorns?' the spirit asked fearfully.

'I haven't drawn them yet,' Adri said. 'I wanted to make this peaceful and quick.'

'What's the deal? What do I get if I leave?' the spirit asked.

'I will let you move on to the next Plane. I'm qualified for that.'

'Prove it.'

Adri sighed and brought his tattoos, glowing in the dark, forward.

'Ah,' the spirit said. 'A Necromancer.'

'You have died recently, isn't it?' Adri asked.

'Why, yes. How did you know?'

'It's because of how obnoxious you are. Let me guess—you are not interested in moving on, am I right?'

'Yes, definitely! I want to see more of this place. I'm in no hurry! You got me right, man.'

'Out of all the spirits, why did it have to be *you* who entered Gray?' Adri said, his heart sinking. 'Okay, look spirit. You have two choices. I can either torture you inside this circle to the point of no return, where your existence is extinguished and my friend can regain control of himself again. Or you can leave him now, and float about and go wherever and wander forever. I will not absolve you.'

'No deal,' the spirit snapped. 'Some Tantric will call me to his service before I know it. I am not powerful enough to refuse yet. Get me a body and we'll talk.'

'I cannot find you a body here, wherever we are,' Adri said. His patience was wearing thin.

'Oh, it's the Ondhokaar. We are in the Ondhokaar,' the spirit said.

Adri was quiet.

'We must leave as soon as we can, Tantric,' Fayne said behind him.

Adri nodded. It was very risky, staying here. He reached into his bandolier and withdrew a bullet. Gray's eyes travelled to Adri's holsters, but the spirit saw they were empty. Adri's guns, of course, were still in the courtyard along with his bag.

'You don't have your guns,' the spirit smirked.

'Oh, I'm not going to shoot you,' Adri said, calmly unscrewing the top off the bullet. A bullet filled with holy water. He threw a little on Gray.

'Leave the body!' he hissed.

The spirit yelled in pain. The skin, where the water had touched it, released smoke immediately, like acid.

'Leave the damn body!' Adri yelled again.

'NEVER!' the spirit shrieked, Gray's entire body convulsing in pain. 'I want to live! Why won't you let me live?'

'You had your chance!' Adri shouted back, sprinkling more holy water. 'You had your chance and right now you are dead! You have no right to stop Gray from living his life!'

Gray's hands and legs began to bend at odd angles slowly as the spirit howled in suffering.

'He's a human!' Adri roared, with complete disregard for keeping quiet. 'He's *not* a bloody puppet, stop that!'

In all his pain, the spirit grinned as Gray's arms dislocated with soft snaps.

'That's it,' Adri said in anger. 'I'm going to do something to you that I reserve for the worst of spirits; I'm going to banish you across the River.'

'What? No!' the spirit shouted, more in disbelief than in pain this time.

Adri made swift gestures in air and spoke in the Old Tongue. 'By all that is holy, by the book that records, and the flame that burns its pages, by the crying child and the great divide, by the Angels and Demons, by the truest form of magic and the chaos it inspires, by the power vested in me by the arts I have learned and the forces I command, I banish you across the River!'

'No! I will leave this body! I will—' the spirits voice was cut off as Adri touched him on the arm with his forefinger. Then he withdrew his hand and waited.

'Aargh!' Gray cried in his real voice.

Adri breathed a huge sigh of relief.

'My arms hurt like hell! Ow!' Gray yelled, and Fayne moved towards him.

'This will hurt only for a moment, little man,' the assassin said before setting Gray's arms back with a jolt. 'Minor dislocations, you're fine,' he added as Gray shouted with pain again.

'Adri—' Gray said, panting, once the pain had receded enough to allow him to talk. 'What did you do to him?'

'I sent it to hell,' Adri replied.

'You can do that?'

'I do not do it because it is a cruel thing to do, possibly the cruellest. The spirit awaits torture and suffering there for a long, long time now.'

'You should have let it go. In the end it had agreed to leave.'

'A spirit like that is dangerous, wherever it is,' Adri said. 'No, I did what had to be done.'

'So you could see everything while the spirit was possessing you?' Fayne asked.

'I had just lost control, I was still a spectator. And I haven't been able to see since we fell down here. I can't see anything right now,' Gray said. 'Ow! And I have wounds all over.'

He turned to Adri again. 'Isn't a spirit already dead? How were you threatening to kill it?'

'A spirit isn't dead or alive. It exists, and though it isn't possible for it to live again, its existence can still be ended, taken to nothingness. They are tortured souls, Gray, and they're here for a reason—something they haven't been able to accomplish, or let go of. When we summon them, we offer them a chance to move on in return for their doing something for us. It works for us, and they get their freedom in return.'

'There have been Tantrics who have kept hundreds of spirits as slaves,' Fayne said. 'Refusing to let them go.'

'Necromancers have ethics. Dead-talking is always a morally controversial art, there are people who have never supported what we do. We have a code through which we operate; and there will always be Tantrics who will not respect the code.'

'The government supports Tantrics,' Gray said.

'The government has its own set of morals,' Adri said grimly. 'They do not follow the true path of what a Tantric is meant to be.'

'Hence you are no longer with them?' Gray asked.

Adri did not reply immediately. 'An engaging conversation. But we must move.'

Fayne picked Maya up. 'Which way?' he asked.

Adri's compass was hanging from his belt. He checked it.

'That way, the tunnel leads roughly towards Howrah. We can't go up now, and certainly not here. Let's move.'

'I can't see,' Gray complained.

'Grab my shoulder,' Adri said.

They started walking into the darkness. It was cumbersome and slow, like the walk in the Hive had been—except there were lesser obstacles here, just one main path they followed. Gray had a question.

'What is the Ondhokaar, Adri? I've heard too many references to it by now.'

'The Ondhokaar is a place watched over by the evil eye,' Adri replied slowly. 'It is an ill-fated place, something that has existed since the beginning of the Old City. It is an entire city in itself beneath Old Kolkata; it is a maze, a labyrinth, a network of narrow passageways feeding into one another, and a scattering of huge caverns. There is no light in the Ondhokaar—it is a filthy, dark place that even Angels are afraid to tread. This is where the venoms of the Old City are brewed, this is where the deadliest creatures that roam the city are born. This is a place unexplored, and wisely so. No one knows what the Ondhokaar holds.'

'We need to find a way out quickly,' Fayne said. 'This is not a good place.'

Maya had been following Adri. She had been following him through a lot of the adventures and happenings that had made him what he was, and even though she knew so much about him

364

already, she was still impressed at what young Adri was capable of. Adri burned with hidden power, she realised, as she saw him fight incredibly by himself. There was a reason why Adri never revealed the full extent of his power, only betraying himself in his ingenuity and the unusual way he solved his problems. There was something more to Adri, and it would explain away all of this. Maya kept following him through chapters in his diary, travelling through the different phases of his life and seeing him change as he grew up and became a Necromancer. Relentlessly, she hunted for the reason that made Adri always feel a bit strange and different to her from the beginning. She found it, finally. It was there among the hundred other things Adri had written about. But it was brief, short and simple—almost as if Adri did not want to ponder over it too much on paper.

Maya did not know if the experiences she was having were a recreation of what was there in Adri's diaries, or if she had somehow gained deeper access to his memories. All she knew was that she saw things like they happened, with a level of detail too great, too intimate, to be of her own imagination. No, somehow she was in Adri's memories. She had no clue how. But her other great question about Adri was answered when she followed him once, as usual, only to stumble upon something totally different from what she had come to recognise as Adri's regular schedule.

Adri was hunting a rogue Demon along with another Sorceress, Trish. They were still learning under the government; Adri must have been eighteen at most, but it was clear he was already under the service of MYTH. The two of them were tracking a Demon near the Highlands of Alish' Ur, far from the Old City. They had been tracking the murderer for several days—the Free Demons had not formed back then, and Demons that killed their Summoners had no organised place to go to. They heard no call from Ba'al back then and thus ended up going on rampages, or hiding until MYTH caught up with them and ended them. This particular one had been hiding, but anyone who had seen the Demon was not spared. It had been extremely secretive; they did not even know what kind of a Demon it was, but they were qualified enough according to MYTH to kill it. Both of them were the best in their batches.

They were on a cliff, overlooking a valley below. Trish was standing and Adri was crouching. He was younger, with short hair and an energetic angry young man look to him; Trish was a pretty girl who dressed like a tomboy. Her hair was cut short and she wore jeans and a sleeveless tee, along with mountain boots, everything black, like Adri. Both of them were dirty, and their clothes were weathered. Adri held a rifle in his hands, a long slender weapon that Maya hadn't seen before. Trish was weaponless other than her Sorcerer gauntlets, which glinted in the early morning sun. Their supplies were in a duffel bag lying among the rocks behind them.

'Is that a moor?' Trish asked, squinting.

Adri was squinting as well. The sun was unusually sharp for the mountains.

'Might just be. It would be the most obvious place for it to go right now,' he said.

'Try and sense it,' Trish said.

Adri closed his eyes and there was silence, other than the occasional gust of wind whistling past. A mountain bird cried out and he opened his eyes.

'No good,' Adri said. 'It's either really good at this hiding business, or it's too far away for me to catch.'

'You're not good enough,' Trish snapped. 'You should work more on your meditation, Adri.'

'Bull,' Adri said. 'The Demon is hiding itself with something. Its vibes are totally cut off, which is impossible.'

'I thought the creature was animalistic. But an animalistic Demon wouldn't know how to use artefacts.'

'Warrior or mage, then. I have a feeling it's a powerful one.'

'Why is it hiding, then?'

'Why do you think? It wants to survive.'

Trish paused for a moment, thinking. 'Let's get after it, then. If it's dangerous, the sooner it's put down, the better.'

Adri nodded and got up. Slinging his rifle over his shoulder and picking up his bag, he followed Trish as she led the way down. Maya followed them.

'You know, Trish,' Adri spoke up suddenly, breaking a silence that had built up for the last three hours. 'I don't agree with what you said back there.'

'What did I say?'

'The *putting down* Demons bit. They aren't animals to be put down. They're quite sharp, actually. And many of them are incredibly cultured and well-read.'

Trish laughed. 'Look who's talking,' she said. 'A Demon-killer working for the government. All you and me have done for assignments in the past months is put down Demons.'

'I know what we do and I know what must be done to protect the people,' Adri said, irritated. 'Don't put words in my mouth. It's the *attitude* I have a problem with. We should treat them with more respect, Demons.'

'I think *your* attitude needs change, Adri,' Trish said seriously. 'Tell me what an animalistic Demon is, if not a predator of everything it sees. And take this Demon, for example. You saw the eaten bodies down at the last village. Would you call that *cultured*?'

'I think it looks at everything in a different way. Chickens would look at me in the same way, I guess, if I was summoned into a world full of chicken.'

'Lame logic, Adri. And what are you, a Demon lawyer?'

'Argh. You could *try* to look at it from their point of view.'

Trish laughed. 'All I see is a couple of extremely deadly chickens hunting me down.'

Adri had to laugh too, shaking his head. 'You're impossible.'

'Let's just hunt this bastard down, Adri.'

That was easier said than done. They entered the moor in another hour and began tracking the Demon, Maya behind them. The Demon did not leave many tracks, and Adri had to work hard to find anything. The ground was hard, making it pretty impossible to find any kind of footprint. When night came, the duo did not rest or camp, continuing, instead, to try and track their prey.

Adri finally ended up tracking it using the flower method, something Maya understood because she had studied it. Some Demons had an affinity for flowers, a strange kind of attraction. For some Demons it was a weakness, even. Flowers were not something the Demons would find on their Plane, across the River—but it was never confirmed what it was about the flowers that attracted the Demons. MYTH had run tests using smell, shape, and colour, but nothing had been proven. The tests were still running.

Adri picked up a small white petal and observed it in the moonlight.

'Okay, he's a flowerboy. I saw this back near the foothills where it had eaten the herd of cows,' he said.

'Just have to find the flowers, then,' Trish said, looking around.

It took them well into the night to track the area where the flowers grew. It was deep in the moor, across a long, dry landscape with huge rocks overlooking it, a dry valley of sorts. They could see bushes with the white flowers strewn across the valley, growing sparsely and mostly under hanging rocks.

'He'll be around here,' Adri said softly, looking at the entire stretch of dead land. 'Too many of these flowers here, he'll be naturally attracted here if he has entered the moor.'

'This place screams SETUP to me,' Trish said. 'Can you sense the Demon?'

'Nothing,' Adri said. 'But I'm telling you, this one's different. It's hiding its magic somehow.'

Maya looked at the duo standing in the moonlight before the eerie stretch in front, and she felt a chill go up her spine. This was not something she was used to. She knew she could not be seen or harmed in her current state, and yet she was afraid of the moor ahead of her.

'Okay, so how do we do this?' Adri asked.

'I'll go in, you cover me,' Trish said.

Adri pulled back the safety catch and nodded. Holding the rifle, he clambered off to a high rock without a second's delay. Within the minute, he was sitting on the edge of the rock, legs hanging, rifle ready.

'Try not to shoot me,' Trish said softly, and started making her way down the slope, reaching the dry floor of the valley after a while. She did not look up even once to check on Adri. In all probability, the Demon's eyes were on her now.

Maya did not know where to be; she felt scared of going down to the patch with Trish despite herself. She decided to follow her from above, walking alongside her and watching everything.

There were too many hanging rocks that cast shadows along Trish's path. She conjured fireballs and started throwing them under the rocks as she went, giving each place a brief glance before moving on. Maya glanced at Adri and saw that he was in a direct line of sight. Trish walked on, lighting shadows up.

Things happened. Fast. One of the rocks moved, suddenly, un-forming itself into a living thing, and lunged at Trish with a huge arm. Trish jumped back and threw her arms forward—electricity leapt from her gauntlets, crackling and fizzling and lighting up the darkness. The Demon, unperturbed by the electricity, continued moving forward towards Trish with speed. She rolled away just as a huge hand made of stone came crashing down with a sound like thunder, raising dust. Maya looked at Adri to see what he

369

was doing—the Tantric was changing bullets and reloading the rifle slowly, a cigarette in his mouth.

She stared back at the fight and saw Trish throwing fireballs at the Demon, and for the first time she could see it well. It was a nightmarish thing, and the loud cries that emanated from it were the same. It was a *Hush*, a Demon born of stone. She had read about them—they came in many shapes and sizes and for the first time she could see one; it looked like a bunch of stones put together to form something remotely humanoid. It was much larger than Trish, about fifteen feet in height, though it stayed hunched. Maya could not make out its eyes, though she well understood that the large gash on the face was actually the mouth. It had long, extended arms and legs, and several long rock fingers at the end of each arm. It even had a tail of linked stone that beat around angrily as it tried to catch Trish. The Demon wasn't slow by any means, but Trish was always faster as she dodged and tried different fire and electricity spells to bring the Demon down. Nothing seemed to stop it, but only infuriated it further. Its cries echoed down the entire moor as it fought the Sorceress.

Trish hit it with a blue wave of what Maya assumed was raw sound. It knocked the Demon back for a second. Frustrated, she took a second to look up at Adri—a second which the Demon borrowed to hit Trish with a solid hand of stone. The blow was a horizontal swing, and Trish went flying into a nearby boulder like a rag doll. Maya yelled in shock, and Adri fired. The gunshot was still echoing seconds later; the Demon stood at full height, looking around, confused. Then it collapsed to the ground, raising a lot of dust and making the very earth shake under Maya's feet.

Adri slung the rifle back over his shoulder and made his way down to the stretch, still smoking the cigarette. He silently walked to where Trish lay, and this time, Maya followed him. She hoped Trish was okay. When Adri reached Trish, he checked her pulse first. Then he sighed with what Maya hoped was relief, and walked over to the Demon and inspected it closely. Adri swept aside the white flowers that were on its rocky body, clamped in mud, he swept away the grass and the dust—he seemed to be looking for something. He found it after a bit of searching; it was a ring as large as a human bracelet on one of its fingers. A ring with runes inscribed on it. Maya could understand nothing, except for the shape of a moon among the runes.

Adri unslung his rifle and turned around. He began to laugh. 'All right, just who are you fooling? This is pathetic,' he said. The laugh was not genuine. It was under pressure, maybe even a little nervous. For a shocked second Maya thought he was addressing her, but no, he was looking elsewhere and all around. There was no reply, only the silence of the moor.

'The Hush liked flowers,' Adri said. 'It was a simple being, not capable of hiding beyond its natural ability to pose as a rock. It would not wear an artefact of the moon to hide its magical vibes. You must be following me, you must be here. Show yourself!'

There was nothing for a while, and Maya did not expect a reply to come. But it did, and it was a mere whisper in the wind.

'That was a damn good shot, Adri Sen.'

Adri lifted the rifle to his eye, peering all over the horizon, seeing nothing.

'Who are you?' he shouted, without lowering his weapon.

'Lose the rifle, Adri,' another voice whispered. 'We are unarmed, and will not harm you.'

'Well, you shouldn't be scared of this weapon if you mean me no harm, isn't it?' Adri shouted.

'We will reveal ourselves in good faith,' yet another voice spoke.

Adri said nothing. And then suddenly, the first figure appeared out of nowhere. Then another. Then another. They kept appearing around Adri, at varying distances; and after the fifth one appeared, Adri lowered his weapon. He was outgunned anyway. When they finished, there were twelve of them around Adri.

Adri looked at them. They were just silhouettes, dark and shadowy, with a hint of a flicker, a slight tremble to them. Their shapes indicated there were both men and women, but Adri could see nothing but black in them. When they spoke, it was still in the same whisper.

'We planted the artefact on the Demon, Adri. We wanted it to catch MYTH's eye. We wanted you to be sent here.'

'Why?' Adri asked, as Maya listened, spellbound.

'Because we could not possibly tell you what we are here to tell you back in the Old City, in the halls of the government. No, we had to draw you away from MYTH. For what you are about to know is not for the ears of everyone.'

'But who are you? And how do you know me?'

'You may have heard of us in stories and legends, Adri. We are called the Eclipse Guard.'

'The Eclipse Guard? The Soul Hunters who went missing from the banks of the Ganga?' Adri asked in amazement.

'Yes, though the truth in those stories is only a grain's worth. We know you because you were a friend to us, Adri.'

'A friend—to *you*?'

'We understand your confusion, so let us elaborate. You see, there are many secrets this world has to keep—many secrets that have been kept secrets to stop myriad machinations that would break the foundation of what these secrets stand for in the first place. Hence secret societies, hence secret text. You are, unknowingly, a part of what is a well-kept secret, Adri Sen. And now you are of age, and you will know what you are to know.'

Adri slung the rifle back over his shoulder and lit another cigarette. He looked up to find everyone quiet. 'Oh, I'm listening,' he said quickly, and they began talking again, nodding amongst themselves.

'In every hundred spirits, one is allowed to return to this Plane and take birth once more, starting the circle of life once again,' they whispered. 'In every twenty billion spirits that are allowed to come back, one is allowed access to the memories of the past life he or she has led. It is a gift, and a unique one. We call those *Raishth,* the Reborn.'

Adri stubbed out the cigarette with a stupefied expression. 'That—would explain a lot,' he muttered.

'We are glad that it does.'

'Who was I—in my past life?' Adri asked.

'That is something all of us have to find out for ourselves, Adri. It is not difficult. Ask the right questions and visit the right places, and you will know who you were. The few visions that you have had which you cannot explain are all from your deep past.'

'I guessed as much right now. They were not just visions, then.'

'They are memories, Adri. The power of your past shall always wait within you, waiting to be unleashed. You will always learn things much quicker and more intuitively if they are things you have already learnt well in your last life—and all the memories of your last life shall come flooding back to you as you live out this one. With each memory of the last life that you unlock, you will only grow stronger—and mentally, you will always be older, no matter what your current age resembles. The experience of an entire life lived out shall always back you up, and this past existence shall forever watch over you.'

'Thank you,' Adri said. 'This changes everything. It explains a lot of my doubts. I know I was a Tantric in my past life. Of that I am certain.'

'We are under a code to neither agree nor disagree. Do not question who made us tell; it is our duty to inform every Reborn of what they are and what it means. It is a rare gift, Adri. Use it well.'

'I will,' Adri said, as the silhouettes began to fade away one by one. The moor was empty once again except for Adri, the unconscious Trish, and the dead Demon. And of course, Maya, who was now privy to one of Adri's biggest and most well-kept secrets. This was what had always been amiss about Adri; this was why he had felt much older than he looked. It explained why he seemed to hide most of his power and abilities, and why he kept to himself so much. Maya had stopped feeling guilty about invading Adri's memories a long time ago—there had been a time when, momentarily tired of following the Tantric everywhere, she had tried to walk away, only to realise she could not put much distance between Adri and herself. If she did, she would be transported back around him, where the memory was the strongest and most fresh. She was a prisoner in what seemed to be Adri's mind. There were times when she had hated it and tried to escape again and again, times when she cried out loud and endlessly for days at a time for help. But at the end of the day she accepted her position and her curiosity about the young Tantric would return once more.

Adri was now waking Trish up, and the world was beginning to blur. They were moving into another memory, and Maya was going along for the ride.

25

'Maya's condition is worsening again,' Gray said. 'She's beginning to sweat like before.'

'The Dreamer's Brew is wearing off,' Adri said. 'We cannot use it on her any more. We need to find the Mask, and soon.'

'The smoke,' Fayne said, pointing. 'That way.'

They had exited the Ondhokaar a little while back, finding a small way out through a sewer system. The forest had ended long behind them and there was no sign of the Horseman, thankfully. They had, however, overshot, and were now in the outskirts of Howrah, well past their goal. Now they had to retrace their steps back into Howrah, and the Howrah Bridge, looming far in the distance, was the best beacon they could ask for.

Adri now had charge of the Sadhu's Shotgun. Gray had still been in possession of it when he had been carried off the courtyard of the Dark Goddess. Adri did not have too many shells for it, however, nor did he have his bullet alchemy case, or empty shells to make some more. Gray had also kept his violin slung across his back, and as a result it had also survived, annoying Adri immensely. Adri was depressed about losing both his shooters, especially considering all the work that had gone into making the excellent weapons, but he knew he could not brood over it for too long. He needed to figure out more ways of dealing with the enemies they would now meet, and more importantly, the Devil Mask.

'Why can't the Devil Mask be distracted?' Gray asked, swatting mosquitoes as they walked.

'It is a Necrotic. Its senses do not work the same way as ours.' Adri replied. 'To put it simply, its senses are focused all around it all the time, making it impossible to distract.'

'That sounds like a tough enemy to fight.'

'It does take an impossibly large number of warriors to bring one down.'

'Then what is our plan?'

'Like I told you earlier, I will discuss it when the time comes.'

'Is there something you could do to take care of these bloodsuckers?'

Funny, I used to refer to vampires with that title, the Wraith said.

'Err, maybe a spirit could have done it, but I don't have any ingredients with me. Can't summon anything.'

'Walk faster, you two,' Fayne said, turning around. 'We should reach Howrah before dark if we are to find the Devil Mask tonight.'

'So we will find it by tonight? Excellent,' Gray said.

'Maya does not have much more time,' Adri said seriously. 'And that's why the assassin thinks we should walk faster.'

They walked faster, Fayne leading the way, and Maya, slung lifeless over his shoulder, was a grim reminder that stared at Adri, making him feel guiltier than ever. And the closer they got to the Devil Mask, the worse he felt. The assassin was responsible for protecting her, but he was responsible for *reviving* her, something both Gray and Fayne seemed to think him capable of accomplishing. So what if it had never been done before? It was possible theoretically, and if Kali had been correct, then the key to everything was distracting the creature. But how did one distract a controller of the dead?

Devil Masks were not commonplace. The only purpose of a Devil Mask was to feed itself, to grow, and to make revenant, nothing else mattered to them, which explained why they weren't on either side of the ongoing territory wars. They were deadly, much more so than the average Demon, and there had been absolutely no research done on them. Only whiffs of rumours, stories, and speculations. Adri had been hearing about them ever since his days in MYTH Castle, when all the young Tantrics, while discussing urban legends, would inevitably talk of the ritual used to summon a Devil Mask. There were also the stories of a wooden mask being found somewhere, and the Necrotic finding its first host through the mask. But no one knew for sure.

Adri wasn't sure about distracting the Mask. Old stories came back—the maiden who sang and distracted the Necrotic—but fairy tales would not help. Adri would see to it that the Mask was distracted. He had a plan, something untested. He was not losing Maya. Not after everything, not after running across the Old City, running from death. He had run enough. He needed to see her wake up.

They kept on walking until they reached an area, which Adri guessed was Beniatola, near Sovabazar. They could see a Settlement a little ahead of them, but a lot of smoke was rising from within. They walked up to the main gates of the Settlement and saw the entrance destroyed and the Settlement beyond it partially on fire. They stood at the gates, watching the Settlement burn, until a sharp voice called out.

'Hey!'

They turned around and saw a figure waving at them from near a cluster of old buildings. Adri recognised the Sorceress' robes from a distance, as well as the young woman wearing them.

'Will she be a problem?' Fayne asked gently as they approached her.

'No, she shouldn't be,' Adri replied.

As they neared her it was evident she had been in battle—her robes were dusty and torn, she sported a bandage around her forehead, apart from the usual bruises and cuts. The Sorceress was a good-looking woman with an unusual alertness to her eyes. She leaned against a broken lamp post, looking at them, her dark brown hair floating in the wind.

'Damn, I thought it would be someone from the government,' she said, as they walked up to her. 'What are *you* doing here, Sen?'

'It's been a while, hasn't it, Natasha?' Adri said, trying to grin.

'Certainly has,' she said with the same stab at a smile. 'It's good to see my name wasn't lost to your memory.'

'No, I have a good one. We were just *passing through*.'

'Why does that not sound right? Ever since you were banished you have been up to something, Sen. I heard rumours, though a lot of them will make you laugh.'

'Rumours will happen. I have been happier since I was banished, but that's another story. Who did this to you?'

'Not a who, but a *what*. I was sent from the camp at the Lake of Fire to deal with a problem here. A Devil Mask. It took us by surprise, and I lost eleven Commandos and a Sorcerer in one night. That's right, twelve!' She looked into the distance angrily.

'A Devil Mask? Here?' Adri asked, his eyes wide. 'Where is it right now?'

'Mullikbazaar, the next Settlement. It has devoured every single person in the Settlement and is now busy making revenant, the bastard. I'm going to kill it personally, but I have no chance alone. I have sent a dragonfly to headquarters for reinforcements, and I mistook you for the advance guard.'

'All right, best of luck with that. I think we best get going. We're in a hurry of sorts.'

Natasha raised an eyebrow. 'You guys look like hell, why don't you stick around for a bit? We have supplies here. Supplies for twelve men who're no more, I daresay we won't run short.'

'You were the only survivor?' Gray asked suddenly.

Natasha looked at him directly for the first time. 'No,' she said at length. 'No, two Commandos also made it out.'

'Adri, no offense, but I need to eat,' Gray mumbled to Adri, who immediately felt guilty. He did not sense much danger here, not until the reinforcements arrived anyway.

'We all need to eat, I guess. Have been hungry a long time, and it's been a horrible day,' Adri said. 'Natasha, I guess we will take you up on your offer.'

She nodded and led them through a couple of buildings and then up another. They entered through a dusty garage and went up three floors through a thin metal staircase until they reached a roof choked with potted plants, the sky open above them. Natasha led them to a stash of blankets. Two Commandos slept quietly in a corner. Fayne gently lay Maya down on a blanket and stood up, looking around. He scanned the rest of the buildings from all four sides of the roof, determining their position and all possible exit routes.

The Commandos had excellent supplies. And even though the food was all cold, Adri and Gray wolfed everything down in minutes, not bothering with washing hands or even taking their shoes off—they'd laid hands on meat and fresh vegetables after a long time. Fayne sat on the highest point the roof had to offer; a cement water tank. He looked down at them silently and then up at the city, taking swigs from his hip flask. Natasha watched the duo eat with innocent wonder.

'You guys were starving!' she exclaimed.

Gray tried to reply and nearly choked. Somehow managing to swallow what he had been chewing on, he chose to down more food rather than reply to the Sorceress's comment. Adri managed a few words.

'How long have you been here?'

'We arrived two days ago and the massacre happened the day we arrived. There were still a few people left alive in the Settlement; we were rescuing them from a fire when the Mask caught us by surprise,' Natasha paused. 'You didn't answer my question about what you are doing here. This *is* government business here, though to be honest, I am in no mood to detain or arrest you.'

'Can I just be done with this?' Adri pleaded with a mouth full of food.

'Of course,' Natasha waved it aside. 'Eat in peace.' She moved off to the other end of the roof with a pair of binoculars.

'She seems pleasant,' Gray mumbled, chewing.

'She can't know our reason for being here,' Adri said warningly in a low voice. 'Her priorities, after all, lie with MYTH. She is just looking to end the Necrotic.'

Gray nodded and that was the main thing; Adri knew Fayne never talked out of place. It would, in all probability, have been an unwarned Gray who would have let their secret out. Natasha could be handled easily, but she had been kind to them, and Adri did not want to go against her. Better they pass through.

You should eat more regularly, fool. You hardly keep your strength up, the Wraith hissed.

'Oh look who's getting motherly,' Adri snapped.

I don't want you to die of starvation at the very least.

'Then let me eat, Mazumder.'

The Wraith fell silent, seeing a sort of point in the logic.

'How's the Wraith doing?' Gray asked.

'The usual. He's been quiet lately,' Adri replied.

They took their time eating. Once done, they washed their hands and faces, and slowly walked around the terrace, feeling much better. Adri reached for a smoke as he walked towards where Natasha stood watching the Bridge with her binoculars.

'What's on the Bridge?' he asked.

'Checking for movement on the other side,' she replied without lowering the binoculars. 'It's getting too isolated here for some reason. The survivors are becoming more and more sparse, the streets are getting emptier. Rumour has it that they're all moving off someplace deep south, as near New Kolkata as they can get. Some bands have been trying to get into the new city but to no avail, of course. It's like they're all afraid of something.'

Adri peered at the Howrah Bridge, now silhouetted against the setting sun, a thing of unbelievable might and beauty. 'Any movements then?' he asked.

'None,' she replied. 'Would you know something about this migration, Sen? Because I'm getting the distinct feeling that you're withholding information.'

Adri scratched his dirty hair, and grinned. 'I don't know what you're implying.'

Natasha shook her head. 'Don't give me crap, Sen. Stop sidestepping my questions and give me one straight answer.'

'It's got something to do with Doomsday,' Adri said, breathing out smoke.

'The Apocalypse?' Natasha asked, surprised.

Adri nodded. 'The end of all things and the beginning of a new era.'

'But that has always been a stupid series of stories. How can it inspire such fear?'

'Hate to be the one to break it to you, Nat, but there have been signs. The storytellers have been telling stories of the Apocalypse. Madmen have been singing songs, there have been messages scrawled on walls.'

'Weird, but not as weird as you calling me Nat. I feel like we're back at the academy.'

'Should I stop?'

Natasha thought for a moment. 'No. Life is complex now,

Sen. Fast. Goodness knows I can't spend time with old friends like I would want to.'

'I was never really a friend to you, though.'

'Yes, but my friends called me Nat.' She sighed. 'I know it's stupid, I don't know why I even commented on that. Here you are telling me about something that has caused mass panic and here I am—'

'Hey—it's okay,' Adri said, trying to sound reassuring. 'I mean, we *are* human after all, right?'

Natasha looked at Adri, her face torn between a smile and a grimace. Adri looked back, serious; a dry tune broke the silence. Adri and Natasha jumped and looked behind them where Gray sat in a corner, playing his violin.

'Is it safe here? The violin, I mean,' Adri ventured.

Natasha shrugged her shoulders. 'Nothing moves,' she said. 'The Mask is in the next Settlement, and I'm not angry at anything else.'

'I'll let him play, then. For his peace,' Adri said.

'Who are they?' Natasha asked. 'Who's the man in the mask?'

'This one here, with the violin, is Gray, a friend and photographer, though his camera is long gone. The other one, the man with the mask—an assassin from Ahzad, Fayne.'

'Whaaa—' Natasha's eyes went wide and Adri interrupted her. 'He's with me. He's okay.'

'He's an *assassin of Ahzad*?'

'Calm down. He's okay.'

'He's *not* okay. He's giving me the creeps!' Natasha hissed in a low voice.

'Err, he can probably hear you, he's got excellent senses—' Adri mumbled, looking at the floor. 'But then again, he's on my side. He's not someone you have to worry about. Nat, listen to me, *listen*—'

Gray was definitely out of practice. His bow moved with reluctance as he tried to follow a tune he couldn't. Nevertheless, he kept playing as evening descended upon the rooftop, and Adri tried to calm down an almost hysterical Natasha.

'Why do you always have to end up doing these weird things with these weird people? Why couldn't you simply stick to your MYTH assignments and stay a Tantric for the state?' Natasha was almost screaming.

'Let's not take it there, c'mon! You don't mean all this!' Adri said in a voice as hushed as possible. The two Commandos were beginning to stir.

'Is she an old flame?' Fayne asked Gray from the water tank.

'Stole my thoughts,' Gray replied. 'She could be. The way they are squabbling; there's good chemistry there.'

'The way she accuses, *myrkho*,' Fayne said. 'The way she accuses gives away a lot.' And the assassin laughed. It was a low, rumbling laugh that was short and did not last, but Gray did respect it by pausing his playing for a moment and looking at Fayne in wonder. It was the first time the assassin had laughed, and somehow Gray felt better now that he had.

The two Commandos, woken up by all the noise, got up and were taken aback by the company; one of them even drew a shooter in alarm. Natasha took a moment to brief them about the visitors before returning to Adri, who was telling her about why they were here.

'The bloody hypocrite,' Gray said, trying a new play pattern. 'Does he think I can't hear him speak?'

'And you can?' Fayne asked, now sitting beside him.

'In parts,' Gray said. 'He's giving the game away.'

'He must trust her, Gray,' Fayne said. 'That's good enough for me.'

'Wait a minute, weren't you the assassin who was with us only because of Maya?'

'I *am* only with you because of the *fatiya*. But I have come to trust the Tantric's judgment. He is a good warrior, and he cares for you and your sister. He might be reckless, but that is why I enjoy his company. He brings me to amazing fights. No, *myrkho*, I trust him on the battlefield, and that is more than what I say for most of my fellow assassins.'

Gray reclined into deep thought, still playing the violin. Then he paused, and said, 'I trust him too, which is why I've allowed him to take Maya and me wherever he has wanted. But this is not my place; this city is dangerous and I cannot see the thrill in the danger. I'm afraid the first thing I'm going to do when Maya is back is take her right back to New Kolkata, even if it means ditching Adri. And I won't feel bad about it. '

'Your decisions concerning the Tantric are yours to make. If my charge is not lifted, I shall accompany you into the new city. However, you do not understand the essence of Old Kolkata because of a simple reason.'

'Which is?'

'You cannot defend yourself.'

'What? I carried that shotgun for half the bloody city—'

'You misunderstand, *myrkho*,' Fayne said. 'I am not talking about weapons. I'm talking about training. The Old City is a vicious place, as cruel and chaotic as the magic it is filled with. However, it is also generous and rewarding to those who earn it.'

'I don't quite see what you mean. What generosity?'

'Generosity is finding the food which you did and which is now in your full stomach. If only you had training, you would not be afraid to go out and embrace whatever the city threw at you. If you can take it head on, the rewards are never far behind. The city is never unfair.'

Gray said nothing, turning to his thoughts once more, and playing his violin again.

'I need to save her,' Adri said quietly. 'I need to, and this is the only shot I've got. Nothing is stopping me from trying.'

'A Devil Mask used to *save* a life?' Natasha shook her head. 'Sounds crazy, but then you are just crazy enough for this, Sen.'

'I will not back down from this one, Nat. I owe her.'

'You seem fond of her.'

Adri was silent.

'What's your plan, then?' Natasha asked.

'Tonight, I will go and plant her in the Mask. Tomorrow, I will go and remove her.'

'That sounds simple enough, except you can't remove a living host from a Devil Mask. She will have to die, one way or the other.'

'I have to try,' Adri said. 'I haven't come this far to put a bullet through her head now. I'm looking for something, Nat, something that will help me distract the Necrotic. What if ten spirits encircle the Devil Mask, and use different voices to distract it—'

Sounds of movement. Natasha looked up at Adri. He signalled Gray to stop playing. They waited. Silence. And then they heard it once more. Shuffling footsteps in the streets, the rattling of the metal staircase.

'Revenant,' Fayne said, walking over to an edge of the roof. Natasha and Adri rushed to the edge and saw a spectacle. Hordes and hordes of revenant were surrounding the building. The narrow alleyways beside the building were all filled and teeming with revenant, desperately and wistfully looking up. They had entered the garage already, and were making their way up the narrow staircase, which, mercifully, could only accommodate a single file as they climbed.

'Revenant! Suit up!' Natasha screamed at the Commandos, rushing over to her own bag. Adri followed her, his eye on Gray as he rushed to pick up the Sadhu's Shotgun.

'Are there any Tantric weapons you might be having?' Adri asked sheepishly.

'Couple of Sorcerer gauntlets, but I doubt you'll be able to use them,' Natasha said, wearing her own gauntlets.

'I'll, err, *try*. I know how the things work.'

'Don't kill yourself. They're in that bag over there.'

Well, well, this should be a laugh, the Wraith said. *Somehow I don't think the great Adri Sen is going to be particularly brilliant with tools of Sorcerers.*

'Shut up, shut up,' Adri muttered, rifling through the bag. 'That's just a voice in your head, Adri. Just a voice.'

Block me out, yes? That's even funnier.

Adri found the silver gauntlets and started wearing them. Everyone else had already started. Fayne and Natasha were repelling the revenant at the stairs while the Commandos and Gray were firing over the side of the building. Adri noticed briefly that the scales on his right hand had spread drastically before he clicked the gauntlets shut on both hands.

'Okay, this is it,' he murmured.

'Fireballs, Sen!' Natasha shouted briefly, flinging fistfuls of fire at the climbing revenant. The revenant kept on coming; they would be destroyed only after taking a great deal of hurt. Fayne was hacking his way down the staircase towards a sea of revenant.

Adri's attempts at using the gauntlets were disastrous. After half-hearted attempts at generating several different kinds of energy, all Adri could summon was a lightball, a glowing spirit orb whose only purpose was to light up dark areas. He flung it at a revenant in rage, and the lightball stuck to its head, lighting up the other revenant near it. It made targeting the revenant easier for the Commandos, but Adri threw off the gauntlets, muttering curses, and grabbed a Commando firearm.

Repelling all the revenant took a lot of time, but they did it. They were all exhausted when they returned to the roof, one of the Commandos keeping a watch downstairs.

'That was sudden,' the other commando said, resting his rifle. 'Bastards came out of nowhere.'

'They're quiet,' Natasha said, frowning. 'But still, I haven't seen them *creep* up like this before.'

'This idiot's music hid their noises until they were upon us,' Adri said, looking at Gray.

'How was I to know?' Gray whined.

'The same thing happened the last time,' Fayne said quietly. 'How is it that there are this many revenant walking around?'

'It's the Devil Mask,' Natasha said. 'That vile thing keeps creating them from dead bodies. As if revenant forming by themselves wasn't enough.'

'How did they find us though?' the Commando questioned. 'They can smell meat, but they can't *herd* together like that.'

'I agree. It's like they were *attracted* here,' Natasha said.

Adri stood up. 'Wait,' he said, with the evident air of being on to something. 'Attracted isn't the right word. It's *summoned*.' He walked up to where Gray's violin case lay and took the violin out.

'What are you—' Gray began, but Adri cut him short.

'I wonder why I didn't hear it before,' Adri said. 'Each and every time the violin was played, it was there, hidden among the notes.'

'Summons?' Natasha asked, surprised.

'Not just a summons,' Adri said. 'More. It breaches the boundaries of the dead; this instrument can talk to the dead in their language.'

'What?' Gray gasped. 'That's just a violin! My violin!'

'A violin infused with ancient magic, magic of the dead,' Adri said seriously. 'Where did you get this?'

'It was a gift!'

'A strange sense of humour, giving one of the instruments of the Damned as a gift to one who doesn't know anything about it. It would probably have gotten you killed someday.'

'Instruments of the Damned? What are they?' Gray asked in amazement.

'I'm no storyteller. Ask them if you ever run across another one again,' Adri said shortly, looking at the black violin. 'Though who gifted you the violin of the Damned is as good as question as any.'

'What does it do? The violin? What do you mean, it talks to the dead?'

Adri saw everyone was listening keenly. 'When we Tantrics talk to the dead, we force them onto our Plane and talk to them in the Old Tongue mostly, which they understand. This instrument, however, breaches all boundaries of language and Planes and reaches out to them in the purest form of communication possible. When simply played, it attracts the dead—it calls them like a summoning horn. If played like a master without a single error' —he looked at Gray— 'it can control them as well. To the dead this music is like a simple emotion, almost like a direct message to the brain. The dead will obey it if the music gives a command.'

'Oh my God,' Gray said.

'You have been carrying one of the most powerful weapons *ever* made all this while,' Adri told Gray. 'Something skillfully made, something hidden. And now, I think I know a perfect use for it.'

'The Devil Mask?' Natasha asked.

Adri nodded. 'This development was exactly what I needed; the Old City never lets down the faithful. I have a plan, and a simple one.'

26

'You can't kill the host already in the Mask!' Natasha hissed.

'I should not have let you come along,' Adri complained.

Women are an eternal pain in the behind, the Wraith said.

They were creeping along side alleys, trying to not attract any kind of attention. The moon was high in the night sky, and everything was more visible than usual as the moonlight washed down on them. The group consisted of the four of them and Natasha. And she was having a problem with the first part of the plan—the one that involved killing the host already in the Devil Mask.

'If you know a way to extract the host without killing him, then do it for this host as well,' Natasha argued.

'That will kill the Devil Mask and we won't be able to heal Maya,' Adri said.

'So one life is not as important as the other?'

'I owe Maya. I do not know anything about who is currently being used by the Mask as a host, and I am not responsible for his or her death. Your team would've killed the host either way in order to kill the Mask, so what are you complaining about?'

'Do not try and twist my words, Sen. I—' Natasha tripped over a raised footpath. Adri instinctively caught her, and she regained her footing. The hand Adri had used to catch her, however, was the scaly one.

'Thanks. Err, your hand felt weird,' she said, raising Adri's hand to the moonlight. She reacted with a gasp that Adri was expecting.

'What is this? All this while I thought you were wearing a glove!'

'It's all right. It's just a little *temporary* issue,' Adri said. The growth had spread. The scales had perfectly and uniformly covered Adri's right hand, and were now slowly growing towards his elbow. They were black and polished, and felt extremely tough, like armour. It felt a bit different, but his hand felt stronger. It was a feeling he would have liked if he had been in control.

'Temporary? I've never seen this before!' she said.

'Can both of you keep it down?' Gray hissed, looking about nervously. He had the Sadhu's Shotgun in his hands, his violin case slung across his side.

'We will discuss my, err, *condition* later,' Adri said. 'If it is to be discussed at all.'

'What *have* you been up to, Sen?' Natasha said, shaking her head.

The Settlement where the Devil Mask was lurking soon came into view. Revenant stumbled around the entrance; everything else appeared to be quiet. The outer wall of the Settlement was a mixture of bricks and cement and steel and everything else that could be put together to keep intruders out. A crude, desperate attempt at defence, and they skirted around the perimeter till they found an entry. It didn't take long to get in; they removed some tires and furniture as quietly as they could and entered the Settlement. The place reeked of death; blood splattered almost everywhere. The streets within were mostly empty, though a few revenant silhouettes were visible in the moonlight.

'Where is it?' Gray whispered.

'Ssshh!' Adri said.

Fayne fell into the rear as he was carrying Maya. Adri took up the lead, holding a Commando sidearm that he did not like at all—a semi-automatic shooter pistol that held about fourteen holy rounds. Natasha was right behind him, and then Gray and then Fayne. Adri led them through shadows of empty houses. They were as silent as possible; Adri wanted to spot the creature before it spotted them. They cut across a small garden and then through the backyard of another abandoned home. A few revenant bumped into them, and Fayne took care of them with a well-aimed dagger, silent. They reached the central square of the Settlement; the creature was there, in the very centre of the square.

Adri drew the others back as soon as the beast came into sight; slowly, after a moment, they peeked from behind a wall. The Devil Mask was big; that was the first thought Gray had as someone who had never seen one before. It was constructed out of dead tissue, so its muscles and tendons were visible, twisting and turning with incredible intricacy around dead bone to form four long and powerful-looking limbs. Each limb was made out of hundreds of bones bound together with dead muscle to form huge legs and arms, though it rested on all fours. Its midsection was large and round, with bones knit into its exterior like a rib cage. Its head was clearly visible; a muscle mass that was the neck had an odd kind of bulge at the end—where there was a wooden mask of a *rakshas*, with bulging eyes and horns and teeth all carved into the woodwork. It was about twelve feet tall, looming over all other beings in the area.

'Bastard!' Natasha hissed.

'What's it doing?' Gray asked, fascinated, horrified.

Good question, Adri thought. The Mask was busy doing something. Its limbs moved occasionally and its muscles swirled in wavelike motions. A tentacle suddenly erupted from its back and then disappeared within its mass.

'Not meaning to be a smart-mouth here,' Natasha whispered, 'but it is actually *distracted* right now.'

'Too bad we're not here to extract Maya,' Adri said.

'But if you can figure out what it's doing, then we can get Maya out while it's busy like this,' Gray said. 'Instead of having to depend on your stupid violin plan.'

Adri looked at the creature with doubt. 'Fayne, any clue?' he asked.

'I don't know what it is up to,' the assassin replied. 'But I suggest you take the shot right now. It won't get simpler than this.'

Adri unslung the high-powered rifle from his back. He didn't have his bullet alchemy kit with him anymore, but he had still managed to modify some bullets for this weapon. It was already loaded, and Adri did not need to check. He clicked the scope into place and silently moved off to the next house for a better line of sight, the others staying where they were.

Adri settled comfortably in the darkness of the house's front porch. Raising the rifle, he took aim and observed the creature tensely. He wished he could smoke, but the smell would alarm it immediately. He was very curious about what it was doing—he had never seen or heard of a Devil Mask being distracted—that could essentially be the key to saving Maya, but he also needed to take the shot and kill the present host. And he would not get the leisure of making the shot if the creature was provoked. The setting was perfect.

Adri aimed carefully at the creature's belly, its carrying cage, where the host stayed once the Mask enveloped him or her. The ribs around the carrying cage would deflect the bullet easily; he needed to put the bullet in between the ribs, where the stomach flesh was. And the shot needed to be fatal for the host. If the host was merely wounded, the Devil Mask would merely heal him or her in some time. Adri was almost ready to make the shot when the full weight of what he was doing hit him. Sure, everyone was okay with it for now. But he was about to kill an innocent being imprisoned inside the Mask for his own purposes, and however well he had justified it to himself up until this moment, now that the shot was lined up, Adri realised he could not pull the trigger. He cursed silently.

'Why isn't he firing?' Gray hissed.

'He's a damn good shot,' Natasha whispered back. 'He'll take his time, but he won't miss.'

'Are you kidding me?' Gray asked. 'This guy uses a couple of revolvers just to prove bullets are free!'

'If he wants to hit a target, he hits it,' Natasha said simply. 'He had many strategies earlier when I used to know him. For example, he used to think that a bullet that missed instilled more fear in its target than one that hit. There was a time when he used to consciously fire off rounds not aimed at his enemies before he would take the killing shot.'

'That sounds—very weird.'

'Adri was always like that.'

'That also sounded sadistic.'

'I think Adri was more into experimenting with the whole thing. He was always *so* confused about his beliefs.'

Adri was beginning to sweat. There was no backup plan for this, no other way. He didn't need his conscience coming in at a time like this.

What are you waiting for, fool? Fire! the Wraith urged.

'Shut up, damn you,' he mumbled.

The Devil Mask trembled suddenly. Its face was looking down. All of a sudden it trembled again and released a black tarlike substance on the ground from a gash in its neck.

'Don't tell me the bloody thing is dying!' Adri muttered, but he knew the symptoms, having seen Devil Masks die before.

Fayne tapped his shoulder, giving Adri the shock of his life.

'Don't do that!' he yelped. 'When did you get here?'

'Apologies,' Fayne said. 'But did you see it release darkblood? It is dying.'

'But why is it dying?' Adri asked Fayne, and then answered it himself, his eyebrows expanding. 'Oh hell! Fayne, get Maya. Now! The host inside the Mask is already dead.'

Fayne moved off soundlessly and Adri followed him back to where the others were.

'Well?' Gray and Natasha asked.

'The host is already dead,' Adri said urgently. 'We just have to give Maya to the creature and get the hell out of here.'

'A pity we cannot just watch it die,' Natasha said.

'You will watch it die, but not now,' Adri said, and then turned to Fayne. 'Fayne, how far can you throw Maya?'

'Throw?' Gray squeaked. 'You want to break her neck or what? No one's *throwing* my sister anywhere!'

Fayne cricked his muscular neck. 'I can make her reach the Mask,' he said.

'Excellent. Let's do this, then,' Adri said.

'Hey, you can't ignore me!' Gray hissed. 'Have you gone nuts, throwing Maya at the Devil Mask?'

'She's going to be the next damn *host,* Gray,' Adri said. 'Get a grip on yourself.'

Fayne climbed to the roof of the house beneath which they were hiding. He held Maya by her ankle with one hand and by her shoulder with the other, like the world's weirdest javelin. Then, with brief aim, he shouted loudly, and threw Maya through the air. The shout immediately attracted the Mask's attention—it whipped its neck in their direction and immediately, three tentacles from its body caught Maya in mid-air, lowering her, bringing her to itself. Fayne leapt off the roof and out of sight; they saw the Mask check for him as it looked towards the roof again and again. Then it turned Maya round and round with its tentacles, inspecting her.

'That looks—so *wrong,*' Gray whispered.

Then its belly opened up horizontally, bone ribs sliding aside. It was a sudden move; mucus-like fluids and slime dripped heavily from within as a lifeless body dropped from inside to the ground. The tentacles moved Maya towards the open belly, and white cilia from within started wrapping themselves around Maya as she was accepted as the Devil Mask's new host.

'Excellent,' Adri breathed, slinging the rifle across his shoulder and getting up cautiously. 'Time to leave, guys.'

Gray was still staring at the Mask, horrified. 'Are you *sure* that's safe?'

'The corruption was about to kick into Maya once more,' Adri said, grabbing Gray's shoulder and pulling him away. 'I'd say it was one hell of a good time for this to happen, never mind safe.'

'What? It's not safe?' Gray exclaimed, finally looking away and following Adri.

'It's never been done before, Gray!' Adri snapped.

They stole out of the Settlement.

'How long is this going to take?' Natasha said as they walked back. 'This process, I mean.'

'Are you both deaf?' Adri remarked. 'I don't do this on a daily basis! I don't know how fast the Devil Mask can heal.'

'So when are we coming back?' Gray asked.

'We'll see the Mask tomorrow night. If it's doing fine, then, in all probability, Maya will have healed by then,' Adri said.

'I hate this,' Gray said.

'It was distracted because it was dying. The host had already been killed,' Adri said. 'It will not be distracted again. We will have to use the violin.'

It took them about twenty minutes to get back to the temporary camp at Mullikbazar, but Fayne sensed something as soon as they got near the building.

'Stop,' the assassin said softly. 'There are others.'

Adri closed his eyes for a brief second. 'I can sense a major magical vibe,' he said.

Slowly, they moved towards the building from the side alley. There, below the building, instead of the one Commando, there stood five guarding the entrance.

'Oh, it's the reinforcements from MYTH,' Natasha said, stepping out of hiding. 'Come along, its fine.'

'Uh, are you sure?' Gray asked.

'We have to last another night here and not let them attack the Devil Mask right now,' Adri hissed. 'We don't have a choice here. Let's go.'

The three of them followed Natasha as she walked towards the Commandos. They saluted her. 'They're with me,' Natasha said, pointing at the three following her, and made her way into the garage. They climbed up the staircase to find a group of seven more Commandos and a very familiar Sorcerer. It was Arshamm, and he glared at them.

'Natasha! Harbouring enemies of the government, I see!' he cried.

'Cut it out, Arshamm,' Natasha said. 'They haven't hurt anyone.'

'The Tantric is banished!' Arshamm protested. 'He's a danger to the men I lead!'

'God, what is it with you and theatrics?' Natasha complained.

'I don't care about what you have to say, Natasha,' Arshamm said. 'I'm having these three arrested and deprived of their weapons as a necessary precaution.'

'You're *what?*' Natasha said.

'Get out of my way, Natasha,' Arshamm said.

Natasha stood between Arshamm and the others. She was stiff, her eyes glaring into Arshamm's.

'So you won't even *listen* to what I have to say?' she said angrily.

'I won't let anyone stand in my way when it comes to this scum,' Arshamm said. 'You want to take me on, Sorceress?'

Adri stepped in between them, surprising both of them.

'You want revenge so badly it makes me sick, Arshamm,' he said, looking at Arshamm.

'Why, you—' Arshamm cried, and tiny sparks of electricity began generating in his gauntleted hands.

'Won't be necessary, Arshamm,' Adri said, raising his left hand to Arshamm's face.

Arshamm glared, horrified, at the ring Adri wore. The electricity in his palms died down.

'Ring of the High Angel Kaavsh,' Adri said. 'Official permit, if you will, stating we are friends of the government. Now back down, Sorcerer.'

Arshamm continued to glare at Adri, his hate spilling. Then he glanced briefly at the Commandos who were watching them and Natasha's ugly expression. His posture relaxed. 'Your permission is legal,' he said. 'This time, I will let this pass.'

'What are you so worked up about?' Natasha shouted. Arshamm ignored her and retreated to another part of the roof.

'Leave him,' Adri told Natasha. 'He should learn to lick his wounds.'

'What *did* you do to him to have him this angry at you?' the Sorceress asked, shaking her head.

'A long story,' Adri said with an apologetic grin.

'I'm all ears,' Natasha said. Adri and Natasha moved off towards the other side, away from where Arshamm had retreated. At any other time Gray would have been curious enough to follow and listen, but not right now. He simply went to where the Commandos were sitting and slumped in an empty space. Fayne followed him, and once again, sat next to him.

'Back at home, there was always a strict schedule to be followed,' Gray said. 'Sleep in the night and work and study during the day. Over here, it's whatever suits us the best. There are no such rules.'

Fayne said nothing.

'How do you sleep standing up?' Gray asked him. 'How can your body rest that way?'

'It's all about training,' Fayne said. 'If you dedicate yourself to anything, a lot can happen which may seem unattainable in the beginning.' The assassin paused. 'But it is not my sleeping habits that are bothering you, *myrkho*,' he continued quietly.

'No, it's Maya,' Gray said softly, looking at his feet.

'Understandable. It is not in your hands anymore, Gray. Your worrying will not help her.'

'She's my sister, I can't help but have the worst of premonitions about this.'

'Have faith. Trust in Adri Sen,' Fayne said.

'I cannot fully trust Adri still, Fayne,' Gray said. 'He's too reckless for my taste. There should be a certain amount of control in a warrior.'

'The *pashlin* has a lot of power which he does not reveal,' Fayne said. They looked at Adri telling something to a wide-eyed Natasha. 'He is older then he looks, and he burns with hidden power. I sensed it the first time I laid eyes on him.'

'You mean he hasn't shown us his full capabilities?' Gray asked, surprised. 'I mean, we've seen him do a lot of things, fight a lot of creatures. Are you talking about the Wraith?'

'No. The energy the Wraith gives him is different. Adri has power of his own which he hides and hides well. For what reason he hides the power I do not know. He did not unleash it even when we were all about to die in the Hive; he depended upon the Wraith then. But he hasn't shown you even a fraction of his inner power.'

Gray looked at Adri in a new light, in partial awe. 'You would never realise that looking at him, would you?' he asked. 'Adri has too many secrets, too many stories to tell.'

'Far too many,' Fayne said.

The Commandos had been murmuring among themselves for a while now. One of them finally came up to Gray and Fayne. 'Err, hello,' he said nervously. 'We were all wondering who you guys are—and on what business of the Angels you are here.'

Gray looked at him blankly, thinking about what to say. The Commando waited awkwardly for a reply that wasn't coming. And right then, all of a sudden, something blocked out the moonlight on that part of the roof, throwing the Commandos, Gray, and Fayne into shadow. Everyone looked up.

There, on a higher part of the roof, where the water tank was, crouched a creature, a silhouette in the light of the huge moon behind it. It watched them soundlessly, its eyes burning white. For a moment no one could react, except for the assassin, who was on his feet in a heartbeat, pulling out blades from his abdomen. Everyone gazed, stunned, at the monstrosity, at the haphazardly shaped creature on all fours, quietly perched above them. There was silence, except for the sound of metal scraping as Fayne withdrew dagger after dagger into his hands. Then it roared, and everything sprang to life.

The roar was guttural, hollow and powerful. It froze everyone's blood and sapped at their courage. 'Devil Mask!' a Commando roared.

Adri did not move while the rest scurried away, creating some distance from the gigantic thing. He stood where he was, coldly eyeing the creature. He was thinking.

'Kill it!' Arshamm screamed, generating fireballs and throwing them as he bounded across the roof to where the Commandos were. Natasha looked at an unmoving Adri, still staring at the creature on the roof.

'I'm sorry, Sen, but there's nothing I can do now,' she said before joining the fray, her gauntlets generating electricity.

The Mask roared as the Commandos began firing holy rounds at it. Tentacles immediately burst out of its sides, a deadly bone spike at each end.

'Watch it, tentacles!' a Commando roared.

The Commandos dodged and continued firing as the creature struck out. The holy rounds did not seem to be doing much damage to it; the creature struck out again and impaled two Commandos, raising their dead bodies to the air as the rest of the tentacles attacked more viciously than before.

'No, no, STOP!' Gray roared, running and tackling a Commando. The Commando, taken by surprise, was thrown off his feet. 'What's wrong with you?' he roared, grabbing Gray and roughly shoving him aside.

The Devil Mask could see everywhere at once. No one took it by surprise, not even Arshamm with his boomerang fireballs. The fireballs and holy rounds pounded into the creature's dead flesh without effect; it struck back with lethal accuracy, impaling Commando after Commando. Natasha poured pure electricity into the Devil Mask, again without any result. At best, the electricity seemed to subdue it mildly. The beast roared, and Natasha yelled for the Commandos to find cover. Cover though, was tough to find as the Mask had the advantage of altitude and that of surprise. Fayne stood beside Adri, quietly watching everything, his hands full of daggers.

'Impossible!' Arshamm hissed, as the creature ignored his attacks. 'How can it just resist my fire?'

'Change your attacks, Arshamm!' Natasha screamed.

Gray had been punched by the Commando he tried to disarm. The punch sent him reeling to a wall, where he crumpled to the floor, staying there. His will was sapped, he merely looked at everything happening in front of him as though it were a dream.

'Don't kill my sister,' he murmured.

The Mask jumped and landed where they were. It was moving quicker than before now. One of its bone limbs reached out and crushed another Commando. The others retreated across the roof, firing away at the Necrotic. Arshamm and Natasha poured in all the electricity they could muster.

'Adri,' Fayne said.

Adri was still gazing at the creature in wonder, his mind working furiously. Then it all clicked. 'Of course,' he mumbled, and then turned to Fayne. 'Ready?' he said. 'Stand by.' Fayne nodded.

The creature was now like a twisted pincushion of death, corpses waving about at the ends of its tentacles, the eyes in the Mask burning white and cruel as it ignored Adri and Fayne and walked towards the group of the two Sorcerers and the few surviving Commandos. Adri turned to Gray and saw him lying immobile across the roof, away from the Devil Mask. He ran to the white haired figure.

'Gray! Gray! It's time!' Adri hissed.

'Leave me here, Adri,' Gray muttered. 'I want to die here.'

Adri slapped Gray hard.

'OW!' Gray roared. 'You did that on purpose!'

'Get the hell up and play the violin!' Adri shouted. 'There's no time!'

Gray's eyes opened wide. 'But Maya?'

'We are extracting her *now*! Play the bloody violin!'

Gray nodded and scampered to where his violin case lay, luckily undamaged. Adri looked at the Mask as it rapidly bore down upon the survivors. It was now or never.

'Fayne! Right when the music starts!' Adri shouted.

Fayne was running towards the Devil Mask. The creature had its back towards Fayne, but it never missed anything. A couple of tentacles lashed out at the assassin as he ran.

Gray started to play. It was imperfect and horrible, and even more so because of all the pressure Gray was under. His hands trembled and he got his basic notes wrong. But the moment the music began it talked to the Necrotic in a language it could comprehend clearer than anything else. It dropped all its attacks immediately and whipped around to face the music.

Fayne completed his run, slicing through the two tentacles and burying two daggers into the Devil Mask's stomach. The next second, he turned both the daggers to cut two enormous arcs in its stomach, completing a full circle through bone and flesh. The Mask froze, Gray played. A section of the stomach dropped out with black slime and translucent fluid—the assassin stepped aside nimbly to avoid getting hit—and inside was Maya, white soft cilia keeping her in place like a puppet in the Devil Mask's centre. The creature had completely stopped moving, but Fayne was still very quick at slashing away the tentacles and catching Maya's limp body as she fell out. The Devil Mask roared and looked at its cut, bleeding stomach as Fayne rushed away with Maya. The creature roared again, fighting the music, but it could not help listening to the violin for a few seconds more even as the Sorcerers behind it pelted it with fireballs. Gray stopped suddenly, and the spell broken, the Devil Mask leapt onto the roof of the next building, and disappeared.

Everybody was stunned. 'Well, after it!' Natasha screamed the next instant and the four surviving commandos nodded and rushed off towards the staircase. Arshamm and Natasha went with them, briefly glancing at Maya now in Fayne's arms.

Gray ran to Fayne. Maya was motionless.

'Adri,' Gray said, looking at Maya. 'Was she healed?'

'The Devil Mask knew the way here because it had access to Maya's memories,' Adri said. 'That's how it found us here. Which leads me to believe that the Mask had completely integrated Maya as a host; she should be perfectly healed of the corruption.'

'Maya's memories?' Fayne asked.

'Yes, and I know what it implies. It seems Maya, even in her coma, has been perfectly aware of our movements and our surroundings,' Adri said. 'It is surprising.'

Gray looked back at the soaked Maya, lying unconscious, but breathing. Her face seemed to be returning to a more normal colour. Was she really cured?

'Let her rest,' Adri said. 'I believe she has a lot of catching up to do when she does wake.'

27

When the morning sun rose, Adri was not on the roof with the others. He was quite a distance away, alone, walking through empty streets. There were not many birds that still called out in the mornings and it made Adri feel better to hear them. Things were changing for the better now. He was quite sure Maya was cured; perhaps he could send the three of them back now. Fayne would be as good an insurance as any that they got back into New Kolkata safe and sound—the siblings would probably be dying to leave anyway. The bridge was nearby and so was the road to Pestilence. What waited for him now was his to deal with. And deal he would. Alone.

'Which way?' he asked.

The next right, the Wraith said.

Adri walked some more before he saw the gates of the graveyard in the distance. It was small, not as big as the one in Park Street.

'Well Wraith, to tell you the truth it wasn't bad, this you being in my body. Towards the end you had become so quiet that there were times I forgot you were there,' Adri said.

Isn't that nice to hear, the Wraith said drily. *The time is almost upon us, either way. You have bound me to my word, and I will show you where I want to leave.*

Adri looked down at his right arm—the scales had spread and were covering the entire arm, glinting in the sunlight.

'About time, too,' he said, entering the graveyard.

Maya was in Adri's room, watching him sleep. She had been feeling better as of late, but something about the world was changing. Colours were gradually beginning to fade away, things far away were beginning to blur. She was wondering what it was, yet she never had a choice but to stay and watch. She sat on a chair near the bed now, looking around the room for something new. It was a room she had seen too many times in her memories, so much so that she was intimately familiar with everything about it, with every object in it. And yet she looked for something new, and a small new statuette on Adri's table caught her eye. She had never seen it before. She would to have moved to pick it up, but Adri began talking in his sleep.

It started off with random words, unusual muttering. Maya had seen him sleep before; he usually slept for a long while, and that was the most boring time to be around Adri. This time it was different. Adri woke up with a shout. Maya gasped, and looked at him. He was covered in sweat, tangled among his sheets, his face hidden. He was panting, but slowly, his breathing calmed down, and he looked up, straight at his table. His face was wet; Maya could not tell if it was sweat or tears. Adri climbed out of the bed, and the colours in the room slipped another degree towards black and white. Maya followed him as he went to his table and opened one of the drawers. He took out a small box, kept it on the table, and opened it. There was a single envelope inside. Light brown, with a red wax seal, long broken. Adri turned it over in his hands again and again before he slipped his fingers in and took out small letter. As he kept the envelope down, Maya saw tiny, slender writing on it. *Adri.*

Adri was opening the letter his mother had left him, the only thing she had ever had to say to him. Maya gazed at it in wonder as Adri unfolded and opened the letter. In the centre of the page, was a word, a single word, written neatly in the thin, cursive writing that was his mother's.

Live.

The world went black and white and everything blurred. And Maya woke up with a start, gasping for air.

It was a long time ago, the Wraith said. *I remember I was afraid. I had been taught well by my masters, but I was never absolutely fearless. At that time I did not view vampires for the filth that they are. Back then, I was constantly amazed by their power, envious of their control over the night. Killing them was tough and I had been trained to believe that. My first real test was to actually put into practice all I had learnt, starting from the little magic tricks to the massive weapon training. Apprehension, uneasiness took me as the vampire crawled out of its coffin. I was sure I would mess it up somewhere, do something wrong.*

'But you killed it, of course,' Adri said, walking through the graveyard. It was small, ill-maintained. Most of the statues and large tombstones were falling apart. A lot of graves were dirty, moss having taken over the stone slabs, names having been rubbed off by the elements. Adri did not like such graveyards. They were where magic caused things to go wrong, revealing its inherent chaotic nature. A place like this gave the magic in the air a room to play its own little games.

I froze, initially. The vampire went by me, its long tongue licking my ear as it went. My sensei, watching from behind, looked at me disapprovingly, unsheathing his sword. Clearly, he planned to fail me after quickly ending this vampire. My career as a vampire hunter would have come to an end before it had even begun. If you remember, I had frozen, and I did not even turn back as the vampire passed me and reached my sensei. I heard quick slashing noises; I turned and saw my sensei fall to the ground, dead.

Adri nodded. 'Not quite the ordinary vampire, then?'

It was a blood reaper, Tantric. And as I saw my sensei die, I felt my fear desert me. In front of me was one of the deadliest vampires, and I had been trained all my childhood to fight these things. I unsheathed my sword. The vampire looked at me and grinned savagely.

'How old were you?'

I was ten.

Adri whistled. 'Not bad.'

The vampire came at me with the speed of the bat. I swung, but of course its power lay in the fact that it could sense my moves beforehand. Then I unleashed my energy blade, a weapon I had developed in secret even from my own sensei, and not one I could have ever used in front of him. The design of the blade I had stolen from the deepest, most well-kept files of the vampire hunters. And, of course, I had created the blade slowly, like an amateur. It was years later that I could perfect the weapon, but even then it served its basic purpose. It was not a tangible weapon so the vampire could not sense it coming; with every wound I landed on the hellspawn, one of my own wounds would heal immediately. I had not meant a stab at power when I had made the blade—it had simply been a precaution—one my sensei could have done with, I might add now. He was an old fool and he died. And I, Mazumder, Bane of Vampires to come, was born on that night. I collected the ashes of the blood reaper after I killed it and wore them in a cloth bag around my neck for my entire life.

'Where did you kill it?'

There, by that white grave.

Adri walked to the white grave. It was nameless, just another grave in the weed-choked grass. He stood there for a while, taking in the silence of the graveyard. He looked up at the landscape around, feeling warm in the sunlight. Then he looked down at the grave.

'Well, I guess this is it, Mazumder. It was a fun run.'

Goodbye, Adri.

And that was it. Adri thought he would feel a surprisingly heavy weight lifting off his mind, or something else—a part of him he would miss immediately. He sighed, slowly. The Wraith was gone. All those thoughts of sharing a body with another soul that scared him had been proved false. His head was blissfully silent, and he felt much more in control. Adri smiled inwardly, clenching and unclenching his fists. Then he looked down at his arm and saw that the scales were still there.

'Wait a minute. Wasn't this supposed to go away?' he cried out. *It will leave when I do,* the Wraith had once said. *Getting rid of that thing is not going to be as easy as you think,* Fayne had said.

'Mazumder! Mazumder!' Adri shouted angrily. Silence. 'Answer me, goddammit!' he cried.

I spoke the truth, Tantric. I told you it will leave when I do, the Wraith spoke.

'You also told me you would leave! That's why we're here in the first place!' Adri shouted, knowing at the same time that this was turning into something ugly, something he didn't want.

I cannot leave.

'I have bound you to your word. I will force you out of me!' Adri said.

I did mention a graveyard near Howrah, but I did not mention which one. The story about the blood reaper was perfectly true, Tantric, except it did not happen here. I am not bound to be released here.

'Then where?'

You think I want to be released, Tantric? The Wraith was perfectly serious; its voice carried no traces of amusement, the usual sarcasm or spite. *I have done terrible things in my time. There is no way that I'm going to the next Plane where the Angels have come from. No, I shall be summoned across the River. And I'm not going somewhere I sent thousands of vampires, where their spirits wait for mine.*

'I do not care about your situation and I told you that, Mazumder! We had a deal!'

I never had any honour, fool. Things such as deals don't matter to me. I plan to keep on living as a Wraith; for that purpose I am transforming you. When the transformation is complete I shall have taken over your body. You can then sit and spectate for a while as I have.

'You did it in the Hive,' Adri said, slowly understanding the gravity of the situation.

You gave me complete control, Tantric. I made my move; who wouldn't have? The assassin was right, the pompous brat. I AM after this body. And if you hadn't shouted out right now and just gone back, I would have been silent until the takeover was complete.

'How long do I have?'

Do you expect me to tell you that? I'm not stupid, Tantric. I've seen what you are capable of. All I will tell you is that I shall not torture you for long, but soon you will be a prisoner in your own mind, the way I was a prisoner in yours.

'Mazumder, there may still be a way to get you to the next Plane. What if we can find it? Will you consent to leave my body then?'

I don't really want to move on, Tantric. I was in the eternal sleep when you woke me up and forced me on this tour around the Old City. I'm seeing everything after so very long, and I like what I see. No, I want to live now.

'You know the Horseman is after me. How long can you survive? I have been running after something for this long, Wraith, and you've seen what I've been through. Let me complete what I've started. Let me, at least, get to the bottom of this conspiracy.'

As long as you wear the pendant, I can keep dodging the Horseman and hunting vampires forever, Tantric. I'm no kind soul, and I have never cared about this conspiracy or Doomsday. Do what you will; you know you have little time. When I take over, I'm going hunting.

Adri's mood changed completely, his resolutions changed rapidly. It was time to reprioritise and quickly so. Not much would change. What was needed to get the Wraith out was a Wraith exorcism, a process that took at least a week to pull off, not to mention he couldn't do it to himself. He would need another Tantric. He knew he didn't have a week. Far lesser. The scales had been growing at a phenomenal rate of late, and now he understood what the black shiny growth actually symbolised.

Think all you want, fool. You are not getting me out, that's for sure. I suggest you divert your energies to finding out what you came here to find.

That was actually the road he would have to take. There was no time now for exorcists and rituals. He had lesser time now to find out what he was after, but he had a feeling he was close. He needed to take the next step.

Pestilence, in a cave beneath the Howrah Bridge.

Adri got back around noon. The first person he saw was Maya; it seemed to him that he was seeing her for the first time. He had seen her still and lifeless all the time, and had forgotten what she was like when she walked and smiled. Which she was, towards him.

Gray seemed angry and sore about something. He was talking to Fayne in a low voice. Fayne watched Maya go towards Adri and looked back at Gray. Maya stopped a little distance away from him. Had he been expecting a hug? Adri hadn't really been thinking about one, but he was surprised to find that he was inwardly—*disappointed.*

'Adri,' Maya said. 'Thank you.'

Adri looked at her expressionlessly. 'You were my responsibility,' he spoke simply.

'Yeah,' she said, still smiling. 'And I screwed up big time.'

'You were stupid,' Adri agreed. 'But we've come a long way from there and a lot of things have happened. And right now, you're okay and I guess that's what's important.'

Maya looked at the floor. 'I would like you to know some things,' she said.

'You do not need to explain anything to me,' Adri said.

'No,' Maya said, looking at him again. 'There are some things you should know.'

Adri and Maya moved to another part of the roof and sat down.

'What has she been through?' Gray asked. 'What made her change?'

'You should understand, Gray, that your sister has seen something about Adri while she was in her coma. And *that* has made the *fatiya* want to stay on with him right now.'

'But that means even you'll stay on!' Gray exclaimed. 'And me,' he added.

'Correct,' Fayne said.

'I want to leave! I want to leave this place and these insecurities! I don't care about anything—my camera is still lying in that bloody forest in my bag. I don't even need that anymore. I want to go home; can't Maya understand that? She should have had enough by now, of all people!'

'If the Apocalypse does happen, *myrkho*—New Kolkata will not be spared. Nothing will be,' Fayne said.

Gray looked at him with distaste. 'Whose side are you on?'

'I will of course, protect the *fatiya* until the charge is lifted from me,' the assassin replied.

'No, I didn't mean that so literally, you idiot.'

'I do not take very kindly to being insulted,' Fayne said, sounding ruffled.

'Sorry, sorry!' Gray exclaimed nervously.

'I am so sorry,' Maya said as genuinely as she could sound.

'You read my diaries?' Adri asked again, not being able to believe what he was hearing.

'I know it's a really bad thing to do. I'm extremely sorry.'

Adri stared at Maya, all sorts of thoughts going through his head. Then he burst out laughing. Maya panicked, not knowing what to think as Adri laughed and laughed, and laughed some more. Maya tried to laugh along, but she couldn't. Adri recovered, gasping for breath, and turned to her.

'A student of Demonology from Jadavpur now knows more about me than my own father?' he asked, laughing again. 'I mean, I've tried to guard my past so well, and all the time I never thought someone could just waltz into my house with me and take my diaries to read.'

'I know it's not done,' Maya said. 'But I didn't trust you at all back then.'

Adri stopped laughing. 'So you trust me now?'

'I know who you are,' Maya said, looking down. 'I admit I read the diaries by choice, but the visions, I did not have any choice but to watch them.'

'Those visions you had, they are exactly what happened in my past,' Adri said quietly. 'You saw the world exactly as I saw it back then.'

'You know why they happened?' a surprised Maya asked.

'Yes and no,' Adri said. 'The Dreamer's Brew, which kept you alive all this while, had one ingredient which must be added secretly. It is a personal ingredient, and not one that is announced. A drop of blood; the one I added was mine.'

Maya stared.

412

'If I had known you'd read my diaries, I wouldn't have added my own blood, but I reasoned that it was the safest thing to do as you knew about me the least. Thus the dreams you would have would be minimal, the brew would mostly keep you in an endless sleep. I did not add Gray's blood as there would be too many memories of his past, maybe things you wouldn't not want to see, or he wouldn't want you to. And yet this is debated; the Dreamer's Brew is a mysterious concoction, and the effects of the blood have never been fully defined. I could never know what it would be that you would see, if at all. Guesses were all I had. But going by what you said— you must know a lot about me by now.'

'An awful lot,' Maya said. 'I wish I could keep apologising, Adri.'

'No, it's good to see that you're up. No more apologies. You're going home now with your brother and your personal bodyguard.'

'What?' Maya cried out.

'Listen to me before you start protesting,' Adri said. 'There are dangers ahead that you cannot possibly comprehend. After all I've done to save you I cannot risk you to danger again.'

'Then you might as well have hired Fayne,' Maya said. Her attitude had changed completely in seconds. A stubborn light shone in her eyes as she looked at Adri. 'You had sworn to protect me, Adri, and you honoured that. And for that I thank you. But if you think I will abandon you after all you've done for me, you're wrong.'

'It's not about *abandoning*. The Old City—you're not supposed to be here.'

'I don't remember you saying that when you needed us to go with you for your own reasons,' Maya said.

'It's true that I needed you to come along,' Adri said. 'But I never thought back then that the city was like this, like a ticking bomb ready to explode. I did not know that it had changed in its danger, or perhaps the years had made me forget. If I had known, I would have reconsidered.'

'Then where are we supposed to go, Adri? Are we supposed to leave everything on your shoulders and go back to New Kolkata and wait for the Apocalypse to find out whether you survived the Horseman or not? I know who you are, Adri Sen. I have followed you around, I have watched you sleep, I have walked a thousand kilometres with you. Don't you try and push yourself into a heroic self-sacrifice here. You deserve better than that.'

Adri stared at her.

'You have more than one enemy, Adri,' Maya said. 'I'd say it's about time you figured out who your allies are.'

In unconsciousness, Maya always had a sense of where she was going, where she was being taken. It was unlike being asleep or in a coma; this feeling was much more real, and it proved to be remarkably accurate as well. The only thing was that it all came to her immediately on her waking up—places they had travelled to, snatches of conversations around her, what she had smelled, and the taste of the liquid food they had poured down her throat. She took a while after waking up to assimilate everything; her mind hurt terribly still, but she was alive. Gray summed up what had happened while she had been gone, and the more she heard about what the Tantric had been up to, the more in awe and shock she went into, even after knowing that someone like Adri was perfectly capable of experiencing phenomena like he did.

The entire existence of Fayne was a shock to her as well—apart from having no clue as to who would pay for her protection, she was very uncomfortable with the idea of a bodyguard. Fayne became more alert about where she went ever since she woke up; Maya knew and resented that. She, however, made it clear to Gray that she was staying with Adri as he investigated things further. She was not going to be one to run away after all Adri had done; though Gray, somewhere within, knew that she was right, he was still disappointed. He had been thinking of home.

Maya got to know about Adri's next objective, and without hesitation she decided to support him. No longer would she question Adri where he did not need to be questioned. No, what Adri needed was reassurance, and she would try and be there for him.

'I'm going to kill Death,' Adri said. 'It isn't going to be easy, and it definitely might have collateral damage. I want you to understand that and then think about this.'

Maya nodded. 'I have already been told what your plans are,' she said. 'And I'll come with you, even if I only stand and watch when you take on the Horseman. If he is threatening to bring in a new age of terror, then you're right. There is no other way.'

'And how do you propose to kill the Horseman?' Gray asked. 'Last I checked, the mad Tantric was going on about how they are not a foe you can beat.'

'I repeat myself,' Adri said. 'If Death is not immortal, I will kill it. Kali talked about the cave of Pestilence beneath the Howrah Bridge. I think we should move.'

Everyone nodded, except Gray. They had packed supplies for a short duration on Natasha's orders. They picked those up now and slung the bags across their shoulders as they left. Before they left, Adri took Natasha aside.

'Nat,' he said. 'There is something I must tell you.'

Natasha smiled. 'Don't say something stupid, Sen.'

'There was a guy in our Tantric batch, same year. His name was Aman.'

Natasha's face scrunched up as she tried to remember. 'Aman, Aman. I can't really place him, sounds vaguely familiar. What about him?'

Adri looked at Natasha. 'He was in love with you,' he said.

'What?' Natasha cried in surprise.

'He was, and then he died. A Demon got him. But his spirit could not move on because he was still attached to you.'

'Good God,' Natasha said. 'I had no idea.'

'I bound the spirit from telling you what he wanted to. And slowly, I helped him pass onto the next Plane. He's long gone, but I wanted you to know. He was a good friend to me, once.'

Natasha could only nod softly, not knowing what to say.

'Sorry to have to tell you this. But—'

'Thanks for telling me,' Natasha said, shaking her head. 'And thank you for helping him move on.'

Adri nodded. 'Thank you for everything. You helped me save a life, and I owe you.'

'You owe a lot of people, Sen,' Natasha said, a ghost of a smile on her lips. 'Now get out of here.'

Adri smiled and lit a cigarette as he walked out. They walked down a couple of side alleys until they reached the main road and began to follow it towards the Bridge.

'You want to quickly let the Wraith go? I mean his graveyard should be somewhere around here right?' Gray said when they passed a lone coffin by the side of the road.

Adri was silent. They kept walking.

Maya looked at everything around her in a new light. She had seen a lot of these places in Adri's memories, and now everything had changed, everything was deserted. They were the only ones on the road now, walking. The Devil Mask had escaped the night before, and if it had not found a host, it was probably dead. The presence of a Necrotic had a direct effect on the revenant; no longer fuelled by the creature, they were not visible like before. Adri only glimpsed the occasional revenant, dragging itself sadly down a random alley

The Bridge wasn't far. They had a new objective now, and Maya was perhaps the only one whose resolve was freshest; even Adri was beginning to have doubts despite himself. But he could not give up and he knew that. Not without trying. As they reached the Bridge, Adri thought about his father and what could have possibly happened to Smith who'd been tracking him. There had been no news from Smith since they had last seen him, and Adri did not have a messenger dragonfly with him. He hoped Smith was all right, but the change in the city's mood seemed to be an ill omen. Even the sun could not stay for long, as clouds began to gather, the sky darkening.

'Wait,' Fayne said suddenly, stopping. Everyone stopped and looked where Fayne was looking. The Howrah Bridge was very close now, and there was something on the Bridge looking at them.

'What is that?' Maya asked, squinting.

'A Demon,' Fayne said. 'It's watching us.'

They stopped and looked at the figure, small in the distance, standing on the edge of the bridge. Then in a moment's blink, it was gone.

'Someone blinked,' Adri said. Fayne nodded quietly. Adri looked at the sibling's confused faces and explained. '*Blinking* is a powerful form of magic that not many creatures are capable of; it's something that takes a high level of magical power to pull off. It gives one the ability to teleport over short distances, provided someone looking at the teleporter blinks his eyes.'

'What?' Gray exclaimed. 'If we hadn't blinked the creature couldn't have teleported?'

'Yes. That's how it works. In the moment that you close your eyes, the user gets his opportunity to make the visual jump. Short distances only, but that Demon is now gone.'

'*Yeteyer.* I don't like this,' Fayne said. 'We should be more careful from now.'

'When I tell everyone to stare from now, no one blinks their eyes,' Adri said darkly. 'If that Demon can blink, it's dangerous.'

417

They moved slowly, cautiously, but were not interrupted or attacked. Fayne was more alert than anyone had ever seen him be. The usually calm assassin was positively jumpy now, increasing the sense of threat and danger and suitably scaring the siblings. 'Kali did not mention *which side* the cave was on,' Gray said after a while. They had taken a small mud road after the buildings gradually ended and were walking through an abandoned slum towards the base of the Bridge.

'We might have to cross the Bridge, then.'

Adri nodded. 'That will not be easy. We'll be sitting ducks for anything that might be stalking us.'

They were, however, in luck. As they crossed the slum and reached the River bank, they could see the black outline of a cave carved into a large rock beneath the Bridge. Beside them lay the mighty Ganga—unaffected and unperturbed by all that was happening in the Old City, continuing to flow with all its power. There were no ferries, no fishermen. A couple of abandoned boats floated in the current, held in place by ropes. They walked slowly towards the cave, looking up at the imposing, powerful Howrah Bridge, standing guard over this part of Old Kolkata, one of the largest magical hubs in the Old City.

'That is how Pestilence can hide his aura,' Adri said. 'By living beneath the Bridge it won't be detected by outsiders, or the government. The Bridge sends out too much magic, completely overshadowing the Horseman.'

'Why will Pestilence help you?' Maya asked.

'I don't know,' Adri said.

'Are you sure big brother Death won't be visiting him?' Gray asked nervously.

'I don't think they can meet each other while the seals are unbroken,' Adri replied. 'At least, that's what the theory is behind a seal curse.'

Adri began feeling a new vibe as they approached the cave. A new, powerful, magical vibe, one he had never felt before in his life. It did not radiate of power like Death's, but had a different taste to it. It spoke to him of hidden things and secrets.

'Curious,' Adri mumbled.

He had the shooter he had been using, outfitted with holy rounds, but he knew he could not possibly battle the Horseman if things got out of hand. No, it would be best to go in unarmed. And alone. They stood in front of the cave now. It was dark and silent, and nothing seemed to exist beyond its doorway. It was large, large enough for any Demon to enter, yet unnoticeable from a distance, almost camouflaged among the other large rocks which were around it. This was where the second Horseman lived.

Adri handed Gray his shooter and took off his supply bag. 'I have to go alone,' he said. Maya was about to protest, but he caught her eye before she could. 'I *have* to.' She looked at him, and finally nodded. Adri looked up at the sky. The sun was hidden, and dark clouds were gathering, faster than before. Taking a deep breath, he entered the cave.

Complete darkness greeted him. He took a small step, testing the footing the ground offered—solid rock, stable. Slowly, he began to walk, one hand on a wall for guidance. Spirit vision was always an easy way out, but now Adri did not want to have anything to do with the Wraith. He did not have to bear the darkness for long, however. Soon, a faint light appeared in the tunnel, and he realised that he had been on a gentle slope, going downwards. He walked faster now, as his eyes got accustomed to the light. Then he saw the torch. Wall mounted, magical fire burning within. He passed it and walked on, crossing another similar torch a while later.

His body began to itch slowly, everything except the right arm. He stopped and scratched—the itching flared up, then ebbed, but did not leave. He looked at his hand in the light of the next torch and drew a sharp breath; it was covered in an angry red rash. Then, before his very eyes, his fingernails started to grow slowly and a general tiredness crept in.

'What's happening?' he mumbled.

Nothing good, the Wraith said. *Get a move on, and hurry, fool.*

Angry as he was at the Wraith, the advice was sound. Adri started walking faster as the itchiness slowly spread to his scalp. He scratched his hair, and a clump of hair came away in his fist. He was losing hair. He started running now; the tunnel went on and on and on, as did the torches.

'Where is the end?' Adri shouted, running.

He felt his face. Boils. The panic in him rose. He nails were quite long now, which helped him scratch himself all over, but he was horrified with what was happening to him. He ran on and on, then finally saw the door. He ran into the door, pushing it and hoping it would open. It stood firm. He took a step back and observed it in the light of the torch above it—a door cut directly out of the bark of some great, ancient tree. It looked tremendously heavy, with gnarled texture and millions of lines across it. It had no knocker. Adri used his right hand to knock, and was surprised momentarily by how strong his armoured hand was as he thumped on the door loudly and audibly. The sound resonated in the tunnel for a while. Then silence. Adri was going to knock again when the door swung open on its own accord, softly, soundlessly. Adri peeped inside, and then entered.

He was now in a large circular room, well lit by over twenty to thirty torches burning fiercely. He looked around, ignoring the burning that had now started in his skin. This was some kind of a laboratory. Crystal beakers and test tubes filled the shelves along the walls, every single one sporting its own shade of liquid and gas. There were no labels or notes or files to be seen anywhere— the Horseman seemed to commit everything to memory. The room was wooden, as was the floor, and apart from tables filled with more equipment, more burners, beakers, and devices Adri had no possibility of recognising, there was nothing else in the room other than a large throne at the far end. A throne made of pure crystal, glimmering like a million diamonds in the firelight.

Pestilence sat on the throne, watching him. The Horseman was shorter than Death yet taller than Adri, even though it sat. It had a thin frame, with long, bony arms and legs—over which it wore grey robes that flowed softly around it, fuelled by an unseen force. Its skin was deep yellow in colour, and was in a constant flux—things appeared on its skin immediately, to be replaced by something else the next second; things like boils, spikes, scales, and rashes that came and went with liquid rhythm, a process that seemed as natural as breathing. Its face was that of a young man—a sharp, leering yellow face with blood-red eyes and fangs that glistened as it stared at Adri silently. Above its large forehead was wild mane-like hair, growing in every direction possible at the same time, the colour a bright and vivid red. Like its brother Death, its hands and feet were enveloped by gauntlets and mail boots that shone dully in the light.

'A visitor!' It screeched in the Old Tongue. 'Ah, pardon me, *Visitors*. How curious.' Its voice was an excited one, and gave Adri the impression of someone trying to control his thrill through a voice long torn up.

'Pestilence,' Adri said, looking at him in unsettlement.

'My aura is not good for you, human,' the Horseman said. 'You must have contracted quite the collection of diseases by now. I do love visitors, but you will die if you stay here for more than a few minutes.'

'I have come to talk to you about your brother, Death,' Adri spoke.

Pestilence's red eyes widened. 'Oh, wonderful!' it said in delight. It opened a palm and gestured towards Adri, calling something back. Adri felt something lift from him and rush away

421

towards the Horseman. Immediately, he felt better. The itching and pain was gone, the rashes had left; he knew his hair had stopped falling, his nails had stopped growing. Pestilence closed its palm and then twirled its fingers.

'There,' it said. 'It has been quite a while since I did that for someone. But then, I *do* love to hear news about my brothers! But tell me first, who told you of this place? Was it Death? But then I doubt that; he's not very *talkative*.'

'I was told about your location by Kali, the Tantric,' Adri said.

'Ah, Kali. Yes, I have heard about this Necromancer in the *Bishakto Jongol*, though I haven't ever bothered to pay him a visit. He's quite dull, isn't he? All he does is worship the Dark Goddess, when there are *so many* truths to be found around us. How is Kali doing?'

'Well, I hope,' Adri said.

'Ah, yes,' Pestilence said. 'When we do not see someone for a while all we can do is hope, is it not? Like I keep hoping for my brothers, and then you come up and talk about Death!' It grinned. 'Not the brother I'm closest to, I might confess, but it's still remarkable to hear from him!'

'No, you misunderstood. I am not a messenger from Death,' Adri said. 'I have come to talk about him.'

Pestilence raised an eyebrow. 'Oh, a discussion then? Wonderful, but you better keep your points well in your head. I warn you, I'm damn good at debate!'

'I am the last soul Death has to claim in order to break its seal,' Adri said. 'The Apocalypse might be what will unite the four of you, but it will destroy everything my ancestors have worked to build. Naturally, I cannot allow it while it is in my capabilities; I have decided that your brother Death must be killed if possible. I want to kill him myself and forever stop the coming of Doomsday.'

Pestilence was silent for a while. It breathed gently, looking at Adri.

'My, my,' it said finally. 'Cutting to the chase, I see. Did you notice my moment of silence a moment ago? Did you?'

'Err, yes.'

'I was contemplating, human. I was considering extracting your soul right here and sending it to Death as a gift, perhaps.'

Adri took a moment before he actually managed to ask the next question. 'And what is your decision?'

Pestilence scratched its head. 'I don't know, human. You amaze me and intrigue me. You come to where I live and declare your intention of executing my brother. What is your point?'

'I don't know how,' Adri said. 'Death is old and powerful. I want you to tell me his weaknesses.'

Pestilence laughed, a high screech that hurt Adri's ears. WHAT?' it asked in mock disbelief, and laughed again. 'Is this for real?'

'I want your help,' Adri said, grim.

'And why would I help you?' Pestilence asked, still recovering from his laugh.

'Others have asked me the same, and my reply remains the same—I don't know. All I know is someone with wisdom told me you might, and it was the best shot I had.' Adri looked down at the wooden floor. 'I want to find a way, and it is tough. Time is short. The other presence you felt in me; it is taking over. Soon there will be nothing left of me. While I still have control, I want to do what I can. What I must.'

'You are honest with me. Why is that? Do you think I respect honesty, or that I will help you if you are honest? Maybe a nice clean lie would have gotten you the information you needed, and maybe you would've gotten away safely as well.'

'I've lied a lot in my life, Horseman,' Adri said, looking up into Pestilence's leering gaze. 'I've lied myself out of every situation possible, and I've lied whenever it has been convenient for me. But I think I'm changing now, after the things I have done of late, after the things I have seen of late, after I know what it going to happen to me in the end. I'm not going to lie anymore.'

'Hah! Your noble air burns me!' Pestilence cried in mock pain. 'We have a hero in our presence today, it seems!'

'I am not a hero,' Adri said quietly.

Pestilence's eyes flashed red; a sharp black coloured tongue licked its fangs as it looked at Adri.

'You have a very curious web,' it said, its tone more serious.

'Huh?' Adri exclaimed. 'A web?'

'It is *The* Web, rather,' the Horseman said. 'It is simply the structure behind; it is what connects everyone and everything. Things move in it, things are born and things are finished. It spans across existence, stretching from life to beyond death, ensnaring the fabric of time itself in its mesh. Everyone is in the web, human. You, me, Death, your comrades who wait for you outside. It is something of amazing complexity, something certain people have tried to study unsuccessfully, withering away their lives. It is something certain creatures have tried to gain power over, only to be trapped in horrific situations for all eternity. The web defines a person, human—the web will change according to who is present in it and at what time. When I see you, I see the web around you— and it tells me everything I need to know about you.'

'It is the first time I'm hearing of this,' Adri said.

'Even for a Reborn, you are not that old yet,' Pestilence smirked. 'There will be many things you have not heard, many things you have not mastered. I can see you have hidden power, but that is not enough to defeat my older brother, human.'

Adri hid his surprise.

'Don't be surprised, please—though I love to hear those little gasps that prove my superior intellect.' It paused. 'Your web tells me of things you have done and things you might end up doing. And I'm the one surprised when I see where you are about to

424

go and what you are about to get into. You have courage, for a human. And you have repentance for your actions. I will help you.'

'Why will you help me?' Adri asked immediately.

'Don't be an idiot, human. Just accept the help,' Pestilence said.

'No,' Adri said. 'No, if I am to accept your help I have to know what your motives are.'

'Perhaps it is wise to not trust anyone,' Pestilence said, sighing. 'Human, my brother Death once made a promise to me, a promise he did not keep and a promise I do not like to talk about and will not until it is kept. I do not want the Cataclysm as much as I want my brother to pay for his mistake. And you—your web is interesting. You are in dire need of help, and since I'm not the one after your soul, I don't see why not.'

'I will not ask any more. Thank you,' Adri said.

'Oh no, this is where you begin asking. Ask away!' Pestilence said.

'How can I kill Death?' Adri asked.

'The only thing that can help you now,' Pestilence said, 'is a certain kind of weapon. It is *very* rare, forged in *Nedrashish,* the forge of Dominion. A certain kind of blade of incredible magical prowess, called an *ebb blade.*'

'An ebb blade.' Adri repeated softly.

'My eldest brother's weapon is a scythe called *Quietus,*' the Horseman spoke. 'It has two blades, one beneath the other. The blade above is a *malgarsh blade.* It is a killing weapon, one that's only purpose is to slay the foe efficiently and effortlessly. The blade below is an ebb blade. This blade is what Death uses to collect the souls it has to; the blade has the unique characteristic of extracting the soul from within when plunged, destroying the material body in the process. The soul is transferred into a soul gem at the base of the scythe, and can be removed, stored, or as in this case, used in a ritual to break a seal. Do you understand, human?'

'Where can I get an ebb blade?' Adri asked.

'Unfortunately, like I said—ebb blades are extremely rare and not found lying around. Apart from Quietus, there is just one more ebb blade to be found in Old Kolkata. It is called the *Araakh*.'

'And where can I find that?' Adri asked, mentally gearing up for another journey.

'Oh, right here,' Pestilence said. 'Ever since the Spider King died, I have been guarding the weapon for him, waiting for him to rise again and claim his beloved.'

Adri stared. Pestilence grinned, fangs flashing.

'Um, so are you going to give it to me?' Adri asked.

'If you ask for it—yes, I suppose.'

'Uh, can I have the Araakh, then?'

'You didn't say the magic word,' Pestilence said, wagging a finger.

'Can I have the Araakh, please?' Adri asked.

'I didn't mean *please*. I meant the *real* magic word, one that will summon the Araakh to the caller.'

'But how can I know that?'

'True, you can't. You're not a descendant of the Spider King after all.'

'So are you going to tell me the word?'

'If I say it out loud it's going to be summoned by *my* side, not yours.'

'Can't you just hand it over to me?' Adri asked desperately.

'I don't know. Would that work?'

'Why not? It's a sword after all, right?'

'No. It's a dagger.'

'Just try summoning it then, why don't you?'

'Hmm. All right, here goes. *Ilk Li Seyth Araakh!*' the Horseman cried.

A blinding flash of light erupted in mid-air, and a dagger enclosed in a sheath appeared beside the seated Pestilence, hovering in mid-air, waiting to be taken.

28

'Is this the place?' Gray shouted. A roar of thunder almost drowned his voice out.

'That's what it sounded like,' Adri shouted back over the howling wind. 'Fits the description!'

'The weather's almost cyclonic!' Maya screamed.

'The church! We can take shelter in there!' Gray shouted.

'That might just be the church he mentioned,' Adri shouted again. 'What colour is the roof?'

He could not see the colour himself, nor could anyone else for that matter—not in this gale. Dust, darkness, and dry leaves were in the air; a storm was brewing, and fast. They hurried towards the church as the rain started. It came down hard and fast, like a sudden hail of arrows, taking them by surprise. As they came closer to the church, Adri peered up at the roof. A flash of lightning. A figure on the roof. Huge wings outstretched.

'This is the place!' Adri shouted as they pelted towards the large twin doors. Aurcoe flew down in front of the doors as they ran. A massive awning above kept them from getting drenched; it was night already, and the storm seemed like it was about to get worse.

'I've done my part well beyond the call of duty, Sen,' Aurcoe spoke. Adri saw that his demeanour had changed slightly; evidently, he was done with the necessary steps he had to take to secure his coming back and registering as an

Angel. His last responsibility remained, and he was getting it over with right now.

'Yes. Tell me,' Adri said.

'I'm not the one who should do this,' the Angel said. 'Inside. Your answers are waiting.'

Adri paused for a second, and then nodded. Aurcoe nodded back and then pushed open the church doors with both arms in a display of strength. They entered, Aurcoe shutting the entrance behind them. The doors groaned above the wind and the rain as they finally rested shut. No one said anything. The church was quieter now, the sounds of the storm partially muffled. Adri looked around. The church had recently been abandoned, yet not everything was gone. Some benches remained, as did the statue of the bringer of light, the saviour. A lot of objects were stacked where the aisles were, things that were packed to be taken away and hadn't been. The path leading up to the Saviour was wide and empty; at the end of the path, on a marble slab beneath the statue, sat a man.

Adri's eyes were wide. He slowly started walking towards the man. The man was well-built, in his fifties, with sharp features and powerful, perceptive eyes through which he now watched Adri. His hair was beginning to grey at places, and other than that, he did not have many signs of age. He wore a dark green suit, clean and well-pressed. He stood as Adri approached.

'Adri!' he greeted.

'Father,' Adri said. 'So it is you.'

Victor Sen adjusted his hair, a grim smile on his face. 'Of course it's me, Adri,' Victor said. 'It's been me all along, and I'm surprised you did not figure it out before this, until I decided to call you here.'

'Aurcoe is working for you,' Adri said.

The others were still near the door, watching and listening in confusion, in awe.

'He never worked for you, my boy,' Victor said. 'And yet again, I'm surprised you depended *this* much on the Fallen. Your old man had to do everything for you!'

'Like what?'

'Like give you the *Ai'n Duisht*, the confounded Pendant of the Crescent Moon! How else do you think a Fallen would get its hands on something that powerful?'

Adri looked at his father for a moment, then ripped the pendant from his neck, letting it drop. 'I don't need this,' he said, breathing heavily.

'*Now*. Or *any longer*, maybe. You sure needed it all this while, and I was there to get it to you when you did.'

'I did not need your help,' Adri snarled.

'What would you have done without your father, Adri?' Victor asked, laughing. 'What? I taught you everything you know; I had you put through the exams in MYTH when you couldn't manage on your own. I brought you up. I taught you how to control spirits and Demons. I *built* you! Where would you have been without me?'

'Not here, that's for sure,' Adri said grimly.

'This isn't too bad a place to be,' Victor said. 'Even though it *is* the end of the road, you've walked long and walked well.'

'I might still end up surprising you, Father,' Adri said. His hand had a cigarette, which he lit.

'It's not just the Tantric smoking to avoid spirits, is it?' Victor said, closing his eyes briefly. 'No, it's a show of defiance, whenever you smoke. It comes from a deep-rooted feeling of being uncomfortable. Afraid.'

'Don't *you* go about analysing me!' Adri said with force.

'Afraid again, Adri?' Victor smirked. 'Afraid as the day you were born, afraid to come into my arms after such an important event, afraid to face your only living parent.'

'You were the one who was afraid,' Adri said. 'Afraid to tell me about Mother. You were *afraid,* and there is no other explanation, Father.'

'I was not afraid, Adri,' Victor said. 'Telling you then would simply break the curse, and we couldn't have had that, could we?'

'What?' Adri exclaimed, in spite of himself. 'What curse?'

'*Now* you may know, Adri. Now that you are twenty-three and about to die. But then again, death is but another state.'

'What curse?' Adri cried.

Victor's eyes narrowed and he put his hands in his pockets. 'A blood curse, one of the oldest. A sacred and protected ritual, one that was long banned by the government and locked away in one of MYTH's innumerable secret vaults. Guarded extremely well, actually. But when could MYTH ever stop me from doing what I wanted? All they could ever do was welcome me back with apologies of their own. Heh.'

'The curse, Father,' Adri said quietly, his eyes burning. 'Tell me how my mother died.'

'The *Oka Draugr,* the sealing of the breath, it would be called in the Old Tongue. But then I should tell you why, Adri, it would not be good for you to not know. You see, Adri, after you live as long as I have, and after you have done the things you have wanted to, there comes a time when a man must ask himself—*what more?*'

Adri stared at his father. He was sweating, feeling unwell.

'I have done it all, Adri. I have breathed life out of a dying demigod. I have hunted Demons across the star light highways of the Abyss. I have retrieved the secrets I have wanted to know from the Old City. I have changed parts of my body with old forgotten spells, incantations. I have sheltered a hundred souls in my body to know what the feeling of sharing is like, all without losing control. I have ripped the wings off Angels and given lifeblood to Fallen. I have fought a terrible battle with an Alabagus, far above the Old City and far below the heavens, a battle that lasted an entire day.

I have raided tombs and crypts of the greatest Necromancers and Sorcerers of old, discovered their secrets, taken their weapons. I have earned the title of the most powerful Tantric in the world. And I have done it all for the sake of knowing.' Victor paused, and took a deep breath.

'This is but one life,' he said. 'I wanted to *know*. That can never be considered a crime, only a mistake by some. Because if you do choose a path, you cannot take responsibility for anything or anyone—everyone you know is there to only help you get to the greater truth, to help answer the questions you have always been asking.'

Victor walked around, scratching his nape. 'I'm afraid that's how I've always been, Adri. Love for me has always been a love for finding out, a love for knowing. I am the only person who worked for the government, then for the resistance—the Defenders of Old Kolkata—and then MYTH again, only this time, I was their most celebrated Tantric. It is all because I wanted to do it. I wanted to know if I *can* do it. My ideals can change immediately, Adri, if it suits what I have wanted to find out. Are you beginning to understand, even slightly?'

'You think that could be an excuse?' Adri asked. 'Searching for more? Is that why I was never raised as a son? Is that why you were afraid of responsibility? Because you did not *care* enough?'

'Everyone is raising children and settling down, Adri,' Victor said, gently shaking his head. 'I'm afraid there were very few people who I could connect to, and who could connect to me. You were never one of them.'

'What did you do with my mother?' Adri hissed.

'I loved her. I have never understood love, Adri—but if I was to say I have been in love, it was with your mother, my wife. She had an incredible power to make it all okay, son—a gift, not a magical capability, and after her death there has not been a single day when I don't miss her. But you have to understand that there was no other way—the curse demands that the owner perform it on his most treasured possession, something he has protected the most. No one else had enough power in the Old City to actually perform the curse.'

'Why? Why did you have to do it at all? You could have stopped anytime! You could have let it rest! But then it was knowledge, wasn't it? Knowing the effects of the curse and seeing your wife twist and die, like another one of your little experiments!'

'I knew the effects already. But I went on with it, though with a heavy heart, because I wanted to see something else—not the effects of the curse on your mother, not that. I could not watch her suffer, and I did turn away when she was in her final moments of agony. No, I wanted to see something else.'

'And what,' Adri asked, 'was that?'

Victor looked at him in the eye, and Victor's grey eyes seemed to light up with a sudden mad shine.

'The Apocalypse!' Victor exclaimed. 'Armageddon, Catastrophe, Cataclysm, Doomsday—it has many names. The birth of a new era, a fresh start with terror, destruction, blood, purification, the greatest of them all! The Horsemen riding together again, the dark prophecies getting fulfilled one by one; I have wanted to see this since the day I have known of it. I have but one life, my son, and I will not have it wasted trying to rule over a mere country. Or be a hero until a grisly death makes me a martyr. No, I have *seen*, and I will see more. I will be a part of the Apocalypse. I will BRING the Apocalypse upon the twin doors of this world!'

Adri took a step back.

'The *Oka Draugr*,' he said breathlessly. 'It didn't—'

Victor looked at him.

'It did,' he said. 'While you were in your mother's womb, it infected your soul, making you *akshouthur*, a soul the Horseman would *need* to break a seal. That is the power of this curse, and

432

it is because of this power that the mother can never survive the childbirth. A necessary sacrifice, but she left wanting you to live.'

'Her spirit,' Adri said in horror. 'Where is it?'

'Consumed by the curse,' Victor replied simply. 'Which is why you can never call her spirit to talk to you, despite all your efforts. The spirits stay silent because they fear the *Oka Draugr*; I thought you would be *Baal Ob* by now, son. I thought you would've gained this information from the Spirits of Old by now. But you have disappointed me—all your years. Your soul matured when you became twenty-three, and the Horseman Death was informed of your presence. There are rules, however, and I knew you would use the twenty-four hour gap. I expected better from you, though. You just trusted everything important to the imbecilic Fallen and got busy securing blood for its transformation. I *had* to send the artefact to you—now that you had begun, we couldn't have it ending so fast.'

'You played cat and mouse with me,' Adri said.

'I wanted to give you a chance, to see if you could change anything, but you were always so reckless, always so much on the edge. It was fascinating to watch your journey—though your end was always inevitable. It would always come down to a father-son meeting, me being symbolic of the *other*, the nemesis—and then you making a last attempt at attack or escape before dying a pitiful death, unworthy of the Sen name.'

'Father?' Adri spoke.

'Yes, son?' Victor asked.

'I'm going to kill you,' Adri said.

Adri threw his hands at his sides and bent down in a perfect warrior's posture. Suddenly, everything around him exploded—invisible, powerful forces appeared about his body, razing the wooden floor down to the mud beneath. A sudden wave of power erupted from Adri, sending everyone a step back with its sheer force, more powerful than the gale outside. Adri's eyes were on fire, and hate burned through him.

'What is *that?*' Gray whispered in amazement.

Maya was silent, as was Fayne. Aurcoe was gone.

'Impressive!' Victor said. 'I did not see this coming, Adri. You *have* grown, then. I can sense your magic, and it is strong. Not strong enough though, to do as you claim.' He grinned at Adri. 'Hit me then,' he said. 'If you can.'

Adri shouted in fury and leapt at Victor, right hand raised. Victor moved to one side almost carelessly and Adri hammered a wooden pillar, smashing it completely. Victor laughed. Adri recovered and spun around.

'I will crush the life out of you, old man,' he spat.

He rushed at Victor again, this time giving him no space to dodge, his energy searing around him like a chaotic, angry force. Victor teleported. Adri's fist drove deep into the marble where Victor had been, shattering it into a million little pieces.

Recovery. Amazement. Adri looked around. Victor stood high up in the rafters of the church. He was laughing.

'How can you—*blink?*' Adri asked in anger.

'You have not understood magic yet, my boy,' Victor said happily. 'You never used any of your gifts or talents properly. In fact, you started out in such an irresponsible way, dragging a poor defenceless girl all across Old Kolkata.'

Gray looked at the both of them. 'Fayne,' he said. 'Can you take Victor Sen out while he's talking?'

Fayne looked at Victor, then at Gray. 'Apologies,' he said.

Maya looked at Fayne and understood.

'Of course I hired Fayne,' Victor said. 'It was the right thing to do, to even things out a bit. My sense of fair play demanded it; she was a poor little girl, wasn't she? She needed a protector, and clearly you weren't up to the task. Also, I doubt you would've survived the journey without the assassin.'

Adri grimaced as Victor turned to Fayne.

434

'Your charge is complete, by the way. I have sent your payment to your vault in Ahzad already. Thank you for your services, I shall not be needing them any more.'

Fayne nodded lightly.

'And you, dear girl,' he spoke, looking at Maya. 'You need not thank me. You're welcome.'

Maya looked at Victor. 'You disgust me,' she said.

Victor laughed and looked up; and the next moment he wasn't there. Adri smashed through the rafters where Victor had been a second ago, dropping to the ground far below directly on his feet. Splinters and wood blocks rained from above, disintegrating before they reached Adri. He spun around. Victor now stood where Adri had jumped from.

'Coward,' Adri said. 'Fight me instead of running around.'

'Oh, I'm not a coward, Adri,' Victor said. 'In case you think I was afraid and thus staged my own kidnapping, you're wrong. No, it was essential that you did not suspect me—I wanted you to make this journey on your own. I wanted to see how far *you* could go. The Infernal that I had burn down my house is loyal to me. Even now it waits behind the church. Rain hurts it like crazy, I suppose, but its faithfulness is beyond that.'

'Where is Smith?' Adri asked.

'One of the unfortunate collaterals. Nothing would have happened to him had you not involved him personally; all I wanted to see was you get some supplies from him and move on. But no, I underestimated his friendship. He was dormant for *years*, I never imagined him picking up his pack and trying to trace me out. He was handed over, to be exact. The *Flesh Eaters* of *Nemen Sui*. If he is not dead already, he will be. A sad waste, but there is no saying, of course, that the coming of the new era wouldn't have claimed his old life anyway.'

'He was your friend and he paid the price,' Adri said through gritted teeth. He charged at Victor again, the forces around him flaring wildly. Victor disappeared while he was midway; he reappeared behind Adri, in the middle of Adri's dash, and spoke to Adri over his shoulder.

'Fool,' he said. He grabbed Adri's shoulder lightly, with incredible speed, and before Adri could even realise what was happening, Victor, using Adri's momentum, flung him into a wall. Adri fractured the wall with tremendous force. A large crack sped up the surface. The forces surrounding Adri disappeared immediately, leaving his body smoking. He slumped to the ground.

'Adri!' Maya screamed and started to run. Gray grabbed her hand.

'No,' he said, holding her back.

Adri wasn't out. He crawled up to a sitting position, spitting blood. Victor stood, without a scratch on his suit, watching him fondly.

'You couldn't have done anything about this, if that helps,' he said gently. 'Your fate was decided from the moment I performed the curse on your mother. I trained you. Hoping, dreaming that perhaps you would surprise me, but you fell short. And it was meant to happen. I was an old fool, thinking that maybe . . .' His voice trailed off. 'But never mind. What has to happen has to happen. I hope you are ready, my son. I can feel the Horseman getting impatient.'

'Death . . . is here?' Adri coughed out.

'Yes, it is. It had been waiting for my words with you to end.'

'Considerate,' Adri said.

'Death is many things but considerate. No, this was always part of the deal in which I hand you over. Death honours deals.'

Adri could feel it now, the raw power of the Horseman—as opposed to his father, who had masked all of his power, not giving away even a shred of his capabilities before Adri attacked him. Death's aura was almost familiar to Adri by now. Despite himself, he smiled inwards. He was ready.

'Horseman,' Victor spoke. A back door flew open, and Adri saw a familiar frame crouch and enter. Death stood straight after it entered; its face turned to the Saviour's statue for a moment and it observed silently. Then its twisted mask turned to Adri.

'It's been long, human,' Death rasped.

'Yeah, yeah, that's right,' Adri said, staggering to his feet.

Victor Sen moved backwards, near the statue. He was evidently going to be a silent observer. He looked at the other three for a moment, now transfixed with fear at the Horseman's presence. Then he looked back at his son.

'I told you before. You cannot keep Death out of your house,' the Horseman hissed. It started a slow walk towards Adri, the wood beneath its feet rotting with each step, the cloak of chains dragging behind him, rattling. Adri seemed unsteady. He wobbled towards Death, almost as if he was about to fall, and then acted quickly. The deed was done—the Araakh was buried in Death's chest. A beautiful dagger, with a hilt made out of dark, inscribed wood—a purple-shaded, wickedly curved blade at one end, a soul gem at the other. Adri held on to the dagger, waiting for something to happen. Nothing. The liquid darkness surrounding Death repelled the Araakh the next instant, and Adri stepped back, the dagger in his hand, looking at Death unbelievably.

'An ebb blade,' Death said. 'Incredible. I didn't know another one existed in the Old City.'

Adri took a step back, breathing heavily. 'Why?' he asked.

'Ebb blades work on souls, human,' Death said, approaching Adri as he backed away. 'My soul rotted away into nothingness ages ago. The blade is useless against me. I remember telling you this as well—weapons do not harm me.'

Adri's mind raced. He had missed something. Something which did not fit. He did not have the time here to figure it out.

'My turn now,' Death rasped. Its scythe swirled into existence in its right hand.

The sight of the gigantic, rusty weapon did not affect Adri. He thought furiously. Something about what Pestilence had said. But what?

Death looked at its weapon, and the first blade retracted and disappeared. The ebb blade remained. It turned its gaze to Adri.

Adri's mind raced faster than it ever had. A split second. He went through his conversation with Pestilence, remembering every little detail, remembering what Pestilence had said, what *exactly* Pestilence had said. Then suddenly, everything clicked into place.

The only thing that can help you now, Pestilence had said. It had never mentioned anything about the Araakh ending Death, or Death's weaknesses.

Death raised the scythe. 'Your time is up, human,' it said.

Adri turned his head and looked at Maya. Realisation. She looked back at him, helpless, tears in her eyes. Desperation. Adri looked at Maya and spoke through his eyes. Volumes. Confessions. Precise instructions. He looked at her long and hard, yet a split moment. One last time. Then he moved quickly and deftly in a move that Death could not see—he stuck his chest out and plunged the Araakh in his back.

His entire world was set on fire. Everything burned, burned instantly and brightly. An incredible suction. A black hole. Demanding everything. His entire existence. His memories and thoughts. His well-guarded feelings. His very soul. Everything that he was. The Wraith resisted the pull automatically, instinctively— and Adri gave in immediately. Adri was pulled into the Araakh as pure energy, as a soul, at the same moment that the other ebb blade burst into Adri's chest. The Wraith now knew what Adri had done; it had nowhere else to go now, but into the Horseman's scythe. Adri's body burned shortly in a sudden, incredible rush of fire and then disintegrated. His face burned away. Teeth. Hair. Then the flesh. Muscles. Organs. Bone. It took seconds, and only Adri's clothes collapsed to the ground, unharmed.

Death detached the soul gem from the base of its scythe.

'Finally, finally,' it whispered, looking at the soul moving about in the gem. It whipped around and walked out of the room without another word.

Victor Sen looked at his son's collapsed clothes, shook his head, and then adjusted his hair. He looked at the others, who stood looking shocked, sickened. 'Good day to you,' Victor smiled, and followed Death out of the door.

EPILOGUE

Where is it that I can look for you?
I talk to you, I tell you things
I stand tall above your crumbled buildings
I stand deep beneath your darkest recesses
I am here where you are

In your stagnancy I smell life
In your arms I will feel death
In your embrace I will breathe my last
I will return to you, from whence I came.

'He's *dead*?' Gray said, his voice choked. 'Adri can't be dead.'

They stood in front of his clothes. Nothing else remained. Maya bent down and rummaged among the clothes, finally withdrawing the Araakh. She unhitched the soul gem from the base and looked at it. It was a translucent gem within which a small light moved about, peacefully, at ease.

'He's not dead,' Maya said, smiling. 'This was Adri's deception, the biggest trick he ever pulled in his life. That seal is not going to open with Mazumder's soul.'

Gray gazed at the soul gem in disbelief.

'The clever bastard,' he whispered.

'He didn't plan on it,' Maya said. 'But he figured it out in the end.'

'But what do we do now?' Gray asked. 'You have Adri's soul. So what?'

Maya turned to Fayne. Her attitude had changed once more. A new fire burned in her. One very similar to what Fayne remembered seeing in Adri. Maya's mind was set. She knew what was to be done. 'Are you free to accept a new charge?' she asked.

'Yes,' Fayne replied.

'I charge you with helping us as we go about the task of attempting to restore Adri back, if that is possible, and to prevent the coming of the Apocalypse,' Maya said, grim. 'Your fees will be paid to you after successful completion.'

Fayne was silent for a moment. Then he nodded. 'I accept gladly,' he said.

'We all owe Adri something, huh?' Maya said, the slightest hint of a smile on her lips.

Fayne was silent, but Maya knew that beneath the mask, his face had probably given way to a reluctant smile.

'Maya,' Gray muttered. 'What are we going to do now?'

'We don't have much time, that's for sure,' Maya said. 'I don't know where Death is headed to break its last seal. It won't be long before it discovers it has the wrong soul. It will hunt us. We must move fast.'

Gray picked the *Ai'n Duisht* off the floor. 'We'll need this,' he said.

'Where are we headed?' Fayne asked.

'I have heard rumours of the Keeper for a long time, and the Soul Library where he sits. If there is someone who will know how to restore a soul to a body, it will be him.'

'The Keeper is legend,' Gray protested, as they started walking towards the twin doors of the church.

'So are the Horsemen. So is the Apocalypse. Don't you see? Everything is real. Everything was always real, just hidden away,' Maya said.

'How are we going to track down the Keeper?' Fayne asked.

'I know someone who should know. We have to track *him* down first,' Maya said.

'Who?' Gray asked.

Fayne opened the twin doors. The streets before them were in chaos. The storm. Lightning lit everything for mere seconds before the gale blew everything away. The trees around the church were close to collapsing. Thunder roared across the night.

'Demon Commander Ba'al,' Maya said. 'The first Demon Adri ever summoned.'

They entered the night, and the storm swallowed them.

ACKNOWLEDGMENTS

A book is a journey, perhaps both for the reader and the individual who wrote it; one that is not over with the last word on the last page. Once the destination is at hand though, this writer, this individual, might want to sit down, rest, catch his breath, but more often than not, he will look behind at the leagues he has travelled, and more often than not, he will reminisce about what it felt like to make the journey in the first place. There is a simple way for him to relive this expedition he so misses by now, and he flips the first page open to start again.

Writing Acknowledgments is a Herculean task; this is not a journey I made alone, and it is perhaps impossible to pen down the gratitude, the love I feel for those who supported me when I was tired. One might call it overrated, this thanking business, but then again, for every person out there who has ever written, their book is their *world*. It is everything, and yet again words must try to describe the indescribable.

I would like to thank my parents, Mayuri and Kishalay Bhattacharjee, and my grandmother, my Dunna, Mira Purkayastha, my uncle, Rahul Purkayastha for being ever so patient and supportive. I know it's not easy to see a couple of years fly by with nothing really happening except for a little boy typing away, but it is your faith in me which made *Tantrics of Old* possible. PP Da, thank you for igniting the flame; I assure you, it will continue to burn, and burn well. Achintya Jethu, for believing in me, for believing I can try

445

to go back to my roots through the English language. Promona Sengupta, for seeing past the syntax and trusting the book enough to sit down with me and hold the book's hand, and for the first, unofficial edit and the lovely poem, a gift, one I have chosen to start the book with, something that sums up *Tantrics of Old* and Krishnarjun Bhattacharya.

Of course, none of this would have been possible without Fingerprint! and the lovely people there. Thank you, Shikha Sabharwal, for your enthusiasm and for giving me so much of a free reign; I'm very grateful. Thank you, Gaurav Sabharwal and Bharti Taneja, for supporting me, and humouring the many questions I was constantly bringing to the table. And of course, thank you, Gayatri Goswami, for editing the book as if it were your own, for investing in the universe and the characters, and for putting up with me. I know I have been extremely difficult and moody throughout.

Dipankar Sengupta I cannot thank enough; for your patience, your blind trust, and the hours of conversation over conspiracy theories, and of course, for the book cover and the animated book trailer, both masterfully executed, for the months of pure effort involved. Thank you, Adri Thakur, for the excellent cinematography in the live action book trailer, and for heartening my sojourn into writing. Thank you, Jyotish Sonowal, Kavya Agarwal, and Shantanu Salgaonkar, for your design inputs and expert font critique. Thank you, Dinesh Bharule, for the compositing and the effects. Thank you, Abhinav Swynenberg, for the excellent music in the animated trailer. And thank you, Anupam Alok, for being an excellent legal advisor—it feels amazing to have a lawyer!

Thank you, Samira Thakur, Ma'am, for carrying the lamp in the dark, for that glimmer of hope when I needed it the most.

Thank you, Samit Basu, for finding the time to calm down these nerves frayed by publicity and marketing.

All my loving relatives, thank you. My friends, companions, you who have stood by me—Moinak, Sid, Ratul, Reshudi, Pallavi, Ateesh, Goru, Doya, Aloka, Arka, Avirup, Tumpi, Enakshi, Ria, Samar, Devendra, Pranav, Manas, Ado, Bittu and my brother Rangon.

KRISHNARJUN BHATTACHARYA

is a graduate in Film and Video Communication from the National Institute of Design, Ahmedabad, and a post graduate in TV Editing from the Film and Television Institute of India, Pune. A wanderer of cities and a passionate game reviewer, he's an absolute lover of all things dark and grotesque, and has deep respect for Ursula Le Guin, Darrell Schweitzer, JRR Tolkien, George RR Martin, and HP Lovecraft, among many others. He dreams of writing compelling fantasy fiction for a living, madman that he is, and telling stories lost to those who would remember. He resides in a post apocalyptic world, terrified of aliens, the walking dead, and secret government WMDs, not to mention what lives under his bed. *Tantrics of Old* is his first novel.

His email id is krishnarjunbhattacharya@gmail.com and his Twitter handle is @Akta_Golpo_Shon.